NOW
THEN
AND
EVERY
WHEN

ALSO BY RYSA WALKER

The Delphi Trilogy

Novels

The Delphi Effect
The Delphi Resistance
The Delphi Revolution

Novella

The Abandoned

The CHRONOS Files

Novels

Timebound
Time's Edge
Time's Divide

Graphic Novel

Time Trial

Novellas

Time's Echo
Time's Mirror
Simon Says

NOW
THEN
AND
EVERY
WHEN

CHRONOS ORIGINS ⧗ BOOK ONE

RYSA WALKER

47NORTH

Published by 47North, Seattle

www.apub.com

Amazon, the Amazon logo, and 47North are trademarks of Amazon.com, Inc., or its affiliates.

ISBN-13: 9781612189192
ISBN-10: 1612189199

Cover design by M.S. Corley

Printed in the United States of America

For Maddy, Ian, and Ryan, three intrepid time travelers I've had the pleasure of watching grow into kind, bright, and generous young adults. My greatest hope for the future is the knowledge that our fate will soon be in the hands of your generation.

FROM THE *NEW YORK DAILY INTREPID* (AUGUST 3, 1966)

Boycotts and Bonfires over Beatles' Remarks

(Birmingham, Ala.) Disc jockeys from around the country have banned songs by the British band the Beatles in the wake of John Lennon's comments recently printed in teen magazine *DATEbook*. Lennon's statement that the Fab Four are currently "more popular than Jesus" has sparked outrage and calls for a boycott of the band's upcoming thirteen-city US tour.

A spokesman for the group has confirmed that Lennon did, in fact, make this remark in an interview with London journalist Maureen Cleave back in March. The singer also noted that he was unsure which would last longer—Christianity or rock 'n' roll.

Two Birmingham DJs have called on listeners to send any Beatles albums, posters, or souvenirs to their station, WAQY, to be used in a "Beatles bonfire" on August 19, when the group is scheduled to perform in Memphis, Tennessee. Other disc jockeys throughout the South and elsewhere have scheduled similar events. The Ku Klux Klan has also entered the controversy, with Dale Walton, Mississippi's Imperial Wizard of the Knights of the Green Forest, imploring teens to "cut their Beatle wigs off" and contribute them to a public burning to protest the upcoming tour.

∞ 1 ∞

Richard Vier tips back the last of his drink and looks me directly in the eye. "You need to relax, Tyson. A minor mistake like that isn't going to have a ripple effect. If it had caused so much as a blip on the timeline, you'd have gotten a message from Angelo, and you wouldn't be here right now. You'd be back at HQ, working with a cleanup crew to undo whatever you did. Believe me. That's what happened to Armin, the music historian who preceded me."

"Did they fire him?"

"Yep. Reclassified as a manual laborer. I think he's on a water-reclamation project somewhere in Australia now."

Richard manages to hold a straight face, but only for a moment. "No, they didn't fire him! He finished out fourteen years and retired from fieldwork, like anyone else. He's off teaching somewhere now, raising kids. Living the good life. I'm just saying mistakes *do* happen from time to time, but they'll let you know. And they'll work with you to fix it. No message means *nothing happened.*"

He's probably right. Had I triggered a major change, something that altered the timeline in any way, I'd have found a note in my

CHRONOS diary instructing me to return to headquarters. Even a small change—some tiny wrinkle that smoothed itself out in a year or so—would have earned me a warning. There was nothing like that in the diary, so I probably *do* need to relax. But it's reassuring to have confirmation from someone who has a few years' experience under his belt, especially when I've spent the past several hours being lectured back in 1963 by the woman who owns the diner where I'm working. Ida has no clue that I'm a time traveler, but she clearly thought my mistake was a very big damn deal, big enough that I was sure she was going to send me packing.

That would have meant scrapping the project until I could scout out a new location in a different town. Not the end of the world, but also not something that I want to happen. I've taken a few day trips on my own, but this is my first major research trip without a supervising partner, and the very last thing I need on my record is a disaster that would require a cleanup crew. Or worse yet, a retraction. Retractions are rare, but the one historian I know who was in the middle of one says they really mess with your head. You get saddled with double memories, where one side of your brain remembers making the jump, but the other side remembers spending that time back at CHRONOS. And if you have to retract a series of jumps, rather than a day trip, you spend a week or so in the isolation unit to avoid spreading double memories to other historians you might run into in the halls or at meetings.

"You'd probably have felt it, too," Rich adds. "If there was a change, I mean. When it happened to Armin, he said it was like getting kicked in the gut, although those of us here at HQ were far enough removed in time that we didn't feel anything. But that's exactly why they stick us in the out-of-the-way spots for the first few solo jumps. Even a minor error in a city like Washington or Birmingham during the summer of 1963 *might* have cascaded into a problem. But in Spartanburg, they're observing the major historical events as much as you are. The only difference is that they don't have to travel back two and a half centuries to do it. Although, to be honest, I still don't see how a box of contraband fried chicken could have tipped the scale even if you *were* closer to the action."

"It wasn't just the chicken. The problem, apparently, is that I went through the front door to *deliver* the chicken."

"Instead of going through the 'colored entrance'?"

"No. See, that's what tripped me up. There isn't actually a 'colored entrance' at that courthouse in 1963. I watched a black man in a suit mount the steps and walk through the door that same day, just as I was rounding the corner. The deal is that most of the restaurants are still segregated, and the judge *should* have ordered his chicken box from The Dixie Chicken on the north side of town, like all of the other white folks. But Ida used to work for this judge's family, and he had a hankerin', as Ida would say, for her hush puppies. So he rings up the Southside Diner and orders a four-piece box with extra pups. Ida assigns me to deliver it. Somehow I was supposed to know that this sort of clandestine delivery had to be done at the *back* door."

"And that's probably why it didn't affect anything, Tyce. This is the kind of mistake you could have made if you really *were* just new in town. You can fully understand that a town is segregated, can even have an encyclopedic knowledge of the history of segregation in the United States, and still not grasp the specific political intricacies of a fried-chicken war. So, when are you headed back in?"

"Thursday. I was scheduled to go back tomorrow, but I got someone to swap jump-slots with me. And no, it's not just because this chicken thing unnerved me. I think I've sweated off ten pounds in the past week. Ida doesn't air-condition the kitchen or the apartment upstairs that I'm renting out. I need a few days to rehydrate." I glance around the club's main lounge. "Are you sure Katherine's coming?"

"Of course, she's coming. Have you ever known Saul to skip one of Campbell's events?"

I'm about to remind him that Saul has been known to come on his own, without Katherine, but he's probably right. Even though Katherine thinks Morgen Campbell is an ass—a view with which Rich and I fully concur—she rarely lets Saul out of her sight these days.

All sections of the Objectivist Club are opulent, even the main dining hall downstairs. This area, Redwing Hall, is normally members only, except for the few times a year that Campbell hosts a CHRONOS event. Entering this room feels almost like we've traveled back in time to the era when men of wealth and distinction gathered in dark, richly paneled rooms like this as a respite from the daily grind of ruling the world. That appearance is definitely one that Campbell likes to cultivate, and the fact that a portrait of his younger self hangs on the wall along with other leaders of the group who preceded him leaves no doubt that he considers himself a titan of society. Even at these CHRONOS mixers that include lesser mortals like me and Rich, Campbell can't resist a touch of exclusivity—there are members-only side rooms where men (and the occasional woman) can retreat for brandy, cigars with real tobacco, and a game of chess or backgammon.

I usually steer clear of these parties, partly because there's always a risk that I'll be one of the historians Campbell corners for a chat. The man has more money than Croesus, but even with all that wealth, he still can't buy the only thing he really wants—the CHRONOS gene. His parents would have had to purchase that for him before he was born. I don't know what genetic gift his family chose. Probably an intelligence boost, although based on the conversations I've had with the man, I think it's equally likely that they boosted his ego. At any rate, since he can't travel back in history, he surrounds himself with those who can and pumps us for information to use in the historical simulations he likes to play with Saul and a few of the other historians in his immediate circle of friends.

As usual, Campbell is holding court in one corner of the room, with a drink in one hand, a cigar in the other, and a ruby *OC* signet ring on his pudgy pinky finger. Katherine once said he reminds her of this historical figure from the nineteenth century, a corrupt politician everyone called Boss Tweed. One of the guests must have said something to amuse him, because Campbell laughs and nods approvingly, then flicks the ash from his cigar onto the floor, taking care to avoid singeing the ancient beast sleeping at his feet. Rumor has it that the dog, a fat, lumbering Doberman named Cyrus, is nearly thirty. Most of the small clear bubbles floating around to filter pollutants out of the air hover near that side of the room, clearing away the noxious fumes from Morgen's cigar and Cyrus's faulty digestive system.

On the plus side, however, booze flows freely at any event Campbell hosts—and it's half-decent, unlike the watered-down swill that the food units spit out. When I showed up after work stressed out over the chicken incident, Rich argued that what I needed was to unwind. Have a few drinks. A decent dinner. Maybe even socialize a bit.

And while he may have been right, he also had an ulterior motive. He wants someone to talk to while he waits for Katherine Shaw to arrive. Someone to make it look like he's just hanging out with his roommate, enjoying the party. He'd still have come even if I'd refused, but odds are good he'd have spent the entire night sitting alone, hoping Katherine would grow tired of listening to Saul and Campbell argue about some mundane bit of history and grace him with her presence for a few minutes.

A blond woman is approaching the table, but it's not Katherine. This woman is the other reason I generally steer clear of these events. Morgen Campbell's daughter, Alisa, almost always puts in an appearance. It's usually a brief appearance, lasting only long enough for her to have a few drinks, find someone to take back up to her apartment—and, of course, make sure that her father sees her leaving with said someone.

I have been that someone on several occasions. More than I'd like to admit, actually. Alisa is a few years older than me, and undeniably gorgeous. She's smart, too. And she's actually *not* a horrible person. But Alisa Campbell has major daddy issues. Morgen doesn't seem to give a damn about who his daughter has sex with or anything else she does—which may well be the root of Alisa's problems. I always wind up feeling a little used after these encounters, even though I guess I'm using her, too.

Alisa has one of the younger historians in tow tonight. I don't recall his name, but he's currently in his second year of field training, so he's eighteen or maybe nineteen. I'm torn between feeling relieved that Alisa has already picked her companion for the evening and feeling an odd combination of envy and pity for the kid, who is staring at her like he can't believe his luck. He's going to have a very interesting night or two, and then—almost certainly—a broken heart and a shattered ego. I'm grateful that she can't ask to join us. The table will only accommodate two stools, and I don't want to witness any more of this guy's impending heartbreak than absolutely necessary.

Alisa places a proprietary hand on my thigh. She's already had a few drinks, judging from the scent of whiskey on her breath. Probably a few of the mood enhancers Campbell has at these events, too.

"Tyce! You naughty boy. Why didn't you tell me you were coming?"

Her companion's face crumples.

"Spur-of-the-moment decision," I say. "And I needed to talk to Rich about . . . some work stuff."

She pouts. "Are you done?"

"Nope," I say cheerfully. "Haven't even started."

Given that Rich is my roommate, we can talk work anytime. If Alisa wasn't already mostly buzzed, she might have remembered that.

But she's never paid the slightest attention to Rich. He's not a bad-looking guy by any means, but she has a type, and thin and bookish ain't it.

Alisa exaggerates the pout a bit and gives my thigh a playful little slap. "You are no fun at all, Tyson Reyes." She presses her body against the side of her companion. "Guess it's a good thing I already have plans."

They head back toward the bar. The guy doesn't look quite as smitten as he did when they walked over. Maybe that's just as well.

Rich's head jerks up, and I follow his gaze toward the lift at the back of the club. His eye seems to have been drawn to another flash of blond hair, but it's definitely not Katherine. Tate Poulsen is a half meter taller than Katherine, and a solid wall of muscle.

"She's coming," Rich repeats, when he sees my grin. "I didn't actually think that was her."

"I'm not doubting you. But that reminds me." I pause for a moment to pull up a couple of images on my retinal screen and then send the first one over to Rich. "Look like anyone you know?"

He's silent for a moment. "Where did you get this?"

"Spartanburg 1963. Drugstore newsstand."

"That doesn't make any sense. Poulsen doesn't do modern. How could he have posed for a drawing like this?"

"Well, he did make one jump to study some neo-Viking group, although that was the 1990s, I think. But wait. Check out the next one before you rush to any conclusions."

His mouth drops. "You're kidding me. This is a joke, right? You had someone draw these."

"No. Swear to God. These are vintage 1960s comics. The first one is the cover of Marvel's *Journey into Mystery* #83, where the Mighty Thor is swinging a giant hammer. And the one you're looking at now is from 1963. The Amazing Spider-Man's alter ego, Peter Parker."

"I know who Spider-Man is." He stares at the images for a moment longer and then says, "I just never really thought that I looked like him until now. But I guess it does explain these damn glasses."

Rich has often complained bitterly about his design team's decision to give him substandard vision. It could easily have been fixed, either in utero or later. But they argued it would make him more *authentic*, whatever the hell that means.

"If my genetic designer decided to give me this Parker guy's face and body—and his piss-poor eyesight—why not at least let me shoot that web stuff out of my wrists?"

I laugh. "Exactly how would that help a music historian in the field? I'm pretty sure Edwina would tell you form follows function."

"Oh, great," he says. "That's just great. *Edwina.* So now you're on a first-name basis with the head of our genetic-design team. That's messed up, Tyson."

"Messed up? How?"

"It's just . . . I don't know. It's kind of like tracking down the doctor who presided at your birth. It's weird."

He probably has a point. There's no hard-and-fast rule against talking to your genetic designer, but it's not the sort of thing people tend to do. For one thing, the designer probably wouldn't even remember doing your adjustment. By the time a historian heads out into the field, his or her design team has encoded thousands of embryos with the chosen gifts selected by their parents. But most of those are fairly straightforward assignments, usually involving a single genetic tweak. Encoding the CHRONOS gene is more involved and actually gives them a chance to flex their creative muscles a bit. I'd been pretty sure that the designer would remember encoding a Viking historian, especially if she'd used that comic as a template.

"How else was I going to get answers, Rich? Are you telling me that if you'd seen this on a 1963 newsstand, you wouldn't have tracked her down for confirmation? Thor caught my attention first—I mean, take away the gaudy costume, and that's one hundred percent Tate Poulsen. But then I start poking around in some of the other volumes, and I see half a dozen other faces that look familiar, including yours. And there's some villain named the Chameleon, too. No face on that one, but . . ."

He nods. CHRONOS tends to turn a blind eye to mild hazing, unless it gets physical, and some wit gifted me with the nickname "Chameleon" during my first year in the classroom. It stuck. Back then, the name had been used primarily by obnoxious upperclassmen, but a few of those obnoxious upperclassmen are now senior historians. Most of them matured, but old habits seem to die hard for others.

For a while, I resented the name, but I can't deny the accuracy. Of the thirty-six historians currently at CHRONOS and the dozens in the cohorts that preceded us, I'm probably the only one who could pose for a family portrait without anyone thinking I was adopted. My family is fairly typical. On my mom's side, we're mostly European and Latino, with a dash of African. My dad's family is African, Latino, and Southeast Asian, but my great-grandmother on that side had eyes almost as blue as the contacts I often wear in the field.

Until recently, CHRONOS deemed multiracial historians of limited use and routinely added a variety of physical tweaks to the package of genetic manipulations that allow us to time travel. For example, even though her mother is primarily of Asian descent, Katherine Shaw is a pale, blue-eyed blonde. Abel Waters, one of the senior members of our cohort, has skin four or five shades darker than his brother, who works with CHRONOS security. And while both examples *could* in theory be due to a random toss of the genetic dice, they were in fact the result of very conscious alterations, performed by the genetic-design team before Katherine and Abel were even born, in order to make them the best possible physical match for the specific research agendas to which they would be assigned.

My design team, however, left my features neutral enough that the folks in costuming can make a few subtle changes in hair or eye color, and send me out into the field as a person of almost any race. I worked with three field agents of different races during training, instead of the one assigned to most trainees. The stated goal was to give me perspective and allow me to investigate and compare multiple sides with minimal bias.

While I do think that's part of it, CHRONOS is also facing pressure to dial back the number of genetic tweaks they've traditionally pitched as "necessary" alterations for time travel. It's not just race or appearance that they adjust. In addition to the elements that allow us to use the medallions, diaries, and other time-travel equipment, our genetic designers routinely increase our intelligence, strength, language aptitude, and a host of other things to help us acclimate to the eras we study. For legal reasons, however, they're very careful to use the term CHRONOS gene, singular, in all official documents. Otherwise, the agency could be in conflict with the international covenant that restricts parents from obtaining more than one genetic alteration per child.

"And this Edwina person admitted these books were her inspiration?" Rich asks.

"Well, I wouldn't say she admitted it. She *did* say that her father had a collection of antique comics. And she said artists have to get their ideas from somewhere."

He rolls his eyes. "That's an admission."

We both look back at the images on our retinal screens as I point out a few of the other historians who seem to have stepped off the pages of classic comic books. Neither of us realizes we have company until Saul Rand claps me on my shoulder. The move is perfectly calibrated—hard enough to slosh half of my drink onto the table, but not hard enough to look intentional.

"Are you guys actually *working*? Drink up, Cham. Rich here may not have a social life, but that's no reason he has to drag you down with him."

And that's how you know a nickname isn't going anywhere. If some jerk like Saul has a short, snappy version, you might as well embrace it.

The short blond woman next to him huffs in annoyance. "Saul! Look what you made him do! And don't call him that. People will think you're racist."

Katherine Shaw says these words as though no one could ever seriously believe that Saul is racist. To be fair, I'm not sure I believe it, either. I've spent a lot of time with racists during my field training, and I think it's entirely possible that Saul is an equal-opportunity asshole.

Saul either doesn't hear her or ignores her. Probably the latter. He spies Campbell and some of his fellow club members across the room and heads off to join them. Katherine grabs some napkins from the buffet and begins mopping up the mess on the table. "I'm sorry. He's so clumsy."

Rich smiles at her. "No need for you to apologize."

The emphasis on the word *you* is so subtle that I don't think Katherine even catches it. But I've been Richard Vier's roommate for two years, and I've heard him rant on numerous occasions about Saul Rand. Those rants have increased tenfold since Katherine moved in with the guy.

I take the napkins from her. "It's not a problem."

"The drink or the nickname?" she asks.

"Both. It's an open bar, and I'm perfectly happy to waste more of Morgen Campbell's money on a refill. And to be honest, the name has started to grow on me."

Katherine raises a skeptical eyebrow, but it's not entirely untrue.

"Okay," I amend. "Let's just say I don't object to *friendly* use of the nickname."

"And that's definitely Saul," Katherine says, beaming. "He's too friendly for his own good. Like an overgrown pup. He wags his tail and now half your drink is on the table."

The only thing that keeps me from laughing out loud at the image of Saul as a big, friendly dog is the look that Rich gives me. Although from the way his mouth is twitching, I think he's finding it hard to keep a straight face, too.

I offer to get refills, and also a drink for Katherine. She declines, and glances over to where Saul is talking to Campbell. I'm certain she won't be here when I get back unless I throw Richard a lifeline.

"Hey, Rich, while Katherine's here, maybe you should discuss that joint research idea you and I were talking about the other night. The nexus of gender movements and music, right?"

I grab both of our glasses and stand up before he can kick me under the table. He came here fully intending to talk to her about the project, but I've known him for the better part of a decade. While Richard Vier is one of the most skilled CHRONOS agents I've seen in the field, Katherine is his kryptonite, or whatever the equivalent is for Spider-Man. Without a nudge in the right direction, he'd spend the rest of the night thinking about what he *would* have said if only she'd stuck around for a few more minutes.

"It's actually gender *and* race," Rich says, raising his eyebrows for emphasis.

Which is his signal that he's finally decided he wants me to sign on for this project, too. He's been weighing the pros and cons of that for the past few weeks. On the one hand, he'd like to spend some time alone with Katherine. But on the other hand, she's much more likely to say yes, and much *less* likely to catch flak from Saul, if I tag along.

When I get back with the drinks, Katherine is staring at something I can't see, so Rich must have sent the proposal description to her retinal screen. He does the same for me, even though I helped him brainstorm ideas for a project that would pull in her research agenda without exposing his underlying motive.

"I like the title," she says. "*You Say You Want a Revolution: The Nexus of Sex, Race, and Rock 'n' Roll in 1960s America.* Pretentious enough to pass academic muster with the snooty types on the committee, thanks to the colon, and you included the word *sex* to pull in the rest of them." Katherine grins up at Richard. I'm really glad for his sake that it's dark enough to at least partially camouflage his blush. "So I take it they've already given approval?"

"I got tentative approval today," he says. "Angelo was the one who suggested I talk to you about adding it to your schedule. He said you were thinking of observing a mid-twentieth-century countermovement to compare to the antisuffragists of the previous century."

This version of events is not entirely accurate. I was in the room when he first pitched the idea to Angelo, and it was the other way around. Richard stammered like mad when he suggested adding Katherine, but if Angelo noticed, he didn't mention it. Or maybe he decided to ignore it. Angelo is Katherine's mentor, too, and he clearly regrets pairing her up with Saul as a research partner. Anything that puts distance between the two of them is probably okay in his book.

And I don't think Rich needed to worry about anyone questioning the proposal too closely, anyway. The committee is little more than a rubber stamp. They'll approve almost anything, as long as it's reasonably risk-free, has a pretentious-sounding title, and is at least tangentially connected to your research specialty. The members are mostly middle-aged former historians who are now stuck in desk jobs and classrooms, but they've all been where we are. Out in the field, curious, eager to track down leads and solve history's mysteries.

"It's an interesting proposal," she says, a bit hesitantly. "But I'm worried that I can't contribute much on the music side. I'm not well versed in 1960s pop culture."

"Not a problem," Richard says. "I've got that part of the research covered. And I can send you over a playlist so that you'll have at least a passing familiarity. It's the one I put together for Tyson last year."

Her blue eyes grow hazy again as she focuses on her screen. "These are some powerful newspaper images. What made the KKK so angry at this band that they torched all their records?"

Richard opens his mouth to answer, but I jump in. "The Beatles were adamantly against segregation," I say, giving Rich a sharp look across the table. Left to his own devices, Rich would bombard her with tons of background information, just as he did me. Under normal circumstances, I'd let him roll with it. He knows this bit of history better than I do, and it would give him a chance to show off. Katherine's a historian, so she's not put off by minute detail. But if Rich tells her the *full* story of why the KKK is burning records by the Beatles in 1966, he's going to end up talking about religion. And that will almost certainly give Katherine the bright idea to bring in Saul and make this a four-person research project. Religious extremism is one of Saul's specialties.

"That's right," Richard says, apparently catching on to my logic. "They refused to play segregated venues on their previous American tour. This time, a black trio, the Ronettes, was opening for the group, and there were rumors that one or more of the Beatles had dated one or more of the girls in the group—pretty sure those were at least partially true rumors."

"So, were women actually *in* the KKK?" Katherine asks.

"Generally not," I tell her. "Although there were a few exceptions, most groups didn't allow women as members. They all have a Ladies Auxiliary, though. Bake sales, organizing activities for the kids, and so forth. In the klavern I joined with Glen for my final training project, the Grand Dragon's wife headed it up. I got the sense that's the usual pattern. Plus, a lot of people come to the cross lightings, as they prefer to call them, just for fun. And by 1966, there's a lot of chatter in their newsletters about how the feminist movement is wrecking things for real women. Of course, I don't know how much of that is—"

"Is driven by the men?" she asks with a wry smile. "Probably not as much as you think. I spent several weeks with the *Werk Glaube und Schönheit*—basically a Junior League for young Nazi women—during field training. They had odd ideas on women's empowerment, both in their literature and the conversations I had with members. But I got the sense that it was mostly organic. Subservience was a part of their personality by that point."

"It doesn't have to be just the Klan, though," Richard adds quickly. "There was a strong backlash by younger women, fans of the Beatles. We could see about attending some of their protests, too."

Katherine nods absently. I don't think he needs to sweeten the pot, though. She's already interested.

"Can I give you an answer on Monday? I need to check my jump schedule to see if I can squeeze this in. And," she adds, glancing toward the tall, dark figure on the other side of the room, "I need to make sure it's okay with Saul, of course."

In one sense, it's a perfectly reasonable thing for her to say. Saul isn't just her usual research partner, but also her *partner*-partner. I'd like to think that if I ever slow down enough to get to that stage in a relationship, a girl would extend that same courtesy to me, as I would to her. What bothers me is Katherine's expression, which tells me that Saul's decision on this jump will be the deciding factor.

"Speaking of," she says, "I should probably get back over there."

"Sure, sure," Rich says. "Take your time. I mean, on the decision. As long as I get back with Angelo by midweek, we should be able to hold on to these jump-slots."

Once she's gone, he turns toward me. "Hey, that went even better than I'd hoped! She seems interested."

He means interested in the project, but I can tell he's also hoping it's something more. I nod and smile, clinking my glass against his. Rich is an eternal optimist. It's one of the things I like most about him. And even though I'm almost certain that Katherine Shaw is too far gone for him to stand the slightest chance with her, the guy is my best friend. No way in hell am I going to be the person to point that out.

FROM *A BRIEF HISTORY OF CHRONOS*, 4TH ED. (2302)

The scientific principles of time travel were discovered in the mid-twenty-second century by a small team of researchers, headed by Ian Alexander, Ryan Jefferson, and Madison Grace. Funded primarily by the US government, the specific details of their research were never fully revealed to the public, although media outlets published a flurry of exposés in 2161, claiming that government operatives had been manipulating the timeline to benefit US and European interests for at least a decade.

The most prominent of those media outlets, the *New York Hourly Intrepid* (published as the *New York Daily Intrepid* before 2046), has since disappeared almost entirely from the historical record. The masthead suggests that the journal was in circulation for nearly 250 years, but the only record we have of their investigation into timeline manipulation, or of their very existence, is contained in a cache of government records that were protected from chronological tampering and released to the public in 2270.

It is still unclear exactly how much history was altered in those early decades of time travel.

∞2∞

Late-afternoon sunlight ripples through the willow in the back-yard, creating playful dots that dance across the lawn. This view has become part of my regular routine over the past few months—pour a glass of wine; make a simple dinner of cheese, bread, and fruit; and carry it out to the table on the patio to watch the sunset light show.

Tonight, however, I have guests. Dinner will be pasta and a salad, the best that can be hoped for given my limited cooking skills and the ancient food-processing unit in the kitchen. It was top of the line forty years ago, but a much better replicator came standard in the one-bedroom economy flat I helped move my mother into before I left London.

"This is all private land?" Alex asks as he exits the house onto the patio.

I nod, ignoring his slightly judgmental tone. "It's been on my father's side of the family for generations. Part of my job while I'm here is to get it ready for market."

That saddens me a lot more than I thought it would when I moved here back in August. Yes, this house is much too large for one person, and yes, it's a bit lonely sometimes. But I feel more at peace here than I have in a very long while, possibly because there is an entire ocean separating me from the ongoing Grace family drama.

"The neighborhood was rezoned for mixed development decades ago," I continue. "So a few years from now, this house and yard will be either an apartment building or an office complex like the one next door. My great-grandfather was exempted from the zoning—"

"Let me guess," Jack says with a grin. "A grandfather clause?"

Alex rolls his eyes. He's right. It's a dumb joke, but I can't help a small chuckle. Jack's grin is contagious.

"Exactly. But Grandpa James's exemption won't transfer to a new buyer. So goodbye yard, hello hi-rise."

"Couldn't you make a case for historical preservation?" Jack asks.

"Theoretically, yes. But the current state of my family's finances means we'll be looking for the highest bidder, and I suspect that will be a commercial developer."

Eighteen months ago, before my father died and my mother took over as the family's financial manager, Jack's suggestion would have been a viable option. Her role was supposed to be a temporary arrangement until we could hire a firm to handle everything. I actually lobbied for it to be permanent, since my mom had worked with my father for years and I thought she would understand things better than a stranger. Nora, my grandmother, nixed that idea, and in retrospect, she was right. My mom took some horribly bad advice, made some truly unwise investments, and at the end of her reign of financial terror, this land, this house, and the contents of the library upstairs are pretty much all that is left from the estate of my great-grandfather James Lawrence Coleman, one of the most renowned and controversial authors of the past century.

I had three primary reasons for returning to the United States to finish my master's degree. The first is that Coleman lived in this house, and his library is a veritable treasure trove of information about his life. The second is that Georgetown University agreed to waive my tuition for the next two years, an offer I really couldn't ignore given our financial situation. The tuition waiver is partly because they're interested in my research. Many scholars have written about Coleman, but none have had unfettered access to his papers and diaries—documents that were willed, along with this house, to Nora, as his only living child. The thing that clinched the tuition deal with Georgetown was our promise to turn all correspondence and manuscripts over to their archives once I have them organized and, with any luck, have landed a publisher for the definitive biography of James Coleman—penned by yours truly, Madison E. Grace.

My third task is selling the house, but that's last on the agenda, both because his library is here and because I need a place to live. Nora kept meaning to put the place on the market after her father died, but it sat empty for years because she couldn't bring herself to deal with the task. She just hired a maintenance service and put it out of her mind. I guess, in the end, that was a stroke of good fortune for me. The place is a bit creaky, but it was built in 1997, so that's to be expected. Great-Grandpa James had it renovated, but that was over forty years ago, so the decor is dated and the appliances are archaic. But he added a swimming pool in the basement, and that earns him forgiveness for a multitude of sins. Plus, the library is like something out of a storybook, if you can look past the clutter, which is honestly still a bit difficult to do, even after several days of going through boxes and assorted debris. I actually found an antique pearl-handled pistol in one of the desk drawers, along with several boxes of ammunition. Even the computers are clogged with ancient, disorganized files and random programs, with cryptic names like *Totals* or *Anomalies*. Some of them are so old I have no clue how to delete them. The man was a literal and virtual pack rat.

"I'm impressed at what you've done with the yard," Jack says. "You should have seen it, Alex. Grass up to your knees. Did you do it all on your own?"

I laugh. "Most of it. Although you say that as though I got down on hands and knees to trim each blade of grass. There's a practically new GardenGenieXL in the garage. It's an older model, but all I had to do was program in the specs and move some of the larger branches."

"Still, you should have called. We'd have been happy to help."

By which Jack means *he* would have been happy. Alex rarely ventures out of his lab during daylight hours, so I'm quite certain he'd have passed on any invitation that included yard work.

When Alex is a few paces ahead of us, Jack leans a bit closer and whispers, "I like the dress. Didn't know you were into vintage. But I kind of miss the blue streaks in your hair."

I smile and my cheeks grow warm. The dress is a bit much for a casual dinner with friends. I probably look like I'm trying way too hard to impress. But there's no point in explaining that more casual attire would be horribly out of place for where—and when—I'll be going shortly. Neon hair accents would probably get me arrested. Jack will understand soon enough.

We pass the small work shed, which is in dire need of an overhaul. That's one project I really *should* hire a professional to deal with. It's not the sort of thing that can be handled by automated help, and I've never hammered a nail in my life. But there's a part of me that wants to get out here and give it a try. I suspect it's the same part of me that wanted to plant the garden we're walking toward, even though it's a bit late in the season. In fact, it's probably the same part of me that's eager to take on pretty much *any* side project that doesn't require me to be in the library upstairs working on my thesis.

The garden stretches for a few meters just inside the fence that surrounds the property. A small greenhouse encases rows of seedlings, mostly tomatoes and herbs. All of the plants look a little anemic, and I make a mental note to ensure that I have the atmospheric controls set properly.

I point toward the mound of earth. "For the garden, however, I did have to get my hands dirty. And it's a good thing, because I doubt the GenieXL would have made this discovery. Hold out your hand, Jack."

After pulling the wafer-thin medallion from my pocket, I center it on his palm. There's a tingle when my fingers brush his skin, but that has absolutely nothing to do with this medallion and everything to do with the kiss we shared two nights ago.

I push those thoughts firmly aside and take a step back as he looks down at the medallion.

"And what exactly am I holding?" Jack's smile seems a bit forced.

"What do you see?"

"Um . . . I see a bronze circle. There's an hourglass in the middle."

"Does the sand in the hourglass move back and forth?"

"No. It's etched into the metal, along with these . . . spokes, I guess?" He holds it away from his body, clearly eager to get rid of it.

"I've seen the design before," Alex says. "It's a religious pendant for the Cyrists. My aunt used to be a member. Where did you find it?"

"Right there. Under the tomato seedlings. Well, under where the tomato seedlings are *now*. So . . . you don't see an orange light, Jack?"

Jack shakes his head. "No orange light. What's this all about, Madi?"

"Just bear with me, okay? Let Alex try."

He hands Alex the medallion, and I repeat the questions I asked Jack. Alex looks at me like I've gone entirely insane, and I haven't even reached the truly crazy part.

I take the medallion back from Alex and place it in my own hand. "To be honest, I was hoping that one of you could activate this. It would make explanations a lot easier. But, here goes. This medallion— which is apparently called a CHRONOS key, at least by a group of Cyrists in 1906—doesn't look bronze to me at all. It's a vibrant, glowing orange. You could put it in your pocket and I'd still be able to see the light. I stuck it under one of the sofa cushions this morning, and I could see amber light peeking out around the edges." I nudge the medallion with one finger to center it in my palm. "When I hold it like this, an interface pops up with rows of tiny video screens. I thought it was a virtual-reality game at first, but then I made the mistake of blinking on one of those screens and very nearly drowned just off the coast of Florida. In 1906."

Alex laughs. It's a friendly, uncomplicated laugh that obviously translates as *good one, guys, you got me.* Jack is also laughing, but his laughter sounds a bit more nervous. He's probably thinking back to Friday night and wondering how he can gracefully back out of any future involvement with a crazy woman.

"Okay, now that you've both had your little joke on the temporal physicist," Alex says, "I think I *will* take that drink you offered."

He starts to walk back toward the house, but I call him back. "It's not a joke, Alex. And Jack doesn't know any more than you do. Hold on for a moment, okay? I'm going to bring back some proof."

I pull up the interface, locate the stable point for Harlem, New York, and set the date for October 24, 1929, at 16:03. When I'm certain that both of them are looking directly at me, I blink.

This is the third time I've traveled to this particular spot, but the traffic noise that assaults my ears is still a shock. I don't know much about the vehicles people drove in the early twentieth century, but I can now say for certain that they were horribly loud. Smelly, too. It's better than the first time I blinked in, thanks to the rainstorm that cleared the air a bit, but the alley still reeks of fuel, with a faint undertone of trash.

I chose this specific date because it's around the time of the stock market crash that's generally viewed as the beginning of the first Great Depression. I picked this time because it's a period when the alley is empty. And I picked the specific location because out of the various places I've visited today, it puts me closest to a newsstand.

The first time I jumped here was simply to scout things out. I stood at the edge of the alley and watched for about five minutes, medallion in hand, ready to jump home if I attracted too much attention. What surprised me most—aside from the noise and the smell—was the vivid color. I know that's stupid. On a strictly rational level, I understand that life didn't play out in black and white or sepia tones in the early twentieth century. But that's how it always seemed in books and movies. The color around me made everything feel surreal, like I wasn't in the past at all, but simply watching some odd historical reenactment.

The other surprise was the realization that if I was going to spend any time in the past, I'd need clothes and money. I've heard Nora talk about carrying cash, but all of my financial transactions are handled by a comm-band on my wrist, which I've worn since I was a kid.

The credits on my comm-band are far more limited now than at any other time in my life, so the money situation required a bit of creative thinking. When I got back from my scouting trip to 1929, I located an antique shop in Baltimore that deals in both rare books and old currency. The owner was willing to exchange a few books for two twenties and a handful of coins from the 1910s. In fact, he seemed to think he'd gotten the better end of our trade, and perhaps he did. One of the perks of inheriting the house where the late, great James Coleman lived and worked is that I have several other signed copies of the books I traded. In fact, there are a few dozen boxes of books autographed by my great-grandfather. He didn't do many signings in person after the scandal, so those books are probably worth quite a bit.

Once I had old hard cash in hand, I jumped back to 1929 and bought this dress and a hat for just under five dollars. My plan is to sell back the change to that same antique dealer, hopefully for more than I paid for the antique twenties. I believe he'll agree that the smaller denomination bills the store clerk gave me as change are in amazingly good condition for having been printed two centuries ago.

I tuck the medallion into the bodice of my new dress. It's much closer to what the women are wearing than what I wore on my original jump, but I'm wishing I'd bought something thicker. The orange light of the medallion is still clearly visible through the fabric. Jack and Alex apparently can't see it, and the woman I met in 1906 made it sound as though that's true for most people. But I make a mental note to devise some sort of pouch to hide the thing better, and maybe get a chain to secure it. If someone decides to snatch it while I'm traveling, I'll be totally screwed.

That thought freezes me in place for a moment, as I'm hit by the weight of what I'm doing. Either I'm two hundred years in the past and fully reliant on a gadget that I barely know how to use to get me home, or else I've gone entirely mad and this is all in my head.

The second possibility scares me far more than the first. I need outside confirmation that I'm not insane. I need someone to believe me, which means I need proof.

A kid on a bicycle whizzes past me in the alley, splashing my shoes and reminding me that standing here thinking about my dilemma isn't going to solve a damn thing. I make it to the news-stand without attracting attention and quickly browse the newspaper headlines. After a few minutes, I select the *Brooklyn Daily Eagle*. It's not a paper I've heard of, but the headline is perfect—*WALL ST. IN PANIC AS STOCKS CRASH*, and just below, *Attempt Made to Kill Italy's Crown Prince*.

The outside of the newsstand is plastered with advertisements for cigarettes and snack foods. One ad, for a beverage called Dr. Pepper, shows a couple at a table with the caption *Drink a Bite to Eat at 10, 2 & 4 O'Clock*. On a whim, I order a bottle and grab a chocolate bar as well.

"Where you from, miss?" The vendor takes his time opening the soda, and his eyes keep moving from my face to my chest as I search among my coins for two dimes. Can he see the light from the medallion, or is he simply checking out what Nora refers to as my *rack*, which I guess was the polite term for breasts back in the 2080s?

He hands me the bottle and my change. "Your accent, I mean. It don't sound like—"

"Just outside of London." That's partly true. I've spent nearly as much time in the US. We lived in Colorado until I was in my teens, and I spent most summers at the shore house near Dublin, where Nora lives now, or at her house in London. But regardless of whether the man is staring at the CHRONOS key inside my dress or the breasts inside my dress, I really don't want to get bogged down in a conversation with him. The oddness of my accent is probably even more attributable to a two-century time difference than to the fact that I've lived in the UK.

I scoop up my purchases and say, "Have a good . . . one."

Did people actually *say* that in 1929? I have no idea, so I hurry back to the alley and pull up the stable point that I set earlier near the work shed in the backyard. I can see myself, Jack, and Alex talking near the garden plot, so I skip forward until I disappear, add another ten seconds, and blink in.

Jack and Alex are still staring at the spot where I was standing.

"Over here."

Poor Alex startles so badly that I feel guilty.

"I'm sorry. I should have set another point closer to the garden."

"Where the hell did you go?" he asks.

"Yeah. One second you were *right there* and—" Jack breaks off and looks nervously toward the shed.

"New York. 1929. I bought snacks and reading material." I hand the newspaper and candy to Alex and take a swig of the soda. "Oh dear God, that's *much* too sweet. I feel like I need to shave the sugar off my tongue. Want to try it?"

Jack takes the bottle I'm holding and sniffs. "Despite your ringing endorsement, I think I'll pass."

Alex stares at the newspaper. He's gone so pale that I'm a little concerned he might pass out. "Okay," he says. "I don't know how you did that disappearing thing, or where you got this paper, but the joke's over. It's not even that original. Everybody thinks it's funny to pull a time-travel punk on temporal physicists. But our lab is one of the top research facilities in the world. We've made some progress—more than we usually let on, to be honest—but we're nowhere near this level. So this has to be a stunt."

"It's not a stunt. If you need more proof, you can pick the date this time. Although it probably needs to be within the same decade, or I'll have to get different currency and different clothes . . ."

But I'm talking to his back. Alex is already halfway to the patio.

Jack stares at me for a moment. I can't tell if he's mad or just confused. Then he takes off after Alex. I'm not sure what he says, but Alex stops, and when I catch up with the two of them, Jack gestures toward the house. "Let's go inside and have that drink while we sort all this out."

None of us is especially hungry yet, but I grab three glasses and the bottle of Shiraz I uncorked earlier. Jack takes a plate from the cabinet and begins slicing the Baby Ruth bar.

Alex watches him with one eyebrow raised, which I completely get. Who the hell *slices* a candy bar?

Jack catches our expression. "Hey, I'm just following the instructions." He nods toward the red-and-white wrapper, and sure enough, it says *Slice and Serve for All Occasions.* "I didn't want to ruin the fancy appetizer you've apparently brought all the way from 1929."

There's a note to his voice that troubles me, and a slight emphasis on the word *apparently.* The truth is, I can't read Jack well enough yet to tell whether he believes me. We've been friends since I arrived on campus back in August, but that's still only a few months. Like me, Jack Merrick is working on a master's in history. Like me, he's new in town. But unlike me, Jack is not an introvert. He has excellent social skills. Thanks to his intervention, I've actually met some people, including Alex, who is Jack's roommate, and a few of the other graduate students in the history department.

It's been nice having a companion for lunch the two days a week I'm on campus. It's been nice having him drag me out of the house most weekends. We have similar interests, and he's easy to talk to, especially since he understands firsthand the pain of losing a parent. His mom died when he was twelve. But I didn't figure out that his interest was romantic until he leaned in for a kiss when he dropped me off two nights ago. Nora once said that any guy who was interested in me would have to launch a full advertising campaign, complete with flashing lights, before I'd catch on. I thought I'd gotten a bit better at picking up on these things, but Friday's experience suggests that I have not.

We carry the wine, the neatly sliced candy bar, and a cheese plate I prepared earlier back into the living room. Once we're seated, Alex takes a long sip from his glass and then says, "So. You found a time-travel device—one that only you appear to be able to use—buried in your backyard. Let's start with an easy question. Why would anyone bury it? I'd think dropping it into the ocean would be a wiser choice if you wanted to dispose of it and couldn't just . . . disable it."

"True. But I don't think it was a *person* that buried the key. And the thing actually did drop me into the ocean yesterday, which was the first time I used it. Perhaps it was trying to tell me something." I pull two oddly shaped items from under the coffee table. "As you can see from the etching on the side, these are called Nylabones. There was also a different sort of dog toy buried there, but it didn't hold up as well. I had to toss it."

"You think a *dog* buried that medallion?" Jack says. "Why? And when?"

"No clue. But Nora called while I was planting the garden, right after I dug the thing up. She said her father never owned a dog, but she's pretty sure his mom did, and she also said the medallion looked like something that her Grandma Kate owned. Nora recognized it as a religious medal, too, although she said her grandmother hated the Cyrists. And Nora is convinced that her grandmother's medallion was buried with her, although I don't know why anyone would want to be buried with a symbol of something she hated."

"Maybe she had two of them?" Jack says.

I shrug. "Maybe. I didn't even realize it had religious connections until Nora told me. It looked like one of those handheld VR toys to me. When Nora said it was something of her grandmother's, I offered to send it to her. But she told me she had plenty of things to remember Grandma Kate by. She actually said it was drab looking."

"Well, she's not wrong," Alex says. "It's kind of ugly."

"We'll have to agree to disagree on that point. I wouldn't say it's pretty, exactly, but it's very much the *opposite* of drab for me. Anyway, I was looking at the key while talking to Nora, and a holographic display popped up. Nine squares, three rows of three, each with an image. Some of them seemed static, but I'm pretty sure now that it's just because they're closets or dark alleys or whatever. The visual navigation is fairly standard, so I swiped with my eyes and discovered a second set of screens. One of them caught my attention—an underwater scene, with a concrete crypt of some sort on the ocean floor. Fish swimming around. It was pretty. Kind of hypnotic. I got caught up in watching the fish move in and out of the picture, and I missed something Nora was saying. She said my name again, louder, which startled me into blinking. And the next thing I know, I'm in the ocean."

"Actually *in* the ocean?" Alex asks.

"Yes. I still thought it was a VRE. A damn good one, but . . . what else could it be, right? I was tempted to just start breathing and see if I'd sprout gills or something, like you would in a game. But I've been swimming since before I could walk, and the don't-breathe-underwater thing is hardwired at this point. So I kicked off from the bottom and headed toward the surface. Didn't make it before my air ran out. When I came to, I was on the beach with a teenage girl trying to resuscitate me. There was a guy with her, and some woman approaching from a house up the shore. They were all dressed weird—I mean, all three of them were on the beach, but pretty much every bit of skin was covered."

"Maybe they didn't want to burn," Alex suggests.

"I guess. But the clothes were just . . . wrong. Bulky skirts, odd shoes. And the woman, a doctor named June, had one of these medallions. She told the other two to go back to the compound or commune or whatever. Long story somewhat shorter, that beach was Estero Island, Florida. The date was October 12, 1906. This June person tried to convince me to stay. Said that the Cyrists could use more jumpers, that I could be part of this glorious new world they were planning. When I made it clear I wanted to leave, she reluctantly showed me how to use the interface to change the date. I eventually made it back to 2136, but the closest I could get to here was a stable point at the Lincoln Memorial. I paged a car, and that's when I called Jack and invited the two of you over for dinner tonight."

"Why do you think you were in 1906?" Jack asks as I grab one of the candy-bar slices.

"Well, the woman *told* me, for one thing. The display on the medallion—the CHRONOS key, as she called it—confirmed it, as well. But I think the thing that really convinced me was getting dumped back into the ocean."

They both look confused, so I continue. "I had to make a quick exit. Another one of these Cyrists showed up unexpectedly, and I didn't have time to scan for a stable point in DC. So I just changed the date. I'd been sitting on a bed, inside a beach house a good hundred meters from the shore back in 1906. But when I reached 2136, I found myself underwater again. That entire end of the island is submerged now, except for a tiny strip where the group erected a giant Cyrist symbol—you know the one that looks a bit like an Egyptian ankh?"

Alex nods. "I've seen them. Like I said, my aunt is Cyrist—at least she used to be. Not sure if she's still a member, but she has one of those lotus-flower tats on her hand."

I nod. We've all seen those tattoos. Occasionally they're worn by someone younger, but more often, it's a faded pink relic on the hand of someone's grandmother. Or blue, if it's their grandfather.

"Anyway, the water was fairly shallow at the location I'd set, so I easily made it to what's left of the Cyrist symbol—" I stop, realizing that I can show them what I saw. "Hold on. Jarvis, pull up a map of the southern end of Estero Island and send it to the wall display."

My virtual assistant turns on the screen. After the map appears, I tell him to zoom in on the sandbar and the concrete pillar.

"Now superimpose a Cyrist symbol over the map." An image pops up—basically an ankh with an infinity symbol for arms and a lotus flower in the middle. "See that upside-down *U* in the sand? That's one of the arms. The statue must have gotten damaged in a storm."

They're both silent for a moment and then Alex says, "No offense, but this doesn't prove anything. You could have searched for a location on the map and built your story around that."

"True," Jack says. "But that slice of candy bar you're eating, the newspaper on the table, the sickly sweet soda over there, and the fact that Madi vanished and reappeared? That clearly indicates that *something* is going on."

"It could be a portable cloaking device. Maybe she cloaked and then walked over to that shed, where she had this stuff hidden." Alex runs one hand through his short blond hair and gives me a pleading look, like he feels he should apologize for calling me a liar. He's a nice guy, who generally hates making waves, but he's also a scientist. I can't really blame him for wanting to find a rational answer.

"But why?" Jack asks. "What reason would she have to lie about this?"

"It's okay, Jack. I probably wouldn't believe me, either. But . . . I dug around in the library today and found something odd. Something that I'd have thought was just one of James Coleman's weird alt-history books if not for this medallion, but . . ."

I open the drawer on the side of the living-room console, extract a thin book, and hold it out toward Alex. The title, *A Brief History of CHRONOS*, is embossed on the front cover. I found this particular volume wedged inside one of the climate-controlled cabinets surrounding most of the bookshelves. There was no title on the spine, and I'm not sure if I'd have found it at all if not for the clunky, error-ridden file catalog in the house's computer system. It's nearly useless unless you know precisely what you're searching for. Fortunately, I had a specific keyword—*CHRONOS*—to guide my search today.

"It's a . . . book," he says, arching one eyebrow. "Not exactly an *odd* find in a library."

"Open it to the preface," I tell him.

He does, although I get the sense that he's humoring me. As he reads the first sentence, color drains from his face.

The scientific principles of time travel were discovered in the mid-22nd century by a small team of researchers, headed by Ian Alexander, Ryan Jefferson, and Madison Grace.

"I don't know this Ryan Jefferson person," I say. "But I'm going to go out on a limb and guess that people call you Alex because your *last* name is Alexander?"

He nods, still looking kind of numb.

I take the book from Alex's hands and give it to Jack, who reads it and then looks back at me. "You've met Ryan Jefferson, too. Alex's cousin. Goes by RJ? He and his wife, Lorena, were at the soccer game last week."

The names bring up a hazy image of a couple in their late twenties, but I can't remember speaking more than a few words to either of them. Jack's weekly soccer games have a shifting roster of players and are really more an excuse to drink and goof off than serious sport. I even took the field once when they were short a player, and my football skills are limited, to put it mildly.

"When did you find this?" Jack asks.

"Last night. It was odd, because I'd already told you to bring Alex and then I saw his name listed there. Although . . . maybe not so odd, since he's the only temporal physicist I've ever met. It did take me a moment to connect the two . . . I don't think I've ever heard anyone call him anything other than Alex."

"You could have found out my last name," Alex says. "It's not exactly a state secret. And you have to know how easy it is to forge a book."

"True," I admit. "This would be a lot easier to fake than me using the equipment. I just thought you might want to see it. But, if you need more evidence . . ."

I tell Jarvis to put up the list I made earlier today of stable points. Each entry includes the physical location, the specific date and time that has been preset into the key, and also a date range that the location is usable. The only things I didn't type in were the long strings of numbers that I'm pretty sure are encoded versions of the geographic locations.

"Pick a new date and place from that list. I have a preference for the New York stable point—"

"Why do you call them stable points?" Alex asks.

"Because that's what the doctor at Estero called them. If I had to guess, the dates listed give us the period of time when these geographic points are stable . . . thus, *stable points*. But that's just a guess. As I was saying, I have a preference for New York, because there is a newsstand really close by. And a date in the 1920s or 1930s would be best, because my time-traveling wardrobe is currently limited to what you see. But I'll jump to any of these you want—"

"Wait a minute," Jack says. "How many times have you used that thing today?"

I mentally tabulate the various jumps. "Seven . . . no, wait. Eight. I think."

His eyebrows shoot up. "Seven jumps to 1929?"

"No. Three jumps to 1929. One to Memphis, 1952. One to Montgomery, 1965. One to Liverpool, 1957. Whoever had this key was into music, because the only thing I could find significant about that last date was that it was when two members of some band first performed together. The others were concerts. All of them were quick in-and-out trips, just to see if I could do it. I wasn't really dressed to stick around. But, after I bought the dress, I actually did hang out for a bit at the Lincoln Memorial in April of 1939 so that I could hear Marian Anderson sing. I recorded it, even. Jarvis, play—"

Alex cuts me off. "I don't know who that is, but if it's someone famous, you could have gotten it from—"

And then Jack cuts *him* off. "Maybe some precautions are in order? Did you ever stop to consider that there might be limits on how often you can use that thing? What if you get stranded in one of those places?"

"He's right," Alex says. "You don't even know how it works."

"Of course, I considered the risk."

It's true, although I wouldn't really say it gave me serious pause until that last jump, when I thought about the possibility of someone stealing the key. Earlier in the day, I'd been too caught up in the sheer excitement of what was happening to really think about potential problems.

After taking a deep breath, I continue. "I needed to get proof, okay? I needed to figure out some way to convince the two of you that I'm telling the truth. That this is really happening, and not the product of a mental breakdown. I *need* someone to believe me."

We're all silent for a moment and then Alex says, "It's not that I don't want to believe you. It would actually help confirm some research I kind of . . . stumbled upon earlier this year. Old stuff, from decades ago. Do you have any idea how incredible this discovery will be if it's real? I *want* it to be real. I want the paragraph in that book to be real. But the fact that I want to believe is precisely why I can't *let* myself believe it. I'm already biased."

"Okay," Jack says. "You're a scientist. You need scientific proof. I get that." Then he turns to look at me. "But I'm *not* a scientist, and I'm willing to go on gut instinct. So if it makes you feel better, you've convinced one of us. I can't think of any reason you'd have to lie to us about this."

I'm not entirely certain if Jack means he believes what I'm saying is true, or if he believes that *I* believe it's true. But either way, it's a start.

"As for our skeptic," Jack says, "go ahead and pick a date and time. Or several, if you'd like. But could we place a moratorium on Madi actually using this thing again, at least until tomorrow?"

"Sure," Alex says. "That will give me some time to dig a bit deeper into the theories of the handful of physicists who believe that time travel is possible for human beings, rather than just packets of information. Or, you know, *lunatics*, as my colleagues call them."

FROM THE *NEW YORK DAILY INTREPID* (AUGUST 28, 1963)

Crowds Flock to DC to Attend March for Jobs and Freedom

(Washington) Over 200,000 attendees, both Negro and white, gathered today at the memorial to Abraham Lincoln, "the Great Emancipator," demanding an end to racial discrimination. Today's massive "March for Jobs and Freedom," the largest demonstration in DC history, was organized by civil rights leaders seeking equal education and the removal of all race barriers to employment.

Marchers made their way to the capital via plane, on a specially chartered train, in thousands of buses, and by private automobiles, with some even entering the city on foot. Gathering at the base of the Washington Monument, the group proceeded toward the Lincoln

Memorial, singing the civil rights hymn "We Shall Overcome."

National Guard and police patrolled the area, dispersing a small counterprotest by the American Nazi Party. Despite concerns about possible violence, the march was orderly and peaceful, with remarks by more than a dozen civil rights advocates. The highlight was a stirring speech by the Rev. Dr. Martin Luther King Jr., leader of the Southern Christian Leadership Conference, who shared his dream of a nation where all people are equal and judged by their character, rather than by the color of their skin.

∞3∞

Tyson
Spartanburg, South Carolina
September 3, 1963

"Hold on, hold on." Miss Ida drops a second foil-wrapped package of hush puppies into the brown paper sack, then folds the edge over three times and creases it neatly. "I almost forgot his extras. Knowin' Judge Turner, he'd send you all the way back to get them. I expect he'll have someone downstairs to meet you this time, but if he don't, his office is the third from the right, up on the second floor."

"Are you sure this is a good idea?"

"No." She laughs bitterly. "I think it's an awful idea. Then again, so is tellin' a sittin' judge *no* when he calls up and orders a chicken box. No good choices here. But, sweet Jesus, go through the back door this time, Tyson. I don't know how folks are doin' things up in Chicago, but that ain't how we do down here."

Ida must realize it's a bit unfair to rehash my error two weeks later, because her dark eyes soften and a tiny smile lifts the corners of her mouth as she pushes the bag into my hands. "Go on, now. Take your break on the way back if you want. But I need you here for the lunch rush, so don't dillydally reading the funny books at Woolworth's."

I'm confused for a moment, and then realize *funny books* must be some weird vernacular for comics. One of her many gossipy patrons has been telling tales.

Once outside, I lift my face to catch the faint breeze. It's still hot and humid, but it's at least ten degrees cooler out here than it was inside. Ida claims it's pointless to try to cool down the kitchen. She's probably right, but when you're stuck over a steaming sink—or worse yet, the deep fryer—it feels like you're being boiled alive.

This is almost certainly the only fresh air I'll catch until my shift ends at nine tonight. The double shift is my own doing, though, not Ida's. I paid the regular waitress a dollar to swap out so I can work the dining room this afternoon, in addition to my usual split shift bussing tables during the breakfast and dinner hours. Today is Tuesday, when the deacons from Mount Moriah Baptist have their weekly fellowship lunch. They don't tip worth a damn, and the waitress clearly thought I was crazy to fork out a whole dollar to get that shift. But this is their first fellowship meeting since two of them returned from participating in the March on Washington. They'll have a lot to say, and I don't want to miss it.

Of course, I'd really rather have been in DC, watching King's speech in person. There were at least a dozen CHRONOS agents in that crowd. For that matter, it would have been more interesting to make this trip to the Spartanburg of three years ago, in the summer of 1960, when Woolworth's national office ordered stores to integrate their lunch counters. Spartanburg's city council responded with a proclamation against the order, and the black community responded in turn with a sit-in at the local Woolworth's. That would have been something worth witnessing.

The town is relatively quiet and less historically interesting in the summer of '63. And that's kind of the point. If I make a rookie mistake and something I do or say changes the opinions or actions of a deacon at Mount Moriah Church or one of the patrons at the

Southside Diner, the odds are good that the timeline will keep rolling right along without the slightest hiccup.

Or, at least, that's the theory. And I really hope it holds true, because as I round the corner, approaching the courthouse, I spot trouble, in the form of two white men leaning against a car parked on the side of the road. Trouble spots me, too. I keep my eyes down, hoping to avoid interaction. It's pointless, though. I can see from the shadows on the sidewalk that they're heading straight toward me.

Both men are dressed in what seems to be standard male summer business attire for this era—a short-sleeved dress shirt, usually white, with black or gray pants. Add a hat if the guy is balding, and a tie if he thinks he's important. Both of these men are sporting ties, and the short, tubby one is wearing a hat.

"Hey, boy," the slightly taller and considerably thinner of the two men calls out. "Where you goin' with that bag?"

I glance up and get a clearer view of his face. He looks familiar, with dark hair and a square jaw. It's hard to be certain, but I think I've seen him before. Maybe in the local papers or in my research prior to the trip.

"I'm just makin' a delivery over to the courthouse, sir."

"Mmm-mmm-mmm." The tubby man steps into my path. He leans in toward the bag I'm holding, and inhales deeply. "Smells like somebody ordered up some nigga-fried chicken."

My jaw tightens, and so does my grip on the bag, but I know better than to meet his eyes. I'm here to *observe*. To experience events as someone living in this time would experience them. This is the sort of crap a black man in 1963 South Carolina has to deal with all the time. It's part of the experience, and I took an oath not to interfere.

Right this minute, however, I'd love nothing more than to punch this fat fuck right in the face.

Square Jaw spits on the sidewalk, just missing my shoes. "What's your name, boy?"

"Tyson Roberts, sir." It's actually Reyes, but if these two are police and they ask for my ID, Roberts is the name they'll find on my Illinois driver's license. I don't think they're cops, though.

"You ain't from around here, are you?"

"No, sir. Not originally."

"'Not *originally*,'" Tubby says, and they both snicker.

"You must be that high yella college boy Ida hired," the taller man says. "Wanna tell me who ordered that chicken box?"

"Don't know, sir. I was just told to—"

"I did, Mr. Scoggin." A gray-haired black man comes around the side of the building, limping slowly across the lawn. "My lumbago been botherin' me somethin' awful, and Miss Ida said she'd have someone carry it on over."

I'm not sure if this is the person the judge sent downstairs to fetch his lunch or just a Good Samaritan who decided to intervene. Either way, I'm glad to see him.

"Maybe you oughta just fix yourself a shit sammich next time before you leave the house," Tubby says. "Save your money for when your lumbago gets so bad you cain't work no more."

The old guy laughs uneasily. "That's good advice, sir. I prob'ly *should* bring somethin' from home. You got my extry hush puppies like I asked?"

Well, that answers my question about whether the judge sent him. "Yessir. They're in the bag."

He gives me a dollar bill in exchange for the food and heads back to the rear entrance of the courthouse, moving much faster now. In fact, he's barely limping at all. I risk a quick glance up at the two white men and can see from the wry twist of Square Jaw's mouth that he's also noticed the old man's miraculous recovery.

His face still looks familiar. *Where have I seen him before?*

"You know Eddie Franklin?" he asks as I stuff the dollar bill into my pocket.

"Yessir," I say, but don't elaborate. Eddie is Miss Ida's fry cook, and also her nephew. He's a few years older than me, and he's introduced me to a few people. Invited me to have a beer after work a few times. I'm not sure if being friendly was his aunt's suggestion, since I'm new in town, or Eddie's own choice. Either way, he seems like a decent guy.

"Well then, you tell Eddie to watch hisself," Tubby says. "We know all about that girl over at Arkwright."

I have no idea what girl they're talking about, but I can put the pieces together. Arkwright is a textile mill, one of many in the area, and the vast majority of mill workers are white until the end of this decade.

"Yessir," I repeat. "I'll tell him."

"Get on back to work, then," Square Jaw snaps.

They return to their car, peeling away from the curb as I head down the sidewalk toward the south side of town. I continue that way for a bit, until I'm certain they aren't following me. Then I turn onto Dunbar Street and walk the two blocks to Woolworth's.

The manager smiles broadly when I step through the door. "Tyson! We got some of them new Marvel books you were lookin' for."

I don't know if this manager, who is white, was for or against segregation during the sit-ins three years ago, but he's always delighted to see me. That's almost certainly because I've dropped about half my meager salary from the diner on magazines and comics during the three weeks I've been here. The CHRONOS archives have copies of most major publications, but a lot of pop-culture stuff wasn't preserved. Historians usually look for a few things to carry back with us, even stuff outside of our own research agendas.

The particular items I'm looking for today, however, won't be going to the archives. Edwina didn't have to answer my questions about her genetic designs, and she definitely didn't have to be nice about doing it. And September 1963 was a big month for comic books. Marvel released the very first issues of both *X-Men* and *The Avengers*. Given the immense popularity of both series well into the next century, I'm certain that our archive has both of those issues in digital format. But they're rare enough that Edwina might not have print copies in the collection she inherited from her father. And at twelve cents each, it's a pretty cheap thank-you gift.

Two of the Mount Moriah deacons are already seated at their usual table when I get back to the diner, but between the morning shift in the kitchen and the humidity outside, my shirt is drenched. I take the stairs up to the small apartment over the diner to stash the comics and change into fresh clothes. Even though I need to get back downstairs, the encounter at the courthouse is bugging me, so I pull my CHRONOS diary from under the mattress and flip it open, bracing myself for a message.

And just like last time, there's nothing. No indication that my little run-in at the courthouse affected the timeline in any way.

"Everything go okay?" Miss Ida asks when I bring the first round of orders back to the kitchen.

"Yes, ma'am."

Eddie is dropping a basket of chicken into the fryer. I decide not to mention the two men yet. Regardless of whether there's any truth to their claim, Sharon—Eddie's on-again, off-again girl—is the other waitress on duty today. I'm certain it's not the kind of thing he'd want discussed in front of her, and even more certain it's not something he'd want discussed in front of his aunt.

For the next few hours, I deliver plates of roast beef, meat loaf, pork chops, and fried chicken. I fetch iced tea and coffee, and "maybe a few more of those good biscuits" for Deacon Faircloth, who will furtively wrap them in a napkin to take home for tomorrow's breakfast. In between, I watch, and I listen. I'm under no illusion that I'll see or hear all of their conversation, but I don't need to. There's a tiny audio device at the table to pick up what I miss while shuttling plates to and from the kitchen, and I've set numerous stable points in the dining room to cover the visual side. I can use that data to fill in any gaps in my notes once I'm back in my own time. And CHRONOS isn't really looking for a verbatim account of what was said and done. If that's what they wanted, there are less risky ways of getting it.

In fact, historians tried the remote-recording route for a few decades, dropping cameras and microphones at the various stable points. They soon realized, however, that context is vital. Even day-trippers miss a lot. If I'd simply jumped in this morning, parked myself at a nearby table, and ordered the lunch special, I'd probably have heard more of the deacons' conversation. But I wouldn't have understood as much about who they are. I wouldn't have caught the things that lie beneath their words. I wouldn't know that the oldest among them, Deacon Fry, was born a slave or that the preacher's brother-in-law thinks Martin Luther King Jr. is a stooge for the Communist Party. I wouldn't know that Deacon Smith's dismissive comments today about the significance of the march and King's speech were almost entirely due to him being passed over in favor of Deacon Faircloth when the congregation chose someone to travel to DC along with the preacher. All of that subtext would be missing for a day-tripper.

I can't help but wonder how many other things beneath the surface are hidden from someone like me, who has been in town less than a month. You can live for years in places like this and still be considered an outsider. But you have to strike a balance. Most historians want a bit of variety. I've only known a few CHRONOS agents who were willing to put down roots and stay in one historical location permanently.

The lunch rush gives way to dinner prep, and then I work the dining room until we flip the *Closed* sign at a little after nine. Sharon is sweeping, and I'm bussing the last table when a motor revs outside.

Miss Ida, who is counting out the register, wraps a rubber band around a stack of dollar bills. I still haven't had a chance to talk to Eddie and decide this might be a good time while the other two are busy.

The engine roars again. "Some fool needs a new muffler," Sharon says.

As soon as I step into the kitchen, I smell the smoke. Not cooking odors from the fryer, but the sharp, pungent smoke of a gasoline fire from outside. The fumes are being pulled in by the fan wedged into the window facing the road that runs alongside the diner.

Eddie stands frozen a few feet from the window, watching the bright glow through the blades of the fan as they spin. The burning object is a cross, about five feet high. As the flames spread up and out, three men in white hoods—the modern kind that proudly show their faces—climb back into the cab of the truck. I'm pretty sure one of the three is the tubby guy from the courthouse. And even though he isn't with them, the hoods are what make me finally recognize Square Jaw's face. He's one of the Klan leaders in the photographs Rich included in the proposal for our upcoming research trip with Katherine.

Eddie grabs the fire extinguisher from the wall near the fryer. "Sharon! Get Aunt Ida upstairs and stay there. Both of you." Then he turns to me. "You sure nothin' went wrong with that delivery today?"

"Nothing went *wrong*, except for two men who told me to give you a message. Something about a woman you're seeing over at Arkwright."

His eyes shoot toward the dining room, and then he curses. "This ain't about no woman. Get the other canister from the dining room."

Ida pushes through the swinging door seconds before I reach it. "What you yellin' at me about, Ed—" She stops when she sees the cross outside. "Sweet Jesus, Tyson. You said everything went okay today! That don't look like okay to me."

By the time I make it outside with the fire extinguisher, Mr. Larson, the owner of the little store across the street, has joined Eddie and is spraying the cross with a stream of white foam from his own extinguisher. Eddie's canister is now empty. He snatches the second one from me, smacks the top against the sidewalk to open it, and puts out the last of the flames.

"Any idea what's got 'em riled up?" Larson asks.

Eddie shoots a glance at me, and then at his aunt, who is standing in the doorway, hugging her arms to her chest. "Judge ordered a chicken box today. Lenny Phelps saw Tyson making the delivery."

"All they *saw* was me giving it to some old man who worked there."

I want to protest some more, to argue that this isn't my fault, or at least not entirely my fault. For one thing, I'm not sure that it is. While he may be dating Sharon, Eddie has, as they say in this era, a wandering eye. I've been out with him on two different occasions, once here in town and once over in Gaffney, and I've witnessed that eye wander across the color line.

I'd like to think that Eddie's smart enough to keep the rest of his body from following, because there's no faster way for a black man in this place and time to get himself killed. Of course, it's also the perfect excuse for the Klan to target a successful black business that's seen as a threat to a white business's profit margin.

But the worst thing that happens to me if Ida decides this is my fault is that she fires me. I might have to head back home early, although I suppose there's nothing to stop me from hanging around town for a few days until I can gauge community reaction to the Birmingham bombing. So I don't protest further. I just give them what little I know. "They didn't use the name Phelps. The old guy said Coggins. Or something like that."

Eddie spits into the grass. "Scoggin is their leader. Tall guy, dark hair. Phelps's sister owns The Dixie Chicken. And Phelps goes ever'where Scoggin goes, like a fat, ugly shadow. Kinda strange to call him muscle when he's barely got any, but he's the one in charge of enforcement. He's got half a dozen guys who'll do pretty much anything he wants if he gets them liquored up."

"He sure does," Larson says. "That's four crosses they burnt this summer alone. Only saw one more 'n that all last year. My brother says they're the ones killed those two Whitman boys a couple years back. And Louise Freeman swears her girl Emmy didn't just run off. I still think they had somethin' to do with it."

Nothing in my research for this jump mentioned cross burnings in Spartanburg this summer. There's no mention of Klan-related killings, either. After three weeks here, though, that doesn't really surprise me. The only African American newspaper from this area in the CHRONOS archives was a short-lived enterprise that operated for a few years in the 1920s. And things like this generally don't make the white-owned papers.

Once the fire is fully out, Eddie gives the cross a few hard kicks, and it topples onto the sidewalk. We spray it down with the hose until it's cool enough to drag around by the dumpster and then go back inside.

Ida is in the dining room, writing something on a note card. She looks up when I walk by.

"I'm sorry, Miss Ida. I would have gone around back, but those men cut me off. Started asking questions. The judge's man came out and got the chicken, though, so I didn't think there was a problem. I guess I was wrong. You want me to work out the week, or go now?"

"No," she says. "I'm countin' on you to stay on through mid-September like you promised when I gave you this job. This ain't your fault."

I glance down at what she's writing. *IDA'S FRIED CHICKEN* is scrawled across the top.

"I'll have to give him the recipe for the hush puppies, too," she says. "It'll prob'ly end up in the hands of half the people on this side of town."

"I bet Dixie Chicken will get it," Sharon says.

"Dixie Chicken already *has* my recipe. I had someone say they stole it from me and offer to sell it to that woman right after she opened, hoping Judge Turner would order from her. He's the only white folks who ever orders from me, so it's no skin off my back. That Phelps woman paid five dollars for the recipe, but she thinks her food is better, so she ain't ever switched. And I suspect that's exactly what will happen if I send it to the cook at his house. So this is goin' to the judge's wife."

"You think she'll cook it for him?" I ask.

Ida and Sharon both look at me like I'm crazy. "No," Ida says. "But maybe she'll tell her cook to follow the recipe. And if that don't work, I'll just have to carry the durn thing over to his office myself. 'Cause if he don't quit orderin' from me, those fools are gonna burn my place clean to the ground."

FROM THE DIARY OF

KATE PIERCE-KELLER

March 9, 2074

History has changed again.

It was a gradual change this time around. I'm sure it took months of organization at every level of government to ensure that people in the United States, as well as those in our allied nations, were in compliance with the new law.

It was gradual in another sense, as well. The seeds for this change were planted in a time shift that happened more than half a century ago. No one activated a CHRONOS key to set it in motion. I don't even know if there's anyone alive who can use the thing, although I'm sure there are government scientists working on that by now. They probably started the wheels turning on that project as soon as they removed the bullets from Simon Rand's body and patched him up. They had my Aunt Prudence, too, and my mother told me that the reason Prudence's coffin was closed at the funeral was that there was no body inside—as soon as they removed the medallion grafted to her arm, her body simply vanished.

Unlike the time shifts that occurred when I was a teenager, this one didn't make me dizzy or panicked, although I'll admit I was a little unnerved when the medical technician arrived about a month ago for our appointment. Aside from that, the only thing I felt was the tiny prickle against my skin as they stamped my left arm with the immunizer. Thankfully, it didn't imprint a temporary lotus tattoo this time. When I saw the stamping tool, I asked the med tech if she could apply the stamp to the back of my hand—a joke that Trey got, even if no one else did. She said no, and the other tech pointed out rather unnecessarily that I am old and my hands lack the necessary padding to absorb the medicine. And then the two of them moved on to the apartment complex next door, probably thinking that this old lady was a little soft in the head.

Or maybe she thought I was one of the people opposed to the program. It's being billed as a mandatory vaccination against a particularly virulent strain of the avian flu that the CDC and World Health Organization are predicting for this year. That's true, in a sense, but they left out the part where the virus has been genetically altered. And the part where we dodged this very same bullet fifty-five years ago by destroying the virus before Saul's people could distribute it.

The main difference between now and 2015 is that there's been plenty of time for the US and our allies to stockpile a vaccine and be sure it's distributed. There may still be a few deaths, but it will just seem like a nasty flu season for us. Back then, we had almost no warning. The only hope was to stop the attack before it happened.

Although it feels like this current vaccination program is altering the timeline, I don't think even Katherine would object. My grandmother was always adamant that a CHRONOS historian was only there to observe, but as I pointed out, I've never been a CHRONOS historian. For all I know, something CHRONOS did could have caused this disaster in the first place. And even if this attack was *supposed* to happen at some point in world history, whether or not time travelers screwed things up, the death toll would have been staggering. I saw that in my own time travels. Rules or no rules, you don't just let something like that happen if you can stop it. Not if you have a soul.

So, I was perfectly okay with the government taking the vaccine that Dr. Tilson and his colleagues developed and saving hundreds of millions of lives. Tilson had hinted that this was likely before he died. I was even kind of proud as I watched the rollout of the program, the careful coordination between allied governments that frequently squabble, and the decision to train unemployed people to go door-to-door to administer the vaccine. It was how governments *should* function, but all too rarely do.

And that's why the images on my newsfeed today have shaken me to the core. I *know* we are currently at war, even though it's been so long and so low-level that it feels like a constant state of affairs. I know that this virus was planned as a terrorist attack on civilian populations. I know it was an illegal weapon under international law, and I'm not so naive that I think you can let something like the use of biogenetic weapons slide without punishment.

I'd be perfectly okay with punishing the supposed *doctor*, Elizabeth Forson, who developed the weapon, fully aware that it would kill many of her own people, too. She'd been willing to risk that as long as it meant killing far, far more of the enemy.

But at least some people within our government knew that this attack was going to happen. The fact that they distributed a vaccine to protect the US and our allies *proves* that they knew. And yet they did nothing to protect the innocent people on the other side. They could have sneaked the serum into a vaccine program sponsored by a group like Doctors Without Borders, which still operates in most of those countries. They had over nearly six fucking decades to plan this. They could have done *something*.

But they didn't. I opened my newsfeed today to see stacks of bodies piled twenty or thirty high. They looked a lot like the bodies Kiernan and I saw at Six Bridges, Georgia, so many years ago—desiccated, dried-up husks, consumed by the virus.

Trey, who I could tell was as horrified as I was at the images, tried to calm me down. He said the government was probably worried about a conundrum. If the war in Africa didn't unfold the same way, would we even have had the sample to develop the serum?

Maybe he's right. But it doesn't change the fact that I'm going to see those bodies in my dreams for a very long time.

And that is why this will be my last diary entry. I don't know how much time Trey and I have left in this world, or how much time we have to spend with our sons or our grandchildren. Kell stops by on a regular basis, since he works downtown, but Nora hasn't been to the house since her father's trial five years ago. She's met me and Trey in New York on occasion, but this time, I think we'll go to her. I'll schedule a flight to London for next week. Trey and I can treat it as a late fiftieth-anniversary trip. We haven't been to London since our ill-fated excursion in 2015, when Cyrist bodyguards chased us across Forum Magnum Square. Maybe we can relax and take in the sights this time, with Nora as our tour guide.

It's time to let go. Trey has spent fifty-two years married to a woman obsessed with the things I didn't change. Things that I *could* have changed, maybe *should* have changed, when I was young enough to use the CHRONOS key. And I've continued to wear it long after I could use the thing because, as I told President Patterson long ago, if there was a time shift, I wanted to *know*.

The CHRONOS key is in its pouch—the leather pouch Kiernan made—inside my dresser drawer now. My neck feels bare without its weight, unnatural, like my ring finger does on the rare occasions when I remove my wedding band. And when Trey and I go to London, the key will stay here. If there's a time shift, I can't fix it. My sons can't fix it. Their children can't fix it.

Even though it's a bit late, I *will* learn to accept the things that I cannot change. But the only way I can be *serene* about doing that is to make sure I never, ever know if another time shift happens.

∞4∞

Madi
Estero, Florida
October 7, 1906

I don't actually lose my balance when I blink in, but it's a close call. The problem is partly the loose sand beneath my feet and partly the slope of the hill. Mostly, however, it's the wind, which is far stronger than I'd imagined when I viewed this location through the key.

Holding my hair back to keep it from whipping into my eyes, I scan the area again to make certain I'm alone. This small hill is the highest spot on the southern end of Estero Island. The bay lies to the east, the ocean to the west. Both are visible—not because the hill is especially high, but simply because this strip of land is less than a kilometer across. Looking northward, the stark, white beach stretches on as far as the eye can see, empty aside from clusters of birds scattered along the shore. Off in the distance to my left is the southernmost point, where a narrow inlet separates this stretch of land from the next in a chain of barrier islands. A beach house sits between here and the point, but I know from my last visit that it's probably empty. June, the doctor who helped me get back to my own time, said that the Cyrists rarely use the place this time of year, aside from Saturday excursions.

Now that I'm sure I'm alone, I kick my shoes off and place them in the shadow of the tall, white Cyrist cross behind me. The wind whips one of the shoes away as soon as it leaves my hand. I retrieve it, then turn both of them over and shove the toes down into the sand, wishing I'd had the foresight to leave them at home.

Once I'm reasonably certain the shoes won't go flying off, I tuck the medallion back into my shirt and hike the hundred meters or so down to the beach. Shorebirds are scavenging along the tide line. They scurry out of my way as I approach, except for one curious creature that cocks its head to the side and tries to stare me down. I don't know what the bird is called in the United States—my summers at the shore were mostly with my grandparents in Ireland—but it looks a bit like the bird that Nora called a *gannet*. The creature seems to have found something tasty that it doesn't want to abandon. I've no desire to disturb it, so I veer a few steps to the right. Apparently, this is still too close for comfort. The creature squawks loudly, flaps its wings, and takes off toward the ocean.

Now that the feathered sentry has abandoned its post, I step closer and let the water swoosh over my feet. It's warm, at least ten degrees warmer than the surf at Bray in the height of summer. Even though my last experience with this beach wasn't exactly pleasant, I would love nothing more than to dive in for a long swim along the coastline. There are very few locations in my own time with water this pristine, and those spots are in such demand that I could never afford to vacation there. And even if I could afford it, the crowds and the noise would make it unappealing. I'd rather swim in the basement pool. There's no sunshine or ocean breeze, but at least it's peaceful.

This particular strip of land is completely submerged in my time. In 1906, however, it's a paradise. Not a soul in sight, and the only sound is the gentle rush of the waves and the screech of the seabirds. It would be nice to spend a day here. I need some alone time. Or maybe alone-with-Jack time. One annoying thing about finding this medallion is that the excitement has kind of overshadowed the relationship we're starting to build. I'd love the chance to spend a little time with him to figure out exactly what I'm feeling.

But even if I could somehow transport Jack here, which I can't, it would probably be hard to relax on this beach knowing that the weird colony of Cyrists is only a few kilometers away. Some of them know far more about this medallion than I do. Last time I was here, June seemed to be wavering between her duty as a physician to keep me from harm and her duty to her god, or prophet, or whatever she believes this Brother Cyrus character to be. I think there's a good chance she'd make a different decision if she stumbled upon me casually soaking up the sunshine instead of washed up on the shore like a drowned rat.

I drag my thoughts back to the task at hand. Four people are waiting for this sample of ocean water two centuries and nearly two thousand kilometers away, so I'd best get moving. Although . . . I guess I could take a weeklong vacay here on the beach and still blink back in with their blasted proof and they'd be none the wiser. Truthfully, I'm getting a bit tired of scientists and their skepticism. It's not too surprising for Lorena and RJ, since this is the first they've seen me time travel. Alex, on the other hand, has watched me use this key at least a dozen times now. He knows this is real, and yet he still can't seem to fully tamp down his inner skeptic. When I blinked out, he was slumped down into the sofa, arms crossed, almost like he's angry at me for disrupting his worldview.

Jack says it's not anger so much as frustration. Alex is one of those people who isn't happy with unknown variables. He wants to know what makes the thing tick, and he won't be content until he's able to take the key apart, analyze it, and replicate it, preferably with a few new-and-improved features. The first step toward that goal is to learn why I'm the only one who can use it, which is where Lorena comes in. She is a geneticist, and she wants physical proof that I'm telling the truth, preferably something she can analyze and quantify. And so here I am on a Florida beach in 1906, scooping up seawater.

I collect the sample, seal the vial, and reluctantly hike back up the beach toward my shoes. I'm nearly halfway there when I hear a popping sound, followed by the faint *putt-putt-putt* of a motor. A small boat has just rounded the bend of the island.

Did they even have boat motors in 1906? I suppose that's a moot point, though, if some of the locals can travel through time. I'm taking a vial of seawater back from the past. Who knows what these Cyrists might have picked up on their travels to bring back from the future?

Since I suspect I'm trespassing on their land, I pick up the pace. The boat is moving faster than I'd have thought, and the engine backfires again in protest. I'm certain I can make it back to the stable point and my shoes before it arrives. But I'll have to lock in my return location, which takes a few seconds, especially with the wind whipping my hair into my eyes. June seemed to think it would be a bad idea for any of the Cyrists to know that I have one of these medallions, and I know next to nothing about the damn thing. What if they have some way to track me? What if they have some way of blocking the signal or whatever it is that enables me to jump home?

Either way, they now have a clear line of sight. The person driving that boat is going to know I disappeared into thin air, but maybe they'll think I was an optical illusion if they're still at a distance.

Screw it. Money is tight, but I can afford to buy a new pair of shoes.

I drop to my knees in the sand and pull out the key. When the holographic menu hovers above my palm, I navigate to the stable point I set a few minutes ago in the living room.

As I blink, I hear the loud popping noise again. I have the fleeting thought that my back, clad in this red shirt, would make a nice, crisp target against the white sand if it turns out that it's a gunshot and not a motor backfiring. And then my knees are on the rug, not in the sand, and I'm back in 2136.

"What happened?" Jack has seen me jump in multiple times. I generally don't land on my knees, so I'm not too surprised that he's worried.

"Had to make a quick exit. A boat came around the bend as I was hiking back up to the stable point. Pretty sure it was one of the Cyrists."

RJ and Lorena exchange a look. They've only been here for about an hour, but I've already seen them do this at least half a dozen times. It's clearly a couple thing, and I get the sense that entire paragraphs of information are being communicated in those short glances.

I give the vial to Lorena. "One sample of seawater from the Florida coast, circa 1906."

She holds the clear ampoule up to the light to examine it for a moment before opening it to sniff the contents. Then she hands it to RJ and searches in her bag until she locates a small handheld device.

Jack laughs, shaking his head. "Madi just blinked out, right before your eyes. And then she blinked *back in* ten seconds later with sand all over her knees, holding a tube of ocean water. Do you really need to do a chemical analysis?"

RJ shrugs. "The popping in and out of sight could've been a portable cloaking device. They're expensive, and illegal as hell, but—"

"Except *you're* the ones who decided which one of more than twenty stable points I'd be visiting. Even if I'd anticipated the sand, I don't think anyone could have guessed you'd want a sample of seawater. What are you even going to be able to tell from that?" I ask Lorena as she adds a few drops to a small window on the device.

"Acidity. Rising CO_2 levels mean seawater has become more acidic over time. That's why some species of coral are extinct or endangered."

"And that meter is really going to give you the date of the sample?"

Lorena looks up from the screen at my question, tilting her head in a way that reminds me of the bird I just saw on the beach. It's not a physical resemblance—the bird was all white and gray angles, and Lorena Jeung is a study in browns, with a round, dimpled face. I think it's more the expression. Her dark eyes have that same slightly imperious look, as though I'm a minor nuisance distracting her from something important.

"No," she says, with exaggerated patience. "It's going to give me the level of acidity in the sample."

"Sorry," I say, a touch annoyed. "I'm a literary historian, not a scientist."

"Then my final step should be more up your alley. Once I locate a table with *historical* acidity levels, I'll be able to tell the date of the sample."

This exchange, of course, reminds me of the historical analysis I *should* be doing instead of trying to convince three people I barely know that this device allows me to time travel. As I'm thinking about that, Alex says something I miss. I'm about to ask him to repeat it, but then I realize he's staring at my bare feet.

"Yeah. Like I said, I had to make a quick exit."

He frowns. "You can't leave high-tech joggers in 1906."

"I'm not the only time traveler who's been on that island," I tell him. "And if I go back now, the person in the boat will see me. I *think* the noise I heard was the motor backfiring, but I could be wrong."

"Then go back to a minute or so before he shows up," Alex says, his voice taking on the same tone that Lorena used a moment ago. "If you walked down to the beach, your back was to the shoes, right?"

That's true. I feel a little stupid for not having thought of it myself. But I've spent my entire twenty-three years thinking of events occurring in proper chronological order. The habit is hard to shake.

"Is that a good idea?" Jack asks. "The woman . . . that doctor you mentioned. Didn't she say it was dangerous to cross your own path?"

"I think her exact words were that it wasn't worth the headache. But I really shouldn't leave them there, and Alex is right. There are several minutes where I'm looking at the bird and getting the water sample. I'm facing the water, not the shore."

Jack still looks worried. I'll admit it's nice knowing he's concerned. But I *am* a bit troubled at the thought of leaving a historical anachronism behind. And truthfully, while I can afford to buy a new pair of trainers, they'd have to be off the rack, not custom-made Fleets like these, which Nora bought me before our investments went south.

So I pull up the interface again, locate the stable point on Estero Island, and roll forward one minute from the time of my last jump. As I pan toward the beach, I see the earlier version of me has almost reached the tide line. The bird will have my attention for the next thirty seconds or so. And my thought about the red shirt making me a perfect target was spot on. My hair and skin are only a few shades darker than the sand, but the shirt stands out in stark relief.

I glance up from the interface. Jack looks like he's about to protest again, but I really do need to do this. I give him a quick, hopefully reassuring smile and blink myself back to the beach.

As I expected, me-from-ten-minutes-ago is oblivious because she's focused on the bird. I'd hoped that I'd be able to simply reach out an arm and snag the joggers, but unfortunately, they're a bit too far from the stable point for me to reach.

I take a few cautious steps toward the shoes. Down by the water, the bird—whose eyes I clearly remember remaining locked on mine until he flapped away—whips his neck in my direction. My movement toward the shoes must have caught his attention.

And then I'm staring straight into my own face, twenty meters away.

Our eyes lock. It's the strangest feeling, almost like a feedback loop. With considerable effort, I finally force myself to look away. As soon as I do, I grab the shoes, and blink home to 2136.

When I arrive back in the living room, I stare down at the carpet, confused. It looks different. Before, there were clumps of sand everywhere from when I landed on my knees. Now, the only sand is on my feet. The carpet where I'm standing, however, is definitely damper than before.

"What the hell?" Jack says.

"I'm fine," I tell him, even though that's not entirely true. I guess this is what June meant by it not being worth the headache to cross your own path. My head is indeed pounding, and I'm very, very glad I haven't eaten dinner yet.

That feeling multiplies exponentially when I look up to see a second version of myself staring back at me.

FROM THE *NEW YORK DAILY INTREPID* (MAY 3, 1969)

Four Klan Leaders Sentenced for Contempt of Congress

(Raleigh, NC) Robert Shelton, Imperial Wizard of the United Klans of America, has been sentenced to one year in prison for contempt of Congress. Bob Jones, Grand Dragon of the North Carolina Klan, and Robert E. Scoggin, Grand Dragon of the South Carolina Klan, were also sentenced to serve one year. Calvin F. Craig, Grand Dragon of Georgia, was fined.

Three additional Klan leaders were cleared of charges. The indictments are the result of a 1966 investigation by the House Un-American Activities Committee, during which the men refused to produce subpoenaed Klan records. They also refused to answer questions from the committee concerning Klan activities, invoking the Fifth Amendment.

∞5∞

TYSON
CHESTER, SOUTH CAROLINA
AUGUST 11, 1966

The wind shifts toward us, carrying a plume of black, oily smoke as flames snake upward. Within seconds, they ignite the cardboard rectangle the man in the green silk robe nailed to the vertical beam when the ceremony began. And then, with a faint whoosh, the fire fans out to light up the arms of the cross.

This again.

Hoping for a bit of untainted air, I take a few steps backward. But clearer air brings with it a clearer view. My mouth goes dry, and my heart begins pounding so hard that it almost drowns out the music blasting from the giant speaker mounted on the flatbed truck behind us. I have to fight the urge to tell Richard and Katherine to get back in our rental car so we can get the hell out of here.

My reaction is completely irrational. I am a member in good standing of the Pitt County, North Carolina chapter of the United Klans of America. Glen Barrett, our southern US specialist and my primary trainer, was embedded with that group for several years before his retirement from fieldwork. He introduced me as his nephew, Troy Rayburn, and then I attended two years' worth of Klan meetings and various events with him during my last four months of training.

It was really difficult to stay objective at first. When they'd start with the racist comments, I'd just repeat over and over again in my head the CHRONOS mantra that we are only in the field to *observe*. I nearly chewed a hole through my tongue from biting it so often, and I clenched my fists so hard and so regularly on those first trips that I was worried my knuckles would cut a groove clean through the skin on the back of my hands. My poker face, as they say, must be decent, though, because the members of the klavern never questioned me. Most of their comments were about my bright blue eyes and suntan. One of the younger guys kept calling me *Hollywood* and said I'd better not bat those baby blues in the direction of his girlfriend. He was joking. Sort of.

Luckily, we weren't expected to be at every event, because I supposedly worked with Glen as a traveling salesman for a kitchen-knife company. The whole knife thing was Glen's idea, and I'd like to kick him for it, because it means I'm stuck lugging around a knife display case on any jump where I'm likely to encounter members of the Klan. Seems like he could have come up with something a little less bulky. But the traveling-sales side of the cover has worked out really well otherwise. Glen was asked on two different occasions to carry documents to leaders in other states. Klan leaders don't trust the US Postal Service. A few of them suspect their phones are tapped, too.

Anyway, my cover with the group is solid. I've popped in for a couple of meetings since Glen retired from active fieldwork—or, from the Klan's perspective, since he got a promotion with the knife company and moved to Chicago. I know the passwords, the challenges, the latest on the federal investigation into the Klan, and all of their truly ridiculous nomenclature. Two weeks ago, I dropped off a letter from one Grand Dragon named Bob to another—from Bob Jones, the North Carolina Grand Dragon, to Bob Scoggin, the green-robed, square-jawed man currently feeding teen magazines into the fire. We drank coffee down in his basement and ate his wife's peach pie while we talked about the federal investigation and shared recruitment strategies. His wife even insisted on buying a couple of Cutco knives from me when Scoggin told her what I did for a living.

Scoggin didn't recognize *me*, even though my skin isn't any lighter than when I worked at Ida's place. Eye color and hairstyle are the only changes they made in costuming. That wasn't even six weeks ago for me, so I'm the same age—early twenties—as the young man Scoggin and Phelps tried to intimidate in front of the Spartanburg County Courthouse. But that man didn't have blue eyes that met theirs directly. That man's eyes were dark, and he kept them locked on the sidewalk. His hair was longer, and it wasn't slicked down with Brylcreem. He kept his voice soft and nonconfrontational.

Scoggin and Phelps hadn't considered that person a man at all. He was just *boy*, and he'd have been just *boy* even if he'd been thirty years older.

Rich, Katherine, and I drove through Spartanburg on our way down here today. The Southside Diner is closed, its wide front window boarded up. At some point during the three years between my visit in 1963 and now, Miss Ida must have decided it was too risky to keep fighting. The Dixie Chicken, however, is doing just fine. Integration seems to be coming gradually. I didn't see any black patrons at their tables when the three of us went in, but several were standing in line for takeout. And even though I really didn't want to give them my money, I had to know.

The chicken wasn't bad, but it was still nowhere near as good as what we served at Southside. Those hush puppies, though, were definitely Miss Ida's recipe. Pretty sure the biscuits were, too.

Richard nudges me. "You okay?"

"Yeah." I step back again as the wind shifts the smoke our way. "Just . . . a bit of a flashback."

"Be sure to put that in your official report," he says dryly. "The committee will be ecstatic."

He's right. I'm certain my reports get scanned not just for historical information, but also to assess my personal reactions. *Will he side with the oppressed or the oppressor?* I haven't made a big deal out of it, but Rich knows I don't much care for being their social experiment.

Scoggin leans forward to add an oversized poster to the pyre. Four dark-haired young men, photographed against an orange background, smile back at us. The edges of the poster curl and blacken, and then the entire thing is engulfed in flames.

A whoop goes up from the crowd, which is a bit larger than I'd have expected for a Thursday-night rally. Scoggin has another, potentially more lucrative, fundraiser in Raleigh over the weekend, so it had to be a weeknight. But it's August. No school tomorrow and people are always looking for something fun to do with the kids on hot summer nights.

The mood is now far less solemn than it was ten minutes before, when several dozen men in robes and hoods held their torches out in unison to light the fire and marched in a wide circle around it as a woman sang "The Old Rugged Cross." Her voice was high and thin, almost as hard on the ears as the feedback from the amp. She must be the regular singer at these events, because one kid standing in front of us stuck his fingers in his ears before the first note even sounded.

Katherine dropped Rich and me off earlier today, around three. The men in white robes—then dressed mostly in jeans and T-shirts—had just finished nailing together the beams of the cross. Richard and I helped them wrap the damn thing in burlap, sharing stories from the klavern I'm part of in Pitt County, North Carolina, and the one that Richard is supposedly trying to start in rural Ohio. That's the cover story we came up with for him and Katherine so they didn't have to constantly worry about getting the accent right.

Once the cross was wrapped, they doused it with gallon after gallon of fuel and we hoisted it upright. Around five in the evening, a hot-dog vendor arrived, followed by an ice-cream truck and a steady stream of vehicles, including Katherine in the Ford Fairlane we'd rented up in Charlotte this morning. The local klavern's Ladies Auxiliary then went to work setting up tables for a bake sale, stacking piles of plastic-wrapped brownies, cookies, and thick slices of pound cake. Richard and Katherine were both slightly disgusted by my hot dog piled with relish, onions, and neon-yellow mustard, but I was hungry. And neither of them turned down the Rice Krispies square I offered. Yes, the dollar I spent will go into the legal-defense fund for that green-robed, race-baiting charlatan, but it won't matter. I already know that he'll be in a federal prison in a few years.

Scoggin drops another batch of magazines onto the fire. He seems immune to the stench of burning petroleum, burlap, and vinyl. Of course, this is far from his first cross burning. It might be his first record burning, though.

The only good thing about being close to the fire is that the smoke does a decent job of warding off the mosquitos. They're not a problem in terms of disease or discomfort, since we were coated with insect repellent before we left the costume unit, but I'm tired of hearing the horrid little bloodsuckers buzz past my ears. That's one extinct species no one has mourned.

"Did you see which album it is?" Richard asks, craning his neck to see the record Scoggin nailed to the cross before he set it on fire.

"*Meet the Beatles.*"

He nods solemnly. "That's the one I'd have picked, too. If you play 'I Want to Hold Your Hand' backward, you can clearly hear John and Paul singing *all hail Satan* in that last verse. It's spelled out in one of the footnotes at the end of that pamphlet you're holding."

The tract in question had been shoved into my hands by a gangly teenage boy when we walked out to meet Katherine earlier.

Communism, Hypnotism, and the Beatles. A sickle-and-hammer, a large garish eye, and a crude drawing of the Fab Four decorate the front. The pamphlet was published a year ago by a group known as Christian Crusade. They must have distributed the booklets widely, because there are multiple copies in the CHRONOS archives, some with red covers, some with blue. And the fact that it was published a year ago, in 1965, makes it abundantly clear that the current furor isn't really due to the comment John Lennon made a few months back about the Beatles being more popular than Jesus.

The other clue that something else is going on under the surface is that anyone who bothered to read the full quote, in context, could see that Lennon wasn't saying this was a good thing. Back in England, where the interview was originally published, most ministers were honest enough to admit that he had a valid point. In the summer of 1966, the quartet of John, Paul, George, and Ringo drew much larger and more enthusiastic crowds in Great Britain than the churches' standard quartet of Matthew, Mark, Luke, and John.

Here in the US, however, where evangelical fervor is stronger, Lennon's comment prompted Pan-American Airlines to rebuke the band silently by leaving copies of the Bible in their seats when they boarded the plane. Deejays, most of them in the South, refused to play their songs, and ministers around the country altered their weekly sermons to address the evil influence of rock 'n' roll.

But Lennon's comment alone wouldn't have inspired the Grand Dragon of the South Carolina branch of the Ku Klux Klan to have his hooded minions dig a hole out here in the middle of nowhere, erect a giant cross, and turn a pile of Beatles memorabilia to ash. All four Beatles have made their views on racism quite clear. On their previous American tour, they refused to play to segregated audiences or stay in segregated hotels. And rather than just insisting quietly that the various venues obey federal law, they issued a press release on the matter.

This isn't about John Lennon's views on Jesus Christ. It's about his interference with Jim Crow.

"I'm just glad he didn't burn *Revolver*," Rich says, even though I think it's a safe bet that at least one copy of the band's latest release is currently melting in the toxic heap at the base of the cross.

"*Revolver* is good," I admit. "But not as good as *Abbey Road*."

He snorts. "You know *nothing*."

Admittedly, I'm not a music historian. But I am his roommate, and after the past few months, mine should count as expert opinion. The Beatles' entire discography played pretty much nonstop while Rich wrote this research proposal.

Scoggin calls out to the crowd, "Okay, I think we got a decent blaze goin' now, so come on, kids. Step up and send those records back to the hellfire they came from. Who do you pick? John, George, and those others, or Jesus?"

A chorus of *Jesus* rises up, and then about a dozen kids step forward with their offerings. One girl, who looks to be around thirteen, hangs back. As the others toss their items into the fire, she clutches the small stack of 45s to her chest and looks at a woman on the edge of the crowd, clearly hoping for mercy. But the woman's frown deepens, and she jabs her finger toward the cross, so the girl just sighs and adds her treasures to the flames.

"That's right," Scoggin says. "We ain't gonna give 'em our money or our attention. We got a reporter here tonight who will make sure our message gets out. Here in America, we don't need no Communist agents blasphemin' and tellin' us how to run our country. We don't need this McCartney kid calling America a lousy country because we don't believe in race mixin'. And I can promise you that at least here in South Carolina, there ain't *nobody* more popular than Jesus."

That's apparently the prearranged cue for the woman with the bad voice to start singing again. We move away from the staticky speaker in self-defense, and I scan the crowd for Katherine. She's hard to spot, mostly because she's short, but also because her hair is puffed up and lacquered in the prevailing style, like most of the other women. I finally locate her over near the table with the baked goods, where the Auxiliary women are talking. One of them is Scoggin's wife. Judging from the closed expressions the Klan women are wearing, I doubt they're going to open up to a stranger, especially one who isn't from the South.

I lean toward Rich. "I'm going to try and give Katherine a boost with the Auxiliary. But if they don't start talking to her, get over there. You busted your ass to get her included in this project so you could have some time alone without Saul distracting her. Don't waste your chance mourning over a pile of melting vinyl."

He gives me an annoyed look. "I don't want to seem obnoxious. Or pushy."

"Just go, okay?"

All evidence to date suggests that Katherine is actually *into* obnoxious and pushy; otherwise she'd steer clear of Saul. But I skip that part of the lecture, and cross over to where the women are standing. The girl who held on to her record collection a few seconds too long is next to one of the tables. She's staring down at her penny loafers, probably dreading the "seat warming" she's likely to get after the festivities are over for not being the first in line.

Katherine's back is to me, so I tap her on the shoulder.

"Hey. I'm gonna take care of some business real quick, and then we prob'ly oughta hit the road. Miz Scoggin, I should have introduced the two of you earlier. I don't know if Kathy here mentioned it, but her husband"—I nod toward Rich—"is planning a new klavern up near Lima, Ohio. I know how important it is to get the ladies on board, so any tips you might have would be much appreciated. And, Kathy, I see Miz Scoggin still has one of her pies back there. Rich will want to marry you all over again if you're smart enough to buy it."

I'm surprised to hear Mrs. Scoggin laugh. "I'll get her address, Troy, and mail her some literature. Bob said y'all are plannin' to be in Raleigh this weekend?"

"Yes, ma'am. We'll have the whole klavern out." I can state this with absolute certainty, since it happened nearly a year ago for me. That was one of my field-training trips with Glen.

"Are you coming up to North Carolina, too, Mrs. Scoggin?" Katherine asks. "Rich and I haven't quite decided whether to stay in Raleigh or head back up to Lima."

"Oh, no. I'll stay here with the kids. Bob says there'll probably be *trouble.*"

I nod, understanding that by *trouble* she means a counterprotest.

"And," she continues, "he'll be holed up with the attorneys the next day, figurin' out how they're gonna deal with these contempt charges. I still think they did the right thing by refusin' to cooperate, but I'm not as certain as Bob that the feds will back down."

"I'm sure it'll all work out fine," I tell her with a sympathetic smile.

And it does, in my opinion, but Mrs. Scoggin and I probably have very different views of what *work out fine* means. The contempt charges she mentioned were levied against seven United Klans leaders, including her husband, earlier this year when they refused to divulge membership lists and other information subpoenaed by the House Un-American Activities Committee in the wake of several murders of civil rights activists last year. Scoggin and two others will serve a year in jail. And as icing on the cake, Scoggin will return home to find somebody has snatched leadership of the South Carolina Klan away from him while he was incarcerated.

I light one of the fake cigarettes from the front of my pack as I approach the group of men on the other side of the crowd. One of them is Phelps, a.k.a. Tubby, and while I couldn't swear to it, I think the two men leaning against that red pickup were with him when they lit the cross outside Ida's place. For the next ten minutes, I mostly listen as they talk about the defense fund for Scoggin and a speech that Martin Luther King gave at the Coliseum in Raleigh two weeks ago.

"No way that crowd was five thousand," one of them says. "Although my brother told me they had nearly that many at the Klan march anyway. Woulda been more if King hadn't rescheduled on us."

"Paper said those Beatles had twenty-eight thousand in *Dee*troit," Phelps says. "Hard to believe."

"Not really," Scoggin says. "It's Detroit, after all."

They laugh. I paste on my well-worn fake smile and join them.

"Hey, at least we kept 'em out of the South," Phelps says. "Memphis City Council canceled the concert."

I'm debating whether to correct this bit of misinformation, but Scoggin beats me to it. "Nope. It's back on. And hey, maybe that's okay. I hear there may be a few surprises waiting for Mr. Bigger than Jesus."

This isn't news to me. The cherry-bomb incident at the Mid-South Coliseum is well-documented. Rich says it's the main reason that this was the Beatles' last tour.

"Whatever they're plannin', they better be careful," someone says. "Those concerts are crawlin' with security."

Scoggin sniffs. "Most of the security ain't Beatles fans. And more than a few of them are our people. They're not plannin' anything too major, anyway. Just a little something to put the fear of God in those boys. Humble them a bit, you know?"

"My younger sister lives outside of Memphis," Phelps says. "I might just keep on driving that way after we're done in Raleigh. Ain't too keen on hearing their sorry excuse for music, but those limeys getting humbled a bit might be something worth seeing. Personally, though, I think we oughta just line 'em up and shoot 'em."

This seems to be the general consensus of the group, and from that high point, the conversation devolves into theories about the racial heritage of Ringo, who one guy says has a Jewish nose and eyes. Apparently, George Harrison is half-black. One of them pulls in some of the crazy speculation in the little pamphlet making the rounds about how the band's music hypnotizes impressionable teens and turns them into godless communists.

In the past, I've joined in with rumors or the occasional joke about whatever they're discussing. It's part of my cover. It's why I'm here, to learn what makes these people tick in a way that you could never learn from reading pamphlets or even watching the few videos of them speaking in this era. But slipping back into the role isn't as easy as I thought it would be after spending a month at the diner. Before, I'd always felt that these rallies were elaborate charades. Just a bunch of grown men playing dress up. I *knew* they weren't innocuous, and there were certainly rumors about "wrecking crews" and "corrections" by the inner circle in Pitt County. But those were history. Things that happened centuries before CHRONOS decided to make me their little social experiment.

It feels more personal now, after watching these guys torch a cross in front of an old woman's business and destroy her livelihood over something as petty as the occasional across-the-color-line sale of a box of fried chicken. And the men standing here around this tree could well have been involved in the murders that Eddie and Larson were talking about outside the restaurant that night.

"You're kinda quiet this evenin', Troy," Scoggin says.

"Yeah." I give him a tired smile. "It's been a long day. And I was just thinkin' about the whole HUAC thing. It's a damn shame."

I leave it at that, and they all nod in agreement. But what I meant is that it's a damn shame Scoggin is the only one out of this crew who will end up in jail.

FROM THE *NEW YORK HOURLY INTREPID* (NOVEMBER 19, 2098)

Cyrist Bicentennial Meeting in Southern Florida

(Fort Myers, FL) Nearly eight hundred clerics from around the world will gather this week near the banks of the Estero River in Florida to commemorate the Cyrist International bicentennial. A highlight of the week will be the anointing of a new Sister Prudence, the prophet and titular head of the church.

A hundred years ago, a mandatory synod for all Cyrist clerics would have been unthinkable, given their vast numbers. Synods were restricted to district Templars, and even then, attendance was in the thousands. Today, however, Cyrist temples are fewer and smaller, and their leaders are easily accommodated at Estero, often hailed as the birthplace of the Cyrist faith, even though this was far from the first Cyrist community. In fact, a group that followed the religious texts known as the *Book of Cyrus* and the *Book of Prophecy*, both of which date from the 1400s, founded one of the very first North American colonies.

It was reportedly a prophecy from the latter book that enabled Cyrus Reed Teed of Chicago to purchase land for the Estero settlement, which he named Nuevo Reino. Nearly fifty people, mostly women, followed Teed south over the next few years, hoping to create a religious community based on Cyrist tenets.

What made Estero and Nuevo Reino unique was the central role they played in the rapid growth of the Cyrist faith. The death of Cyrus Teed in December 1901, barely a decade after the group moved south, might have meant the death of the community, as often happens with small sects centered around a single charismatic leader. Instead, a woman known as Sister Prudence assumed leadership, claiming that she was the resurrected Brother Cyrus.

A string of remarkably accurate prophecies and astute investments followed, and the religion spread rapidly to all corners of the globe. While a schism in the 1950s split the Cyrists into two groups, Orthodox and New, it did not stem the growth of the church. By the late 1990s, Cyrist International was one of the largest religions in the world, counting many leaders in government, finance, and industry among its adherents.

In 2015, an attack by an extremist group within Cyrist International killed more than a dozen Cyrist leaders, but the second phase, a planned bioterror attack on the general public, was narrowly averted. Government authorities estimated that the casualties could have numbered in the tens of thousands. In the wake of the scandal, Sister Prudence (presumably the daughter or granddaughter of the original prophet) stepped down as the head of the church and assumed a largely ceremonial role.

The decline of Cyrist International during the years that followed stemmed largely from financial malfeasance on the part of its leadership, many of whom were charged with (and several convicted of) investment fraud. Member surveys also showed a growing disenchantment with some of the more rigid rules of the faith, and disappointment with the quality of the financial advice being passed along by their religious leaders in exchange for their monthly tithe.

Cyrist International has quite a bit to celebrate this week, however. In addition to ushering in a new prophet, they seem to be reversing more than seven decades of steady decline in membership. This resurgence is due, in part, to publicity after their *Book of Prophecy* predicted the worldwide terror attacks of March 2092.

∞6∞

Seeing the other version of myself is almost like looking in a mirror. The primary difference is that this other me doesn't move when I do. There's no sand on her knees, no hi-tech joggers tucked under her arm, and she's still holding her vial of seawater. She also looks slightly ill, as if someone recently punched her in the stomach. Although, that might be a similarity rather than a difference. I can't see *this* version of my face right now, and her expression is pretty darn close to how I'm feeling.

And we're not the only ones who look ill. Everyone in the room appears on the verge of throwing up.

After a moment, RJ lets out a low, shaky whistle. "You're not going to need that chemical analysis, Lorena. And Madi seems to have solved Alex's question about how to replicate those medallions."

He points first to the key in my hand and then to an identical key, hanging from an identical black cord, which is currently around the neck of the other me.

"Except I also repli . . ." I was going to say *I also replicated myself,* but I stop in midsentence, realizing that my words are coming through in stereo.

The other me manages to get the word *replicated* out, and then she stops, too.

"Are the rest of you . . ." Lorena winces, rubbing her temples. "Are you remembering two different things? Because I sure as hell am."

"Yeah," Alex says. "This is wrong. Really, *really* wrong. Madi, you need to go back and fix this."

Jack glares at him. "No! Absolutely not. This was *caused* by you suggesting that she go back and fix something!"

"What?" Alex protests. "I didn't tell her to spin off a fucking clone! I don't even know how—"

Lorena holds up her hand. "Everybody calm down. We need to think things through. You're the physicist, Alex. What could cause this? How can two versions of the same person—two copies of the same *matter*—exist simultaneously?"

All eyes turn to Alex, who is clearly uncomfortable at being put on the spot.

"Like I just finished saying, *I don't know.* My best guess would be that . . . maybe . . . the device emits some sort of field. A protective—" He stops and barks out a nervous laugh. "Or not so protective."

I'm not sure what he means until I follow his gaze. The other me is now gone.

Just . . . *gone.*

"Did she use the key again?" Lorena asks.

"I was looking right at her," RJ says. "She wasn't even holding it. So if Madi is right and she needs to have the thing in the palm of her hand to use it, then no. She simply vanished."

"When did she *arrive*?" I ask.

"A few minutes ago," Jack replies. "What exactly do you remember?"

I give them a brief recap. Getting the sample. Realizing that a boat was approaching. Deciding I'd have to leave my shoes behind.

"Then I came back here. I asked Lorena what exactly she was going to do with the sample, and she explained about the acid levels. Then Alex noticed my shoes were missing and said that I couldn't just leave them there. And partly because I thought he was right and partly because I really wanted my damn shoes back, I decided to pop in and grab them during the short period while I was facing the ocean. Things got weird, though. A stupid bird on the beach startled when I jumped in, and the other me turned around and looked straight at me, just as I was grabbing the shoes. And then I jumped back and *she's* already here . . . and . . ."

They all start talking at once. The only thing I'm getting from it is that they have two competing and very different memories of what happened.

"I'll be right back," I say. "There's something I need to get from the library."

Whatever failings my great-grandfather may have had—and, according to Nora, they were many and egregious—James Coleman kept a well-stocked bar. The fact that he kept this well-stocked bar in the library where he worked suggests to me that he may have followed at least the first part of Hemingway's possibly apocryphal advice to write drunk and edit sober. After a brief inventory, I select a bottle of bourbon, along with five shot glasses.

Lorena declines. She's breastfeeding and has noticed that her daughter doesn't sleep as well if she drinks. I didn't even know they had a baby, but then I know almost nothing about them, aside from the fact that RJ is listed in that little book with me and Alex as part of the team that invented time travel.

I pour a shot for the rest of us and toss mine back. The bite is sharper than I remembered, since I generally stick to wine. But that's a good thing. It takes the focus off my tangled brain.

After the burn subsides, I lean back into the sofa. "Okay. *Now* I'm ready for your version of what happened. And then I'd love to hear any theories Alex may have on how I managed to duplicate myself."

"Well," Jack begins, "the other you remembered seeing you grab the shoes. She watched you blink out, and then she waded into the water to collect the sample. But the boat was a lot closer when she noticed it."

"Most likely she was distracted," RJ says. "From trying to figure out why you jumped back to steal her shoes."

"*My* shoes."

He gives me a shrug. "Same difference."

"Anyway," Jack says, "she jumped back as soon as she spotted the boat."

I nod. "Makes sense. She didn't have to worry about going back to the stable point for the shoes, because she knew they were already gone."

"Yes, but she also realized the guy in the boat had a gun," Alex says.

Oh. So maybe the other me *did* look worse when I first saw her.

"I heard something, too. But I thought it was probably the boat motor backfiring. I left before I knew one way or the other."

"Do you have the sample?" Lorena asks.

"No. I gave it to you before I left."

She shakes her head. "The other you was still holding the sample when she disappeared."

"I *know* that. I saw it in her hand. But *I* gave you the sample I collected before I left."

"Not in this reality," RJ says.

"She's not going back," Jack tells him as I pour myself another shot. I'm trying to figure out whether I like or dislike the fact he's stating this so definitively, without even asking me. But he's right. I'm *not* going back.

"Of course not," Lorena says, although she sounds a bit reluctant to me. I guess she sounds that way to Jack, as well, because he stares at her for a long moment, eyebrows raised.

"It's just academic curiosity," she explains. "About the acidity levels, not the time travel. You can mark me in the *convinced* column for that. I guess there *could* be an alternative explanation for what we just experienced, although I can't really imagine what it might be. So . . . maybe this would be a good time for Madi to explain where she found that device."

I spend the next few minutes telling RJ and Lorena about finding the medallion, my first trip to Estero Island, my near drowning, and my encounter with the members of the Cyrist colony nearby.

"Is the orange light only visible when it's activated?" she asks.

"No. I can see it right now, even through my shirt." I tug on the cord and center the medallion in my palm. "And now, in addition to the light that surrounds the medallion, I see the interface that allows me to select or set a stable point."

"Can I try it?" RJ asks.

"Sure." I pull the cord over my head and toss him the key. "But if you're not seeing a bright light coming from the thing already, I don't think you're going to get the interface to pop up."

"Jack and I tried," Alex says. "Nothing."

Nothing is exactly what Lorena and RJ get, as well. "Is it just skin contact that activates it, or specifically your palm?" she asks, handing the medallion back to me.

"Good question. I've been going on the assumption that it only works in my hand, since that's how June, the doctor at Estero, told me to use it. But I don't really know."

We spend a couple of minutes testing it out. I can see a hazy version of the interface when it rests on my leg and a slightly clearer one if I balance it on my inner arm. But the only way to stabilize the display enough to make it usable is to hold the key in the palm of my hand.

"It probably works better in your palm because you have more nerve endings there," Lorena says. "That's just a guess, but it makes sense. And it's clearly activated because it detects something in your body that's missing in ours. The next step is to figure out exactly *what* it's detecting. I'd like to run a blood analysis, if that's okay?"

"Now?"

"Well, I'd *take* the sample now. But I want to do a full-spectrum analysis, so this portable unit isn't going to be adequate."

Reluctantly, I roll up my sleeve. She taps my upper arm with one of the microneedle gadgets, and I feel a slight suction as the sample is drawn.

Once she's done, I turn to Alex. "Could we get back to the duplicate me? Where did she go?"

He laughs nervously. "You seriously think I'm going to have an answer for that off the cuff? This is way beyond my current level of understanding. My best *guess* is that you just spun off a bubble universe. An unstable bubble. And I'm not at all sure what the ramifications of that might be."

"So . . . why was she the one to disappear? I mean, why her, instead of me?" What I really want to ask is whether there's a way I can make certain that it will always be her instead of me if this ever happens again. That sounds kind of absurd, given that she *is* me, but I really don't like the idea of this me being the one to disappear.

"There's this theory called quantum Darwinism," Alex says. "It's kind of like . . . well, like Darwinism. Except . . . quantum. Usually it pertains to slightly different information about quantum states, though, not to people. But the idea is that when you have these different versions, only one can continue to exist. And the one that survives is the one that is best adapted to the environment. The one with the most complete and coherent information. If you extrapolate that to the current situation, the one with the most complete information is you. You're the one who went back and crossed your own, earlier, path. Does that make sense?"

RJ and Jack nod.

"Kind of?" I say.

Lorena says, "No. It doesn't."

Alex rolls his eyes. "It's tied into Everett's Many-Worlds Interpretation. Come on, Lorena. I know you understand that one."

"Yes, but the MWI is just talking about mathematical possibilities, not *literal* universes. And not unstable universes."

"I said it was an extrapolation. Do you have a better explanation?"

Lorena begins talking rapidly, pulling in quantum entanglement, Schrödinger's cat, thermodynamics, and a whole bunch of other stuff that might as well be ancient Greek. When she finally pauses for breath, I cut in.

"Do you think I should stop using the key?"

Alex considers my question for a moment. "No," he says, finally. "Although I do think you need to be more cautious until we have a better idea how the time travel works."

This is the first time that Alex has actually acknowledged that I'm time traveling. I smile to myself, partly because it feels like a victory, but also because I was a little afraid that he was going to say I should stop using the key. My curiosity has been piqued, and it would be hard to stick it into a drawer and just forget about it. I will definitely avoid crossing my own timeline, though. June was totally right about the headaches that can cause, and even if it seems likely that I would continue to win out in this quantum Darwinism contest, I'm not too keen on taking the chance.

"The biggest problem," he continues, "is that it would be a whole lot easier for me to figure out how it works if I could take it apart. And . . . that's kind of risky when it's the only one we have."

"But according to that book Madi showed us, you invented the thing," RJ says.

"Wrong," Alex says. "According to the book Madi showed us, *we* invented it. Me, you, and Madi. Maybe you need to read up on temporal physics so you can answer these questions yourself."

"Yeah, right," RJ says, rolling his eyes. "I'll be handling the marketing and grant applications. I'm guessing Madi is the historical side of the equation. That leaves the science stuff up to you, Cuz. And Lorena, assuming there's a genetic component."

"Wouldn't it make more sense to turn the device over to Alex's department?" Lorena asks. "I mean, no offense, Alex, but you're just a postdoc. There are people there with more experience and maybe . . ."

RJ is shaking his head vehemently. "Spoken like a true academic. Which isn't a *bad* thing in general. But it's horrible advice if Madi ever wants to turn a profit on this."

"They'd also take all the credit for the *discovery*," Alex says. "This is the research opportunity of a lifetime, and it's exactly in my field. No way am I turning it over to someone else."

"Plus, they'd probably try to copyright Madi's DNA," Jack says. "Which doesn't seem fair to me."

A shadow crosses Lorena's face. Their odd couples-telepathy thing must have its limits, though, because RJ doesn't seem to catch it. He leans forward and says, "Here's the deal as I see it. You can probably sell this thing right now and offer yourself up as a research subject. But you'll make a whole lot more—and have more control over how it is used—if you can find a way to replicate it and lock down the rights. You need to present it as a total package. Not just the technology itself, but also historical locations that are already scouted out. Like the list you had earlier, but a more comprehensive log of stable points."

"That's true," Alex says. "At a bare minimum, we need to understand the science behind it. And I'm kind of afraid that handing things off to someone else would create a conundrum if the book is correct and we're supposed to be the ones who make this discovery."

I rub my temples, where a dull headache is forming. "How can we be the ones who develop the technology when I just dug it up in the garden? What if the book only says we discovered the technology because we stole it?"

Alex shrugs. "Could still cause a conundrum, since it would change the historical record."

"Unless the book is forged," Jack tells him. "Which you seemed pretty sure of the other day when Madi first pulled it out of that drawer."

"I've had time to think it over since then. I have a theory about this that builds on an earlier project that was abandoned nearly a half century ago. So I think the book is probably legit."

"Well, as I said before," RJ says, "I don't understand a damn thing about the tech side. I *am* excited about the potential, but, obviously, it's your call, Madi. And your grandmother's, I guess."

Technically, he's right, since the key was found on Nora's property. But she told me to toss it with the rest of the trash. And since my grandmother couldn't see the orange light, I'm pretty sure she can't use it to time travel.

The one thing I do know for certain is that Nora will adamantly oppose any future travels on my part if she knows about the key. As my grandmother, she'll put my safety over her financial situation. And this really is about *her* finances. I'll be okay either way. I'm twenty-three, and in good health. As long as I'm able to finish my research, someone will be interested in the definitive biography of James Lawrence Coleman. It might not support me for the rest of my life, but I can find a job once I have my degree. Nora, on the other hand, is too old to start over. She made a career of volunteering, serving on philanthropic boards and the like, and her pension is miniscule. And even though it's not rational, even though I'm not my mother and not responsible for her bad financial decisions, I still feel a degree of personal responsibility for Nora's current situation.

Simply put, I'd like to try to restore some of the family assets that my mother lost. So, there's really only one option.

"I have power of attorney over all matters concerning the property and its contents. If there's money to be made from this technology, I'm in. But given the current state of my finances, I can't pay any of you for working on this. And . . . I need to retain a controlling interest. This really belongs to Nora, and I have to look out for her, too. The four of you could split the remaining forty-nine percent. Does that seem fair?"

"More than fair," Alex says. "I'd have taken less, to be honest. I just want to be part of this. The money's not my top priority."

Jack seems hesitant. "It should be split three ways. I'm not a scientist. There's really not much I can do to help."

"So?" I say. "I'm not a scientist, either. Neither is RJ. And while I don't know about him, I can't imagine any reality in which I *could* be a scientist. Math's always bored me, and while I did well enough in science, it's never been anything close to a passion. So my role in this must always have been as a historian."

"Same here," RJ says. "There are only two reasons I'd be in that book. The most important is as a cover for Lorena's involvement. And the second would be handling the sales side of things. Figuring out how to market this. Whether you even *can* market it."

"So not being a scientist isn't a disqualifier, Jack. You'd be helping me with the history side. Plus, you're the only other historian who knows about this medallion. If we're going to start adding more stable points, like RJ suggested, then I'll need your input. Otherwise, the locations are going to tilt heavily toward literary history. And even more importantly, I want someone else helping to assess whether there's any historical . . . blowback, I guess? Changes. That's not a minor task."

"Okay," Jack says. "I'll agree for now. But if we get into this and I'm not earning my keep, we'll have to reassess."

RJ and Lorena engage in another one of their silent two-second discussions, and then Lorena says, "We're both willing to work on this project in exchange for shares of the eventual sale of the technology. My role will have to be silent, though, given my job. I can simply say I'm helping RJ with a business project, if anyone asks, and it should be fine."

The others begin talking about business models and start-up costs, neither of which I had considered in much detail. It's obvious that we'll eventually have to pull in the government, but they all seem to favor delaying that for as long as possible, especially Alex.

"We need to know exactly what we're dealing with. I think . . ." Alex stops, looking around at the four of us. "This is in confidence, okay? There are rumors at the institute about a project involving human time travel. It was years ago, and I'd have staked my life on them being *just* rumors, but . . . maybe not. I'll see if I can find out more through the grapevine at work, but I don't want to push so hard that people get suspicious."

RJ agrees. "We need to keep this under wraps until we understand how the device works and exactly what it can do. And that could take a while, since none of us really has extra cash stashed away to sink into a major business endeavor. I just finished my classes over the summer, so I'm only working part time right now. That's good in the sense that I'll have time to start writing up funding proposals, but not so good for our cash flow."

"There might be another way to free up a bit of cash," I say a little hesitantly. "I could offer lodging, if any or all of you are interested. That would free up whatever you're spending on rent to cover any equipment we need to acquire. This place has eight bedrooms, including one that's a two-room suite, which you could set up as a nursery. Just something to consider. I totally understand if you guys want to keep your own places."

In fact, a little panicky voice in my head is hoping they'll decide not to take me up on the offer. The house is definitely large enough that we'd still have privacy, but I don't know RJ and Lorena that well. And I spoke without even considering how it might sound to Jack. Technically, I just asked him to move in with me. Him and four other people, but still.

Alex says he's not sure if he and Jack could get out of their rental agreement, but they might be able to find someone to sublease the apartment. RJ and Lorena are conferring, using actual words for a change, and it sounds like they're seriously considering it. All of them say they'll get back to me with an answer soon. On the business side, I have everyone transfer their full legal names, contact information, and thumbprints to Jarvis, my virtual assistant, and then ask him to draw up a basic partnership agreement for what we're calling, at least for now, AJG Research. We'll probably need a more in-depth agreement later, and definitely a catchier name, but this will at least get us started.

It's almost dinnertime when we finish, so we call it a night. Alex has plans in DC. Lorena and RJ need to get back to their daughter.

"I guess I should go, too," Jack says reluctantly, after the others leave. "You seem a little tired, and I should probably get some work done."

He's right. I *am* tired. Maybe it's just the sheer relief of having others confirm my sanity. Or maybe the time travel itself is draining. Either way, the slightly frantic energy I've felt all day has begun to drain away. I kind of want to curl up on the couch and watch something. Or maybe listen to a book.

But I also need to get some work done.

"Or," I suggest, "we could order dinner and both work here? There's plenty of desk space in the library, although we may have to clear away some junk."

Jack smiles. "Works for me."

After deciding on Thai and clearing away the glasses and whiskey, I show Jack the section of the library where I found the CHRONOS history. Then we head out back to wait for the aerobot delivery. I take a seat on the low brick wall that runs around the stone patio. Jack joins me, and we both just sit there for a moment, looking out at the large white oak tree that shades the right corner of the lawn. This is the first time we've actually been alone since that clumsy first kiss, and I feel intensely self-conscious, like a schoolgirl sitting next to her crush in an assembly. I find myself stealing quick glances at his profile. Jack has one of those faces that is all angles and planes, almost stern when he's not smiling. The stubble along his jaw is a shade darker than his light-brown hair, and I have a strong urge to feel it against my palm.

Apparently, I'm not the only one feeling awkward. We do that weird thing where both of us start to speak at the same time. Then we both laugh. And then silence looms again.

This is stupid. I'm twenty-three, not thirteen. I've had two long-term relationships, one of which lasted nearly two years before we realized, at about the same time, that we had too little in common to make a go of it. Jack, who is four years older, mentioned a girlfriend in passing when we first met. In fact, I hadn't been entirely sure that she was an *ex*-girlfriend until last week when we were at a bar with some people from the department and he said as much after someone made an offhand comment about long-distance relationships rarely working out.

"Maybe we could have another go?" I say. "Only this time *without* the part where I miss your signals and we bump foreheads?"

Jack smiles. "That sounds like an excellent plan. Except"—his eyes shift up toward the roof—"I think we have company."

A small silver drone maneuvers down to the bright-orange delivery mat near the patio door. I retrieve our noodles from the bag and press my thumb to the paypad. The drone beeps twice and heads off into the sunset. Then, Jack takes the containers from me, places them on the patio table, and pulls me into his arms.

The kiss is better this time. Much, much better.

"I can't let you take all the blame for misreading me the other night," he says when we pull apart. "There were some mixed signals on my end. I hadn't entirely decided whether this was a good idea, and then . . . it sort of just happened."

I'm not quite sure how to take that, so I duck into the kitchen to grab the wine and two plates from the cupboard.

"That came out wrong," Jack says, following me inside. "I didn't mean I was *still* undecided. What I meant was, when we were in the car . . ." He gives me a sideways grin. "It's just that I didn't want to mess things up. I actually *like* you."

"So . . . do you usually only kiss people you *don't* like?"

"No." He laughs. "And you're teasing me now, aren't you? My point was that I didn't want to mess up a perfectly good friendship, if you weren't interested. And having had a breakup not that long ago . . ."

"You're not keen to rush in," I say as I dish out the pad thai. "Makes sense."

I'm tempted to mention my proposal about everyone moving in here, since I'm a little worried he might have taken that the wrong way. But I can't think of any way to broach the subject that doesn't sound weird or presumptuous. So I opt instead for a bit of self-deprecating humor. "Anyway, it's a relief to know that I'm not as hopeless at reading romantic signals as my grandmother seems to think."

"Nora or Thea?"

I don't remember ever mentioning my maternal grandmother by name, but Jack and I have had lunch and/or dinner together several times a week for the past few months. Even though I haven't spent nearly as much time with Thea as I have with Nora, she's a colorful person. I have a number of stories about her travels and her unending quest for spiritual enlightenment, so Thea must have sneaked into our conversation at some point.

"Nora. I love her dearly, but she is . . . a bit much, sometimes. That's true of both my grandmothers, actually, in totally different ways. Nora is a Nordic ice queen, who tries to out-British the British to make up for the fact that she wasn't born there. She took my dad's death really hard, but you'd never know it because 'stiff upper lip' and all that nonsense. And Thea is the polar opposite. I see her maybe once every three years. We go to dinner. She reads my palm or aura or whatever crazy stuff she's into this year, and then takes off again, back to following some new guru around the world. She's fun, but rather exhausting. So . . . what about your family? You've mentioned a sister, but . . ."

"Not much to tell, really. They're in California. My sister is in med school at Berkeley."

A cloud passes over his face as he speaks. There's something he's not sharing. But I can't really expect him to bare his soul on the basis of two kisses, one of them badly bungled.

After a minute, he continues. "Deciding to attend school on the East Coast was seen as a major act of rebellion. Add to that the fact that I'm the only person in two generations not to go into the military or some sort of scientific field, and I guess that makes me the black sheep of the Merrick clan."

"Studying history on the East Coast makes you a black sheep?"

He laughs wryly. "Families are weird. What can I say? And I think that's even more true of blended families. My stepmom is wonderful. We get along great, but she's not my mom, you know? I think she wanted to be, or at least wanted to try to be, but I was at an awkward age. The one time she tried to draw me out, to get me to talk about missing my mom, I just couldn't. She wouldn't have understood, because all the things I missed were odd. Things that wouldn't have made sense to anyone, that I'd have felt stupid even talking about back then. Even with my sister, Jenna, because she was only six when Mom died, and I think the memories faded faster for her. But every time my hair would fall into my eyes, I'd think about the way Mom used to tuck it back behind my ear. I hated it at the time, but later . . ." He shrugs. "There was also this sandwich she used to make with peanut butter, banana, and bacon, which probably sounds gross, but it's good. And the fact that she actually kept a swear jar—do you know what that is?"

I have a vague idea, but I shake my head. "Not really."

"It was this big jar she kept on the kitchen counter. Whenever anyone in the family said a bad word, they had to contribute a credit. The money went to charity at the end of the year. She said her grandma had one, and the first time she caught me cursing she decided to revive the tradition, because she knew that I was picking it up from her and, even more so, from my dad. She was mad at my dad one day and forked over twenty credits. Got her money's worth, too."

"You'd like Nora," I tell him. "She doesn't have a swear jar, but she'd have enough to fund a charity all on her own if she did."

"So, how about you?" Jack asks. "What's the one stupid thing no one else would understand that you miss most about your dad?"

I don't even have to think about it. "He had this nickname for me, from the time I was a toddler. He called me Mad Max. Or later, just Max. It was from an old movie. I was a daredevil as a kid. A bit of an adrenaline addict. I went for the highest diving board, the fastest amusement-park rides, and I always swam too far from shore. My mom hated the nickname—said Dad was encouraging me to take risks—so he never used it around her. It was just ours, the pet name he called me even after I grew out of my wild-child phase. And when he was gone, I realized that part of me was gone, too. That I would never be Mad Max again."

"You didn't grow out of it as much as you might think. Every time you use that key, you're taking a huge risk. I think there's still a lot of Max in there."

I smile. "I'm going to take that as a compliment."

We focus on our food for a few minutes, watching the sunset through the branches of the ancient white oak.

"How long do oak trees live?" I wonder aloud.

Jack has no clue, so I ask Jarvis, who gives me a range from around 150 to 300 years.

"What's with the interest in . . . is it called arboriculture?"

"I guess? It's not the tree itself," I say, "although it's pretty impressive. I was just thinking that my great-great-great-great-grandmother might have sat here watching a sunset over a smaller version of that tree. That it could have been here even before she . . ."

"What?" Jack asks when I trail off.

"Hold on. I'm going to try something."

"You're not planning to use that key again, are you?"

"Not to jump." I walk out to the tree. "I'm just curious."

I set a stable point a few yards in front of the oak, and then join Jack at the table again.

After some quick mental math, I change the year to 2015, which I think is the year the house was purchased by my ancestor Katherine Shaw, Nora's great-great grandmother. As expected, the tree was already in the yard. It was still fairly tall back then, but nowhere near as wide.

Leaving the current time, month, and day in place, I scroll the years backward.

"What exactly are you doing?" Jack asks.

I feel a bit guilty, since he can't see what I'm seeing. Even if he could use the device, he wouldn't be able to see it while I'm using it, based on what June, the Cyrist doctor, told me after I washed up on Estero Island. He probably feels like I'm ignoring him. But my curiosity is stronger than my urge to be polite, even to Jack.

"Just checking in on my family," I tell him. "It hadn't even occurred to me that I could use this thing to see them. Not just here, but in the house, too."

"Please tell me you're not planning to contact them. I'm new to this whole time-travel thing, but even I know that's a bad idea. You could . . . erase yourself. Or something."

"I'm not planning to jump. I'll just watch them through the key without interacting."

Jack laughs. "You have time-travel technology, and you're planning to use it to spy on your great-greats? Have you ever talked to anyone about these voyeuristic tendencies?"

I can tell he's teasing, but my face still grows warm. "I don't plan to set stable points in the bedrooms or the baths."

"That might be safe with a boring family like mine. But are you sure your ancestors confined their sex lives to the bedroom?"

"I'm not," I tell him, now scrolling the days of 2015 backward. It's clear that the house is occupied, because the porch light flickers on and off as I go through. "But I'm also not enough of a prude to let that remote possibility bother me. The people in these images have been dead for many years."

As I speak, I keep watching the small image, which suddenly comes to life. A bright-green something sails through the air, landing on the lawn just past the oak. Is it a bird? Or maybe a moth? I don't think so, though. The shape seems too regular.

"Are you looking for something in particular?" Jack asks around a bite of noodles.

"No. Just . . . whoa."

A large reddish-brown mass blocks my view of the green shape on the lawn. It eclipses everything for a moment, and then I'm able to make it out as a dog. A fairly large dog, with an auburn coat—either a retriever or an Irish setter. The green shape, which I can now identify as a disk-shaped toy, is clasped in its mouth as its tail wags wildly.

But my eyes are drawn to a different disk, attached to the dog's collar. A disk that glows bright orange.

"I really, really wish you could see this, Jack. Can you think of any logical reason for a dog to wear a time-travel device?"

FROM THE *NEW YORK DAILY INTREPID* (JANUARY 20, 1960)

Wrestler Sputnik Monroe Charged with Disorderly Conduct; Hires Negro Attorney

(Memphis, Tenn.) Roscoe Monroe Brumbaugh, better known as "Sputnik Monroe," was charged with disorderly conduct last week for drinking beer in a Negro cafe. He appeared in court represented by a Negro attorney, Russell B. Sugarmon. The wrestler, formerly known as "Rock" Monroe, has gained a degree of notoriety for his protests against segregation of wrestling audiences over the past few years. One of these protests earned him the nickname "Sputnik" when he appeared at a Mobile, Alabama TV studio in 1957 with a black hitchhiker he'd picked up and asked to work temporarily as his driver, a few months after the USSR launched its satellite by that name. A woman who was offended by his open friendship with the Negro said she called him the worst name she could think of, "Sputnik," and it stuck.

After moving to Memphis in 1959, Monroe has waged an ongoing effort to prevent Ellis Auditorium from restricting Negro patrons to the small balcony often called a "crow's nest," turning them away when the seats in that section were full, even if the main auditorium had empty seats. Monroe argued that this cut into his profits and those of the auditorium, since there are always more Negro patrons than white ones at his wrestling matches. The auditorium relented last year.

Monroe and his companion, another white wrestler, were fined $26 each for the offense. The cafe owner, who claimed that the two had not been sold beer but were simply there giving out passes to their show, was warned by the City Licensing Commission that his license was at risk if it happened again.

$$\infty\,7\,\infty$$

Tyson
Memphis, Tennessee
August 19, 1966

There is exactly a thirty-four-second break in the traffic on this side of the building. The alley provides a bit of cover, but there's still some risk of being seen. Since thirty-four seconds is cutting it a bit close for a four-person jump, we split into two groups. A few seconds after Katherine moves out of the stable point, I blink in, and follow her over to the sidewalk. In about three minutes, there will be two shorter breaks. Richard and Saul will join us then.

Rich has been in a foul mood for the past few days. While he's definitely interested in the substance of this research, and very much looking forward to seeing the Beatles on the next leg of the trip, the key reason he proposed this joint project was to score some quality almost-alone time with Katherine, and that's not happening now. After we returned from our last jump, Katherine shared the details of the KKK rally with Saul. The very next day, Angelo told Rich that Saul Rand was being added as a fourth member of the project, given that there were significant areas of overlap with his field. Angelo didn't seem particularly happy about it, so I'm guessing Saul pulled strings with one of the other committee members. The Rand family has money and influence, and Saul is perfectly willing to use family connections to get his way.

I don't want Saul tagging along any more than Rich does. He's a narcissistic asshole. Frankly, I'm surprised that he passed the personality tests that determine whether an agent is allowed in the field or remains at CHRONOS HQ as an analyst. If I were in charge of things, he would be parked behind a desk, and I'm not the only person who feels that way. One of the historians who trained him pushed to have him benched, and Delia and Abel, two members of his cohort, seem to lean in that direction as well.

But I'm not in charge, and to be fair, I have to admit the events we're studying do indeed dovetail with Saul's focus on religious history. The religious angle is being pumped up by the Klan and other groups to cloak their real reasons for opposing this tour by the Beatles, but it's still a factor.

Katherine leans back against the red-and-silver telephone booth on the corner while we wait and surveys the area around the auditorium. "You've been in Memphis before, haven't you, Tyce?"

"Yeah. This stable point, actually. A David Bowie concert in 1972."

She gives me a vague smile, leaving little doubt in my mind that she has absolutely no idea who David Bowie was. Admittedly, I wouldn't know that, either, if I had a different roommate.

"That was one of my training jumps with Rich," I say. "Good concert. And then we came back a few months ago to see Elvis in '56. How about you?"

"First time." A faint breeze pulls a strand of her blond hair from the twin ponytails CHRONOS costuming created for this event. She tucks the hair back into place and sniffs the humid air. "Is Memphis always this . . . pungent?"

She's right. The acrid stench of asphalt mingles uneasily with stagnant water from Wolf River Harbor and the swampy stretch of land on the other side. It's cooling off a bit now that the sun is going down, but it was close to ninety degrees earlier in the day, and the air is still hot and muggy. Having had my fill of summers in the South, I pushed to jump in later, after the event starts. But that would have been a fairly short trip, and this way we can roam around a bit, maybe talk to some of the attendees before the doors open at eight.

This section of downtown Memphis is in a state of constant construction for most of the mid-twentieth century. The stable point we just used is blocked—literally blocked—after 1973 by a giant concrete support for the new bridge that will span not just the smelly harbor and the island, but the Mississippi River beyond. Things will begin looking up a few decades from now, when the strip of land across the harbor will be turned into a rather nice park—or at least it looks nice in the pictures I pulled up during my research for this jump. At the moment, though, it's abundantly clear why the place is called Mud Island.

"Maybe the Coliseum will be better," Katherine says. "It's about six miles inland, right?"

"Yeah, but it will also be more crowded. And if you think that will be an improvement, you've never been in an auditorium full of teenagers. In August. In the South." I laugh. "We'll be wishing we were back here by the time the concert is over."

Katherine looks a good ten years younger tonight than she did at the Klan rally. Her face is makeup-free, aside from a bit of pale-pink lipstick, and she's wearing a knee-length pleated skirt and a sleeveless blouse in a loud plaid print. Even in the period clothing and ponytails, which aren't exactly flattering, she's attractive. A bit too porcelain doll for my taste, but that's probably just as well, since the two guys who will be blinking in any second now will be trying to one-up each other all night. I wish I had the courage to tell Rich what everyone else can see. He needs to move on. Saul and Katherine played coy for months due to their age difference before finally making their relationship public, but everyone knew. Angelo reportedly gave them hell about fraternizing, but I think the die was cast as soon as she was assigned as Saul's research partner. Poor Rich never stood a chance.

Katherine baffles me, though. You'd think someone who studies civil rights movements, including feminist groups, would see through Saul. That she'd stand up to him and wouldn't make stupid excuses for his bad behavior. But she's truly blind where he's concerned. I hope to hell I never fall so hard for someone that I lose all sense of judgment.

"At least we're spared the toxic fumes of burning vinyl this time," Katherine says, then frowns. "Saul was *really* unhappy to have missed the South Carolina rally, you know. I wish you guys had told me that the project had such a strong religious component. It's not like he can just drop in later. The rally was small enough that we'd almost certainly see him and end up with double memories."

"Guess we just weren't thinking of it in terms of religion," I say, hoping she doesn't spot the lie. "You know how it is. I study race, so I see the racial aspects. You probably spot gender issues first. And Rich is mostly interested in the music. Classic case of historical tunnel vision."

Katherine nods. "True. And speaking of music, Richard will probably be wishing he'd waited and joined us at the concert. I think it's a safe bet that the music at this rally won't be memorable."

This particular jump to Memphis was added at Saul's request. Rich and I found out about the addition at the same time we learned Saul was being added to the team. As usual, Saul wasn't content with merely joining the project, but insisted on everyone else catering to his whims. We were initially planning to do a bonfire in Texas, instead. I guess Rich and I can schedule it at a later time, but I can't blame Richard for feeling like Saul is usurping the whole project at this point. The Beatles concert, which will be starting shortly across town, was obviously on the agenda from the beginning, but this event, dubbed the Memphis Christian Youth Rally, is kind of peripheral. There's no indication of Klan involvement, so I'm not sure I'll get much of anything for my own research. And the music will, as Katherine suggested, almost certainly suck.

The event was organized by local pastor Jimmy Stroud as an alternative for Christian teens, once it became clear that the Memphis City Council wasn't actually going to force the Coliseum to cancel the Beatles concert. Stroud originally promised to pack the local football stadium with teens who preferred Jesus to John, Paul, George, and Ringo. As estimates of the crowd size dwindled, however, the event was moved to Ellis Auditorium, just down the block from this stable point. They'll get a decent turnout, but nothing close to the number they'd hoped, and Rev. Stroud himself will even have to acknowledge that the Beatles were the bigger draw.

Two couples cross the street up ahead, signaling the next short break in foot traffic. A few seconds after they pass the stable point, Saul blinks in. He's dressed in the standard white-guy summer uniform, just as Bob Scoggin and his fellow Klansman were when they intercepted me outside the courthouse in Spartanburg. In fact, Saul looks a bit like Scoggin right now. I probably wouldn't have noticed it if he hadn't been in 1960s attire, with his dark hair slicked down tight against his head, but it's not just the trappings. There's also something about his expression and the set of his jaw.

Saul places a proprietary hand on Katherine's waist and whispers something I don't catch. She blushes and gives him a tiny dig with her elbow, just as Rich jumps in. He quickly looks the other way, managing to keep his jealousy fairly well hidden—just that downward quirk of the mouth that I know means he'd really love to punch something right about now.

As we approach the corner, half a dozen or so adults walk past. A gaggle of teens trails behind them, with the boys in one cluster at the front, followed by a slightly larger group of girls. One of the guys turns back as they pass us and yells, "Hey, Carol!" This is followed by a very poor rendition of the last line of "I Want to Hold Your Hand."

The girl makes a gesture I can't see from this angle, but judging from the hoots of the other guys and the shocked expression of the girl standing next to her, I doubt it was the peace sign.

Richard catches the exchange, too, and laughs. "Guessing the Memphis Jesus rally was *not* Carol's first choice of entertainment this evening."

"I can't imagine why," I say. "I mean, who would pass up the chance to meet Dennis the Menace?"

None of the others had the slightest clue who or what Dennis the Menace was until I explained it. That's one of the advantages to focusing on a specific time in history, rather than jumping all over the place. I'm the only one out of the four of us who can sing the theme song from *Gilligan's Island* or *The Beverly Hillbillies*. Which will probably never come up, but in this era, you'd be a little suspect if you didn't at least recognize them. Pop culture matters.

The performer that Rev. Stroud booked to be the Christian alternative to the Fab Four is a teen actor, Jay North, who is best known for playing this Dennis character on a television show a few years back. One of the sources in our archives said Dennis the Menace doesn't even show up for the rally. But either way, the preacher seriously miscalculated the actor's appeal. The Beatles' two shows at Mid-South Coliseum will pull in nearly twenty thousand fans at $5.50 a ticket—which is roughly the price of a top-notch filet mignon dinner at a five-star restaurant in 1966. Admission to the Memphis Christian Youth Rally, on the other hand, is free, but they'll attract fewer than eight thousand. And a good third of the crowd seems to be parents, judging from the folks we've seen passing by.

Katherine also notices the exchange between the two teens. She taps Saul on the shoulder. "Change of plans. You're my uncle. A preacher from Birmingham. We're in Memphis visiting family. I wanted to see the Beatles, but you forced me to come here. And I *hate* you for it." She gives him a sassy grin and takes off to join the group of girls up ahead.

I suspect that their original cover had her at Saul's beck and call for the entire evening. But if he was planning to argue, it's pointless. Katherine is already gone. Maybe she has a bit more spine than I thought.

Saul glances back at me and Rich and gives me a quick visual scan. "You really think they're going to let you in like that?"

"What? Khakis and a sports coat? That's standard mid-1960s menswear."

I'm being purposefully obtuse. I know he's not talking about my clothes. The bright blue lenses are gone today, and my hair is natural. Not quite what they'll call an Afro a few years from now, but no one is going to mistake me for that Dennis the Menace actor.

"Anyway, that's kind of the point," Richard says. "Ellis Auditorium has been more or less desegregated since 1960. So we're testing them."

"How can the place be *more or less* desegregated?" Saul asks. "Seems like an either/or proposition."

"Easy," Rich says. "Leave it up to the group renting the place. I think they'll let Tyson in. They want as large a crowd as possible to counter the other concert, and no matter how segregated the churches are, they won't want to make a scene. Tyce says they'll tell him whites only because their daughters are in the audience. Whoever wins takes the other's next three Q and A sessions."

"Ouch. Wouldn't want to be the loser," Saul says.

He's right. Public question-and-answer sessions are one assignment that almost every historian hates. Someone had the bright idea a few years back that the best way to ensure continued funding for our research was to improve our public image. Interact more. Share our lessons learned. There are thirty-six active CHRONOS agents, so each of us ends up fielding a three-hour shift as the historian on duty roughly once a month. It's a stupid assignment, because we aren't generalists. We each know about our own area of history and a few tangential subfields. I've yet to hold a session where someone didn't ask me about the US Civil War or the Vikings or something else that is way the hell out of my area of expertise. The tour groups would be better served by an avatar that could access everything in the archives, so I'm convinced that Q&A is something that a sadist on the oversight board cooked up as a form of torture. The bet was my idea, and I seriously hope they never let me in the door.

The line to get into the auditorium isn't nearly as long as the one we'll see at the Beatles concert, but it still snakes around the side of the building. Katherine is up ahead, and whatever she told Carol must have worked, because they are now whispering back and forth conspiratorially.

Saul is pushing toward the front of the line. Which probably fits his cover, to be fair. But it also fits his personality.

"I'm going to hang back until the crowd dies down a bit," I tell Rich. "Not really a fair test of the system if I make it in because I was in the middle of the herd."

"Fine with me. Just makes it more likely you get stuck with the Q and A sessions." Rich shifts closer to a group of older teens a few clusters away, and I fade back toward the alley.

Agents often travel in pairs, and occasionally in larger groups like this one. Splitting off allows us to observe more, however, so we rarely stay together, except in cases where safety might be a major concern. The main restriction is that we try to stick fairly close to the stable point, since we have to return there in order to travel back to headquarters. One of the safety protocols to prevent rogue historians from using the equipment without permission is that the system doesn't allow for side trips, which means the key will only return us to the jump room. How long we spend in the location is somewhat fluid. We arrive back at CHRONOS exactly one hour after we left, no matter how long we stay. But each scheduled jump is allowed a certain number of hours, days, or weeks, and we're run through a fairly thorough physical check upon return. It's partly to make sure we don't bring back anything contagious, but also to make sure we haven't aged an extra month or two because we decided to do a bit of unapproved time tourism while we were in the past.

There's a drugstore a few blocks down from the auditorium, still close enough to the stable point that it doesn't make me nervous. I'll hang out there for a bit. Grab a newspaper and a soda, maybe check out what's on the comics rack in August 1966, and then head back.

When I reach the store, I spot a group of girls in the empty lot next door. Three of them are leaning against the side wall, while a fourth, in a tight blue dress, paces in front of them. She reminds me a bit of the woman who usually sings lead for the Ronettes. One of the girls against the wall is reading a magazine. They all look to be in their late teens, except for one who is a good deal younger, maybe ten or eleven. All four are clearly dressed for something more important than hanging around outside the drugstore.

Which probably means they're headed to the Jesus rally.

Damn it. Rich is going to win our bet, and I'll get stuck with his Q&As.

The girl who is pacing stops as I approach the door. Now that I'm closer, I see that she's holding a cigarette.

"You got a light?" she asks.

On jumps to the last half of the twentieth century, I've found that offering a smoke is very often the best way to break the ice. Sometimes you just end up with small talk, but you can pick up bits and pieces even from talking about the weather or sports or whatever. I'd rather have my own—the fake kind that don't rot your lungs—so I usually keep a pack in my pocket with a few of each. I left them at home this time, though, since I wasn't entirely sure about the protocol at a religious concert.

"Sorry," I tell her. "I don't smoke."

She rolls her eyes and starts pacing again.

The girl closest to the door, who looks like she could be the youngest one's older sister, is staring at me. She wears a vivid orange dress, sleeveless with a flared skirt, and her head is cocked to the side, like she's trying to figure something out. As I get closer, she smiles and lifts her hand to wave, but then yanks it back down. She must have mistaken me for someone she knows. And it would *have* to be a mistake, unless I ran into a much-younger version of her before the Elvis concert. But she couldn't have been more than seven or eight back then.

So I nod and return her smile, then head into the store to make my purchases. Rather than heading to the comics rack, however, I add a cigarette lighter to the soda and gum the clerk is ringing up and go back outside. There are worse ways of whiling away a half hour or so than chatting up a pretty girl and her friends.

I flick the lighter as I approach the girl in the blue dress.

"Thanks! You're a lifesaver." She takes a long drag and then walks over to hand the smoke off to the girl reading the magazine, who puffs absently and then hands it to the one who smiled at me. She glances down at the younger girl and then hands the cigarette back to her friend in the blue dress.

"You can smoke, Toni," the younger one says. "I won't tell."

"Oh, yes, you will. First time Mama gets onto you. Or when you want something of mine and I say no. I know you too well."

Definitely sisters. I pull out the pack of Doublemint. They both take a stick.

"Thanks." The older sister folds the gum neatly into thirds and pops it into her mouth. She's still looking at me like she's trying to place my face. "You from around here?"

I shake my head. "Passin' through on my way back to school up in Ohio. Had a summer job down in South Carolina. Tyson Roberts."

Her eyebrows rise slightly. She takes my hand when I extend it and gives me that same smile that tilts up just a bit higher on the left side. "Antoinette Robinson. Toni to my friends. This is my sister, Joanna." She introduces the other girls—Gloria, in the blue dress, and Lois, with the magazine.

"What school are you at?" Toni asks.

"Antioch. Starting my third year."

"I thought I recognized you! You were there last year for commencement." It's more a statement than a question, and her smile widens. "Jo, this is one of the guys who helped Daddy with the car at Opal's graduation, after we spoke to Dr. King. Remember?"

Jo grins. "Oh, yeah! The one who—"

Antoinette jabs her elbow into her sister's shoulder, cutting her off. Jo gives her an angry look, but then seems a little embarrassed.

I really wish she would have finished the sentence, because I need all the information I can get. I'm trying to keep my own expression neutral, but it's hard, since this is precisely the sort of situation agents aim to avoid. While I know exactly what speech she's talking about, I'm still very much looking *forward* to hearing it. That jump—to Yellow Springs, Ohio, in June 19, 1965—is still about six weeks away for me.

When I chose Antioch as my cover, it was partly because the school was one of the first in the nation to admit people of color. It seemed safe to assume that the people I interacted with in Spartanburg might have heard of it but wouldn't know anyone who was actually attending a school that far away. Memphis is actually farther still from the school, so this is really, really bad luck.

"You don't remember," Toni says, her face falling slightly. "But of course you wouldn't. It was a big deal for us. Opal is the first college graduate in the family, and Jo and I had never been that far from Memphis. But I guess it was just another day on campus for you."

"No, no. I remember. Everything was just kind of a blur. Not every day you get to see a man like Dr. King in person. And I'm glad I could help. I hope you had a smooth trip back home?"

"We did." Her smile is back now, and I find myself getting a bit lost in it. "Were you able to get the stain out?" she asks.

Again, I have no clue what she means, so I just nod and change the subject. "Are you ladies heading over to the rally at Ellis Auditorium?"

On the one hand, I hope she says yes. On the other hand, things will be much less complicated if she says no, because I won't have to worry about saying something wrong. Not that it would tip her off to the fact that our meeting at Antioch hasn't happened yet for me. That wouldn't even occur to her as a possibility. She'll just think I'm crazy or that I really did forget meeting her. And even though I shouldn't allow that to bother me, it does.

The girl in the blue dress, who is now leaning against the wall next to her friend with the magazine, snorts when I mention the rally, then releases a slow stream of smoke.

"No," Jo says, pulling something out of her pocket. "We're going to see the Ronettes. And the Beatles, too."

"Assuming Gloria's boyfriend ever gets here." The girl with the magazine rolls it up. I see a flash of orange and a picture of three young women on the cover.

"He's coming," Gloria says. "Some people have jobs, you know."

As if on cue, a two-tone Ford pulls up to the curb. Jo lets out an excited little squeal and dashes to the car.

"You sure they're going to let you in over there?" Toni asks, glancing in the direction of Ellis Auditorium, as she climbs into the back seat with her sister.

"That's why I'm going, actually. To find out."

It's true, in a sense. But the main reason I say it is to impress her. To make her think that even though I'm going to the decidedly less cool concert, I'm doing it for a noble cause.

Antoinette Robinson *does* look impressed. She waves and gives me another one of those killer smiles as the car pulls away. "Be careful!" she calls back through the open window. "And try to stay on your feet this time!"

I stare after the car for a moment, baffled. What the hell did she mean by that last comment?

There's still a half hour or so to kill, so I head back inside and pick up a few comics to take back to Edwina. I also grab an *Amazing Spider-Man* for Rich, mostly to rub in his uncanny resemblance to Peter Parker.

I stash the comics in the inner pocket of my jacket and head back to the auditorium. When I arrive, there are still a few stragglers hanging around outside, but most of the crowd has gone in. Music is playing, much more upbeat than traditional gospel. Some electric guitar in the mix. Drums.

It's not good music, by any means. In fact, it's pretty awful. But it's also not what I imagined they'd be playing at a Christian counterrally for a Beatles concert.

Even though this isn't a ticketed event, I assumed someone would be at the entrance. But the door is unattended. So I follow the music and the couple ahead of me through the lobby.

I scan the crowd as I step inside the auditorium, looking for the light of the CHRONOS keys. It's usually fairly easy for me to spot—I see the light as a vivid purple. Rich sees it as a pale green. I can't remember what color the light is for Katherine, and I don't think I've ever asked Saul. Why we see it differently is a mystery to me and every other historian I've met. It's clearly a variable that someone purposefully added to the genetic design, and the current design teams continue it. Maybe it's simply out of tradition at this point, because I can't really think of a reason we'd all see the light differently.

It takes a minute, but I find Katherine, seated a few rows from the front. She's no longer with the girl she started talking to on the sidewalk. In fact, she seems to be on her own. The other girl is a few seats over, slumped down in her seat, the very image of a disaffected teen.

I can't find Rich, but Saul is at the back of the auditorium, watching a rather heated argument between four angry individuals and a man in a dark suit. The couple yelling the loudest are both almost as round as they are tall, and the man keeps jabbing his finger into the chest of the guy in the suit.

The music is too loud for me to make out exactly what they're saying, so I tap the small clear disk in the hollow behind my ear that allows me to operate some of the peripheral equipment, like the CHRONOS diaries. When my retinal screen pops up, I open the settings and filter out the music so that I can hear the specifics of the argument.

". . . not what I signed up to sponsor, Stroud. Where is Dennis the Menace?"

The guy in the suit, who must be the organizer, Jimmy Stroud, stammers. "He . . . he got held up. Maybe he'll make it in time. I don't know."

"And what the hell is that on the stage? You were supposed to hire *Christian* musicians."

"I did!" the thin man yells. "This is what the kids listen to, Douglas. You know that. At least it has a message, right? I don't much like it, either, but if you'd listen to the lyrics . . . it's the 'Doxology.' *Praise God from whom—*"

"You ask me, it's more like *praise Satan*," the woman says. "If you're gonna have dancing and play the devil's music, we might as well have let them see the Beatles. Come on, Douglas. Let's get our group and go."

Saul catches my eye as the group passes in front of me. He gives me a little nod before heading over to talk to Stroud. The chubby woman sees me, too. She gives me the stink eye. "See? I told you they wouldn't keep it separate," she says to her husband. "Like I said, we might as well have seen the Beatles."

I'm thinking the woman actually wanted to see the Beatles herself. I wonder which one she has a secret crush on. Paul, probably.

Once she and her husband move on, I make my way a bit farther into the auditorium, looking for an empty seat. There are some near the middle, but none along the edge, so I lean back against a column and scan the room to see if I can find a spot that won't require me to squeeze past half a dozen people.

Someone taps my shoulder and I turn, expecting to see Rich. But it's Jimmy Stroud.

"Sorry, son. I'm gonna have to ask you to leave." He leans forward and says in a lower voice, "Although, if you really want to hear the music, I'd be okay with you going up to the balcony. We just need to keep folks happy, you understand?"

Saul is still near the back, in the exact spot where he and Stroud had been talking a few minutes before. He gives me a little two-fingered salute and a smile, then heads back to the far side of the auditorium.

If not for that smile, I'd have assumed Stroud just happened to see me.

I've wondered for a while whether Saul has clued in to the fact that Rich is interested in Katherine. I think this settles the question. He's just guaranteed that Rich will get three months of double Q&A duty.

"Did you hear me, boy?" Stroud says.

"Yessir. I'm going."

My failure to jump the first time he told me seems to have resulted in Stroud rescinding his offer of balcony accommodations. He accompanies me to the front door, and I step out into the tepid night air.

Rich is waiting on a bench across the street. "Damn it," he says when I join him. "You win."

"What did *you* do to get kicked out?" I ask. "Can't have been your pale white face."

"Kicked myself out. That music was shredding my brain."

"You could turn it down—or off—like I did."

"Nah. Let's just go back early. You know the real shame is that there's actually some decent Christian rock in the 1960s. A group called the Exceptions had an album. *Rock 'n' Roll Mass*. One of the guys went on to start this band called Chicago that was pretty influential for about a decade, although . . ."

Rich continues, but I'm only half listening. I can tell from his tone that the music, as awful as it may be, isn't the reason he's ready to go. He's mostly pissed that this project has been hijacked by Saul, and he's probably ready to get the last jump to the Beatles concert finished so that he can move on to something where he isn't forced to watch the girl he loves with a guy he hates. A guy Rich would hate on general principle, even if Katherine wasn't in the picture.

A guy Rich would hate even more if he knew that he was the reason I won the bet.

I'm kind of in agreement on wanting this project to wrap up quickly. I've got two more jumps scheduled before Dr. King's commencement speech in Ohio. And while I know that absolutely nothing can come of it, given that we live three and a half centuries apart, I really want to see Antoinette Robinson's smile again.

Which I guess makes me almost as hopeless and hapless as Rich.

FROM *THE GENETICS WARS: AN ALTERNATE HISTORY*, BY JAMES L. COLEMAN (2109)

Unlike previous international wars where historians have largely been able to agree on precise dates, there is a wide variance of opinion on exactly when the Second Genetics War began or ended. Some historians argue that the term should not be used at all, since smaller skirmishes that employed targeted genetic weapons continued even after the generally accepted end of the First Genetics War in 2095. An international agreement on genetically targeted bioweapons was signed by all members of the United Nations, but there was considerable disagreement on the issue of genetic enhancement. Regional accords on this issue took the place of a firm international consensus. Some experts have argued that the failure to enforce any sort of limits on alterations was a core reason that the peace did not last, and a string of small conflicts again pulled more than a dozen countries into the Second Genetics War.

When hostilities finally ended, the United Nations urged member states to take immediate steps to curb the worldwide increase in genetic enhancements. The International Genetic Alterations Accords were signed by all member states of the United Nations in 2218. Some member states acceded to the Accords with significant reservations, but the core principle agreed upon by all was that each child would be allowed a single genetic alteration or "chosen gift."

An optional protocol, signed by most parties to the treaty, insisted that this single enhancement should be seen as a right, and should therefore be guaranteed by the government. While the United States did not sign the optional protocol, the courts held that alteration was indeed a right, along the same lines as guaranteed access to public education. Those who cannot afford the procedure are covered by a mandatory government subsidy, but in these cases the "chosen gift," and therefore the child's eventual career, is subject to economic and national security needs as determined by the government.

∞8∞

I place a thin leather-bound volume on top of the stack on the right-hand side of my great-grandfather's massive desk. The short book *Flowers for Algernon* is one of his best works, in my opinion. I've read it before, of course. I cried the first time, back in my second year of upper school, and even sniffled a bit during the virtual-reality version, which I viewed twice—once from Charlie's perspective and once from Algernon's.

But I've never held a first edition of the book in my hands, one that is actually signed by the author. I've touched plenty of things that belonged to James Coleman, of course. Most of the items in this house are his. This feels different, though. More personal.

I'm so glad it's not one of the books on the "suspect list." Those works—forty-seven novels in all, along with several dozen short stories—are stacked on the left side of the desk. A few were the subject of lawsuits, but most are works that the handful of literary critics who have deigned to study Coleman's oeuvre have declared to be plagiarized or ghostwritten, based on extensive computer analysis.

During the half century he was writing, James Coleman published an astounding 624 books, along with countless short stories.

That comes out to roughly one book a month, although he didn't start publishing until he was in his thirties. The few scholars willing to give him the benefit of the doubt have argued that he may well have been writing long before the publication of his first book, *Fer-de-Lance*, which launched his popular Nero Wolfe series. But several biographers presented evidence against that theory.

Rubbing my eyes, I force myself to quit procrastinating and get back to the actual task at hand. I made peace with the fact that I am a habitual procrastinator years ago, once I realized that nothing motivates me quite as effectively as a looming deadline. If a paper is due on Tuesday afternoon, I will most likely be dictating the last few words as I scarf down lunch and transmitting the file to my professor as I enter the classroom. The last-minute rush doesn't appear to affect my grades, so I've learned not to fight it. I seem to do my best work with a deadline staring me down like an oncoming train.

Laziness isn't the problem . . . well, not the *entire* problem. I usually start well in advance, but I tend to get lost in the weeds, and wind up researching tangents that have little to do with my specific topic. An assignment on mystery novels of the 1930s might lead to an article on Dashiell Hammett, where I might encounter an anecdote about the playwright Lillian Hellman that mentions the fact that Hellman was the executor of Dorothy Parker's will, and then I find myself curled up on the couch with a volume of Parker's snarky poems. And even though I will have learned many new things by the end of the day, I'll be no closer to two thousand words on the early-twentieth-century mystery genre than I was when I started out with my first cup of tea.

This library isn't helping matters. Before, I only had to contend with digital distractions. Now, however, I'm surrounded by an entire room filled from floor to ceiling with actual physical books. James Coleman was an avid collector—not just of his own books, but of all books. Nora said her grandmother Kate Pierce-Keller started the collection when she was a young woman. Her goal had been to at least partially restore the library that was destroyed when a fire in this very room consumed most of the books that her own grandmother Katherine Shaw had accumulated, although many of them were irreplaceable. Today, the bookshelves sit behind protective fire- and dustproof doors. Climate controls inside each compartment maintain the books at a steady sixty-five degrees and a humidity of 40 percent. There must have been a concern about natural light harming the collection as well, because each chamber is lit from within by a faint orange glow.

And there's so much to explore on those shelves. In the two months I've been here, I've spent dozens of hours in this library, idly browsing the titles on the spines. There are digital versions of many of these books in the household computer, but sometimes I pull one of the family treasures out of its little nook just to enjoy the feel of it in my hands and to breathe in the scent—that sweet, slightly musky aroma that always reminds me of vanilla and freshly mowed grass.

I've tried to convince myself that combing through this collection is research, and I do occasionally find something relevant. But it's really just another way to procrastinate. In the past, while I was taking regular classes, there were always papers and exams and other due dates to keep me somewhat on task. Now, however, I have only one class and one real deliverable—my thesis. With only a few intermediary deadlines, it's been harder to stay motivated. My first major assignment—a paragraph outline of the first three chapters—is due in two weeks, and I've barely gotten started.

And now my curiosity has been piqued even more by the discovery that *A Brief History of CHRONOS*, which I would have cataloged as a James Coleman *novel* based on its title and blurb, appears to be future history instead.

That makes me wonder a bit about the other volumes, maybe two dozen total, that are all subtitled *An Alternate History*. Like everyone else, I assumed that these were part of a series. Just some odd, quirky idea that popped into Grandpa James's head. They were never among his bestselling books, and I'd venture a guess that the only people who bought them were avid collectors who wanted to be able to brag that they owned every book written by James L. Coleman. To be honest, they're all as dry as stale toast. Some seem to be actual alternate history, while others should really be subtitled *An Alternate Future History*. I skimmed through a few of them, including one called *The Genetics Wars*. The book describes two Genetics Wars. The first Genetics War detailed in the book is a real regional conflict that occurred in the 2070s reimagined as a full-scale global war, with a biogenetic weapon that killed over half a billion people worldwide. The Second Genetics War hasn't happened yet, but apparently it will be the result of ongoing tensions over human genetic alterations.

Military and political history have never been my favorite sub-fields. I find them bloody and boring. But I've taken the basic world-history classes. I might forget the names and dates of major battles, but I have a pretty solid grasp of the basic flow of events. There's no way I'd have forgotten what was, essentially, a third world war, so I'm inclined to stick with my original assessment and file the entire *An Alternate History* series under *F* for fiction.

I did get a bit of reading done last night while Jack was here, but my mind kept wandering. Some of the time it wandered to Jack, who was stretched out at the opposite end of the couch, facing me, scanning a book about the second European Union on his reader. A good chunk of the time, however, it wandered to the medallion in my pocket, or to the various jumps I'd made earlier in the day, or to the puzzle of the time-traveling dog from 2015.

Okay, maybe not an actual *time-traveling* dog, but, at the very least, a dog in possession of a time-travel device. Neither of us had the slightest idea why anyone would attach the device to a dog, so once we finished dinner, we called Alex. His best guess was that the device emits some sort of field and maybe it was for protection. That idea seemed to intrigue him—so much, in fact, that he signed off the call abruptly to get back to his research.

Which brings my wandering mind full circle to my *own* research. I grudgingly pick up the first book in the stack next to me. It's a rather insipid biography of James Coleman written in the early 2060s, when my great-grandfather was still the prolific wonder of the literary world. I've skimmed through this particular volume once already and taken a few notes. None of the biographies were authorized. Much of the information is contradictory and based on second- or thirdhand accounts. Coleman was a recluse in his later years, refusing interviews, so biographers had to work with limited sources.

The only living person who knew him well has been angry at him since she was thirteen. Nora Coleman Grace is mentioned—and quoted—frequently in some of these biographies. Nothing she had to say about her father was complimentary.

In fact, if I want to provoke my grandmother into a flurry of profanity, all I have to do is say something nice about the man. For years, I would have sworn she hated him. Nora herself would certainly say that's the case, even today. But now that I'm older, I think it's less hatred and more a deep, painful disappointment. My grandfather once told me that Nora actually idolized her father when she was a girl and was delighted to be known as the only child of the great James L. Coleman.

And then came the scandal when she was a teenager. Her parents divorced, and Nora moved with her mother to London. That's where she met and, eventually, married my grandfather. He tried to convince her to patch things up when they were planning their wedding. But Nora steadfastly refused to invite James Coleman, and had, in fact, been furious when she learned that my grandfather had sent him pictures of the ceremony.

The closest thing to a kind word I've heard Nora say about her father is that he was a prolific writer with a talent for marketing. Her assessment mirrors that of the vast majority of literary critics. James Lawrence Coleman wrote in virtually every genre, and his nonfiction works span so many categories that it's almost impossible to list them all. *Prolific* doesn't even scratch the surface.

I've read most of his fiction. Some of the works are truly horrible, with florid prose, paper-thin plots, and characters so cliché that I resorted to skimming in order to finish. One of his three historical romance series was actually cringeworthy, with appalling gender and racial stereotypes.

Other works are breathtakingly good. A short story called "The Lottery" is among my favorites—not just of Coleman's writing, but of all the short stories I've read. His mystery series with the detective named Philip Marlowe was also worth a second read, and *The Exorcist* was chilling.

My goal over the next two years is to find some coherent theme in his work. I'm not the first to attempt this, but unlike the previous researchers, I have the advantage of unfettered access to his notes. There are supposedly diaries here, as well, but I've yet to find them. So far, my research has largely consisted of organizing the notes— *handwritten* notes, believe it or not, and only some of them in binders—which I have gradually been sorting into piles for digitization. I just hope Jarvis has better luck than I've had deciphering Coleman's scrawl.

The discovery that surprised me the most, however, in my early attempts at organization wasn't written by James Coleman. Nora has often mentioned her own paternal grandmother, Kate Pierce-Keller. They remained close, even after Nora's estrangement from her father. I knew from family history that Kate was a social and political activist, focusing on environmental causes, among other things. The only slightly negative thing I've ever heard Nora say about her Grandma

Kate is that she believed her grandfather would have preferred to lead a quiet life, but his wife was driven to fix the various wrongs in the world, almost as if she felt personally responsible.

"She continually butted heads with politicians on the environment, foreign policy, human rights," Nora told me. "Pretty much everything."

What Nora hadn't told me, and apparently hadn't known, was that her Grandma Kate was also an aspiring writer. There are several unpublished works in the computer files with her name listed as the author. A few even had covers, including one book—*Odds Against Tomorrow*—with tall buildings rising from a red sea.

The books bearing my great-great-grandmother's name puzzle me on more than one level. It's not just that the works were never published. I've read *Odds Against Tomorrow*, and it's actually very good. But I'm sure that there are many, many manuscripts that never see the light of day, for a variety of reasons. My key issue with those books is that they question the narrative—which continues to prevail despite the *not guilty* verdict—that Coleman was a plagiarist.

In late 2069, three people came forward claiming that James Coleman had stolen several of the many works published under his name. Two were relatives of deceased writers, and the third was an elderly man named Cale Madewell. He presented a print copy of a manuscript entitled *The Bleak Season*, which he'd written as a young man. Newspaper accounts of the trial said that the paper was yellowed with age. All three claimed that Coleman had somehow gotten hold of, and taken credit for, unpublished works.

Coleman was judged innocent, although there were rumors that he paid settlements behind the scenes that convinced two of the three plaintiffs not to make their cases as forcefully as they might otherwise have done. The public believed him innocent, but this was clearly due in part to the fact that they *wanted* him to be. Most readers had at least one book by Coleman among their favorites, and he was legendary for his work ethic. On sunny days, residents would record him walking through the neighborhood, often stopping for a break at Timberlawn Park. A stranger might have simply thought him a middle-aged man on the park bench holding a tablet and talking to himself, but the locals (and those who viewed the recordings they posted) knew that it was Coleman dictating another book.

Literary critics, on the other hand, seized on the plagiarism charges as a credible explanation for all of the things about his work that had never made sense to them—the speed at which he released books, the odd variations in writing style, and his penchant for genre hopping. Nora definitely thought her father was guilty. She referred to him more than once as *that fat fraud*.

Kate Pierce-Keller, on the other hand, defended her son until the day she died. What struck me as most unusual when I was first going through accounts of the trial, however, was that when she testified, and in the handful of interviews she gave before and after, she deftly evaded any direct questions about Coleman's guilt or innocence. Instead, she focused on the intrinsic value of the books. It would have been a tragedy, she'd said, if a play like *The Memory of Water*—one of the challenged works, and one for which Coleman won a literary award—had never found an audience.

I went into this project without a firm opinion on the plagiarism issue, although if I'm honest, I was leaning toward a guilty verdict. The unpublished books with *Kate Pierce-Keller* on the cover pull me in the other direction, however. If Coleman was swiping other writers' work, wouldn't unpublished books by his mother have been prime candidates? She'd probably have given him permission. And if not, if he really was a serial plagiarist, would he have been able to resist adding those four books to the dozens he published after she died?

Maybe. But it bothers me. It feels *off*, somehow.

What's bothering me even more, however, is the CHRONOS key in my pocket. Seeing its twin on the collar of that dog back in 2015 means I can't rule out the possibility that one or more members of my family were time travelers. One of the issues the jury seized upon was the fact that none of the manuscripts in the lawsuit were ever published, even partially, in any format, either in print or online. Two of them even predated easy access to computers. The manuscripts were by otherwise-unknown writers and had sat untouched in desk drawers or safety-deposit boxes. It was much easier for the jury to accept the defense's argument that these were skillful forgeries than to believe that Coleman had somehow uncovered them.

But what if he was a time traveler?

That possibility puts a very different spin on things. Yesterday's trip to the beach at Estero taught me that it's quite possible to change events. Going back to grab my Fleets not only spun off my temporary clone, but also screwed with the memories of everyone there to witness it.

If James Coleman was a time traveler, that could have opened a lot of doors for pilfering ideas or even entire manuscripts from other writers. Find a book that hit a bestseller list or won an award. Go back in time and steal the manuscript. If you get back to your own time and discover the book was never published, you release it yourself.

Possible? Yes. But it's complicated enough that I still don't find the explanation *plausible*.

A soft beep in my ear indicates that I have a call coming in. I asked Jarvis to hold all calls, with one exception, so I know it's Jack even before his face pops up on my lens.

His smile fades when he sees me. "What's wrong?"

I laugh, shaking my head. "Nothing. You just caught me in the middle of thinking about my research. I hope you've gotten more accomplished than I have today."

"Not really," he says. "Lorena keeps buzzing me. She tried contacting you directly but didn't get an answer. I told her you probably had your virtual assistant screening calls."

"I did."

He grins. "And I got through anyway. I'm flattered."

"You should be. I made one exception. Do you know what she wants?"

"Nope. She was curt and snippy—so, basically, just being Lorena. But she also said something about privacy issues. I think it's a fairly safe bet that it has to do with the lab sample."

"Oh. Right. Believe it or not, I'd kind of forgotten about that. I don't have her number, though. Can you send it?"

"That won't be necessary. She's actually on her way over. That's why I called—well, one reason I called."

"What was the other one?"

"Because I was just thinking about that cute little twitch you do with your mouth when you're annoyed. Like just now when I said Lorena was coming over. And the fact that you blush when I give you even the tiniest compliment."

I feel my face growing warm. "Stop! You did that on purpose."

He nods, grinning.

"And you make it sound as if I dislike Lorena, which is absolutely not true. It's just that I was trying to concentrate . . . and . . ." I stop for a moment, debating whether I really want to give voice to my suspicions yet. But I need a sounding board.

I give Jack a general summary and then say, "So now I'm wondering if Coleman didn't just go back to when a book was written and swipe the work. Then he returns to the future where the writer is long dead and publishes it."

Jack doesn't look convinced, which is fair, because I'm not really convinced, either.

"It seems contrived," he says. "And risky. You'd never know if you had the only copy. The writer might have notes, might reconstruct . . ."

"Which could have led to the three plagiarism complaints."

"True," he admits. "But if Coleman was actually doing something like this, I'd think there would have been way more than three lawsuits, don't you?"

Jarvis chimes in to tell me that someone is approaching the door. "Should I say you're not in, mistress?"

"Mistress?" Jack snorts.

"It's a historical reference. From these comics my dad liked. There was a character named Jarvis, and he was a butler before he was a computer, and . . . Would you please stop grinning like that?"

"Should I tell them you're not in?" Jarvis repeats.

"No. I'm coming." I say goodbye to Jack, who is *still* grinning, and head downstairs.

When I open the door, Lorena is on the front porch. A baby girl, who looks to be about ten months old, is slung across her hip. The baby has Lorena's round face and RJ's eyes. She's gnawing on the canvas strap of her carrier and looks like she needs a nap.

"Lorena. Come in. I'm sorry I missed your calls. I was trying to get a bit of work done, and—"

She holds up one hand. "It's okay. Some discussions are better handled in person, and I had to leave early to pick up Yun Hee anyway. Two of her teeth are coming in and she's extra cranky."

I smile at the baby. She doesn't smile back—just looks up at me with those big gray eyes and continues her assault on the makeshift teether.

Lorena isn't smiling, either. She's not exactly a super cheery person, and she probably didn't sleep well if the baby is teething, but it doesn't take a genius to deduce that something is bothering her. She wouldn't be here otherwise.

"Would you like some tea? Or coffee?"

"Dear God, yes. Coffee would be wonderful."

The food unit is old, but it makes decent coffee. By the time we're seated in the kitchen with cups in front of us, Yun Hee is nodding off against her mom's shoulder. Lorena adjusts the baby's weight and then looks at me directly.

"We need to discuss your lab results."

I nod. That was really the only reason she would be here. But I'm hit by a sudden fear that she's found some deadly heretofore undiscovered virus lurking in my genome.

"Why didn't you tell me that you're genetically enhanced?" she asks.

"Because . . . I'm *not*. Oh, wait. I had a slightly higher risk of retinoblastoma. So, they did this very routine procedure when I was a baby. Could that—"

"No," Lorena says. "I'm talking about germ-line engineering. I ran a whole genome sequence—basically mapping your entire DNA—and there were some . . . inconsistencies. Not the kind that would show up under a cursory scan. These appear to be traits you inherited. Some from your mother's side and some from your father's."

"What *sort* of traits?"

"There's evidence of enhancement on more than a dozen markers."

"*Neither* of my parents were enhanced, Lorena. My father was born in Ireland, and they were party to the very first round of international agreements on restricting genetic alterations. So was the African Union, where my mother was born. The AU had firsthand experience with genetic targeting a decade before her birth. They wanted that technology locked down tight."

I try to keep my voice level, but this isn't a charge that you toss around lightly. In fact, it's the kind of accusation that can ruin lives and livelihoods, even if you manage to prove your innocence.

Plus, I know it's not true.

Both of my parents were born *after* the heyday of genetic enhancement, *after* scientists began trying to stuff the genie back into the bottle. Advanced nations gradually loosened restrictions on in-vitro genetic alteration during the 2020s. The first exceptions were to correct potentially fatal congenital abnormalities. By the 2040s, however, most nations had legalized genetic tweaks to bring offspring to the "norm." There were protests from those who argued that such programs were ableist and elitist, but even those who were ideologically opposed to alteration often found an excuse when it came to giving their own offspring an extra advantage.

The baseline shifted upward rather quickly. It was an open secret that those with enough money could get a clinic to define average or even slightly above-average intelligence as a "developmental problem." For a few thousand more, a clinic might be willing to change nose size, eye color, predisposition to obesity, and maybe toss in musical talent or eidetic memory as a bonus. And those whose parents couldn't afford the procedure at all slipped further behind, and the gap between rich and poor widened.

Those who were wealthy enough to afford the best clinics had fewer problems, but the middle class, those who scraped together their meager savings to pay for a boost at the smaller, less experienced clinics, faced a higher rate of infant and even maternal mortality. Since the procedure was still illegal, they couldn't sue when things went wrong. Often what went "wrong" wasn't even noticeable until later in life, when they realized that tweaking one section of the brain could have cascading (and often catastrophic) effects on the other sections. Suicide rates were very high as that first enhanced generation reached adulthood.

Things came to a head with a series of biological attacks in the early 2070s. The most serious occurred when the Akan deployed a biological weapon against a neighboring country. Many were killed, and others were rendered sterile. Those who were attacked in this fashion fought back, mostly with conventional weapons, and the United Nations was eventually pulled in for peacekeeping.

The silver lining to the conflict was that it produced a spate of international and regional organizations and treaties aimed at preventing something like that from ever happening again and caused a social backlash against rampant genetic engineering. Several of the people leading the charge were enhanced who recognized the unfairness, but it was largely a bottom-up revolution.

Mandatory testing began in 2094. Those who refused testing were treated, for the purpose of classification, as enhanced. The only legal exemptions were for members of a handful of religions that don't allow blood or tissue to be taken from the body. Enhanced individuals are not allowed into more prestigious academic programs. Some firms refuse to hire them on principle.

In recent years, the enhanced have begun to fight the law, claiming that the blame lies with their parents or grandparents for altering their genetic makeup in the first place. They argue—with some justification—that they are being unfairly penalized for something over which they have no control and cannot change.

On the other side, the masses contend that this is a perfectly legitimate way to level a playing field that has been tilted in favor of the wealthy for generations. Even before genetic enhancement was available, the rich passed their benefits along to their offspring through private schools and college funds, while the poor struggled in underfunded public schools and spent much of their lives paying off university debt.

Lawsuits continue to this day, with enhanced individuals suing the various schools that deny them entry and the geneticists who altered them. Quite a few have sued their own families, and there are cases of parents ending up in prison for breaking the laws on genetic enhancement.

Slowly, the pendulum has begun to shift back toward the enhanced and their families, who usually have money to fund lawsuits. Several landmark decisions have been handed down in the past decade in courts around the world, holding that genetic enhancements purchased—whether legally or illegally—by one generation cannot be used to discriminate against their descendants. Requirements that parents correct for any inherited enhancements at the embryonic stage are increasingly dismissed as posing an undue risk and burden.

But the bottom line for the past forty years has been this: If you are enhanced, you can still get an education. You can get a decent job. Some doors, however, will be closed to you. Some advantages, like scholarships and merit promotions, will be weighted in favor of those who are not enhanced.

I've always agreed with these rules. I still do. The enhancement gives an advantage. You don't get to double-dip.

My department at Georgetown believes in those rules, too. Even with the promise of access to my great-grandfather's papers, I'm technically a foreign student. Had my passport and birth certificate not both shown that I am genetically unaltered, I probably wouldn't be here. I certainly wouldn't have a tuition waiver. That kind of benefit is only available if you can show that you had the native talent and work ethic to get into the program without any sort of enhancement—or, in my case, some of that and a fat bribe in the form of the papers of a famous great-grandfather for their archives.

I passed the official screening at birth. Plus, I've been to doctors in several different countries. So have my parents. You'd think if they were concerned about our status, they'd have passed on that information before I went off to undergrad. My dad *might* have tried to shelter me as a kid from something like this, but he would have told me once I reached adulthood. So this has to be a mistake, or else a really, really bad joke on Lorena's part.

I take a deep breath to rein in my anger and keep my voice down in deference to the baby in Lorena's lap, who looks miserable and is on the verge of falling asleep. "My parents were not enhanced. They were tested. I was tested. And I have papers to prove it."

"I'm willing to accept that you didn't *know* they were enhanced, okay? You'd have been crazy to let me take that blood sample if you knew. And, theoretically, these *could* be alterations that your parents themselves inherited, although some of these enhancements weren't available until the late twenty-first century. A few of them . . ." She shakes her head.

"What?"

"A few of them aren't like anything I've ever seen, okay?" She taps her comm-band and the sequencing results appear in front of us.

I'm not a geneticist, but I can see the red flags—the *literal* red flags—on the report.

"It's possible that your previous tests didn't detect this if they were performed at a smaller clinic. This isn't the type of thing that a normal blood scan would detect. I'd think that your initial testing, though, would have turned this up, not to mention the more thorough scan they'd have performed on both of your parents before they were allowed to conceive. But . . . your family has, or at least *had*, money, right? Wealthy people have been bribing officials since the dawn of bureaucracy. A few thousand credits to the guy running the premarital or neonatal tests, a few thousand more to the family doctor, and no one has to know. You just teach your kid to tone it down. Miss a few questions on purpose. Maybe lose a chess match or settle for second place in track and field."

"My family always encouraged me to do my very best." I don't mention the fact that this was truer of my dad and Nora. Mom, on the other hand, has always been more inclined to discourage my competitive side.

"There's really no mistaking the results," Lorena says. "That's why I took the sample in the first place. I mean something *had* to be different about you if you can operate that device the rest of us can't."

"Different doesn't necessarily mean enhanced."

"No," she admits. "But the evidence is solid. Maybe you need to have a talk with your parents? Or your grandparents, since they'd have been the ones to order the procedures."

"What do you think they had enhanced?"

She gives me an uncomfortable look. "It might be easier to explain what *wasn't* enhanced. Okay, no. That's overstating things, but . . ."

"Are we talking about physical attributes? Or—"

"Yes, but also intellectual. Areas that deal with memory and language aptitude. And some stuff that looks . . . well, not natural. I can't even identify it."

I sit there silently for a long time, staring at the report with the stupid red flags. "Do you understand what this means for me?"

"Of course, I do. That's why I'm here. That's why I haven't told anyone. But you need to recognize that this could become an issue. Georgetown wouldn't have let you into the program if they'd had this information, and . . . they're my employer, Madi."

"So you're going to turn me in."

"No," she says, looking miserable. "Not if I can avoid it. I deleted the data as soon as I transferred it to my comm-band. And then I purposefully screwed up a few other tests for my work project. Told my supervisor that we'd gotten some sort of contamination in the samples. That I had to throw out a set of results."

I feel bad for being angry now. She's taking a big risk, especially when she has a family to support.

"Thank you."

She shrugs. "Errors like that happen sometimes. Maybe they won't look too closely. But your genetic alterations are almost certainly the reason you can use that CHRONOS device. And whether we move forward on this time-travel thing or not . . . I doubt this is something you're going to be able to keep hidden indefinitely."

FROM THE DIARY OF
KATHERINE SHAW

Personal Journal 10262304

We fought again last night. It was the same fight we always have, with only slight variations. I'm tempted to record it next time, and then I can just play it on the holoscreen anytime Saul decides that he needs yet another Game night at the Club, even though he promised that he'd only go two nights a week when we applied for shared quarters.

He always says that I can come, too, but I know he doesn't really want me there. If he loses, he always blames me, saying that I'm a distraction. And I have no desire to spend three nights a week in the company of Morgen Campbell or his dog, who snarls every time I walk past. Campbell is loathsome and lecherous. He delights in making snide sexual innuendos, either about my relationship with Saul, or worse, Saul's relationships before we were together.

I don't believe half of what he says, and Saul assures me that I'm right in dismissing the old man's comments. "He's just trying to rile you up," Saul said after the last time I went. "He likes to see you get angry. If you're going to let him bother you like that, you should just stay home. Or take up a hobby. Make some friends."

Of course, if I do hang out with friends, male or female, Saul gets jealous. He's only happy if I'm sitting at home, waiting patiently for him to return.

Saul says The Game is his only relaxation—which, as his partner, I find rather insulting, since it's not an activity we share. Two sessions a week isn't enough to keep him in top form, he claims, and he's tired of Campbell winning. I swear the man is addicted, although I'm not sure whether it's to The Game itself or to his rivalry with Campbell.

He says he loves me but if I'm going to be this clingy, this possessive, maybe he should apply for separate quarters. Of course, he *knows* I don't want that, and so he has the upper hand. That's why he started the fight, so that he could push me into agreeing to *three* nights a week.

Yes, I'm angry at myself for giving in. But I held firm on three nights a week. And no sneaking off for a minisession in the afternoons. If he needs more time than that, then he can just move in with Campbell and his nasty-tempered, gassy old Doberman.

∞9∞

"Training sessions usually take precedence on the jump calendar when there's a conflict, don't they?" Saul glances at the others around the long table. His eyes pause a bit longer on Angelo—the short, slightly overweight man in charge—and the three other jump-committee members.

There are fourteen active agents at today's scrum, in addition to Angelo and three members of the jump committee. All fourteen of us are, in some fashion, specialists in anglophone countries during the modern era. *Modern* is defined as anything between 1850 and 2160, with the latter year being the firm cutoff for any sort of in-person observation. There are similar meetings held for other regions and time periods. I'm fairly lucky in that my work is strictly modern and Anglo, at least so far. Rich's research has taken him to Brazil and the African Union in the past year, and he's done at least one jump to the late 1700s, so he occasionally has three or four of these torture sessions in each two-week block.

Our team meetings are a bit larger than most. Medieval, which is anything between 1450 and 1849, has half as many historians, and there are only a smattering of ancient specialists. CHRONOS has always had a pretty strong bias toward US history, given that both the technology and the organization began in the United States. There's also a pretty sizable bias toward the modern era, since it's easier to blend in and there are fairly decent historical records, including photographs and video, that we can study during the six years we're in classroom training. Or at least that's the usual explanation. Personally, I think it's at least as much due to the fact that most agents prefer traveling to eras where there are basic amenities like toilets, showers, and food you don't have to kill yourself.

The ostensible purpose of these team meetings is to go around and discuss our most recent jump and whatever project is next on the horizon. It's a way of sharing "best practices and lessons learned," as the old saying goes. A core of regulars is always here, but there are usually three or four floaters, as we call them, who specialize in subfields that cut across continents or eras, like Rich and music history.

Everyone in this room has dealt with Saul before, and it's a fairly safe bet that he'll get his way. He almost always does. Some of it is seniority. He's thirty-one, which means he has only a few more years left in the field. But it's also his connections. And his bulldoggish tenacity.

"In addition," Saul continues, "my training jump with Oakley was on the schedule before Richard's new project was approved. So even if we weren't prioritizing training, we'd need to reschedule the other jump instead of mine."

"Or," I say, "we could take the simpler route, rather than messing with a jump schedule that is determined weeks in advance, and you could skip this second Memphis jump. You were added to our project *after* it started. I doubt you'll get much more from it than what's covered in the newspapers from the era or in the accounts we'll bring back."

Katherine gives me an annoyed look across the table. Normally, I would have stayed out of it. True, I don't like Saul, and I'm also still a bit pissed about his role in getting me bounced from the rally during our last jump, although I suspect Saul thinks he did me a favor by sticking Rich with my Q&A sessions. But my animosity isn't strong enough that I really care one way or the other whether Saul tags along. I am a bit concerned that he might get in the way of me chatting with the six robed and hooded men who will be hanging around outside the Coliseum before the concert begins. But my key reason for speaking up is that I know Rich *won't* do it, because he doesn't want Katherine angry at him.

Personally, I think that's a mistake. Katherine seems to be angry at Saul a lot, but she's still attracted to the guy. Right now, I think she's mostly indifferent to Rich, and I suspect that's worse than anger.

Saul's nose pinches slightly at my suggestion that he drop the next Memphis jump. I guess that's supposed to be his wounded expression. But anyone who knows him—okay, anyone who knows him and *isn't* Katherine—can tell it's fake.

"The committee felt that my expertise would contribute to the project," he says. "To be honest, I'm still not clear why I wasn't added when the proposal was being written, since it's very obviously within my subfield. That's water under the bridge now, but having missed one of the jumps already, I'm not willing to miss a second one. And Oakley needs the field hours. The rest of you will just have to deal with a short delay. Training comes first."

Delia Morrell slowly lifts one perfectly arched brow, and several of the other historians look like they're fighting back a laugh. Saul Rand has bitched and moaned about every trainee he's been assigned. He complained about Grant Oakley, the trainee whose rights he's now defending, at our very last scrum, arguing that he had a full schedule on the upcoming jump to 1911 Atlanta and couldn't afford to be saddled with a noob.

Grant, the noob in question, must be feeling a bit of whiplash from Saul's sudden change of heart. He keeps quiet, though. That's almost always the best course of action as a trainee, especially when you're still trying to figure out the power dynamics in the room.

"He has a full two-week training session coming up with me and Abel next month," Delia says. "Grant could always do this Atlanta project later, as a solo."

Delia and her husband, Abel Waters, are two of the oldest members of our current group of thirty-six field agents. She's been in the field for nearly fifteen years. I think Abel came in with the class right after hers. They've got maybe two more years in the field before they end up taking jobs like Angelo's, stuck behind a desk, overseeing jump committees and training schedules. I've only known of two historians who lasted twenty years in the field. By around age thirty, ability with the CHRONOS key starts to deteriorate. That's one reason we start fieldwork at sixteen.

I preferred my training jumps with Rich. He has a more relaxed style, and we hit it off on a personal level. But to be honest, Delia and Abel taught me more. That's true of Abel in particular. There are a lot of unwritten rules on how to navigate society as a black male any time before the mid-twenty-first century. Abel helped me learn how to blend in and avoid making waves, something that's harder for him, strictly on a physical level, because he cuts a more imposing figure. When Abel Waters walks into a room here in CHRONOS, everybody pays attention. He's six five and powerfully built, dwarfing most people in the present or the past. He doesn't back down from an argument, either. But put him in the 1930s South, and he is capable of shrinking, fading into the wallpaper. It's a survival mechanism that serves him well and allows him to observe the culture without inserting himself into it. He usually takes the role of Delia's driver, and it's almost like he's a different person . . . He's so convincing that you'd swear the man had somehow lost a few inches of height when he landed in the past. If Abel Waters had been delivering that chicken box to the courthouse, I suspect he'd have walked right past Scoggin and his buddy without attracting their attention in the slightest.

Saul ignores Delia and nods toward the calendar hovering over the center of the table. "There are three empty slots a week from Thursday. If we get one other person to agree to a schedule change, we can just bump the 1966 trip to the ninth. Kathy has a jump she can move forward. I'm sure Rich and Cham—sorry," he says, looking not at me, but rather at Katherine. "*Tyson*. I'm sure Richard and Tyson have a jump they can swap out."

Rich curses under his breath. It's barely audible, but almost everyone is now looking at the two of us, and I'm guessing at least a few of them can read the words on his lips. He doesn't protest, though. He knows we're beaten.

Rich says that he has some Q&A sessions he can get out of the way, and I tell Angelo that I can move my 1965 jump forward. Angelo looks relieved, but also a little annoyed. He doesn't like seeing Saul win any more than the rest of us.

Saul leans back, clearly pleased with the outcome. I'm not sure he really cares one way or the other which jump he does first. He just likes sticking it to Richard. I think maybe he also just likes to win.

While I didn't want Saul to win, either, I'm kind of okay with the switch. I've been looking forward to hearing Dr. King speak in person for years, and my mind has been replaying my conversation with Antoinette Robinson since we got back from Memphis the other day. Part of the reason I keep thinking about her is purely physical. She's damn pretty and I'm as susceptible as the next guy. But it's also the oddness of having her remember something that hasn't happened yet for me. It feels like a loose thread, and my mind keeps tugging at it. The sooner I get my life back into some semblance of chronological order the better.

Our usual routine after these team meetings is to head over to the Objectivist Club for lunch. It's only a couple of blocks from CHRONOS headquarters, and even though it's a few credits more than lunch in the cafeteria or from the food units in our living quarters, there's a general consensus that we deserve something out of the ordinary as a consolation prize for the hour or two of tedium we've just endured.

Or at least that's the story that we'd give Angelo or the board if they ever asked. But they were CHRONOS agents at one time, and I suspect the after-scrum lunch was a tradition back then, too. The actual team meeting goes on the books. It's official, recorded into the archives, and, therefore, there are some things we just don't talk about in that setting. Screwups, for example, that escaped official notice but might be good for the others to know so they don't make the same mistakes. Sometimes there's a funny story that you just don't want included in the record. It's also a good chance for newer historians to ask for advice without looking like total neophytes.

Richard, however, is not in the mood to socialize today. He watches the others head for the elevator. "You go ahead. I'll grab something at the cafeteria." Then he adds in a lower voice, "I've had enough of people for one day."

"Then you should steer clear of the cafeteria. It's right at noon."

Even though there are only thirty-six active agents at CHRONOS, more than five hundred people work here as analysts and support staff. Our food units in the living quarters can make anything on the menu at the cafeteria, so the only reason to go downstairs is because you *want* to be around people.

Rich shrugs, making it clear that it's less people in general than *certain* people he'd prefer to avoid. "Good point. Guess I'll just head up to the room and grab something from the kitchen."

He punches the button to go up.

"Hey, wait," I say, "who should I ask about 1960s-era cars? Not driving them, but how they work. And don't say the archivists. I don't have an official reason for researching it and would prefer not to raise questions. It's for the Ohio jump."

I'd given Rich a brief overview of my conversation with Toni Robinson after we returned from the last trip, partly because I wanted to talk about it, but also because it was kind of bugging me. This isn't quite the same as crossing your own path, which is a training exercise everyone has to do where you go back in time and have a conversation with yourself. The whole point of *that* exercise is to convince you that you never want to cross your own path again if you can avoid it, because it's really not worth the headache or the possibility that you'll upchuck your last meal. In this case, though, it's more of a nagging feeling, like things aren't sequential.

"Wouldn't be the first time one of us developed an interest outside his field," Rich says. "The archivists probably wouldn't bat an eye. If you mean one of us, though . . . Timothy, maybe. Or Evelyn. They did one long project in the late 1950s, and they've got that JFK thing coming up. I'm guessing one of them has basic mechanical knowledge in case they break down on the side of the road. But you're overthinking this, Tyce. Like I told you the other night, whatever you did to help that family out was something you already *knew* how to do."

"You *think*," I say. "You said you're not certain."

"I'm *reasonably* certain." The elevator opens and he steps inside. "I mean, theoretically, it would have to be, right? Of course, if you're really curious, you could always ask Angelo."

Rich grins and gives me a wave as the elevator door slides shut.

He knows damn well I'm not going to ask Angelo. That would immediately lead Angelo to ask *why* I wanted to know, and the odds are good that the jump would get canceled. Just to be on the safe side. Someone else would no doubt help Toni's father with whatever was wrong with the family car. History would unfold exactly as it was intended to without me there to observe it.

I'll end up with a double memory if that happens. Not the end of the world, but also not pleasant. My bigger concern, though, is that Antoinette Robinson, who is not under a CHRONOS field, will no longer have any memory of me at all. I know it's kind of egotistical, but that bothers the hell out of me.

The main room at the Objectivist Club is worlds apart from the brightly lit, modern cafeteria at work or the nineteenth-century vibe that Campbell has going up in Redwing Hall. Here, the tables are scattered in small groups inside an atrium that looks more like a park than a restaurant, with greenways and a stream running through the center. The ceiling shows a clear blue sky today, far more pleasant than the actual, rather dreary gray outside. Should you find yourself in the mood for a bit of amusement after your meal—and willing to lose a month or two's worth of credits—a state-of-the-art gaming center sits on the other side of the clubroom.

Most of the team is already at our usual cluster of tables when I get to the OC, although Timothy and Evelyn don't seem to have arrived yet. I'm about to ask Delia and Abel if I can join them when Katherine waves me over to her table.

She's alone. Otherwise, I'd have pretended I didn't see her. Saul skips at least half of these after-meetings to hang out with Morgen Campbell, who doesn't lunch down here with the commoners. The Redwing Room has human waiters and a license to serve real meat—which Morgen swears is far superior to the slaughter-free meat on the menu here in the main clubroom. I've had meat of all varieties on my jumps, and the lab-cultivated stuff tastes identical. I'm pretty sure Morgen just gets off on knowing something had to die to provide him with lunch.

So I join Katherine, reluctantly, hoping Saul isn't in any hurry to come back. Although if she's still pissed about me opposing him earlier, this won't be a pleasant meal either way. She looks more worried than pissed, though.

I tap the center of the table to pull up the menu. "Did you already order?"

"No. I'm waiting on Saul. He said he'd only be a few minutes. Is Richard angry about the change?"

I briefly consider telling her that I don't know, but I opt for the truth instead. "Yeah, he's pissed. With good reason, too. He's the lead researcher on this project, and Saul is screwing up the schedule. If he had a conflict, he shouldn't have asked to join."

Katherine frowns, looking down at the table. "That was my fault. I should have just told Rich no in the first place, but it sounded interesting, and—"

"Then why should you have said no? Does Saul control your professional life, too?"

Her blue eyes flash, and I'm afraid I've gone too far. But then she gives me a tired smile. "You've never been in a serious relationship, have you, Tyson?"

I stare at her over my water glass without answering. Katherine is only two years older than I am, so this wise-elder act isn't cutting it with me.

But she ignores my expression and continues. "Making a commitment to someone involves a lot of compromises. Saul tends to be a bit on the jealous side—although to be fair, so am I. Anyway, he thinks . . ." She pauses, a slight blush rising to her cheeks. "He thinks Richard has a thing for me. I've told him that's ridiculous. Richard and I have been friends for going on ten years. Since the first day we started classes. But Saul is really insecure—"

I snort. It's an automatic response, because that's just garbage.

"It's true!" Katherine protests. "I'm sure it doesn't seem that way, but you don't know him like I do. Believe it or not, you really hurt his feelings today."

The center of the table slides back to deliver my lunch. I'm glad for the diversion, because it helps me fight back laughter at the idea that anything I said might wound someone with an ego as big as Saul's. I take a bite of my lasagna and then say, "Listen. I'm sorry if I hurt his feelings, but he kind of asks for it. And I really don't want to debate the merits of Saul Rand over lunch."

She's silent for a moment, and I think that's the end of it. But then she heaves an angry sigh and the words come spilling out. "Of course, you don't. Because then you're free to continue to judge me without any context. To think that I'm weak-minded enough to let Saul manipulate me."

"I don't think—"

"Yes. You do. I'm not a fool, Tyson. I can tell what people think. Even Richard. But I *know* Saul. I know what he's been through, and how far he's come. His family . . ." She lowers her voice. "They're awful. His parents are dead now, but they both lobbied to pull the Americas out of the IGAA."

The International Genetic Alterations Accords of 2218 were the global compromise reached after a century of rampant on-demand genetic modification. Widespread genetic alteration had produced a deeply divided world, where children of the elite were guaranteed a higher IQ, greater physical strength, and even a longer life span. The unaltered masses, frustrated at having to compete equipped with only what nature provided, eventually rebelled, launching the Genetics War. They'd never have stood a chance in defeating the genetically enhanced minority if not for the fact that a sizable portion of the enhanced had begun to realize that things were getting out of hand. Even so, it took nearly a century of starts and stops, regional agreements, and global tension before nations came together as one to try to find middle ground.

The first generation of children conceived after the Accords was altered to remove all germ-line—inheritable—enhancements. As a compromise, each child would be allowed one—and only one—chosen gift. This was a somatic alteration, something that couldn't be inherited by their offspring. In the years immediately after the Accords were signed, gifts were distributed by lottery, based on the needs of society and tied to the job the child would eventually hold. Children assigned as mathematicians would be given a genetic boost to improve not just their ability in the field, but also their passion for the job. There would be no glut of artists and no lack of teachers. All jobs would pay the same basic income, and each child would be perfectly suited for his or her job.

All in all, things are better since the Accords, but there were problems from the outset. It might have worked better if they'd redistributed financial assets a bit more aggressively at the same time. But that was a sticking point in the negotiations. The prevailing argument—pushed rather effectively by those who held the bulk of the wealth—was that it would be enough simply to ensure that money wasn't a determining factor in the next generation's success. The chosen-gift system did level the playing field considerably, but parents still passed a percentage of their wealth down to their children, along with their ideas about which jobs were more prestigious.

And with extra money in the hands of the few, corruption gradually crept into the system. While the list of allowable chosen gifts has remained fairly stable, the method for allocating those jobs has changed considerably. In my grandparents' era, a small bribe meant that you might get first crack at the list before all of the best gifts, the ones that carried some level of social status, were taken. By the time my parents were born, a bribe was required to get anything that most people considered prestigious, and the rules on inherited modifications began to relax. If someone was an artist, they reasoned, it only made sense that they'd want at least some of that talent to be passed on to their offspring.

Plus, some governments began adding package deals for priority professions. The bribe was a bit higher for those. My parents and grandparents invested a lot of money to get me into CHRONOS. That's true of every historian in the program.

But even though there are work-arounds, and all nations cheat to some extent, the underlying concept behind the IGAA is considered sacrosanct. Nobody wants another genetics war. Nobody wants to go back to a time where the divide between the enhanced and the unenhanced was so wide that it was hard for either side to consider the other fully human.

"Saul's family was fighting the Accords long before he was born," Katherine says. "They tried to purchase multiple enhancements for him and his sister on the black market, but they couldn't find a geneticist willing to do it. His grandfather and great-aunt are still involved in efforts to pull the Americas out of the agreement. Saul's had a tough time breaking free from some of the beliefs that were drilled into him when he was a kid."

I'm not sure that Saul's relationship with his family is nearly as strained as Katherine thinks. He's one of the few historians who is an actual *member* of the Objectivist Club, and that membership is tied to the Rand family. They certainly haven't cut him off financially. We're all required to maintain quarters at HQ, but Richard says Saul frequently vacations at one of several homes his grandfather owns. And whether it's in the form of direct bribes or family influence, someone has definitely pulled strings for him at CHRONOS.

I don't go into that, but simply note that Morgen Campbell is a well-known opponent of the Accords. "And he and Saul seem to be pretty chummy," I add. "You were saying just last week that he spends way too much of his spare time gaming with Morgen."

"He does," Katherine admits. "But I don't think you can really call Morgen and Saul friends. They're more like . . . opponents. Morgen's obsessed with wealth. He thinks the person with the most cash and the most toys should run the world. But Saul understands that there are forces stronger than money. Religion, for example—he could have chosen pretty much any subfield, but that's the one that fascinates him, because he's seen what a powerful influence it can be. Saul's interest in their simulations is to prove Morgen wrong. And, I think, in a way, to prove his parents wrong. To show that there *are* things more important than money."

Even though I don't entirely buy what she's saying, I do believe *she* believes it. And I like Katherine. I really don't want to argue with her.

"Okay. Maybe I misjudged him."

She smiles, then glances around the room nervously. "I shouldn't have told you any of that. Saul would be furious. But I'm hoping maybe you could help Rich understand. We used to be close, but since I started dating Saul, things have been different between us. I completely understand that Saul is hard to like. He's . . . spiky, like one of those prickly creatures up in Canada . . . What are they called?"

"Porcupines?"

"Exactly. Although, I guess that's not the best analogy, since porcupines aren't really ever *not* spiky."

"Except to their mates. Otherwise there would be no little porcupines."

Katherine gives me a little nod of admission. "True. But could you guys try to give him the benefit of the doubt, even if it's possible that I'm the only one who sees his nonspiky side?"

She's *not* the only one—Saul's pre-Katherine sexual exploits were extensive, and Rich claims the guy is still on the prowl every chance he gets. But I decide not to stir things up further.

"You want some bread?" I ask, pushing the basket toward her. It feels weird eating when she's not.

"No, thanks." Katherine blinks her eyes rapidly to switch on her retinal display, and we sit there silently for a few minutes as I eat and she scans through something I can't see. Whatever she finds must annoy her, because she finishes off the last of her iced tea and gets up. "If you see Saul, could you tell him I decided to head home early? I've got a bit of a headache."

"Sure."

As she heads for the exit, I glance around and spot Evelyn and Timothy at the table next to Abel and Delia. Grabbing my food, I head over to join them so that I can pick their brains about auto repair.

Timothy slides his plate a bit closer to his wife's to make room for me. He looks amused. "Lots of drama today. You seem to be smack in the middle of it."

Evelyn glances toward the door that has just closed behind Katherine. "Is she okay?"

"Yeah. I think so. Said she had a headache."

"Why did Richard let Saul on the project in the first place?" Timothy asks.

"Same reason Saul gets away with most of his bullshit. Word came down from above. I'm pretty sure he pulled another one of his stunts in Memphis."

I explain the bet with Richard and Saul's conversation with Reverend Stroud. "Of course, I can't *prove* anything. Just Saul being Saul. I don't know why Katherine puts up with him."

Timothy leans forward, a conspiratorial glint in his green eyes. "Actually, I have a theory about that."

"Oh, hush, Timo," Evelyn says, rolling her eyes. "That's just rank speculation."

He grins. "But it makes sense, doesn't it? You know the design team had to have given Tate Poulsen a testosterone boost or something. They tweaked *all* of us . . . some more than others. The vast majority of Katherine's jumps—with or without Saul—are before the twentieth century, when women were expected to be meek.

Subservient. It makes sense that designers might do something to make women traveling to that era fit in better. And Saul's clearly attracted to the timid type."

Evelyn snorts. "You think Esther is timid? Saul Rand is attracted to any woman who's attracted to *him*."

"Whoa," Timothy says, as another thought occurs to him. "You just made my point. Only . . . backward. Esther's work is with matrilineal societies, and some of them are societies where women are warriors, so . . . maybe that's something they tweaked in both of them, just in different directions."

Evelyn gives a little shrug. "Okay, okay. It's possible, I guess. But the idea that they would alter something like that bothers me. It feels inherently *wrong*. If they tampered with Katherine in that fashion, who's to say they didn't tamper with me? Or you? Maybe we're only together because they found a way to increase my preference for green eyes and my tolerance for really bad jokes."

Timothy leans forward and gives her a quick kiss. "Then I owe the genetic-design team a huge debt of gratitude, don't I?"

She gives him a little smile. "I just hope for Richard's sake that it's not true. I keep hoping she'll wake up and realize she has far better options. She deserves better than Saul."

I'm a little worried that they're going to keep up the discussion on Rich's feelings for Katherine, and even though they both seem to view his infatuation as a given, I don't want to be the one to confirm it. So I shift the discussion over to 1960s cars and quickly discover that neither of them knows much more about auto repair than I do.

"They have this thing called Triple A," Timothy says. "You call them if your car breaks down."

"But no mobile phones for . . . what? Three more decades?"

Evelyn shrugs. "Pay phones in the cities, though. We've only made a few trips into the more rural areas. Never a good idea to get too far away from your stable point. What has you worried about car repair, anyway?"

I could tell them. It's not like I've broken any rules, and I trust them not to say anything to Angelo or the board. But given that Evelyn seems to have picked up on Rich's feelings for Katherine, I think it's possible she'll also guess that my reasons for being a little anxious about the Ohio trip are in part due to a girl. And I'd really prefer not to go into that right now.

"I was just wondering how I'd deal with it if it happens. There was a car broken down in Memphis when we were there, and I was kind of curious."

We finish eating and then mingle with the others for a bit. Delia tells an amusing story about this guy they met in 1939 Georgia who claimed to be clairvoyant. That leads to another story about a purported psychic in Amsterdam, and someone asks if any of the earlier cohorts had gone back to the sixteenth century to interview Nostradamus. And that somehow segues into a comparison of witch trials. Shaila, who focuses on Islamic cultures, mentions a witch panic in the mid-2000s that swept through Saudi Arabia and a few other countries, and that leads to the next thing. It's the sort of free-flowing conversation we can't have in the team meetings, but it's probably even more important in terms of helping us decide which eras and events to study.

Afterward, on my walk back to HQ, my mind returns to Timothy's theory about Katherine. The possibility that she might be with Saul, in part, because of something the design team inserted into her genetic code shouldn't really come as a surprise. They alter everything else. I'm one of the few who can look at my parents and see anything of myself in their faces. Katherine is blond with blue eyes, a far cry from the Asian features of her mother, who is a technician at CHRONOS, or her father, whose race is as mixed as the average person on the street. That's true for the vast majority of agents.

I won't say I've never thought about the differences between the periods we study and now. Back then everything about you—your entire mental, physical, and emotional makeup—was shaped by your family tree and your environment. Life spans were shorter and congenital diseases were still rampant. Genetic modifications have helped millions of people live better lives.

If your one enhancement is the CHRONOS gene, though, everything about you is fair game for alteration. Appearance. Intelligence. Language aptitude.

But I've always believed that underneath all that, my personality, the core of what makes me Tyson Everett Reyes, would have been basically the same even if my assignment and my chosen gift had been something entirely different from CHRONOS.

Now I'm wondering if that's true.

And if they tweaked that, too, then what part is really me?

FROM THE *NEW YORK HOURLY INTREPID* (MAY 3, 2111)

Supreme Court Rules in Favor of Genetically Enhanced Ballerina

The Chicago Ballet must pay damages and reinstate a dancer who inherited a genetic enhancement from her father, the Supreme Court says, in a ruling that may have a ripple effect on other enhancement cases.

Marla Wembley, twenty-seven, had been with the ballet for four years when it was discovered that her father was genetically enhanced. Lawyers for Ms. Wembley noted that the enhancement her father received prior to birth was for gymnastics, not ballet. During her years of training for her career as a dancer, she was unaware of his enhancement, due in part to the fact that an injury as a teen ended his career.

The lower court agreed with the Chicago Ballet's position that regardless of how the alteration was marketed to Ms. Wembley's grandparents, it would have resulted in a general enhancement in physical ability.

In the 8–3 decision handed down on Friday, the Supreme Court reversed that decision, arguing that the earlier ruling was a violation of Wembley's rights under the Equal Protection Clause.

∞10∞

I step to the edge of the pool and dive into the warm water as the music begins. Jarvis is now sufficiently trained to sort out *why* I'm swimming, based on my heart rate and general demeanor. If I'm already relaxed, he plays a mellow mix. If I'm down here because I need to exhaust my muscles in order to have any hope of sleeping that night, he selects something that will keep me moving at a rapid pace.

That pace was rapid enough for me to place first in my age group for swim team every single year I competed. I've always been proud of that. Proud of the fact that I worked hard and accomplished my goal. But maybe I had an unfair advantage. Maybe all of those ribbons and trophies should have gone to someone else.

It's almost enough to make me get out of the pool. To go in search of something else to get my mind off the news Lorena gave me. That bottle of bourbon in the library is sounding pretty good right now.

Instead, I concentrate on the up-tempo mix of drums and bass pounding through the pool speakers—an excellent call on Jarvis's part. I try to empty my mind of everything except the music and the water around me and focus on matching my stroke to the beat.

Nora has complained more than once about the expense her father incurred in catering to the whims of his much-younger second wife. This pool is just one example of many in her litany of ways that Raquel Coleman was spoiled rotten. I suspect that converting two-thirds of this basement into a swimming pool wasn't cheap, but I'm glad Raquel got her way. This is my favorite place in the entire house. It's my retreat, my cave—warm, with cozy amber lights and the slight tang of salt in the air.

The library on the top floor is magnificent, and I'm enough of a bibliophile that it *might* edge out the pool for my favorite place, under normal circumstances. But the library is also a reminder of work I need to be doing. And, as of today, it's a reminder of how very much I do not know about my family. About myself.

Jack called about an hour after Lorena left, asking if I wanted to do something later. I debated crying off, maybe claiming a headache. It's actually true, after Lorena's news, but it's also a bit of a cliché excuse. And I do want to see him. I need to talk to someone about what Lorena told me. As nervous as I am about revealing the results of the DNA test, if I don't talk this through with somebody, I'm going to go crazy. Jarvis isn't an option. He'd just parrot back what he thinks I want him to say.

Although that actually might be informative right now. My mind is in such a state of turmoil that I have no earthly idea *what* I'd want him to say.

I considered calling Nora, or my mother. If my dad were still alive, I probably would have called him. But then if my dad were alive, would I even be here? Almost certainly not. I'd be finishing up my degree in Dublin. There would be no money worries, or at least nothing like we're facing now. Matthew Grace wouldn't have gambled everything on a few closely related investments. He would have *diversified*, because he wasn't a fucking idiot.

But maybe I'm not the best judge of that, since I didn't really think my mother was an idiot, either. If I'd thought she would do anything so colossally stupid, I would have handled the family finances myself, even though numbers and investments really aren't my strong suits. I've tried to convince myself she was just so distraught over my father's sudden death that she made bad decisions. His death came as a complete shock to all of us. He was in seemingly perfect health when I'd visited the week before. We'd even talked about taking a hiking trip at Glendalough, just the two of us, like we did a few times when I was in high school. And then I got the call. His heart had simply stopped.

I know my mother was upset. She loved him. But she volunteered to take over the finances, saying the activity would help keep her occupied. And then she went barreling down a direct path to financial ruin. She couldn't have made worse financial decisions if that had been her actual goal.

So, calling Mom is something I tend to avoid these days. When we do talk, half of the time she spends the entire call telling me how sorry she is for screwing everything up. The other half of the time she spends the entire call telling me that it's not her fault. I wish she'd just pick one and be done with it.

And I don't want to worry Nora. Fear plays a very big role in that. Her son's heart stopped without warning, and he was thirty years younger than she is. I can't stand the thought of losing Nora, too.

I do know that I'll eventually have to talk to both of them about this. I can't fathom a scenario where at least one of them didn't know I'm enhanced. But tonight, I need moral support more than I need confrontation. So instead of making excuses to Jack, I opted for middle ground. He's bringing takeaway and his swimsuit. And hopefully by the time he arrives I'll have completed enough laps to burn off most of my nervous energy.

Most of the time, I find my stress evaporating after only a few laps. Today, however, reality keeps creeping back in, accompanied by a tiny, incessant worm of panic. I keep having to yank my mind back to the rhythm and the water, as I propel myself toward the amber light at the shallow end of the pool. Flip, twist, and back to the other end, counting off another lap each time I turn to the end of the pool where one of the lighting panels is off-kilter and the light shines much brighter.

Flip, twist, swim, repeat.

The music stops abruptly somewhere around lap twenty-five. Normally, I'd know the number for certain, but I lost count a few times as my mind drifted.

"Jack Merrick has arrived, mistress," Jarvis announces in his clipped accent as I surface. "Shall I tell him to join you?"

I say yes and push myself up to the pool's edge. A moment later, I hear footsteps at the top of the stairs.

"Madi? Are you there?"

"Yes. Come on down."

Jack squints around for a moment when he reaches the bottom. Then he places the pizza on the poolside table, which I've already laid with plates, glasses, and a bottle of wine.

"Isn't it kind of dark in here?" he asks.

"A little, I guess." It doesn't really seem all that dark to me, but I tell Jarvis to increase the lighting by 30 percent and to switch from my swim tunes to dinner music.

"We should definitely eat now," Jack says. "I grabbed this from that place you like over near campus, since they don't deliver this far out. And the package only guarantees it will stay warm for half an hour."

I hadn't really thought I'd be hungry. The lump that took up residence inside my stomach after Lorena's visit felt too large to allow much room for food. But exercise seems to have worked up my appetite, and the pizza smells wonderful.

Jack is acting a bit odd, though. He keeps giving me nervous looks as we eat, and he's making small talk about his classes and the history department. That's something he can barely tolerate in others and never does himself. Which has me wondering if he already knows. Lorena promised she wouldn't tell anyone, but I doubt that promise included RJ. And since Alex is RJ's cousin, and Jack is Alex's roommate . . . I think it's within the realm of the possible that he already knows, but he's sworn not to rat out the person who told him.

He tops off our wine and says, "So . . . Lorena told me you were upset but wouldn't say why. Wouldn't even tell RJ."

I push the pizza aside, my appetite now shriveled. As Lorena said earlier, she's really supposed to report this. Not just as a medical professional, but as a citizen. If you know someone is using genetic modification to take unfair advantage in education or business and you fail to report it, you can be fined, lose your job, even be confined to your dwelling. Telling Jack will put him at risk, as well.

When I hesitate, he leans forward and takes my hand. "Lorena didn't tell me, Madi . . . but Alex and I pieced it together. The medallion is obviously keyed to your genetics, and it doesn't really seem like something that would occur naturally. But it will probably be okay. As long as that was the only alteration, the government will be willing to overlook it. I mean, they need someone who can operate the thing, right?"

"But it's *not* the only alteration, Jack. Lorena said there were more than a dozen changes. Baseline enhancements, I think she called them. Not to me directly, but to my parents. Or my grandparents, although I'm not even sure that type of alteration was possible when they were . . ." I trail off and then bark out a nervous laugh. "I was going to say 'when they were born,' but how can I even *know* when they were born if they passed along the genetic ability to use that key?"

We're both silent for a long moment, and then Jack says, "So, what are you going to do?"

I shrug miserably. "I'm on scholarship, Jack. If this is exposed, I'll not only lose it, but I'll put my family at risk. Nora, my mother, Thea—they could all be in serious trouble. On the other hand, the odds seem pretty good that it will be discovered at some point in the future, and I'm now liable because I *know*. And so is Lorena, and now you, and Alex, and RJ."

He grimaces. "Which means your options are either to forget you ever found the key and hope for the best or to exploit the key to the fullest and hope that doing so will keep you out of trouble for the enhancement."

"That about sums it up. Neither is exactly a great choice."

"True. But . . . the government is going to *want* this technology."

"RJ says several governments are going to want it. He seems to think we'll have a bidding war. And . . . to be honest, I'm more inclined to go with an international organization, or not sell an exclusive license. Do we really want any single government to have exclusive rights to this technology?"

Jack shrugs. "Hey, like I told you, I'm from a military family, so I have a slight bias to at least restricting it to US allies. But regardless of who buys the rights, you're the only person who can use it—or, at least, the only person to the best of our knowledge. If you leverage that, maybe you can make leniency part of the deal."

"Or they could hold a hefty penalty over my head—for me, my family, all of us—and force me to do whatever they want. I think that's equally possible, don't you?"

"No. I don't think they'd . . ." He stops and is silent for a long time as he looks around the basement. Then he says, "Yeah. I think that's *at least* equally possible." His voice is tight now. Angry almost. "But I'm not sure there's a way to avoid that."

"Maybe the best option would be to go back and tell myself that planting a garden is a very, very bad idea. Undo the past week and make it so I never even see that orange light coming up through . . . the ground." I stop, looking around at the basement lights. The pool lights, too. Both are the same pale amber as the ones that illuminate the library cabinets. What occurs to me now, however, is that even though the panels they're behind mute the color, those lights are the same shade as the CHRONOS key.

I run to the pool and dive in, ignoring whatever Jack is calling out. When I reach the deep end, I swim down to inspect the lighting panel. It's the one that I noticed was a bit brighter, but the panel isn't loose after all, and the light is much brighter here. I tug on it, and pry at it with my fingernails, but it is held in place with tiny screws and doesn't want to budge.

So I kick back up to the surface. "We need to find a screwdriver. Or something I can use as one. I'm pretty sure there's another key down there. The lights in the pool—and also the ones upstairs in the library—are the same color."

We poke around for a few minutes in a small closet that holds salt and other odds and ends that are used to maintain the pool. I finally locate a small tool kit on one of the shelves. Then Jack changes into his swim trunks and we dive in.

It takes four trips to the bottom, but we eventually manage to loosen the panel enough to push it aside and reveal a small cub-byhole. At the very back, plugged into some sort of interface, is a CHRONOS key identical to the one upstairs on my dresser. The glow seems to be amplified, like it's powering the other lights in the pool. Jack yanks at it, but it doesn't budge. That's probably a good thing. I'm pretty sure we'd be in the dark if he pulled it out of its holder. The fact that it's the same color as the lights in the library also has me wondering if that key is serving some other purpose.

Jack is already out of breath, so he goes back to the surface. Something else catches my eye as I'm about to follow him. It's a package encased in a clear wrapper of some sort, wedged against the side panel of the hole. The package holds several thin books, a squat vial about the circumference of a cherry tomato, and a small yellow stick that looks like a pencil. I've never seen one so tiny, though.

"Books?" Jack says when I place the package on the tiles at the pool's edge. "What kind of idiot hides books in a swimming pool?"

"The same kind that hides a time-travel device there, I guess. They do appear to be in a waterproof wrapper, but you're right. It's weird. Whoever hid it clearly intended for me—or at least someone in the family—to find it."

"How do you figure?"

I look back at the pool. The light at the deep end is even brighter now that the panel is attached by just the one screw. "Would you have noticed anything odd about that pool light?"

"I can barely even tell that there *are* lights in the pool," Jack says. "I mean, I see something. But it's really dim. So you're thinking that whoever hid this wanted it to be found by someone . . ."

"By someone who could use it. They probably had no clue about the one buried in the garden. But that key in the pool and these books? They were left by someone in my family. My best guess would be James Coleman, since this pool was installed for his second wife. She was Nora's stepmother, so I doubt she carried the gene to use the key. That leaves James and . . . I think, his brother? No. It was his nephew. Which would make him some sort of cousin, I guess. He lived here, too. Helped take care of Grandpa James when he was getting up in years."

"Could you contact him?"

I shake my head. "The nephew was twenty years younger, and the wife he built the swimming pool for was twenty-*five* years younger. But Grandpa James outlived both of them. I assume that's why the house reverted to Nora."

Once we're out of the pool, I place the waterproof package on the table and extract two slim, almost identical books.

"Looks like old diaries," Jack says.

"Or maybe not so old." I run my finger along the edge of the pages. "The material is odd. Too thick to be regular paper. More like pages in a modern sketch pad, really, where you can erase or save your artwork."

When I flip open the cover, there's an inscription, written in small neat letters:

Katherine Shaw

1890–1900

"That's one of my ancestors." I point at the name inside the diary. "Nora's grandmother's grandmother. She was the original owner of this house. Well, not the *original* original owner, I guess, but the first person in my family who owned it. And she was alive in the 1990s, not the 1890s."

"Sounds like you might have inherited a certain ability from your great-great . . ." He laughs. "How many *greats* would that be?"

"Four. Although, *Katherine* could just be a family name. I mean, this could have belonged to an umpteenth-great-grandmother, who actually did live in the 1890s, for all I know. That would be the more logical conclusion."

"In most cases, I'd agree. But I've seen you time travel. And I doubt a two-hundred-year-old diary would be in this good of shape, or have pages made out of whatever this stuff is . . ."

He has a point.

The second book also has Katherine's name printed on the inside, with the date 1780–1790. Those words are scratched out, though. Beneath them, in a different ink and different handwriting, is a single sentence.

Use with disk.

And below that, a name that I recognize instantly—Nora's grandmother Kate Pierce-Keller.

FROM THE *NEW YORK DAILY INTREPID* (JUNE 20, 1965)

Reverend King Speaks to Antioch Graduates

(Yellow Springs, Ohio) Nearly three hundred graduates of Antioch College and their families gathered on Saturday as the Reverend Martin Luther King Jr. delivered an address called "Facing the Challenge of a New Age." Dr. King urged students to develop a "world perspective" and to work to alleviate poverty and hunger both in the United States and abroad. He called for an "all-out war" on poverty and for increased efforts to remove any remaining vestiges of discrimination and segregation. In addition, he noted the need to take the final steps toward ensuring voting rights for Negroes in the South.

While King has generally focused on domestic issues, Saturday's message to the graduates also had international themes, touching on nuclear disarmament, the war in Vietnam, and the need to strengthen the United Nations.

Accompanying Dr. King was his wife, Mrs. Coretta Scott King, who attended Antioch College in the 1940s.

∞11∞

TYSON

YELLOW SPRINGS, OHIO

JUNE 19, 1965

I grab an armful of folding chairs from the back of the large white delivery truck and join the student volunteers who are setting up the wide stretch of lawn where commencement will be held. One of the first tricks you learn as an agent is that people are far less likely to question whether you belong if you keep yourself busy at whatever communal task is at hand. With that in mind, I jumped in early, using the stable point that I'd set up on a preliminary trip to scout out the area, and lined up with the other volunteers. A skillfully forged student ID is in my wallet if anyone actually does question me, but that seems unlikely given the number of people who will be arriving in the next hour. The Antioch College class of 1965 is the largest yet, with nearly three hundred graduates, and they're expecting all of the fifteen hundred invited guests to attend, since the college announced that Martin Luther King would be giving the commencement address.

King's speech also means that there will be a sizable security detail in addition to campus police. A near-fatal stabbing in 1958 forced him to take personal safety seriously. There were multiple death threats against him this year alone. It's been almost a year since three civil rights activists, two of them brothers of Antioch students, disappeared in Mississippi while working to register black voters. Their bodies were found weeks later in a shallow grave. Malcolm X was assassinated back in February. Earlier this year, police in Selma, Alabama, beat down a crowd of nearly six hundred peaceful marchers with clubs and tear gas. Several deaths occurred in the aftermath.

But despite the ongoing violence in the summer of '65, there have been recent victories, too. Many of the students on this campus took part last summer in an ultimately successful effort to desegregate a local barbershop, and some have arrest records to prove it. The Civil Rights Act was signed last July. In December, Dr. King was awarded the Nobel Peace Prize. And finally, the Voting Rights Act passed the Senate and was just voted out of committee in the House of Representatives, in part due to public reaction to the death of two white civil rights activists during the protests surrounding the Selma march.

It's a beautiful morning to reflect on those victories, with clear skies above and just the hint of a breeze. You can almost feel hope and optimism in the air. I guess that could be normal for a college graduation, though. This is my first, so I don't really have a point of comparison.

As ten o'clock draws closer, families drift in and begin filling the seats. The driver of the truck tosses the last of the chairs to me and the other three guys who are nearby, then pulls down the back door and heads back across the lawn toward the campus gate.

Our crew of volunteers disbands once the last chairs are in place and each has a commencement program on the seat. I hang toward the back, partly because the front sections are reserved and partly because this suit is hot, and the back rows are shaded by the tall towers that rise above the pitched roof of Antioch Hall.

Two men with rifles are on that roof now, scanning the crowd. Security guards. They were mentioned in one of the articles I read about the event. The author said there were other bodyguards on the ground as well, and I'm sure any guests sitting at the front will be under close scrutiny. That's one reason I helped with setup—it gave me a chance to create three strategically located stable points near the front and to mount a small recording device under one of the folding chairs. This will give me extra data to pore over when I get back home, and I can still hang back in a section where I'm less likely to draw attention.

Most of the people are looking around anxiously, either hoping to catch an early glimpse of their graduate or of Dr. King. I'm watching for King, too, although I'm also keeping an eye out for Antoinette Robinson and her family. It's nearly ten. The band is warming up. I'm beginning to wonder if I missed her and they're already seated. Then I see Toni, her sister, and two people who must be their parents coming in from the parking lot, almost at a run.

Antoinette's gaze slides right past me, and I feel a momentary wave of disappointment. Which is all kinds of stupid. The event that caused her to remember me is clearly *after* the ceremony, in the parking lot, and I still have absolutely no idea what I could possibly do to help her dad with his car. Maybe I follow Timothy and Evelyn's advice and go call this Triple A place? Except . . . that's a conundrum, because I wouldn't have even asked the two of them about 1960s car repair if I hadn't already spoken to Toni about it.

Two couples change seats so that the Robinson family can sit together. The four of them collapse into wooden chairs one row in front of me with an almost audible sigh of relief as the processional begins and the graduates begin to make their way down the aisle toward the empty seats cordoned off at the front.

When the music ends, someone steps up to the podium to lead a prayer. Several short speeches and songs follow. I don't pay much attention to this first part of the ceremony. If there's something I miss, I can always review the event from the stable points I set up. My eyes keep drifting toward Toni Robinson, who sits at the end of the aisle, next to her little sister. They both look bored, and the younger one is fidgety to the point that their mom taps the girl's knee with her rolled-up commencement program and gives her a stern look.

But once Reverend King is introduced, everything else fades into the background. King is here, at least in part, as a thank-you to Antioch for the scholarships given to his wife, Coretta, and her older sister, when the two women attended the school in the late 1940s. Other historians seem to have largely overlooked this speech, possibly because it was those family connections that brought him here. If this were one of King's better-known speeches, I'd almost certainly see at least a few dots of purple light in the crowd today, because I wouldn't be the only agent to have made this trip. I think there's also a good chance, if this were considered a major speech, that the board would have wanted me to have a few more years of experience under my belt before approving the jump.

Major speech or not, I'd argue that it's kind of a turning point for King. Most of his addresses prior to this one focused primarily on civil rights inside the United States. In this speech, however, you get glimpses of his concern about the war in Vietnam and the need for nuclear disarmament, things that will become his primary focus during the final years of his life.

I've read the speech, of course. Dissected it, in fact, as part of the proposal for this trip. But printed words—even the bits of audio that have survived—don't really prepare me for exactly how powerful King is as a speaker. For the next thirty minutes, I *almost* forget that Antoinette Robinson is a few yards away.

As he draws to a close, King calls not only for people of all races, but also people of all religions, to work for peaceful coexistence. The speech ends, as many of his speeches do, with the words of the spiritual, "Free at last, free at last. Thank God almighty, we are free at last," and then King takes a seat so that they can get on with the task of handing out diplomas.

It's a slow, plodding process. When they reach the names beginning with *Y*, I quietly exit and head toward the parking area to be sure that I don't lose the Robinson family in the crush to greet the new graduates. Again, that concern feels stupid, because I already have some clues about what's going to happen. Assuming, of course, that having this advance knowledge didn't make me do something different.

All of this makes my head hurt, so I shake it off and lean against one of the trees at the edge of the parking lot, about twenty yards from the path leading to the stable point I arrived at, which is tucked away inside a small utility building. About ten minutes later, people start to drift toward their cars. It takes another five minutes for me to spot the Robinson family. The older sister, Opal, is with them now, clutching her diploma and wearing a graduation gown. The cap, however, rests on her youngest sister's head.

I spot Dr. King around the same time. He and his wife are headed toward a cluster of vehicles parked near the sidewalk. Two bodyguards accompany them, along with the college president and a few other people in academic regalia. The security guards on the roof are also drifting in this direction.

Coretta King looks up as the Robinsons approach the lot. While there are more black students in 1965 than there were when she attended Antioch, they're still far from the majority. Her smile widens and she tugs on Dr. King's sleeve. He follows her gaze and holds up a hand like he's telling the men he'll be right back, and then he and his wife—along with the bodyguards—make their way toward Opal.

"Congratulations," Mrs. King says, extending her hand first to Opal and then to the others. A small crowd begins to gather, and the bodyguards look around nervously. One of them glances at me, but his eyes keep moving. I don't fit the profile he's looking for today, although I can't help but wonder how he'd react if he saw the barely different version of me that attended the Klan rally.

Antoinette takes a few steps back to make room for the bodyguards. The group is directly in front of me now, so close that the hem of Toni's yellow dress brushes briefly against the leg of my trousers.

"And what are you planning to do with your degree?" Dr. King asks after offering his own congratulations.

"I'm going to teach," Opal replies, in a voice so low that I almost miss it over the sound of cars cranking at the far end of the parking lot. "Back home in Memphis."

"Good for you! The world can always use more good teachers." King then puts one arm around his wife and leads her back toward the school officials in front of their vehicle.

That's when I see the purple light. Not just one flash but four, maybe even five, in the crowd approaching the parking lot.

I remind myself that it's possible these are just agents from a future cohort. Maybe my report on King's speech convinces the next batch of historians that this really is a major speech that marks a turning point in King's legacy, and four—no, I can now see that it *is* actually five—historians decide they need to witness the event in person.

I'd really like to believe that. Because the only other explanation is that I've fucked something up so royally that CHRONOS had to send an extraction team.

FROM THE DIARY OF KATE PIERCE-KELLER

January 26, 2024

When I handed the keys over to President Patterson, I suspected that at some point I was going to regret it, but I thought there would be a bit of a buffer. That she'd be a decent human being at least for a little while. Maybe long enough for me to finish high school, make it through my college applications. Just a short breather where I could focus without thinking about whether I'd made a mistake.

Just a little time to mourn Katherine.

But no. Less than a month after Katherine died, Patterson's allies in Congress began pushing for a constitutional amendment to remove the two-term restriction on the presidency. Non-Cyrists in Congress tried to insert a clause that would have restricted it to future presidents, but they failed. The states ratified it within two months, and Patterson immediately tossed her hat into the ring for a third term. And she won, although I'll confess that I'm not convinced it was a free or fair election.

My dad says that the laws being passed really aren't all that different from the ones passed during her first two terms. Maybe that's true. I wasn't especially political before the time shifts. All I know is that the environmental protections, as well as press freedom, are facing death by a thousand tiny cuts.

The irony is that I'm pretty sure these crackdowns are because they're losing members. When your religion is mostly based on greed, you need something to keep the faithful faithful. You can't fully trust the government statistics, but Charlayne claims that many Cyrists, especially in the Orthodox group, have become disillusioned with the fact that stock tips from the *Book of Prophecy* simply aren't what they used to be. That's really no surprise, since the Cyrists don't have time travelers interfering in the markets now. Without the cash incentive, the religion seems to be losing its appeal, and the mandatory tithe is causing members to leave the fold in droves.

In one sense, that makes me happy.

But it also has me wondering what kinds of oppressive policies they'll resort to in order to stay in power.

∞12∞

Jack bends back the top of one of the interior pages of the 1780s diary, which apparently belonged to Katherine Shaw.

"See? The paper is too thick, and the texture is wrong. It might fool a casual observer, but . . ." Jack fishes around in the bag for the tiny pencil and then tries to draw a line in the margin. It doesn't leave a mark, but as he drags the tip along the edge of the book, the text begins to scroll downward, revealing page after page of handwritten text.

"Hold up," I say when something interesting comes into view.

Personal file KS05092304_05181780_1 saved.

"That looks like a date to me. May 18, 1780."

"Or possibly two dates," Jack says. "If KS is for Katherine Shaw, then we have May 9, 2304, and May 18, 1780."

It looks like it should link to more information, but when I tap the screen nothing happens. Jack tries it with the little stick, and still nothing. The page kind of flickers when you tap the underlined section, but that's it.

We play around with it for a bit and make a few minor discoveries. There are small hand-sketched stars jotted in the margins. If you tap one of *those* with the pencil thingy, an information window pops up on top of the text, which makes me think the diaries functioned as rudimentary computer tablets. Sliding the pencil along the edge, like Jack did earlier, reveals what appear to be links to files at the end of entries, but none of the links are functional.

Another thing we learn is that the equipment seems to work much better for me than it does for Jack. His reaction to this fact is almost comical—he nearly drops the book he's so eager to get it out of his hands. He's not the competitive type, so I don't think that it's because he feels like I'm one-upping him. It's almost like he's decided the thing is some sort of sorcery.

The little vial inside the packet contains four clear, rubbery stickers about the size and shape of the tip of my forefinger.

"They look like the lenses people use to change their eye color," Jack says.

I look at the tiny sticker for a moment. "I don't know. The shape seems a little off, don't you think? More oval than round. And they're a bit too cloudy to see through effectively."

"We could ask Alex," he suggests, "if you want to conference him in. He's usually back at the apartment by now."

I ask Jarvis to place the call. When Alex pops up on the screen, he's on the sidewalk approaching the old house in Arlington where they live. It was once a single-family dwelling but has now been divided up into six small apartments, most of them leased to graduate students at Georgetown.

"Wait," Alex says. "Let me get inside so that we can talk."

We watch as Alex hurries up the stairs to the top floor. Once inside, he tosses his bag onto the counter and then barks a couple of commands at his own virtual assistant. A dull humming noise fills the room.

"Okay," he says. "That should block anyone who might be listening."

His words worry me. I haven't really thought much about the whole security side of things. This house sat empty for months, and while we do have a decent security system, it's really more designed to prevent robbery than spying.

There's not much that I can do at this point, however. If someone has been listening over the last few days, they know pretty much everything already.

We bring Alex up to speed on Lorena's visit. He looks a bit ill when I tell him about the enhancements. "I didn't want to say anything yesterday, but I was worried about something like this. I mean, barring a truly unlikely set of genetic coincidences, you'd need some serious enhancement to use the key. And then there's the various tweaks you might need to be effective as a historian. But yes, this puts a kink in things. Are you still . . . um . . ."

Alex trails off, trying to keep his voice nonchalant. It's still painfully obvious how very much he wants this project to move forward.

"I'm weighing my options. But . . . we do have some good news."

I explain about the second key inside the pool and the diaries, and then we show him the small rubbery sticker. He peers into the camera and shakes his head. "Can you increase the lighting in there? I can't see a damn thing. Seriously, it's like the two of you are inside a torch-lit cave."

Jarvis increases the lights to maximum, but Alex still can't make any guesses about the little sticker. "It could be anything really. I'd need to magnify it a lot more than what's possible with my commband in order to tell if there's a power source or any sort of circuitry inside the thing. At some point, I'm going to need to examine one of the medallions, too. I mean, assuming . . ." He trails off again, bringing me back to the dilemma that's been making me crazy all day.

"There's no easy choice," I say. "Leaving aside the whole issue of someone finding out I'm enhanced, I was having some second thoughts last night. So much could be learned with one of these devices. But I might end up changing something and have no idea how to fix it."

"Are we even sure that you *can* change anything?" Jack asks.

"I went back and got my shoes, remember? Created a spare Madi who disappeared. Screwed with everyone's memory? That was definitely changing something."

"But . . . did it change *history*? The other you disappeared. You have your shoes. And yeah, we have dueling memories, but it's not like that really *changed* anything. Alex and I were talking about that this morning. There are a multitude of theories about time travel, but most of them hold that you can't actually rewrite history, at least not on a large scale. You might be able to change some smaller events, make some alterations around the edges, but—"

"Yeah," Alex says, interrupting him. "About that. We probably need to reassess. I still think it's hard to change history on a large scale. It's unlikely that Madi leaving those joggers in 1906 would have changed anything in our time, for example. But someone in Madi's family seems to have been a time traveler. Possibly more than one person, if Lorena is right about the genetic alterations being from both parents. And now we have Madi, in the past, able to use this equipment from the future. If we're planning to replicate and market that technology, possibly years before it would have otherwise been invented, I think that qualifies as changing history."

"Maybe . . ." I stop for a moment, trying to think all of this through. "Maybe it's not a member of my family who left these clues. What if it's us? *Future* us, and we're just trying to expedite things."

I like this idea a lot. The notion that someone, even someone in my family, left this information for me to find feels like cheating. It feels like plagiarism. I still don't know if James Coleman was guilty of that offense, but I do know that I have no wish to steal the intellectual property of anyone else.

Alex considers this and then nods. "It still could change a lot to have this technology appear years before it would have otherwise. But it makes as much sense as anything else. Maybe someone got the jump on us in terms of patenting the device or figuring out the genetic changes necessary in order to use it. Or maybe there's a reason technology like this is needed earlier than we actually perfect it."

"That seems more credible than it being a family member," Jack says. "They'd be taking a leap of faith that someone in their gene pool with the ability to use the key would find it. But we'd *know* that Madi could use it. We'd know that she'd be here, in this house. That she used the swimming pool. So if there was some reason, some world crisis we needed to change . . ."

"That's part of what scares the hell out of me, though," I say. "Who are we to make that decision? Something like this in the wrong hands could be very dangerous."

"True," Jack admits. "But in the right hands . . . you might change some really awful stuff, too. What if you could stop a major war, a potential World War Three, before it ever began? How many lives might be saved by something like that?"

The number is in the tens of millions, and I know that Jack's point is valid. What really bothers me is the idea that I might play a role in making a decision that momentous. I feel woefully unqualified for that kind of responsibility.

"Maybe we're in some sort of dystopian hellscape in the future and speeding up our research is the last best chance to save the world?" Alex is clearly joking with that last part, but I'm not finding any of this amusing.

"If that's the case, though, you'd think we'd have had the common sense to send back—"

I was about to say *a message or instructions*, but then I realize that whoever hid the key for me to find may well have done precisely that. "We need to comb through those two diaries for information. And I think we need to do a more thorough search of the books in the library. I'm more convinced than ever that there's something odd going on with them. Otherwise, why would they be encased in those cabinets with that orange light?"

Alex repeats his theory that it's a protective field. "It keeps the item or the individual within sort of a buffer zone. I spent most of the day going through that research I mentioned yesterday. One of my professors, Dr. Bhatt, was an assistant on the project back in the early 2090s. I've never spoken to him directly about it, but a postdoc student who's been here longer than I have said that Bhatt had a few tokes too many at the departmental picnic a few years back and mentioned that the project had government funding at one point. He told her they had a teenage boy who could go backward or forward a couple hours. There was an experiment where the kid would go back and change some minor thing. Everyone outside the field remembered only the changed reality, but everyone inside the field remembered the old version. That kid and also the primary researcher were killed during the 2092 attacks. The boy's body wasn't identified, but the security cameras at the main entrance showed that he was there. And the lab took a direct hit. Everyone inside was killed."

"What happened to this research after the attacks?" I ask.

Alex shrugs. "It fizzled. There were a couple of research papers talking about chronotron fields, but nothing mentioning human research after that point. That's one reason I assumed it was either a bogus story they tell new students just for the hell of it, or, at the very least, there were no actual breakthroughs. If there had been anything substantive, even with the lead researcher and subject gone, somebody would have restarted the program after the dust settled. This isn't the kind of thing you abandon if you've seen results. And . . . as I've said before, our current research is nowhere near the point of being able to send people through time. I can't say much more than that because I signed nondisclosure forms, but really, we have *nothing* even close to this. Only now I'm starting to wonder if maybe . . ."

"If maybe the researcher had one of these little gadgets?" Jack asks.

Alex nods. "And also someone with Madi's genetic ability. But . . . there weren't many deaths in the US from those bombings. Just a lot of big-ticket property damage. What are the odds that both the subject and the researcher just *happened* to get killed in the attacks? Seems like a rather odd coincidence, even if they were in the same place. Unless . . ."

He and Jack exchange a look.

It takes me a second longer, but then I get it.

Unless they were the targets.

That thought keeps circling in my head long after Jack leaves for the evening. I'm not sure I really believe that a worldwide terror attack was planned solely to destroy time-travel technology, but Alex is right. It *is* an odd coincidence. And I now have two diaries that might have answers, not just to that question, but to my family's role in all of this.

But it's a massive amount of information. After a half hour of poking around, I finally figure out how to use the diary's search feature. I run a query on the term *2092*, but there's nothing about that year in Katherine Shaw's diary. Her granddaughter's diary mentions the date several times, but there's nothing useful. I try a few other search terms, but eventually realize that the only way I'm going to learn anything from these diaries is to simply read them, because context is important.

And since I can't sleep anyway, I prop a few extra pillows behind my back and settle in. I'm torn over which to read first. It would probably make more sense to start with Katherine's, but when I thumb through, it feels a bit like a travelogue, interspersed with a few personal observations. While that might normally be interesting, I need answers, not descriptions of the 1893 World's Fair. So I put Katherine's book aside and pick up Kate's.

I start at the beginning. April 9, 2022.

It's basically a rant. About the environment, about the Cyrists, about the president at the time. The anger goes beyond that of a mere concerned citizen. To be honest, she seems a little obsessed. It's like she takes every bit of government malfeasance, every breach of faith by certain members of the legislature, as a personal affront.

On the one hand, I completely understand her outrage. The mistakes of that era were felt for generations. But the same can be said for many points in history.

The next diary entry is more of the same. Different day, slightly different specific event that set her off, but pretty much identical points about what needed to be done. About people needing to wake up.

And while I know she's right, I find myself skimming through. Moving on to the next entry. The next rant.

To be fair, they aren't all that way. Occasionally, there are little flashes of light. Some comment about her family, something funny one of her kids did. A joke she heard, although many of those are political, too.

The thing that's truly annoying me, though, are the links and the little stars in the margins. It's obvious that there's more here, but I can't access it. I dig out the little stylus from the spine of the diary and try again, but aside from the link or star slightly graying out when tapped, nothing happens.

Of course, the information in those files could be just as opaque and barely relevant as what I've been reading. The links could just be photographs. Videos of her cat, if she had one. And I'm quite certain that at least some of them are political rants.

But I think there's more. Under the surface, there must be more. Otherwise, why would someone—possibly an older version of me—have bothered to hide these books away, sealed in a plastic container and tucked inside the wall of a swimming pool?

FROM RECORDS OF THE HOUSE UN-AMERICAN ACTIVITIES COMMITTEE

Written Testimony of Daniel N. Wagner (February 11, 1966)

Mrs. Witte [Eloise Witte of Cincinnati, who claimed to be Grand Empress of the Ohio Klan] then told me that the Knights of the Ku Klux Klan had hired a gunman for $25,000.00 to assassinate Martin Luther King, but the gunman had had feathers on his legs and could not accomplish this task so in turn had to give the money back. Mrs. Witte then said it appeared it was up to her to take care of King and if I were interested. I said I would accomplish this for a lesser amount of money.

Mrs. Witte said she would take care of me financially and if I needed places to stay or any kind of support, she would see that I received it, but this assassination had to take place in Ohio. So Mrs. Witte set the date June 29, 1965, at Antioc Colledge [sic] in Yellow Springs, Ohio. Later this date was changed because King was to appear at the administration building at Antioc Colledge [sic] on the 19th of June 1965. Mrs. Witte asked if I wanted the assissitance [sic] of another 10 men, which she had appointed to help, and I said that that sounded better.

We were suppose [sic] to drive up to the speaker stand, and those other ten men in 4 or 5 different cars would blast the crowd all around King, and I was to shoot king [sic] and be positively sure he was dead. Mrs. Witte said this would be a great achievement for the white race.

This was cancealed [sic], or I was told about it earlier the week of the 19th of June, because Mrs. Witte couldn't get it organized as well as the KKKK rally, which was supposed to take place on a farm at the same time. Mrs. Witte told me not to worry but that she would make sure I got another chance to get King.

∞13∞

TYSON
YELLOW SPRINGS, OHIO
JUNE 19, 1965

If the flash of purple light from those CHRONOS keys hadn't caught my eye, I don't think I'd have noticed the movement behind them, on the roof of Antioch Hall. The man closest to the parking area raises his rifle. A moment later, the second man follows suit.

There's no way that I can reach King in time. The only thing I can do is yell out a warning to the others. Then I tackle Antoinette to the ground as shots ring out and the screaming begins.

Dr. King staggers backward once, and then falls when a second bullet hits him. One of the bodyguards pulls Mrs. King behind a car. Another guard crouches in front of King and begins firing at the men on the roof. A man close to King is hit, and people are pushed onto the asphalt as the crowd rushes to get out of the line of fire. Their screams mix with the sound of shattering glass.

This is wrong.

All wrong.

King wasn't shot in 1965.

Not yet. And not *here*.

One of the two men on the roof catches a bullet to the arm. He loses his balance and tumbles from the building, his arms pinwheeling as he flies toward the ground. The other man on the roof is gone now. I don't know if he was hit or if he retreated into the building.

Or maybe he had a stable point up there? While I didn't see a purple flash, I don't know if I would have spotted the light from a CHRONOS key at this distance. I can definitely see the ones in the crowd, though. There are five—two men, two women, and a boy of maybe twelve, which strikes me as the oddest thing of all. Kids don't go into the field. CHRONOS agents don't bring their children to work. In fact, CHRONOS agents don't even *have* children until their fieldwork is over.

All five of the travelers are clustered toward the front. All are watching intently as the bodyguard rips off his suit jacket and presses it against the wound in Dr. King's chest.

Which means this isn't an extraction team. If it was, they'd be looking for me. And they aren't. They're just *watching*.

And then I feel a gut-wrenching nausea ten times worse than the one that hit me in the stupid exercise when CHRONOS made me go back and talk to myself. It doesn't last long, but it leaves me certain that any efforts made to save King's life will fail.

No. It means they already *have* failed.

I'm certain of it. Not just because I can see him there on the lawn, unmoving. Not just because of the panic on the faces of the people around me.

I've also been hit with a massive double memory.

On the one hand, I remember meeting Antoinette Robinson and her friends outside the drugstore. Watching her fold the piece of gum over twice and pop it into her mouth. I remember her saying she remembered me because I helped her father get their car going. Most of all, I remember getting hopelessly lost in her smile.

And then there's the other memory. It doesn't exactly supplant the first one, but it's just as vivid. Just as real. Antoinette was still outside the drugstore, with her sister and her friends. Same orange dress, but she'd lost weight, and it hung oddly on her now. This time, she remembered me because I'm the guy who pushed her out of the line of fire. This time, she said I was there on the day Dr. King was *killed*. This time, there was no bright smile, and she clutched my arm frantically, asking me why everything changed. She said something about the Selma march, too, but I didn't catch it before her friends pulled her into the car and they drove away.

This is not good. This is *so very* not good.

Antoinette stirs beneath my chest. I manage to get to my knees, one of which stings sharply when it touches the ground. Since I still don't trust myself to stand, I just shift my weight a bit to the other knee and move aside.

"Are you okay?" I ask. "I heard the shots and just reacted. I'm sorry if I . . ."

She pushes herself up to sitting, but her eyes don't meet mine. They're fixed in horror on the car behind me. I follow her gaze and see that the rear windshield is shattered from the gunfire.

"Something *happened*," she says. "I felt it. Something—"

"Toni?" Her mother shoves past the people between us, panic in her voice. "Oh, my God, Toni! Were you hit?"

I manage to stand and reach a hand down to help Toni to her feet. She looks as faint as I feel.

"No. No, Mama. I'm okay. But I probably wouldn't have been if this guy hadn't pushed me down." She points toward the car directly behind us.

Mrs. Robinson's eyes grow wide as she takes in the windshield. Then she pulls me into a hug so tight I can barely breathe.

"You saved her life. Thank you, thank you so much."

I'm almost certain that something I've done is the only reason her daughter was ever in danger. But I can't really go into that, so I just smile back, first at her, and then at Toni's dad and sisters who have now joined us.

Her dad introduces himself and shakes my hand absently, glancing over his shoulder at the chaos surrounding Dr. King. "That was quick thinking."

"Something *happened*," Toni repeats, staring at me. "What *was* that?"

The smile freezes on my face and slowly fades as I realize why she was so frantic in my second memory of the drugstore. My CHRONOS key is where I always keep it—on a chain attached to the inside of my jacket pocket. Toni would have been almost as close to it as I was when the time shift happened. That shouldn't be a problem, though, once the physical effects fade. She has no way of knowing that King is supposed to live for three more years.

"It's Reverend King, sweetie," her father says. "Someone shot him."

Toni nods. "I know. It's horrible. But . . . there was something *else*. Not just the guns. I felt it *here*." She presses her hand against her stomach. "And it's more than that. I just know it is. I know something is wrong. Something *changed*."

"We hit the ground pretty hard," I tell her. "I might have knocked the wind out of you."

She narrows her eyes. I think she can tell I'm hiding something.

"Maybe you hit your head, baby," her mom says. "Let's get you to the car so you can sit down."

"I didn't hit my head." Toni grabs my arm. "You know what I'm talking about, don't you? Selma. What happened in Selma? Why did those people die?"

Sirens drown out the last part of her question, keeping me from having to say anything else. One of the police officers must have called for an ambulance. We all take several steps back to make room for it, and Toni's mother pulls her away.

An officer calls out to the crowd, telling everyone to stay put because they need to get witness statements. But I have to get back to the stable point. As much as I'm dreading the reception I'll get when I return, we need to find out what happened.

We need to *fix* it.

Yes, it's only three years. I allow myself to hope that the changes were minimal, but I know better. That kick to the gut I felt wasn't some minor quiver in the timeline. It was more like an earthquake.

I inch my way to the right, behind the car with the shattered windshield. Toni's mom is now leading her daughter to their car, the car that I'm supposed to help get started, but that history seems to have been overwritten. My feet hit the path that leads to the stable point a few seconds after Antoinette slides into the back seat. I turn and hurry down the path, glancing back over my shoulder to see if anyone is following me, since I'm clearly disobeying the officer's order to stick around for questioning.

No one is following me. But when I look back one last time, Antoinette Robinson's frantic eyes lock onto mine.

I try to send her a silent message. I'm going to fix this. I have no clue what I did to cause the change, but CHRONOS will help me fix it. Like Richard said. And when the timeline is back to normal, Toni will be back to normal, too.

FROM THE *LIVERPOOL DAILY POST* (JULY 5, 1957)

The annual Crowning of Rose Queen and Garden Fete will be held tomorrow at Woolton Parish. A procession will begin at 2 p.m., with the opening ceremony by Dr. Thelwall Jones at 3 p.m. in the churchyard. Entertainments include a demonstration by Liverpool police dogs, numerous sideshows, a dress parade, and refreshments.

In the evening, a Grand Dance will be held in the church hall, with performances by the George Edwards Band and the Quarry Men Skiffle Group.

All proceeds benefit the parish charity fund.

∞14∞

I step out of the shadows, tap my comm-band, and page a Dryft to carry me to London. The wait is seven minutes, so I pace around the churchyard, which is mostly grass and (in this decade, at least) carefully trimmed hedges.

This church—Saint Peter's, in Woolton, near Liverpool—is nearly 250 years old. It's also the only stable point in the United Kingdom on this key. It's listed as viable from 1888 to 2150, and it's my cheapest travel alternative for having a face-to-face conversation with my mother in London and my grandmother in Dublin.

The main building of Saint Peter's hasn't changed much over the centuries. Like most religious buildings from the period, it has its share of buttresses, turrets, parapets, and pinnacles. There are even a few gargoyles sprinkled about, and something called a lych-gate at the entrance to the churchyard. The gravestones that dotted the lawn in the earlier centuries are mostly gone now. Only a few, presumably with historical significance, remain.

On the date that was locked into the key for this location—July 6, 1957—the hedges were less carefully tended, and one pointy leaf scratched my cheek a few millimeters below my eye. Back then, headstones took up much of the lawn. Some were relatively new, and others tilted at odd angles, as though they were tired of standing sentry over the bodies beneath them.

This church was the very first location I visited on purpose after finding the CHRONOS medallion. I was so nervous that I simply peeked out from the alcove that hides the stable point long enough to realize that, yes, I had indeed traveled back to 1957, or at least to some point in the mid-twentieth century, based on the houses I could see beyond the church walls and the vehicles parked along the street. After briefly considering stepping out of my cubbyhole to explore the place, I realized my clothes were a bit too risqué for the 1950s. So, I chickened out and blinked back to the safety of my garden in 2136.

I'm more confident now, however, and once I finish the unpleasant business of asking Mom and Nora about this whole genetic-enhancement issue, I may treat myself to a little historical tourism. The 1930s dress currently in my bag is old-fashioned for 1957, and it will probably raise a few eyebrows, but it won't get me tossed into jail for indecent exposure. The shorts and T-shirt I'm wearing right now probably would.

I'm not really all that hyped about visiting 1957. I can't say that it looked all that interesting from the brief glimpse I got. It's mostly just idle curiosity about what made this location important enough to merit a stable point. And I'm also hoping for some clues about the historian who owned this CHRONOS key. Not a name or anything like that. I doubt I'll find an etching on a wall inside the 1957 version of this church that proclaims *Jane Doe was here from the future*. But maybe I can learn something about his or her interests. I'm not sure how that will help me, but I can't help feeling a certain kinship with whoever used the key before me.

Not a *literal* kinship, though. I'm quite certain it didn't belong to Katherine Shaw. I've spent the past two days alternating between the diaries that were stashed inside the pool light, and her specialty definitely wasn't music history. She and her partner did visit a club in Chicago to listen to a pianist named Scott Joplin on one of their trips to the 1893 World's Fair—a destination Katherine visited frequently, judging from the entries in the diary—and if my suspicions about those file links are accurate, they also obtained a recording of that performance. Most of her work, however, seems to have centered on civil rights movements, especially for women. She discusses the suffrage movement in the US and Great Britain in her diary, and also several religious groups that ordained women, as well as abolitionists. But Scott Joplin, who played an upbeat style called ragtime, was the only musical performer mentioned in the entire diary. And with the exception of the odd underwater stable point, all of the locations on this key seem to be music related.

I put this jump off for a day, trying to glean a bit more information from the diaries. I'm still nowhere near finished with either of them, however. These little books may be thin to the casual observer, but each page holds several months' worth of entries, and neither of the two diarists was one to skimp on words. I just keep feeling like I'm missing something, though. I'm really tempted to set up a stable point down in the basement and scan through to find out exactly who hid these for me to find. And when I find that person—regardless of whether it's one of my progenitors or a future version of myself—I'm going to smack them a good one for being so fucking cryptic. Why not just leave me a letter or a video and say "Here is every single thing you need to know"? With bullet points, preferably, and a nice, concise summary at the end.

But no. Instead, I'm stuck wading through rants and reports about Spanish royalty visiting the World's Fair.

When I grew tired of reading, I continued my search through the cabinets in the library; I also found an odd device Jarvis identified as a thumb drive, which was once used to hold data, and several other diaries. One of them had an embossed title on the front—*Book of*

Prophecy—but it must have been someone's idea of a joke, because the entire volume was blank.

In addition to those efforts, I spent a few hours yesterday afternoon helping Lorena and RJ move their things from the small apartment they've been sharing with Lorena's brother and his wife for the past few months. The wife could hardly conceal her glee when we arrived with the rental truck, and Lorena made several snippy comments as we were leaving, so I think I understand why they were eager to take me up on my offer of a place to stay.

Jack and Alex still have six weeks left on their lease, but both of them packed a bag and claimed a bedroom. My place is closer to campus, and it doesn't smell like old gym socks. Alex brought in a new computer system last night, which I suspect maxed out his credits and sent him into debt, along with several odd devices stamped *Temporal Physics Lab*, which I suspect he doesn't have official permission to borrow. He's turned about half of the library into his own personal lab. I just wish he didn't have the habit of singing out loud to whatever he's listening to while he works. The guy can't carry a tune to save his life. It's also a little disconcerting to try to work on that side of the library, so it's a good thing the place is huge. I don't think I've ever seen him working with fewer than six holoscreens open. He sits in the middle, with the screens surrounding him. It's like he's in a data cave. Some of the screens show text or charts, but quite a few just look like weird blobs to me. I don't ask questions, though. Alex is the sweetest guy in the world when he's not engaged in something but seems a little prickly about his work process. And he clearly doesn't like to be interrupted.

Jack seems more ambivalent about the move than any of the others. In general, he's been more on edge the past few days, and I wonder if he's having second thoughts about being involved in all of this. Maybe he's worried, like he said before, about the two of us pushing things too far too fast. Or about being involved with me at all, after the revelation about the enhancements. To be fair, that would be a deal breaker for most guys. Everyone living in the house is committing a class 3 misdemeanor by not turning me in.

He left yesterday morning before anyone else was awake and didn't show back up until we were at the house unpacking the first load from the truck. I didn't ask where he went, even though I wondered, because I don't want to seem pushy. Alex, on the other hand, had no such qualms. He got a vague answer about an upcoming test in his History of Science class, which Alex didn't seem to believe. Neither did I.

Maybe the old girlfriend is back in the picture? This prospect bothers me far more than it probably should at this stage in our relationship.

My Dryft arrives at the curb as my mind is cycling through all of this. It's a shared flight, in deference to my dwindling credits, and also one of the older, less secure models that always make me a bit nervous about the piloting system getting hijacked. The old man sharing the pod seems pretty unperturbed about it, though. He's already half-asleep by the time we reach our cruising altitude, and he snores all the way to London. I take my earplugs from my bag to drown out the racket, hoping to spend the hour reading more of Katherine's diary. As I'm inserting the earplugs, my thumb slides into the curved hollow between my ear and the base of my jaw, and it occurs to me that it's about the same size as the odd, almost-transparent stickers that I found in the bag with the diaries. I fish around inside my bag for the vial, and when I finally locate it, I peel off one of the adhesive disks . . .

Disk. Damn, that's what Kate's note meant. Not a computer disk. Not even a thumb drive. This tiny, rubbery sticker. I feel a little stupid, but to be perfectly honest, it's not round. It's more oval in shape, and that's really not a disk.

The sticker fits perfectly, though. Once it's in place, I discover that tapping the links in the diary with the tiny pencil pulls up a holographic screen that hovers a few inches above the page. It looks a lot like the navigation display for the CHRONOS key.

After a bit of trial and error, I figure out how to get the videos to play. At first, I'm worried about disturbing the old guy, but the little disk must function like earphones, because he doesn't react in the slightest when the audio kicks in. The bulk of the recordings are personal diary entries of a petite blond woman who I assume is Katherine Shaw. She spends a lot of time talking about her work partner, Saul, who is apparently also her romantic partner, although they haven't gone public with that yet in the early entries. Some of the entries are reflections on her work, but most are snippets of her social life. Parties, dinners at some place called the OC, and occasional grumbles about a nonhistorian friend of Saul's named Morgen Campbell who was apparently a pompous jerk.

After watching a few of these early videos, I realize it might make more sense to work my way backward. When I click on the last video, however, I gasp out loud. The old man sharing my pod gives me a querulous look and readjusts in his seat, but I barely notice him.

This entry was recorded several years after the ones at the beginning of the diary, in April of 2305. It's instantly clear that the romance between Katherine and Saul has soured. In fact, it turned violent, right after she made two discoveries. First, he'd been breaking some rules at this CHRONOS place, rules that could get him fired, apparently. Second, her birth control had failed. She never got around to telling Saul the last part, though.

At some point, I'll need to go back and watch the entries that lead up to this. Maybe some of them will have clues as to how this woman wound up in the mid-twentieth century, eventually becoming Nora's great-great-grandmother. But the shock of seeing her in the video, with her face swollen and a red mark around her neck, is too raw. I just stare out the window, watching the scenery below until the Dryft touches down on the roof of a building a few blocks from my mom's flat.

This is not the best area of London, and the flat is without a doubt the least expensive place Mila Randall Grace has ever lived. There were no complaints on that front when I helped her move in a few months back, however. She knew better. If the accommodations are a step down for her, she really has no one to blame but herself. The building is safe and reasonably modern, and the flat is plenty big enough for one person.

Once I'm outside her place, I find a spot behind the building that's relatively inconspicuous and set a stable point. It will be nice not to have to go through all of the hassle and expense of paging a flight-pod if I want to visit again. I'm definitely not going to let *her* know that I can blink in anytime I want to, however. That would only amplify the chaos the next time she's in a dramatic mood. Better to have her assume that I'm a three-hour flight that neither of us can afford away.

I take the lift up to the fifth floor and ring the bell. She's not expecting me. I thought about calling. It's a bit rude to show up unannounced, even when visiting your mother. Also, since she doesn't know I'm coming, there's a slight chance she won't even be here, and I'll have to come back later, something Alex mentioned when we were discussing my itinerary this morning. As we talked about it, though, I realized that it wasn't really a problem. Coming back later simply means setting another stable point in her hallway, then scanning forward and jumping in when I see her approach the door.

And although I didn't go into this with Alex, the simple truth is that I have to catch my mother off guard. I need some answers on this whole genetic-enhancement thing. *Honest* answers.

There's no immediate response to the doorbell. I set the stable point while I'm waiting and then push the button again. This time, the little camera nested in the door scans me and the lock clicks open.

"Madison. What are you doing here?" Mila Grace's voice is thick-tongued and heavy. It might be from alcohol, but the mood meds that her doctor friend prescribes all too freely are a far more likely cause. She's lost weight, too—something she can ill-afford—and the dressing gown she's wearing hangs loosely over crumpled pajamas. Her hair, which is almost always pulled back into a bun, is a mass of dark curls, streaked with the silver that's been creeping in over the past few years.

She gives me a perfunctory hug and then steps back so I can enter the front room.

It's a mess. This would never have been the case before my father died. For one thing, we had household help. But even when we were on holiday and it was just the three of us, she liked a tidy house. I'm more my father's daughter in that respect. When it gets so cluttered that I can't find things, then I'll take the time to pick the place up.

"Why didn't you tell me you were coming?" she asks, scooping up a pile of clothes so that I can sit on the sofa. "And how long are you staying? Can you really afford travel right now?"

"I'm not staying. A friend of a friend at university has a private copter. They were coming over for the weekend and asked if I wanted to tag along." As soon as the lie leaves my mouth, I realize that it's Monday. "We're . . . we're heading back in a few hours. I just had something I needed to discuss with you."

Her blue eyes narrow slightly. We used to be close, and she's my mother. So even with her senses dulled from whatever she's on, she's had years of experience and probably knows I'm lying. She definitely knows that whatever I came here to discuss has me on edge.

"Do you want something to drink? Or eat?"

I kind of do. The food unit here is a lot better than the one at the house back in Bethesda. I don't know if it's the regional settings or just because it's ancient, but even though I entered Nora's recipe exactly, I've yet to coerce a palatable curry of any sort out of the machine. I'm not at all sure how the discussion I'm about to embark upon will go, however, so I decide it might be better to wait and eat when I get to Nora's house.

"No, thanks. Like I said . . . I really can't stay. I just wanted to see you and ask"—I take a deep breath and then just plunge straight into the deep end—"and ask why you never told me that you and Dad were both genetically enhanced."

The question catches her off guard, exactly as I'd planned. But whatever sedative she's on makes it harder than usual to read her expressions. "Why on earth would you think that, Madi?"

"Because I have test results that show I inherited changes from both my maternal and paternal lines."

"Then someone has made a mistake. You can't possibly think that I would—or even *could*—keep something like that a secret from you and your father."

"There's no mistake. And I never said you kept it a secret from Dad. I said that *he* was enhanced, too."

I spend the next few minutes grilling her, but she hems and haws, mentioning the minor gene therapy I had as an infant to protect against an increased risk of a rare eye cancer. When I press her, asking her directly whether she or my father was enhanced, she says no. Repeatedly.

But she's lying. And she's never been especially good at lying. I can only remember a few times before my father's death where I noticed her not telling the truth, and those were fairly minor white lies. Still, she has a few telltale signs, like speaking a full octave above her normal tone or fidgeting with her hair.

What bothers me most isn't the lying, though. I sort of expected that. It's more that she seems *scared*. She definitely doesn't seem surprised to learn that I inherited genetic enhancements. The revelation itself got almost no reaction, and while that could be the drugs dulling her senses, I'm pretty sure she already knew. Her second most obvious reaction was annoyance, although I don't know if that's because the secret is now out or because I showed up unannounced.

"I'm not going to *tell* anyone," I say, hoping to reassure her. "That would be practically suicidal. I just want to know why . . . and how, I guess. The friend who did the test isn't going to turn us in, either. Maybe it was one of your parents who was altered, and it didn't show up with older equipment." I pull one of the syringes Lorena gave me this morning from my bag. "If you'd be willing to give us a blood sample, Lorena may be able to figure out exactly—"

"Absolutely not. This is ridiculous!"

And now she's crying. Mila has always been emotional, and even more so since my father died, but this is borderline hysteria. She drops into the chair opposite me and pulls her knees up, clutching them to her chest. It's almost a fetal position, and I remember it well from the weeks after my father died. She just keeps repeating "Why now, why now," as she rocks back and forth.

After a few minutes, she pulls herself together and wipes her eyes with the back of her hand. "You can't just storm in here with these . . . *insane* accusations and demand a blood sample. Someone is lying to you, Madison, and I won't be part of it. Do you hear me? I won't!"

Until this moment, I was planning to tell her about finding the CHRONOS keys. I wasn't sure if I'd go into the time-travel side of things, but I wanted to see if she had any knowledge about the medallion itself, or even of the Cyrists. Her own mother, Thea, has spent her life cycling through weird religions. I'm guessing she cycled through Cyrisism at some point. Mom lived in several different communes with Thea when she was a child. Almost every time we meet, Thea tells me about this fabulous guru or cleric who is helping her find her true self.

But given my mother's reaction and her current precarious state of mind, I'm not willing to risk sharing any information with her.

She's keeping things from me, which means I can't trust her. That saddens me, even though I can't say it really surprises me.

"It's okay," I tell her. "You don't have to do anything you don't want to. Listen, I need to go. I have to meet up with my friends so we can get back to DC. I'm sorry I upset you." She doesn't respond, so I lean down and press a quick kiss to her cheek. "I'll call you in a few days."

Just as the lift arrives, I hear a door open behind me. I look back to see my mom leaning against the doorframe of her flat, looking small and defenseless. Tears are streaming down her cheeks.

"Madison? I love you. You *know* that, right?"

"Yes. I love you, too. Take care of yourself, okay? Eat something."

The flight to Nora's house takes about an hour. I try to focus on the diary again, but it's a lost cause. For the first half of the trip, my mind keeps going back to my mom's reaction, and her general state of mind. Is she even stable enough to live alone? And then the pod stops to pick up a father with two small children near Manchester, and any hope of concentration is lost.

Nora's cottage is near Bray, a seaside town about twenty kilometers south of Dublin. We sold the larger house in London, and at some point, we may have to sell this place as well. But I hope we can keep it, at least as long as Nora is alive. My best childhood memories are connected to this cottage, to days at the shore with my grandfather and Nora, and to long walks in the Wicklow Mountains with my dad.

The landing pad closest to Nora's cottage is at a hotel about a kilometer away. The sky is clear today, and despite the slight nip in the air, it's nice to get a bit of exercise outdoors. I sent Nora a message while we were in the air to tell her I was coming by for a very short visit, so she's waiting in the garden when I hike up the cliff walk to the cottage path.

Her gray pantsuit, with faint silver stripes, is far more formal than what most people would choose to wear on an afternoon at home. It's possible that she went out this morning—she plays euchre with friends a few times a week and occasionally volunteers at a local school. But I doubt it. On days when she goes out, she usually wears a skirt. My grandfather once said that she was determined to fit in with the people in his social circle when they married. Everyone knew she was James Coleman's daughter, but most had long forgotten the plagiarism case. Nora still felt that she had one strike against her going into any social situation, so she was determined to be the epitome of a proper, refined member of British society.

"Madison Grace, you don't really mean to tell me that you've crossed the goddamn Atlantic and aren't going to stay the night?"

Well, *proper* and *refined* except for the cursing. Although to be fair, a few of her euchre buddies swear pretty fluently, too. Her comment about crossing the Atlantic makes me laugh, although she doesn't really understand why. I *guess* I crossed the Atlantic to get to Liverpool, but it took a lot less time than my hop across the Irish Sea a few minutes ago.

"I'm obviously delighted to see you," Nora says as she hugs me, "but seriously, what are you doing here? I thought you were busy with classes and . . ." She trails off, probably not wanting to say that we can't afford last-minute transatlantic travel.

"It's a long story. Feed me and I'll tell you everything. I've been craving rajma masala for weeks."

The youngest of Nora's two cats, Mercury, greets me when we step inside. Mars, the older and more restrained of the two, gives me a little head tilt of recognition and then goes back to his nap. For as long as I can remember, there have always been two cats, each named after a planet. I guess at some point, Nora will have to cycle back through, although these two are fairly young and they're genetically tweaked for longer lives, since there are few restrictions for genetic enhancement of pets. If you have the money and you want a dog who will live forty years, there's a geneticist out there somewhere who'll be happy to help you.

Once we're both at the table—me with my red-bean curry and Nora with a cup of tea—I tell her about the test results. Unlike Mom, she's completely baffled, and it's clear that she doesn't entirely believe me, even when I show her the report that Lorena gave me.

"It has to be a mistake. I can't vouch for your mother's family, of course, although Matthew took the standard genetic tests before you were conceived. I can, however, tell you with complete certainty that we absolutely did *not* have your father enhanced. Even if I'd wanted to—and I sure as hell did not—your grandfather would never have allowed it. You know how he felt on that issue. Have you asked Mila about this?"

Nora's mouth presses into a tight line when she says my mother's name. They've never been what you would call close, but they got along well enough prior to the financial debacle. Now, they speak only through me.

I fill Nora in on my mother's response, toning down her reaction and entirely omitting the part about her seeming half-stoned. "She said she doesn't know anything about it, but . . . I didn't get the sense that she was being entirely truthful."

"Maybe you should ask Thea, then. Assuming you can track her down. After all, she's the one who would have procured any illegal alterations on Mila."

This is true. Thea raised my mother on her own, so my maternal grandfather has always been a mystery. Mom claims she met him once when she was small, but when she talks about it, she does that thing with her hair—stretching out one of her curls and then tucking it behind her ear—so I'm pretty sure she's lying.

"I tried to contact Thea on her birthday last month, but the call bounced back. I'll give Mom a few days to cool off and then ask if she has more recent contact information."

Nora makes the same slightly exasperated face that she always does when we talk about Thea Randall. She's still annoyed, twenty-five years after my parents' wedding, that Thea dictated the venue and countless details of the ceremony, and then didn't even bother to show. Or help pay for it.

"Well, even if you find her, I doubt she's going to give you a blood sample. I'm actually surprised Mila doesn't claim the exemption—although she never got the tattoo, so it would be harder for her to make the case."

"Make the case for what?"

"For being a Cyrist. Not that Thea has ever practiced, but she has the lotus tat, doesn't she? I've never seen it, since I've never seen *her*, but Matthew said her parents were Orthodox Rite."

I think for a moment, trying to pull up an image of Thea's hands. The truth is, Thea has a lot of tattoos, so many that they blend into a bright mosaic. There could be a lotus flower on her hand, but I'm not certain.

"Maybe. I thought she might have spent some time with the Cyrists, given her ongoing search for her inner truth, but I didn't know she was born into it."

"Well, it would explain a lot about her attitude," Nora says dryly. "The Cyrists have always felt they were better than everyone else."

That's clearly a religious slur, and I'm tempted to point out that there are good and bad people in any religion. But I'm guilty, too, since we both tend to mock Thea's tendency to change religions like other people change socks. Also, Nora is eighty. She's entitled to express a few crotchety opinions without being scolded by her granddaughter.

"Even if she does have the lotus tat, she's not a practicing member," I say. "She flouts a lot of their other rules, so maybe she'd be willing to donate a few drops of blood to the cause."

"I suppose it's possible," Nora says. "What traits does this friend of yours think were altered, anyway? In Mila's case, I'm guessing it wasn't financial acumen."

I ignore the dig at my mother, in part because it's well deserved, and answer Nora's question as best I can. "Lorena said it was multiple enhancements, on both my maternal *and* paternal sides. Some dealing with memory and intelligence. Language aptitude, apparently. And then there's an odd cluster of modifications that she's never seen before, that seem to have something to do with this." I push the now empty plate aside and reach into my bag to get the CHRONOS key.

Nora frowns when she sees the medallion. "What does that ugly hunk of metal have to do with genetic enhancements?"

Before, when my only concern was whether I could make some money off the research, I'd been determined to keep Nora in the dark. I think there's a good chance she'll try to talk me out of using the key once she knows what it does. She'll say it's too dangerous and probably demand that I give it to her. And she's going to be mad as hell when I refuse. But I really don't have much choice but to tell her now, since I need to find out how I wound up with illegal genetic enhancements that are directly connected to my ability to time travel. With my mother refusing to help and Thea currently God-only-knows where, Nora's really my best chance for figuring things out.

"It might be easier to just show you what it does. But first, do you remember the other day when you called me? How I just sort of vanished while I was planting the garden behind the house?"

She nods slowly. "Of course. You scared the bloody hell out of me. If my father could spend all that money on a pool in the basement, you'd think he could have at least installed a decent comm system for the yard so that you didn't have to rely on your wristband. Which is apparently faulty, too."

"It wasn't actually my comm acting up, Nora. I accidentally triggered this device and . . ." I decide to leave out the part about winding up in the ocean and nearly drowning. "And I wound up in Florida. In *1906* Florida."

She arches an eyebrow, but I hold up my hand to stop her. "Bear with me, okay? Just . . . pick a date. Preferably a time when the clothes I'm wearing now won't be considered obscene."

Her expression shifts to one I haven't seen in years, but which I remember very well from my childhood. It indicates that I am on shaky ground, and she's nearly had enough of my nonsense.

"September 3, 2113."

"No. Not my birth date. Something I couldn't have predicted. And, come to think of it, it would help if you make it a time when I could still find a newspaper at a corner store."

"Fine," she says. "May 8, 1999."

It's not a date that I recognize, so I nod. My first instinct is to pull up the stable point in Liverpool or the one I set outside my mother's place. Both are accessible in 1999. But the only cash I have is US currency, circa 1930, which will be odd enough in the US at the turn of the twenty-first century, and doubly odd in the UK. That means I'll need to make another transatlantic hop.

So I pull up the interface and scroll to the stable point in New York that I used when I first demonstrated the key for Jack and Alex. I choose a time in the early morning when there shouldn't be too many people around to notice me popping in.

Nora watches as I set the key, although I guess all she's actually seeing is me staring at the medallion in my palm.

"I'm going to blink out in just a second, so don't be startled, okay? I'll be right back."

I create a local stable point so that I can return here to the sitting room. Just as I'm about to jump out, I realize that I'm still seated and quickly get to my feet. Having landed on my ass on one of my first jumps, I'm in no rush to repeat the experience in an alleyway.

The New York that I open my eyes to in 1999 is a bit more run-down than the 1930s version I last visited. It smells roughly the same, however. The newsstand is no longer on the corner, but I spot a shop just down the street with a large yellow sign that reads *Grocery-Candy-24-Hour Smoke Shop*. As I approach, I see what looks like a bundle of rags in the doorway of the abandoned storefront next door. It moves slightly when I walk past, and I realize someone is sleeping there.

There are many problems in 2136, but in the US and UK, no one has to sleep on the street. No one goes without food or health care, and everyone is guaranteed at least twenty hours of work a week, once you're finished with school. The job may not be something you want to do, the accommodations may not be luxurious, and the food may be little more than nutritional bars, but basic needs are met. The rest is up to you.

I step carefully to avoid waking the person and pull open the door to the convenience store. Any hope of not waking the homeless person ends there, as a loud buzzer sounds, announcing my entrance. The figure beneath the bundle of rags grunts once and burrows down deeper.

Once inside, I grab a copy of the latest *New York Times* and a bag of something called Doritos, which appear to be cheese crisps. The clerk inside the small glass booth is half-asleep. He doesn't give me a second look—just takes the five quarters I stick into the little cup. I tell him to keep the change, then step outside and prop the bag against the wall near the sleeping person. I don't know how nutritional it is, but it's food.

Then I blink back to Nora's place.

"Son of a bitch," Nora says. "Where did you go? And how did you do that?"

"I went to May 8, 1999, as requested. New York." I hand her the paper. I'd sort of expected a major headline, but the top stories are about a couple of politicians leaving office—one in the US and one in Russia. "What made you pick that date?"

"It's the day my grandmother was born," she says, looking down at the paper. "But you didn't answer my second question. How did you do that?"

When I reach the end of my explanation, I can tell that she still doesn't quite buy my story. Not exactly surprising, I guess. "Give me another date," I begin. But then I stop. "Never mind. I have a better idea."

"Whatever you're planning, don't do it. That thing can't be safe, Madi."

"It's safe."

I pull up the local stable point I created before the Harlem jump and set the date for August 15, 2125. That's not the exact date, but it's in the ballpark. I pan around until I see the little table near the window. A blue-and-white ceramic teapot sits in the center, on a crocheted doily.

The tiny teapot was a gift to Nora from my grandfather on their first anniversary. Their names and the date of the wedding were etched in gold on the bottom. About a month before my eleventh birthday, Nora's two cats came tearing through the parlor, and one of them knocked the teapot off the table. My grandfather wanted to buy her another one, but they both knew it wouldn't be the same. Now, a framed family photo sits in that same spot.

I begin scrolling forward until I find the first day where the little teapot is missing. Then I roll the time back one day, blink in, and grab the teapot before the cats wreck it.

When I return to 2136 and place the teapot, now whole, into Nora's hands, her eyes grow misty. "Oh my God. Madi! Where did you find—" She stops. "What's wrong?"

I shake my head. "Just a mild headache. I probably shouldn't have jumped so soon after scarfing down that curry."

But she's not buying it, so I finally admit that bringing back the teapot is giving me some odd double memories. It's not like we spent a lot of time over the past ten years talking about the shattered teapot. In fact, I don't think we mentioned it directly more than a few times, although Nora would often yell at the cats to stop acting like demons before they broke something else.

Now, however, I have a second memory of the event, where we puzzled over a *missing* teapot. It just vanished. The doors were locked, and there was no sign of a break-in. The entire family was home that day, and we only noticed that it was gone shortly before we headed up to bed. It was baffling, and my grandfather actually called in the police, even though the item wasn't expensive, because he was certain that someone had managed to get inside the house. The police seemed to think that I might have broken it accidentally and didn't want to admit it. They even looked through the rubbish bins, trying to confirm the theory that I'd tossed out the fragments hoping to avoid punishment. After they left, Nora ordered a new security system.

The dueling memories make me a tiny bit queasy, but it's not as bad as the feedback loop I got staring at my doppelgänger on the beach at Estero. It's only a vague discomfort, a bit like remembering a story where there were minor differences between the book and the movie versions. Nora is so happy to have the teapot intact again that I don't regret it one bit.

The bigger issue is that I wasn't really expecting this kind of ripple effect. I thought that I'd just jump back, rescue the teapot, and give it to her in the present. I didn't realize that would create an entirely different narrative about what happened that day.

"Where did you find this?" Nora repeats.

"I went back and kept the cats from knocking it off the table that day. Not Mercury and Mars, but the two cats you had back then. Saturn and Neptune, I think. They came running into the room, and one of them bumped into the teapot. It bounced off the arm of the chair and shattered into a million pieces. We were still finding shards of ceramic in the rug months later."

"But . . . that's not what happened," Nora protests. "It was *stolen*. You were here, Madi. Remember the police officer who was such an ass to you?"

I spend the next few minutes trying to explain the whole layered-memories thing. What baffles me, though, is the fact that she doesn't remember both versions. When I changed things after my jump to Estero, all four of the other people currently in the house were hit with the competing memories. But Nora swears she doesn't remember any reality where the cats broke her teapot. I'm now doubly convinced that the CHRONOS key in the pool needs to stay in place until we have a better idea of exactly how the system works. Maybe it's the only thing keeping the entire house inside a protective field.

On the plus side, however, Nora does seem to believe me about the time travel now. I place the key in her palm to see if she can activate it, but she can't see anything.

Nora shakes her head in frustration. "I don't understand how this piece of crappy jewelry is connected to genetic enhancements. It isn't orange. It's just plain brown and just plain ugly to me. Whatever you inherited must have been from your mother's side."

"Or, more likely, the gene skipped a generation or two. This was buried in the yard at Grandpa James's house, Nora. And there's another one in the basement. Maybe Dad would have been able to activate it, although I guess we'll never know . . . for sure."

Except, I *could* know for sure.

I'm amazed that this hasn't occurred to me before. I could go back and put the CHRONOS key in my father's hand when he was still alive and see what happens. I could actually tell him goodbye.

Or better yet, I could get him to the hospital. Maybe they'd be able to save him.

I just used the key to rescue Nora's teapot. Why not use it to rescue my dad?

FROM *TEMPORAL DILEMMA USER'S GUIDE*, 2ND ED. (2293)

Q: *How many people can play* Temporal Dilemma *(TD)?*

A: The SimMaster 2950 is designed for up to eight participants in individual mode. Multiplayer simulations are great fun at parties!

Games with more than two or three players, however, generally result in less realistic outcomes due to the multitude of variables in any temporal simulation. For our more serious players who prefer one-on-one competition, the SimMaster 2950 offers enhanced speed and superior VR resolution.

Q: *How can I join a* TD *team?*

A: Team play is substantially different from individual mode. Each team is composed of up to eight players, with a leader who assigns roles. Intramural *TD* leagues generally hold tryouts at the beginning of the year and follow the same rules as professional *TD*. The best preparation for tryouts is to practice using the latest expansion modules. Contact your school and community organizer for more information on *TD* amateur leagues.

Q: When will new expansion modules be released?

A: Two new releases are planned in 2294. The first is a simple expansion, compatible with the World Dominion simulation series. This expansion adds over two million additional data points, ensuring realistic play across the four quadrants.

The second is the long-awaited Excelsior VR series, specifically designed for individuals whose chosen gift allows them to bypass the controls and form a neural link with the SimMaster.

Parents take note: The Excelsior series can be played by children as young as five. Yearly updates allow the system to grow with your child, ensuring that they will be ready for professional competition, in either individual or team mode, as early as age twelve. Make the most of your investment in the Excelsior Chosen Gift by giving your child the edge he or she needs to enter the Excelsior League and become a "Time Master"!

∞15∞

The jump platform at CHRONOS headquarters is a large circular area at the very center of the room. Whoever designed it was clearly thinking of an old-fashioned analog clock when they positioned the stations for twelve historians, the maximum number in a jump group. Even that was probably decided by someone thinking of a clock, because there's no real reason to have an even dozen agents—or, more frequently, two groups of a dozen—in the field at a time.

Our jumps are to all points around the globe, and many different time periods, so it's often hard to predict the costume any given agent will be in when we all arrive in the jump room. But the *timing* is always predictable. Our group left at ten a.m., and so we were all scheduled to come back at eleven a.m. on the dot. All of us. We jump out at the same instant. We return at the same instant. No matter how long you are in the field, whether it's a few hours or a few weeks, the system is set for you to return exactly one hour after your departure.

As you blink out of the jump room, you see the historian across from you. When you open your eyes upon your return, you see the same historian looking up from his or her key.

Always the same. *Predictable.*

Today, however, I am the *only* historian in position on the jump platform when I open my eyes. Angelo is on the far side of the room with Aaron, the guy who usually operates the equipment. A quick glance at the display on my key shows that the time is 10:02, and the look on Angelo's face tells me that something is very, very wrong.

But I knew that the instant the shots rang out back in Ohio. Before that, even, when I saw the five flashes of purple light in the crowd.

Angelo jerks his head toward the door that leads to the administrative offices and costuming. I follow him without speaking, thankful that I'm at least being granted a private dressing-down, rather than being screamed at in front of the entire jump team. I guess that's why he pulled me back early.

Or, a semiprivate dressing-down, at any rate. Rich and Katherine are already in Angelo's office. Neither of them is on the jump schedule today. It's clear from their expressions that they know something major has happened. I don't think they could have even gotten down here from the dorm level in the space of two minutes, let alone had time for Angelo to brief them. That means they've jumped backward a bit.

Usually there are only two chairs in front of Angelo's desk, but someone has pulled up a third. I sink down into it. "I don't know how anything I did could have caused an anomaly, Angelo. There were rumors about an assassination attempt that day—some kid was arrested a year or so later, and he said that it was planned by a local Klan leader and then canceled. But there were threats like that almost any time King spoke."

Angelo rests his elbows on his desk and rubs his face. "Richard says you had an overlap with someone you met in Memphis?"

Rich gives me a look of apology. I'm not mad at him. I was going to tell Angelo that part of it anyway. Can't see that I have any choice, since he'll be the one figuring out how to fix this mess.

"Yes. But the girl wasn't involved in this. She just recognized my face. Apparently, there was a problem with the family car, and—"

He waves a hand dismissively. "Richard told me. What I want to know is, was that the only time you saw the girl? You're sure you didn't interact with her on one of your earlier jumps? Maybe in 1963, in . . . What was the name of that place in South Carolina?"

"Spartanburg. And no, there's no way. She mentioned that she'd never been out of Tennessee until her sister's graduation from Antioch. And the only other time I've been to Memphis was 1956. She'd have been a little kid."

I know that I should tell him the part about Toni getting a double memory. And I *will* tell him if I have to. It's just that I'm not entirely sure what the consequences might be for her. I don't really think they'd send someone back through time to kill her or lock her up or anything—although I guess I can't entirely rule that out if there were major changes to the timeline. That sort of decision would be made by the government, not by CHRONOS, and I can easily imagine them taking a utilitarian stance and making sacrifices for the greater good.

But King was only supposed to live three more years. Most of the major civil rights legislation was pretty much a done deal by this time. Did his death result in more racial tension? The Watts riots in Los Angeles are later that summer, in early August. Maybe this made them worse. Maybe the riots spread to other cities.

Angelo sighs. "Okay, then. I'll admit I was hoping that we could find some way to connect the earlier events, but apparently not."

"What earlier events? And what kind of impact are we looking at?" I ask, dreading the answer.

"Level five," Rich says. "The Vietnam War goes on for six more months."

"What? Just because King died early? That doesn't—"

"It's not just King," Angelo says. "That's why all three of you are here, rather than me simply going back and telling you to skip that jump to Antioch. We've got *four* early deaths of significant individuals between March 24, 1965, and August 19, 1966."

"That's the date of the last Selma march. I haven't—"

"I know you haven't been there. A sniper picked off five people—three women and two men—in the area they were using as a stage, including"—Angelo flicks his eyes, searching for something on his retinal display—"an author named James Baldwin. Also a singer, Mary Travers."

"I know who Baldwin is," I say. "He wrote *The Fire Next Time* and *If Beale Street Could Talk*. But I've never heard of this Mary . . ."

"Travers. She was with Peter, Paul, and Mary," Rich says. When I shake my head, he adds, "'If I Had a Hammer'? 'Blowin' in the Wind'?"

"I thought 'Blowin' in the Wind' was Dylan?"

Rich sighs. "Dylan wrote it. Well, he sang it, too, but radio stations didn't play him much in the early sixties. Peter, Paul, and Mary brought protest music to middle-class whites. College kids. You've definitely heard of the fourth victim . . . John Lennon. And it happens at the concert in Memphis."

I sit there silently for a moment, trying to come up with some logical chain of events that might result in the killing of those four people—King, Baldwin, Lennon, and a folk singer whose name I don't even recognize. I'm about to make the rather obvious point that it's probably the Klan or a similar group when I remember something important that I haven't told them about the Antioch trip.

"There were five other agents at Antioch. Watching as King died."

Angelo frowns. "But you were the first to make that trip."

"Exactly. They'd have to be from a later cohort. And get this. One of them was a kid."

"A kid?" Katherine says. "You're sure? Maybe it was just someone who's kind of short, like me."

"No. A boy. Twelve years old, at the very most."

"That's . . . troubling," Angelo says. "On several levels, but mostly because it suggests that we don't manage to fix this. I'm not willing to accept that as a possibility. The reason I had Aaron change your return time was to get a head start on figuring out what went wrong. Since the three of you are currently researching this time period, you're my first choice to investigate. If we need more people on it, I'll pull Timothy and Evelyn in, but obviously the fewer people who know about this, the better. And we've already got questions coming in from above."

He doesn't have to clarify that. We all know that there are exactly two buildings in the United States that are under a CHRONOS field. We're inside one. The other is the White House.

"Shouldn't Saul be here, too?" Katherine asks. "He's working with us on the Memphis jump, and—"

"Saul is on a *training* mission," Angelo says. "And as he noted in one of the scrums, training comes first."

I'm not sure if Katherine catches the sarcasm in his voice, but Rich definitely does. He and I exchange a look. Training might *usually* come first, but it definitely doesn't come before a level-five fuckup. Saul isn't here because Angelo doesn't trust him.

"So what's the plan of action?" Richard asks, cutting off Katherine, who was about to protest further. "Do we split up and each take one of the events, or—"

"No. I want all three of you together as much as possible. You'll need some research time to figure out where we should focus first, so I'm sending you back twenty-four hours, directly to the isolation unit. Come up with a plan of operation. Since I obviously can't jump back, I'll send instructions back to myself and join you there about . . . two hours ago, so you can brief me. I need to keep a clear head, and that will give me as few conflicting memories as possible. My goal is to get the three of you back into the field *ahead* of the regularly scheduled jump."

"Can you give us an idea of the impact?" I ask. "I mean, I know level five is serious, but . . ."

Angelo gives me a grim look. "There are significant timeline changes. That's all I'm authorized to say, but given the current political climate, failure to fix this would cost us our funding. They'll shut us down, maybe even retroactively."

"They'd erase CHRONOS?" Katherine asks.

He shrugs. Katherine looks a little pale, because we all know what that means. Every person in this room—hell, every person in this building—was genetically enhanced for their specific job within the organization. If the government erases CHRONOS, goes back and keeps it from ever being formed, that would effectively erase all of us. Oh, we'd still exist in some form, but all of our memories and a huge chunk of our personalities and physical attributes would be different, so for all intents and purposes, we wouldn't be the same people.

I have a hard time accepting complete erasure of the organization as a credible threat, since it would change things in the timeline as a whole. History curricula for the past few generations would be very different, for starters. And who knows how many other decisions might have been changed by that knowledge?

But shutting CHRONOS down? Maybe even sending back a message not to bother with the genetic alteration on the last few cohorts of trainees? That's believable.

The three of us follow Angelo back to the jump room, where only a single tech, Aaron, is on duty. I know Aaron pretty well because we play in the same virtual rugby league. He gives me a sympathetic smile, and I can tell he's worried. How much does he know about what's going on? How much does the rest of the support team at CHRONOS know?

"I have you guys at the first three stations," Aaron says. After we take our places, he adds, "You'll go straight to isolation. Let the crew there know if you need anything."

I've never been to the tank, as the isolation unit is generally known. I expect it to be tiny and stark, like a jail cell. But when we arrive, I see that it doesn't look all that different from the quarters that Rich and I share. A little larger, maybe, with two extra bunks. The equipment at the research station is a major upgrade, too. It looks a bit like the system they have down in the archives.

"Wow." Katherine runs her finger over the top of the console, and a holographic globe shimmers into view. "A SimMaster 8560. Morgen and Saul were talking about this model at dinner a few weeks back. They said it was still in the R and D stage, though. Not due out for at least three years."

"Could be an experimental model," Rich suggests.

"Maybe. But it looks like a finished product. Morgen Campbell would sell what's left of his tiny, shriveled soul to get his hands on this." She glances over at Rich and me. "You've seen Campbell's setup, haven't you?"

"I've played at the Club a few times," Richard says, but I shake my head.

Even though it's considered an honor to be pulled into Campbell's clique, I've never wanted to be part of the select group of pet historians who gather at the Objectivist Club for simulation tournaments to test out classic historical hypotheticals. What if there had been tanks or fighter planes during the American Civil War? What if Hitler had died in jail? What if the US had used nuclear weapons on the USSR before the Cold War began? What if the Genetics War had started five years later?

The official name of the game, which has been popular for a few decades, is Temporal Dilemma, but most people refer to it generically as "time chess," because there are several different copyrighted versions. It's nothing at all like chess, aside from the fact that playing—or at least, playing well—requires a good deal of strategy. Time-chess leagues are organized at every age level once you begin school. Most of the school groups that come to our Q&A sessions are time-chess fans. My father, who played in high school, says it's an excellent tool for teaching history, economics, and related fields. The fact that he enjoyed playing so much is probably why he was willing to cough up a substantial bribe to be sure one of his two offspring was given the CHRONOS gene.

Around here, though, people don't even call it time chess. It's just *The Game*. My aversion to it is partly because playing it means I'd have to interact with Morgen Campbell, Saul Rand, and others like them on a regular basis. It also seems like a massive circle jerk, designed to inflate egos, since Campbell awards prizes to those who prove his pet theories true.

The biggest reason I steer clear, however, is that The Game itself seems like a perversion of our entire mission. We *study* history. We don't change it. I've always been a little suspicious of historians who spend too much of their spare time fantasizing about breaking the prime directive of CHRONOS.

Most of the retired historians play, though. I guess it's kind of a substitute for being in the field. Most of the technical staff play, too. But the majority of the current historians don't, so I suspect I'm not the only one who feels that it's kind of a conflict of interest with the day job. I know that Angelo agrees with me. You can read it on his face anytime conversation turns toward The Game.

"Saul is really good," Katherine says. "As you probably already know. I don't play in the league myself, but I've been watching him practice and play for the past few years. Sometimes, I make copies of his simulations when he's not around." She smiles slyly. "And I've beaten his score more than once, although if either of you tell him that, I'll deny it and then murder you."

I snort. "My, what a fragile ego Saul Rand must have."

Katherine rolls her eyes. "He's still a better player than I am. But if he knew I'd beaten him even once, he'd get all competitive. The Game is important to him, and it's not really important to me. I don't think it's healthy for partners to compete in that way."

I get a vivid flashback to Timothy's green eyes lighting up with amusement as he and Evelyn joked about Katherine being genetically programmed to be more submissive. He would, no doubt, consider this statement Exhibit A for his side of the argument.

But I push that aside to focus on the real issue. I'm about to ask why we even *need* a gaming system right now, let alone someone with expertise, when it clicks. This is how they expect us to figure out what mistake could have resulted in a level-five emergency.

A game. Admittedly, a very complex game on a beyond-state-of-the-art system, but it still seems like a pathetic tool set for solving a level-five disaster.

Rich scans for something on his retinal display. "I've only played standard simulations. Out-of-the-box stuff. Usually you make a change and the system calculates the probability of outcomes, but that isn't really going to help us in this case. Do you know if we can set it to work backward? So that we provide current information and it isolates what set the chain of events in motion?"

"Sure." Katherine taps a control box on the right side of the display. "You just need to enter the changes and set the system for backward induction. Do we have the new data?"

"Syncing with the system to send it now," Richard says.

I pull up the new file in my in-box, which must be the one he's sending to the simulator. The file is labeled simply *Anomalies*, and it's massive. Results are organized into global, regional, and national sections, then states, territories, and local units. There are subcategories for political, cultural, economic, scientific, demographic, and physical data at each level. That last category seems a bit strange, so I open it out of curiosity. It's fairly small, with annual figures for things like air quality, ocean temperature, and frequency of natural disasters, among other things, stretching back to 1960. Some figures are marked to indicate missing data and extrapolations, but it's largely complete. Most of the main categories are broken down into smaller units—for example, the political section for the United States shows a list of twenty-three persons who held a specific national political office in the old timeline but either never existed in this offshoot, or else never won the election. When I click on the link and add in the data for states and territories, the number increases to 248.

"Well, the president is still the same, except for two earlier elections," Rich says, so I guess he's scanning through the top-level changes, too. "I wonder what would have happened if this event changed the current occupant. I mean, the White House is under a CHRONOS field. The president is under a key even when she travels. So would the old-timeline president have vanished, or been protected because of the CHRONOS field?"

Katherine and I both groan.

"Richard actually enjoyed Temporal Conundrums," she says, referring to everyone's least favorite class. "Be glad you didn't have to deal with him in the classroom. We're all sitting there agonizing over these headache-inducing problems, and Rich is piling on the complexity, asking questions even the teacher preferred to avoid."

Richard grins. "When I retire from fieldwork, I'm going to teach that class."

She presses her lips together primly. "Mm-hmm. And if you do, we'll all awaken one morning to the tragic news that the heads of the entire third-year class simultaneously exploded when you presented your special twist on Gödel's time-block theory. On the other hand, I wouldn't have passed the Conundrums final without your help, so I'm very thankful for your geeky side."

Rich's smile fades a bit. I suspect he's thinking that Saul doesn't have a geeky side, other than his obsession with The Game. And maybe wishing *he* didn't have a geeky side, either, which makes me both sad and exasperated at him.

"Do either of you know anything about previous level-five events?" I ask.

Richard shakes his head. Katherine makes a little face that suggests she knows something but isn't sure she should talk about it.

"Come on," Rich says. "If you know something, we need that information, too."

"It's not anything I know for certain," she says. "Just something Saul and Tate were talking about a few months ago, when we were moving Saul's things over to the new quarters. They were joking around about retractions, although I didn't get the sense Tate thought it was all that funny. Anyway, Saul said there was a level five during the first generation of agents. They had to send a massive team back to some village in France. He said they had to kill seven people. But that's all I know, and . . . he could have just been . . . you know . . ." She leaves us to fill in the blank and wanders over to the display. "Whoa. Look at this."

Rich and I join her. A window at the top is scrolling through the categories being loaded into the system, but that's not what she's talking about. She's pointing to a line at the very bottom of the window, which shows the copyright date as 2308.

"Interesting," I say. "Looks like someone in procurement cheated and jumped forward a few years to fill the purchase order. Naughty, naughty."

Technically, that's not allowed. In fact, if you believe the textbooks we used during our classroom training, it's not even possible. The equipment is, supposedly, locked to prevent travel to any time after 2160, when the first time-travel device was patented.

"Of course," Rich says, "Angelo just authorized Aaron to send us back twenty-four hours, so they've obviously decided that this situation warrants a bit of rule breaking. I just wonder if it really matters whether we have a top-of-the-line sim system."

Katherine shrugs. "It will shave a few minutes off each round. Whether that's important depends on how many rounds we have to go through before we can draw some conclusions. Either way," she says, nodding toward the progress wheel hovering in front of the globe somewhere over the Indian Ocean, "we might as well relax for a bit, because we've got at least an hour before we can start. I slept in this morning. Angelo's message woke me, so I didn't even have a chance to shower. But . . . you might want to go first, Tyce."

I glance down and realize that my jacket is still caked with mud from the parking lot at Antioch. There's also a reddish-brown splotch on my pant leg, and the fabric is stuck to my knee where I scraped it.

"Yeah," I say. "Good point."

Once I'm clean, I pop a bandage on my knee and check the closet, hoping it's equipped with one of the newer fabricators like they have in costuming. That way, I can go ahead and order something that would be suitable for the 1960s and not have to bother with changing. But the system is unfortunately a basic model that spits out the generic shirt and pants we call CHRONOS scrubs. I guess that's all they figured we'd need while in the tank. Not like we're going to be hosting a soirée.

When Katherine heads to the shower, Rich immediately looks away from whatever he was reading and asks in a low voice, "So what did you leave out? You were holding back in Angelo's office. It's something to do with the girl, isn't it?"

I consider lying, not because I don't trust him, but because I'd rather not put him in the situation of having to lie, too. But he'd know I wasn't telling the truth, and I don't want that, either.

"You're better off not knowing, Rich."

Of course, he just stares at me, eyebrows raised. And since I know he's not going to let it go . . .

"Fine. When the shots rang out, I pushed Toni to the ground. To protect her. Problem is, the CHRONOS key was in my suit pocket."

"Fuuucck," he says after a moment. "She was *inside* the CHRONOS field? You're certain?"

"Yeah. She felt the time shift, same as I did. Like a kick straight to the stomach. But I guess you felt it, too, right?"

He shakes his head. "Not anything like that. It was more of a twinge than a kick. Angelo said the same thing. He only knew what had happened because of the alert from the TMU."

The Temporal Monitoring Unit, or TMU, is on the same floor as the jump room. It's where we report immediately after returning from the past. They cycle us through a med pod to check vitals, run our blood work to make sure we didn't bring back anything contagious, and make sure the change in our cellular age roughly matches the amount of time listed in the research plans we filed. Once we pass medical, we report to Timeline Consistency for a group debriefing. In every single instance since I began at CHRONOS, this has taken less than a minute. As soon as we're all seated, the technician, usually Marcy Bateman, who I dated briefly during my field training, pushes a key. She stares at the screen for a few seconds, then calls each of us by name, in alphabetical order. After calling a name, she says, "You're free to go." I'd always thought she was running the report in real time, but now I suspect there's someone—or maybe many someones—in the back room checking for anomalies the entire time we're gone.

"You were a lot closer to the precipitating event than we were," Rich says. "That's probably why it hit you so hard. How do you know this girl felt it? Maybe it was just shock from the shooting?"

His voice rises hopefully at the end, but I shake my head.

"She was talking about things changing. And she was pretty distraught about it. She mentioned Selma, said people died at Selma. Which is true, but I guess she meant more people died. I didn't make the connection until—well, until *now*, to be honest. I'm familiar with Dr. King's speech at the end of the march, but I hadn't researched the concert the night before in much detail. But Toni lived through it. Saw it on the news. She'd have known if people died there."

Rich is quiet, but I can tell what's on his mind.

"You think I should have told Angelo."

"I do. But it's not my decision. Unless . . ."

"Unless we can't fix this. I know. And I *will* tell Angelo if I have to. But it wasn't Toni's fault, and I don't know what a retraction team might do to her or her family. You heard what Katherine just said."

He makes a dismissive noise. "Saul Rand lies more often than he tells the truth. I've never heard that story."

"Neither have I," I admit. "But he's been around a lot longer than either of us. And the point is, we don't *know*. I have an obligation to protect them if I can."

"You do realize Angelo isn't likely to accept that as an excuse for lying to him, don't you? And it's not like you can credibly claim it slipped your mind that the girl was inside the CHRONOS field."

"Credible or not, that's exactly what I'm going to tell him. *If* I have to tell him anything. He may not believe it, but I'm not going to put them at risk if I can help it."

Rich gives me a knowing look. "You mean you're not going to put *her* at risk."

I get exactly what he's saying and shake my head. "That's completely ridiculous. She lives nearly three hundred and fifty years in the past. And I just met her."

He glances toward the bathroom door, where I can hear the faint hiss of the sonic shower. "It can happen fast, man."

"You met Katherine when the two of you were *ten*, Rich."

"That's completely irrelevant. When she walked in on orientation day, that was it for me." He mimes yanking his heart out of his chest and tosses it toward Katherine, who's still behind the closed bathroom door. "Doesn't matter that it's hopeless—and yes, Tyce, I *know* it's hopeless. I'm not stupid. My point is that any decisions I make regarding Katherine aren't rational. I'm incapable of being rational where she's concerned. So I'm not judging you. That would be the height of hypocrisy. All I'm saying is, don't fool yourself into thinking that you're making strictly logical decisions here. You're thinking with your heart as much as your head."

FROM THE DIARY OF
KATE PIERCE-KELLER

COPIED FROM OTHER-KATE RE: CYRISTS

Fort Meyer 040302

Okay, I'm writing this out in the hopes of getting everything straight in my mind before I discuss it with Katherine and Connor, especially since Katherine told me not to bother with this jump. She said that Saul gobbled up dozens of tiny cults when he started the Cyrists, and that we already know that the Koreshans were one of them. That I could waste months tracking them all down and my time would be better spent focusing on getting the keys from Dallas, yada, yada.

But this group felt different to me. Heaven's Gate, the Order of the Solar Temple, and the others don't have as many points of overlap. The name *Koresh* is actually *Cyrus* in Hebrew. The Koreshans started in Chicago, around the same time that Saul and Katherine were there for the World's Fair. In this timeline, they moved to Florida earlier and were better financed. Their commune at Estero is much larger in 1902 than it should be, according to the protected files in Katherine's library. There were nearly a dozen people waiting at the dock when I arrived this morning, eager to visit the community and listen to the small orchestra they've formed. That's not the sort of thing you put together if you only have a tiny cluster of people.

Unfortunately, all conversation stopped when I arrived at the dock. I thought at first that it was because I was a stranger. While Fort Myers isn't a small town for this era, everyone else seemed to know each other. But the man who showed up right after me, carrying an instrument of some sort in a brown leather case, acted as though he recognized me.

Katherine is going to be livid that I didn't walk away right that second, as soon as something felt off. But I couldn't shake the sense that I was onto something.

And then when I stepped into the boat, the guy driving it grinned at me so wide that I thought his face would split in half. He's about my age, maybe a little younger. Very good looking, with hair that seems a little long for 1902, but it looks right on him.

He stared at me the entire trip. It should probably have felt creepy, but it didn't.

The fact that everyone else kept looking at me, however, was making me nervous. About ten minutes in, one of the women turned around and started to say how much she and her husband had enjoyed the last concert, and how happy the Koreshans must be that I'd be able to attend today. Had I been traveling? Was I staying long? And it was just so heartwarming to see the wonderful work the group was doing with all those orphans.

I was half tempted to dive over the edge of the boat and swim for shore at that point, but it didn't seem like a wise course of action while wearing an ankle-length skirt. And I couldn't really blink out with everyone staring at me. So I just smiled and gave vague answers, nodding in what I hoped were the right places as she continued talking. I decided to wait until I reached the shore and then find a spot where I could safely blink home.

That didn't happen, though. The boat driver followed me and grabbed my hand before I could pull up the display. I yanked away and debated screaming, but then he said, "Kate, Kate—no, it's me. It's Kiernan. Kiernan Dunne."

Then he reached into the collar of his shirt and grabbed the black leather cord around his neck. There was a tiny leather pouch, but I could see faint rays of blue shooting out through the stitching at the seams.

I didn't recognize his name at all, but somehow, this guy has a CHRONOS key.

And over the next few minutes, I discovered that *somehow*, he knows Aunt Prudence.

While some of the kids taken in by the Koreshans are actually local orphans, this Kiernan guy claims that most of them are, in fact, Prudence's offspring. That's why I need to be careful how I break this news to Katherine. Telling her that the Koreshans really are integrally connected to the Cyrists is the easy part. The part I'm dreading is telling her that her long-lost daughter isn't just helping Saul. She's making him an army of time travelers.

∞16∞

Madi
Near Liverpool, UK
November 12, 2136

"Madison Grace!" Nora grips my upper arm with surprising force. "No. Absolutely not."

I didn't even have to say what I was thinking. She knew from my expression alone. And probably because deep down she was thinking exactly the same thing.

"I'm serious, Madi. Even a minor change like saving this teapot had you rubbing your forehead and looking like you were going to upchuck your curry. You need to wipe that notion right out of your head."

She's right. I know she is. But the idea still hovers at the edge of my mind, taunting me. What's the point of having an ability like this if I can't do something constructive with it? My father was a good man who died far too young, and *so* many things would be different if he'd lived.

"It wouldn't work, anyway," Nora says. "You'd find yourself in a conundrum. If Matthew was still alive, you'd never have been digging around in my father's godforsaken backyard, and you'd never have found that device at all. So if you go back and try to save him, it will just backfire."

She says this with a great deal of confidence—far more, in fact, than I'm feeling on the subject. The part about me never finding the medallion is almost certainly correct. But the rest feels like a rather convenient rationalization.

"You don't know that," I say. "You can't know for sure."

"Well, no. I'm not an expert. But neither are you. Just because you can use the thing doesn't mean you understand how it works. And as much as I would dearly love for Matthew to still be alive, I'm not willing to risk losing you, too. The wisest course of action would be to bury that damn thing back in the garden. Or better yet, let's take a walk on the shore and toss it into the sea."

"I'm not going to do anything stupid, Nora. And . . . you're probably right about saving Dad creating a conundrum, even though I really wish you weren't. But I'm not getting rid of the key. This research is going to happen anyway. It's already begun. And I think there's a very real chance that people will eventually uncover my genetic background. The test Lorena ran was more detailed than the average blood work they do at a physical exam today, but how long will that be true? Her lab equipment could be standard-issue in five or ten years, and you know what the penalties would be. I'd barely be employable with something like this on my record. I'm going to need some major leverage in order to have any sort of future at all."

Nora opens her mouth to protest but closes it again. She knows that part is true. Everyone has heard a story of someone who cheated, who either didn't have their embryonic offspring restored to baseline when the new rules went into effect or bought an enhancement on the black market. The penalties aren't quite as harsh in the US as they are in the rest of the world, but it can still ruin your life and livelihood.

"And, anyway, I think it's already been decided." I pull out the *Brief History of CHRONOS* and show her the part with my name.

"Was this in *his* library?" Nora's nose twitches slightly when she mentions her father, just as it always does. "My father's nonfiction works were even less factual than his novels. This book is probably just one of those alternative-history pieces he wrote. You shouldn't put too much stock in it."

"It has my *name* in it, Nora."

"He could have written that after you were born," she said. "You never met him, but he certainly knew you existed."

"Except"—I tap the other two names—"I *know* both of these people. One is a temporal physicist. The other is a technical writer for research grants. He's married to the geneticist who did the test. And like I said, she's positive that the markers show alteration on both sides. That's why she wanted to get blood samples from both of you—so that she could maybe narrow down who was altered and who simply passed the gene along. Mom refused."

"Well, I can't say I entirely blame her on that front. This is a bit of a shock to the system, even leaving aside the possible legal ramifications. What will it mean for your studies? Are you sure you can trust these people to keep the secret?"

I shrug. "They're friends. I haven't known them long, but . . . Jack, the guy I mentioned before? He's known them longer than I have, and I trust him. So, yeah. I trust them."

And I do trust them. Even if Jack seems a little distant, I don't think for a moment that he'd turn me in. He was there this morning when I left. In fact, the last thing I saw before I blinked out was his smile, although his eyes still seemed worried.

I reach into my bag again and pull out the diaries of Katherine Shaw and Kate Pierce-Keller. Nora is silent for a long time as she stares at the names, and then begins to flip through the pages of Kate's diary.

"You've read this? You can make sense out of it?"

"I haven't read much. They're both really long. But yes, if I use the little pencil thing tucked into the spine there, I can scroll down." She starts to tug the stylus out of the binding. "I don't think it will work for you, since you can't use the CHRONOS key."

It doesn't. She tries a few more times and tosses me the diary. "I suppose you'll have to read it to me, then."

"Like I said, it's long." I flip through the pages, about fifty in total. "Each of these pages holds a lot of data."

"Well, then, I guess you'll have to stay the night, won't you, dear?"

"Jack will worry if I'm not back."

"I thought you said he was just a friend."

"Friends can't worry about each other?" I can tell from her smile that my blush has given her the information she was looking for, even though I'm not sure it's fair at this point to say what we have *is* more than just a friendship.

"And Jack doesn't actually have to worry. You apparently have a time-travel device. I think you can figure out how to get home on time and still keep your old gran company for a few hours."

So Nora and I both spend the evening with our grandmothers, in a sense. Mars curls up in her lap, and Mercury curls up in mine.

It's an odd role reversal. I remember many nights spent sipping chocolate in front of this fireplace while Nora or my dad read to me as a child. My mother was always more practical, arguing that I would learn to read more quickly if I read along with the narration myself. But then she never was particularly keen on reading. There just weren't all that many books from her childhood that she was eager to share with me. Nora had dozens of favorites, though, and when we visited, she'd pull me into her lap each night for story time to share one of her treasures.

And now I'm reading to her.

Judging from the glimpses of her face that I catch when I look up between sections and her occasional nod or slight chuckle, I think Nora gets more out of the diary than I do. Perhaps she's hearing her grandmother in the words. To me, the diary feels cryptic. It's clear that Kate kept it for her own remembrance, rather than as something she intended to pass down for posterity. Otherwise, she'd have spent a bit more time explaining things. Most of the entries were made when she was in her early to midthirties, during her two pregnancies and the years that she was raising James and his older brother, Harry. There were occasional anecdotes about family life, but most of the diary was devoted to national and international events. She seemed to hold an almost-personal grudge against Paula Patterson, who was the first Cyrist (and first female) president. She worried quite a lot about someone named Simon. She also mentioned a woman named June a few times. *Probably* not the same person I met in 1906, but . . .

While most of the entries are written out, there are several links that look like video or audio files. The clear disk is still in the hollow behind my ear, but there's no point playing them now, since Nora wouldn't be able to hear or see them. I make a mental note to check them out later, although I'm a little hesitant after seeing that last video of Katherine Shaw.

After several hours, we reach the point where Nora's eyes are drooping and my voice is raspy from reading aloud too long. We're nowhere near finished—I flipped the page only four times—but Nora puts her teacup on the sofa table and reaches out her hand for the diary.

"That's enough for now. Thank you, Madi. This answered a lot of questions."

"Really?" I hand her the book. "I didn't think that anything in here was exactly a smoking gun. She doesn't say anything about time travel, and it's *possible* that she was able to operate the diary, but not the key. Even in Katherine Shaw's case, the fact that her name is in a diary isn't proof of anything. As you noted with the *History of CHRONOS*, this could just be some alternate-history series that your father was working on. Maybe he just used family names for the hell of it."

I don't believe a word of this, of course, but I know Nora well enough to realize that playing devil's advocate is often the best way to get her to come around to your way of thinking. She likes to argue. My grandfather often said that she would have made an excellent barrister.

"No," Nora says, running one finger across the front of the diary. "My father didn't write this. I suppose it's possible that he entered the information into the diary itself, but I could hear her voice coming through as you read. Those are her words. And while she didn't come out and say anything like *My name is Kate Pierce-Keller and I'm a time traveler*, it's there if you read between the lines."

This surprises me a bit, because I really didn't get that sense from the diary at all.

Nora smiles at my expression. "You didn't know her. She was a lovely person, but it always seemed to me that she was haunted by something, driven to fix things for which there were no easy remedies. Or at least, no easy remedies given the frailties of human nature, like greed and tribalism. Grandpa Trey would have been happier if she'd been able to relax a bit more and just enjoy life. I never really understood what caused her to push herself so hard, but after listening to what you read tonight, I think she felt guilty for something that happened. Maybe something she changed that she shouldn't have. Or maybe something she *should* have changed but didn't. Or couldn't. The young woman who wrote those words had a lot of regrets. And more than a little anger. She still did later in life, when I knew her, but somewhere along the way, she found a measure of serenity to balance things out."

I'm really hesitant to ask the next question, because Nora herself is fairly serene right now and mentioning her father will almost certainly shatter that tranquility. But I need to know.

"Do you think your father could use the key? It would explain a lot about the . . . books. And the trial."

Nora closes her eyes and is quiet for so long that I'm almost certain she's fallen asleep. But then she shakes her head slowly. "No. I never saw him with that medallion. And before we had our falling out, we were actually quite close. I would have known." She gets up to carry our teacups to the adjoining kitchen, then stops, looking back at me over her shoulder. "It's possible that his brother could. Of course, they're both dead now, so unless one of them left you an encrypted message in the library—"

"Or unless I went back and asked them."

She gives me a wry smile. "True. But again, speaking as someone who has read many time-travel books in my eight decades of life, isn't that a rather major no-no?"

"It's not like I actually knew either of them. Or they knew me."

"Ah, but if your presence changes anything, even alters the movement of a butterfly's wings a hundred years ago, what might that mean for this timeline?"

"Absolutely nothing, aside from that butterfly becoming a splat on the side of a delivery drone a few seconds earlier than fate intended."

Nora laughs. "You're probably right. But why take the risk?" She sits back on the edge of the sofa and rolls up her sleeve. "Might as well get the blood drawn now, and then we can get some sleep. I made up the bed in your old room. If you play your cards right, Mercury might even bunk with you."

I do, apparently, play my cards right. Mercury is purring contentedly on the pillow next to mine long before I'm able to fall asleep. My mind keeps cycling between the quarrel with my mother and the fact that this device might be able to bring my father back. It's like that old story about the monkey paw, though—I'm pretty sure that any attempt to save his life would carry a curse. Had Nora's grandmother done something like that? Had she saved someone she loved and paid a price? Or was the regret and anger due to the fact that she had the power to save them and didn't act?

I still can't quite fall asleep, so I pick up the diary again and click on one of the videos. A finger moves away from the display, and then Kate Pierce-Keller's face comes into view. She's saying something about the Cyrists and climate change. It's hard to pay attention to the specifics, however, because four odd things hit me almost instantaneously.

The first oddity is that she's whispering. That mystery is quickly solved, however. As she leans back from the camera, I realize that she's trying to avoid waking the little boy who is curled up in her lap. He's maybe two or three years old, clutching a blanket with stars on a dark blue background.

A second weird thing is that Kate and the little boy are sitting in what I have very quickly come to think of as my living room in Bethesda. All of the furniture is different, of course, but I can see one of the two curved stairways that lead up to the second floor over her shoulder.

Third, just as she begins talking, a new link pops up directly beneath the video. Unlike all of the other file links I've seen in the diaries, which contain initials and two date strings, this one is labeled COPIED FROM OTHER-KATE RE: CYRISTS Fort Meyer 040302.

Last, but definitely not least, is how very familiar Kate looks. For some reason, that fact is jumping out at me more than anything else, but that's silly. *Of course* she looks familiar. I've probably seen photographs of her in a family album, and it's perfectly reasonable that there might be a resemblance among family members.

It still nags at me, though, and I stop the video and zoom in. That's when I realize why the resemblance feels strange to me. Kate Pierce-Keller is *Nora's* grandmother. If there's a family resemblance, it should be to Nora or my father. But this woman looks a lot like my mom.

More to the point, she looks almost exactly like my *other* grandmother, Thea Randall. Kate is younger here, and Thea's eyes are blue, not green. But otherwise, the likeness is uncanny. My mom has a framed image of herself taken when she was around seven and Thea is in her thirties. This woman could be Thea's twin.

None of this makes sense. But what Nora said earlier about tracking down my globe-trotting maternal grandmother seems a lot more pressing now.

I click on the link that mentions Other-Kate. It's not a video, as I expected, which is unusual. All of the other links have been multimedia. Instead, it's a text entry. And I soon realize that there's a good reason Kate might have chosen to give it the extra security of nesting it inside a link. While nothing else in the diary has been a smoking gun, this short entry is red-hot.

I read it through a second time, coming back to the final paragraph:

> *While some of the kids taken in by the Koreshans are actually local orphans, this Kiernan guy claims that most of them are, in fact, Prudence's offspring. That's why I need to be careful how I break this news to Katherine. Telling her that the Koreshans really are integrally connected to the Cyrists is the easy part. The part I'm dreading is telling her that her long-lost daughter isn't just helping Saul. She's making him an army of time travelers.*

The name *Prudence* is, of course, familiar. Anyone who has ever known a devout Cyrist has heard them say "Praise Prudence" before their first bite of lunch. But I've never thought of her as an actual person, a person who might be someone's aunt, any more than I've thought of Krishna or Buddha in that way.

I try to tap into Nora's digital assistant to see if I can find images of Kate, but Nora has changed the password. I don't want to wake her, and even though my head is still spinning, my eyes are exhausted. So I turn off the recording and let Mercury's soft purr lull me to sleep.

Nora is awake long before I am, watching a VRE on her ancient headset. When she hears me coming downstairs, she puts it aside, and we take breakfast in the small sunroom that overlooks the seawall. She's in a cheery mood, and I realize that there is one substantial silver lining in this situation for both of us. Even though she has close friends nearby and a more active social life than my own, it's not the same as having family close by. I call pretty regularly, but I've worried about her being on her own so much at her age. Weekly transatlantic flights aren't in my current budget, but with this device, I can pop in for a visit more often.

Assuming, of course, that I don't wind up imprisoned for illegal genetic enhancements.

Between anecdotes about her euchre club and the wine-making class that she's taking at the university, I ask Nora if she has any pictures of Kate.

"I'm sure I do somewhere." She pulls up her wall screen and does a brief search, and then three images appear side by side. They seem to be in chronological order. The first two are family photographs of her with a tall, light-haired man Nora identifies as her grandfather Trey Coleman and two boys—young in the first photo and in their teens in the second. In both of these, she looks much like she did in the video—long, dark curls and vivid green eyes. The third picture shows a woman in her sixties or seventies, with a cloud of silver hair.

"She looks like Thea," I say.

Nora doesn't seem too surprised. "I never met her, since she didn't bother showing up for the wedding. But I told Matthew the first time he brought Mila to meet us that his new girl looked quite a bit like Grandma Kate. He laughed and said she must have made a good impression on him the few times he met her, back when he was too young to really remember."

"I agree that she looks a bit like Mom. But, Nora—that first picture of Kate is almost identical to Thea in her thirties, and, aside from the eyes, that last picture of her could easily be Thea today . . . although I doubt Thea would ever let her hair go white. I'm serious. They could be twins."

Nora frowns. "Well, aside from the fact that one was born in 1999 and the other in—how old is Thea?"

"A few years younger than you. I think she was born in 2060."

"So twins born six decades apart. I can tell from your expression that you don't think this is a coincidence, but I'm not sure what you think it means."

"Neither am I," I admit. "She could be a clone. That was semi-legal for a while."

"True. That would mean Matthew and Mila were what—second cousins? Or third?"

I tally it up mentally. "I don't know what you'd call them if Thea was cloned. It's close to double cousins, but there's not really a term for it. And—" I stop and shake my head. "No."

"What?" Nora asks.

"I was just thinking that Thea could actually *be* Kate. If she was able to use the medallion, I mean. Maybe my grandmother is also *your* grandmother, and that's why she didn't come to the wedding. You'd have recognized her."

Nora's eyes grow wide, and I laugh.

"No. I don't really think Thea and Kate are the same person. Their faces are eerily alike, but there are tiny differences aside from the easily altered eye color. And that probably rules out a clone, too, although I suppose there could be tiny differences due to environmental factors. That's something I'll have to ask Lorena when I see her, although I really wish I was going back with both of the blood samples she requested. But an embryo frozen in 1999 could very easily have been born sixty years later. And . . ."

I pull out the diary and read the Other-Kate entry. "Do you remember Grandma Kate mentioning an Aunt Prudence?" I ask when I reach the end.

"No. But I do remember her using the phrase *praise frickin' Prudence* on more than one occasion when she was annoyed."

I open my mouth to ask her to run an image search, but she's one step ahead of me. The search results that pop up on the wall screen are mostly religious art, and there's a good deal of variation in the artists' renderings. But even without the two photographs of a middle-aged Prudence from the early 2000s, the resemblance is clear.

"That could be Thea," I say. "I mean, if you add a bunch of tattoos and piercings. Even the eyes are the same."

Nora puts the picture of Kate next to the search results. "She could easily have been Kate's sister. Or aunt, I guess. You need to take all of this back to Mila. She must know more than she's letting on."

I think back to my mom, curled almost in a fetal position in her tiny apartment. "She does know more. But it may be a while before she'll admit it."

"Well, maybe she'll be more reasonable in a few days."

I nod, even though I doubt it.

"Did your grandmother ever mention her grandfather? The one who . . ." I trail off, because I'm not sure how to phrase the rest. "Katherine Shaw's partner."

Nora thinks for a moment, then shakes her head. "I don't think he was in the picture. Katherine Shaw remarried at some point. Maybe multiple times. I'm sure you can pull up the official records once you're back in Maryland."

"Some of them, maybe."

I fill her in on what I learned from Katherine's diary, toning down the more violent aspects, since I really don't want to upset her. She gives a baffled laugh.

"So, you think my great-grandmother was conceived in 2305?"

"Yes. In the very first few hours of that year, if Katherine's suspicions were correct—she said something about a New Year's Eve party. That's the last bit of information though. I'm hoping I'll learn more from Kate's diary once I dig in a bit."

"Speaking of digging in," Nora says, "your oatmeal is probably cold by now. Do you want me to reheat it?"

It's definitely lukewarm, but I tell her it's fine, and we both focus on our breakfasts. The photos of Thea and Prudence remain on the wall screen, however, reminding me that I definitely need to call my mother or, more likely, pay her another visit soon. And not just to ask about Thea, Prudence, and the Cyrists, but to ask for a copy of the medical report from my father's death. I've never seen it, so I have no clue whether his death could have been forestalled. I'm not at all certain what I'll do if I find out that he could have been saved, but if it wasn't something preventable, then I can put it out of my mind entirely.

My grandmother is watching me when I look up from my breakfast. "You're still thinking about it, aren't you?"

"Thinking about what?"

She rolls her eyes. "Stop it. If you need to use that medallion in order to ensure your future, that's one thing, although even that worries me. It's a bit of a slippery slope, just like when they started the genetic enhancements. A little change here. A little change there. You never know how those little changes are going to interact when you put them all together. It's very easy for the whole thing to snowball. But using that device to purposefully change something that has already happened? That's playing with fire."

"I told you before that I'm not planning to do anything stupid."

Nora holds my gaze for several seconds, and then nods. "Okay, then. I guess I don't have any choice other than to trust you."

Which means that she doesn't entirely trust me.

And that's fair enough. I don't entirely trust myself.

I'd planned to jump straight home after breakfast, but instead I slip back into the bedroom and pull on the 1930s dress. There's really no *reason* for me to blink back to Saint Peter's Church in 1957. It's more that I'm curious, and I need a diversion. Something to take my mind off that niggling temptation to just get it over with, to simply jump back to January of last year and tell an earlier version of myself to get my father to a cardiologist.

A tourist trip with the key is a lousy consolation prize, but it's better than nothing. So, after telling Nora goodbye, I set the key for July 6, 1957. The information I found in my search said that the parade began at two p.m. and the festivities at three. I scroll to two thirty, when everyone's attention should be on the parade, and blink in.

∞

MADI
NEAR LIVERPOOL, UK
JULY 6, 1957

The thorn at the tip of the damn leaf scrapes my cheek again, right below my eye, exactly as it did the last time I used this stable point for 1957. I reach out and snap the leaf off. Whoever set this point must have been taller than I am. The leaf isn't the kind of thing that would be especially annoying at my neck or chest, but it's a little disconcerting that close to my eye. The person who programmed the stable point clearly failed to consider the fact that shrubbery *grows* over time and gardeners aren't always vigilant about trimming back the greenery, especially on the side that faces the building.

While I doubt I'll use this location again, my job in this business we're starting will apparently be to vouch for the safety and accuracy of these stable points. I haven't figured out how to edit or delete them yet, so I simply take two steps back and make a new entry. Maybe

I'll leave both and make a note that this new trolley stop is for short people who don't want their eyes poked by pointy leaves.

The afternoon sky is clear, with just a few puffy clouds, and the air is filled with scents of popcorn, sugar, and automobile exhaust. Off in the distance, I hear music that sounds vaguely like a marching band. I hope the musicians are children still learning to play, because they're bad. *Really* bad.

I stay back a bit, not wanting to be too conspicuous as I approach the crowd gathered along the sidewalk to watch the slow procession of flatbed trucks. Some of the trucks are festooned with colored paper and other decorations, and most have a group of young people sitting on the back, holding signs with the name of a club, school, or church, dutifully waving at the crowd. Farther down the way, a cluster of kids runs along the sidewalk, keeping pace with the parade. One of the boys is wearing a weird hat that looks like an animal hide, with a striped tail hanging down the back.

The sound of the marching band tapers off as the musicians reach the end of the parade route, concluding with a few off-tune squawks. Over the engine noise I hear more music coming from a few trucks back. There's an opening in the crowd, so I move up to the curb as the truck approaches, hoping to catch a glimpse. Six teenage boys with musical instruments—guitars and a drum set—are standing or sitting in kitchen chairs on the open back of the truck. On each side, there's a rope with red and white triangular flags dangling down. The rope stretches diagonally from the top of the truck cab to the rear bumper. Like all of the parade floats, it doesn't really look safe.

I recognize one of the two guys sitting with his back against the cab as John Lennon, one of the two Beatles here today. The other guy, Paul McCartney, apparently shows up later. Lennon is dressed in a plaid shirt, and he and one of the other guys are playing guitar. I wouldn't really call it a performance. It's more like friends goofing around with some random chords as they near the end of the parade route.

There's a muffled *oof* as one of the little kids running along the sidewalk crashes into a portly middle-aged man standing a few people away. Someone says, "Mind where you're going, Davy Crockett," and I get a brief glimpse of the odd fur hat as the man jerks backward, shoving into the two people next to him, who, in turn, shove into me.

My foot slips off the edge of the curb, and I tumble onto the road.

I catch myself with my forearm. My first thought is that I'm going to have a nasty scrape. Then I hear brakes squealing, and my second thought is that a scrape is going to be the very least of my worries. I squeeze my eyes shut and roll toward the sidewalk.

Luckily, the truck isn't going very fast. The driver swerves and misses me by half a meter as the truck comes to a full stop. There's a crash from the back of the truck, and then someone says, "Oh, bloody hell."

I can't see what caused the crashing noise, but it must not be too major, because several people are laughing. "Nice work, Eric!" one of them calls out. "Nearly went arse over tip off the lorry."

A woman reaches down a hand to pull me up. "Are you hurt?"

"Thanks. And no, I'm just scraped a bit." My ankle also twinges, but it holds my weight as I step back onto the sidewalk.

One of the guys on the back of the truck—Eric, I presume—is getting to his feet. John Lennon frowns, rubbing the back of his head, and another member of the band leans down to pick up the snare drum that toppled over.

"Could have been far worse," the woman tells me. "You were lucky."

The crowd begins to drift to the back of the churchyard. I wander around for a few minutes, reading the gravestones. Only one of the stones is still standing in 2136. I don't know if they relocated the bodies or just did away with the other headstones, but they left the one bearing the name of Eleanor Rigby. There's also a plaque on the building in my time, explaining that the headstone was the inspiration for one of Lennon and McCartney's songs.

My ankle is still throbbing, so I take a seat on the low garden wall to listen when the Quarry Men begin to play. The first song has a bunch of doo-wahs and doobies, and while they're not bad for a bunch of sixteen-year-olds, I'm not all that impressed. Maybe it would be more enjoyable if I wasn't alone, or if I had more knowledge about this subject and era, or even if I had heard more than one or two of the songs by the band—not this band, but the famous one that Lennon will eventually form. The historian who owned this key was probably as thoroughly into music history as Katherine Shaw was into that World's Fair she visited or the various social movements she wrote about in the diary. He or she probably found this jump fascinating. But my ankle and arm are both sore, and most of the fun has gone out of this excursion.

The one odd thing that catches my eye is a flash of orange light in the small group of people clustered near the wall on the opposite side of the churchyard. It's almost certainly a reflection from the sun. My view of the group is mostly obstructed by the crowd, but it's four adults and a child. Not a *small* child, but a boy of maybe eleven or twelve, with dark hair and eyes. He's paying attention to something else—probably the band—when I first look their direction, but he must feel my eyes on him because he meets my stare and holds it, clearly annoyed.

I look away, and when the song is over, I limp back to the stable point, since it's one spot I already know has decent cover for me to blink out. I'm maybe a meter away from the hedge when something hits me. Not something I can see, but it has an intense physical impact. I feel a gut-wrenching blow and barely manage to stagger behind the holly bush. Leaning against the bricks, I slide down to the ground and focus on my breathing, trying to fight off waves of nausea and dizziness. I sit there clutching my knees to my chest, relieved that I made it somewhere out of view of the crowd.

The feeling gradually subsides, and I realize it was probably a delayed shock reaction from nearly getting hit by the truck. I've had anxiety attacks in the past. They were fairly frequent after Dad died and our economic situation bottomed out. But this was by far the most vicious, and it seemed to hit me out of nowhere. I've never had a panic attack that literally drove me to the ground.

What scares me most, however, isn't the physical reaction, but the thoughts running through my head. I can't quite shake the feeling that none of this is real. My mother wasn't at her flat. She's moved away. So has Nora. Both the flat in London and Nora's cottage in Bray were vacant. I called but couldn't find them.

It's like the dreams I had right after my dad died. The dreams were so vivid, like I was awake and going about some mundane task, but I also knew I was asleep. If I could only scream, I thought, someone would hear me. They'd help me. I'd wake up. But each time I opened my mouth, no sound came out. I'd thrash about, trying to wake up. Jarvis pegged them as false awakenings, when I put him in psychotherapy mode. He said they were possibly caused by anxiety and also that they were fairly typical abandonment dreams, not unusual after the death of someone close.

I've never had one of those dreams while awake, though. Maybe the feeling was triggered by the panic attack?

When I finally calm down enough to steady my hands, I take out the CHRONOS key so I can go home. But my mind is very much torn between two different meanings of that word. There's my physical home, the house in Bethesda, in 2136, where Jack and Alex are waiting for me to return. But another voice in my head says that *home* isn't a place, but a *time*. A time when my father was alive, the family was solvent, and I had no clue that I was a genetically enhanced time traveler.

The voice also reminds me that I have the tool in my hands that could—just maybe—make *home* exist again.

I pull up the stable point I created in Nora's sitting room and scroll back almost two years to Christmas Eve 2134. The last normal Christmas, the last time I was really and truly *home*. Through the key, I see the sofa where Nora sat last night as we read her grandmother's diary, except there's a red-and-green knitted blanket draped over the back. Holidays at Nora's are an odd pastiche of customs from her childhood in the US and local traditions from my grandfather's family. For as long as I can remember, she always had the place decorated when we arrived, except for the stockings and the last small box of ornaments, the special ones that she saved for me and my dad to add to the tree. Mom has never really understood the hoopla over Christmas—it just isn't something her family did—and she clearly thinks Nora goes way overboard with the cookies and the lights and the quaint gumdrop tree on the kitchen counter. So hanging those last ornaments was our special tradition, just me and Dad.

I'd planned to keep scanning through until I found a time when Matthew Grace was alone in the front room. All I'd need is a few seconds. Just long enough to tell him to make an appointment with a cardiologist. But I get pulled into the memory when I see him walk into the room with the box. I'm a few steps behind him, laughing about something I wish I could remember now as I put the tray of eggnog and cookies on the tea table. Once again, I wonder why there's no sound on this device. It can transport me through time and across the damn ocean, and it can't let me hear his voice again?

But I don't really need the sound. I remember this conversation vividly. I'd recently broken up with David, the guy I'd been dating for several years, and my father was a little surprised that I was in such good spirits. I admitted that the split had been kind of a relief. David had been with me at Nora's the previous year, and it hadn't felt right. He didn't fit. And even though David never said anything out loud, I had the sense he was smirking at the Grace family traditions. I really liked David most of the time, maybe even loved him a bit, but I'd known then that he would never be part of *home*. And I think maybe David knew it, too. It had just taken us almost a year to break the habit of being a couple, mostly because we both hated doing things alone.

I was facing the tree as I talked to my dad, searching for the perfect spot to hang a tiny silver bell, so I never saw the shadow cross my father's face as I talked about the breakup. But I see it now through the key. Dad was never all that crazy about David—something I knew, even though he'd never have admitted it—so it's not that he was sad about us ending things. It's something else that's bothering him, and it bugs me that I don't know what. That I can't make the me who is scanning the tree for a bare spot turn around and ask him what's wrong.

By the time the earlier version of me looks back at him, the shadow is gone. All I see is his warm smile.

I watch now, the words in my memory syncing with the image of him saying, "You're a smart girl, Max. Hold out for someone who makes you happy. There are worse things than being a little bit lonely."

My dad would have liked Jack. And even though it's too soon to know for certain, I think Jack would have fit at Nora's. I think he could eventually be part of that feeling called *home*.

And it's that thought that gives me the strength to look away from my dad standing there next to the tree with the box of our Christmas treasures. I squeeze my eyes shut and feel a few stray tears coursing down my cheeks. Then I pull up the stable point in the library back in Bethesda. I pan around until I see Jack, sitting next to the computer where Alex is working.

That's odd. He was in another chair when I blinked out, closer to the stable point. It's been about thirty-six hours for me, but only a few seconds have passed for him. He should still be in the chair looking at the stable point. Giving me that slightly nervous smile.

I scroll back and see the exact moment when he leaves the chair. It's almost instantaneous after I jump out. He and Alex both startle and then hurry toward the desk in the far corner of the room.

Each time I've used the key, when I've looked back at the stable point, the scene has always been the same as when I left. The only exception is when I doubled back to the beach at Estero to retrieve my shoes.

And that almost certainly means something has changed.

THE *NEW YORK DAILY INTREPID* (MARCH 7, 1990)

Twenty-Fifth Anniversary of "Bloody Sunday" Commemorated in Selma

(Montgomery, Ala.) Twenty-five years ago today, a group of nearly six hundred civil rights activists gathered for a protest march across the Edmund Pettus Bridge, named after a former US senator and Grand Dragon of the Alabama Ku Klux Klan in the late 1800s. The 1965 march was organized by Dr. King's Southern Christian Leadership Conference, whose members had come to Dallas County to aid local groups in voter registration. Efforts to organize were blocked by local courts and law enforcement. Prior to the march, police raided a group at a rally in a neighboring town, shooting a black teen, Jimmie Lee Jackson, who was attempting to protect his mother from the onslaught.

Several journalists covering the march were also severely beaten.

Leaders of the SCLC were determined to undertake a peaceful march from Selma to Montgomery to protest the escalating violence against African Americans and their continued disenfranchisement. Alabama Governor George C. Wallace banned the march, but organizers were not deterred. At the end of the bridge, they were met by the local sheriff and state troopers, some on horseback, armed with tear gas and billy clubs.

Marchers had to retreat. Several claimed that the armed police had attempted to force them over the side of the bridge into the Alabama River.

Images of the violence prompted people from around the nation to travel to Selma in protest. Many of them were ministers, heeding a call by Dr. Martin Luther King Jr., the leader of the SCLC. On March 9th, King attempted to lead 1,500 marchers across the bridge, but they were forced to turn back. The only concession made was that the state troopers allowed them to kneel and pray before retreating.

James Reeb, one of three Unitarian ministers who joined the second march, was beaten by a mob of angry white men after eating at an integrated diner in the town. Reeb's death two days later prompted action by President Lyndon B. Johnson, who said at a press conference on March 13th, "What happened in Selma was an American tragedy. The blows that were received, the blood that was shed, the life of the good man that was lost, must strengthen the determination of each of us to bring full and equal and exact justice to all of our people."

Johnson also expressed the belief that Gov. Wallace would work with him in protecting the right of the marchers to peacefully protest. When Wallace reneged on their agreement, Johnson nationalized the Alabama National Guard, and sent several thousand federal troops and law enforcement officers to Selma as peacekeepers.

On March 15th, Johnson stood before Congress to speak on the proposed Voting Rights Act, saying, "Their cause must be our cause, too. Because it is not just Negroes, but really it is all of us, who must overcome the crippling legacy of bigotry and injustice. And we shall overcome."

Several days later, the final march from Selma began, with the protection of state and federal troops. The numbers waxed and waned, but around ten thousand arrived in Montgomery on March 24th, camping at Catholic mission City of St. Jude. Dozens of celebrities, including Harry Belafonte, Sammy Davis Jr., Joan Baez, and the folk trio Peter, Paul, and Mary, held a concert that evening on the church grounds. The next morning, approximately twenty-five thousand joined the last leg of the march to the Alabama State Capitol.

One of the people in attendance was an SCLC volunteer, Viola Liuzzo, who was murdered by members of the Ku Klux Klan while driving marchers back to Selma.

The Voting Rights Act passed the US Senate in May by a vote of 77–19. It would go on to be passed in the House in July, and was eventually signed into law on August 6, 1965, with Dr. King and other SCLC leaders in attendance.

∞17∞

Angelo walks in a few minutes before nine a.m. He's carrying the small leather satchel I remember seeing him with back when he was an instructor. His normally ruddy skin is pale, and he looks much more frazzled than he did when he met me in the jump room yesterday. Or, yesterday for *me*, at least. All of that will happen a little over an hour from now for him, which means he's already battling double memories. That will be the case for the next few hours, at a minimum. A small part of Angelo's brain is no doubt telling him that he started out the day in his office, sipping a cup of that truly awful-smelling herbal tea he likes and chomping on his morning bagel while reading through jump reports and proposals. The other part is reeling from arriving at the office to find a message from himself, telling him that a level-five event is about to upend the entire organization, not to mention the timeline, if we don't find a way to prevent it.

Even though Angelo is only in his late fifties, he's moving like an old man right now, and it's unnerving to see him like this. For most of us who finished training in the past few years, Angelo is like a second father. We start classroom training at age ten, and we don't see our families much after the first year. By the fourth year, we have less in common with them than we do with the instructors here at CHRONOS. It's not just a matter of similar interests, but also similar language and customs. So much of our training is practical, making sure that we can actually fit into the eras and places we visit without disrupting anything. Before Angelo took over as jump coordinator, he was an instructor and residence-hall adviser. He was the man with the answers, the one who could usually fix whatever problem you brought to him or, more often, give you solid advice on how to fix it yourself. But given that Angelo is well past the age where he can use the CHRONOS key, he has to rely on us to fix this problem. And it's one vicious bear of a problem.

He puts the satchel on the edge of one of the bunks and sits down next to it. "So give me some good news." The look on his face tells me that he already suspects we don't *have* good news.

Over the past twenty-three hours, Rich, Katherine, and I have been sleeping in shifts, while the other two tweak the parameters of the simulation and personally comb through every news article, video, or photograph that we can find concerning the three events from both the old timeline and the new. The goal is to pinpoint a single change that could feasibly have caused a time shift that killed over thirty-two thousand people and erased or altered millions more. Truthfully, I'd argue that the death-toll statistic should be much higher, because one of the more significant changes to the timeline is the fact that the Genetics War starts a year earlier, but anything more than twenty years out from the dates of those first four significant early deaths in the 1960s isn't calculated into the total.

After forty-two separate simulation runs, we still don't have anything definitive. Only one thing stood out, and it's a long shot. We're looking for answers, and it's possible that my mind is making a connection that doesn't actually exist. But there are now two additional people in the photograph of the Klansmen protesting outside the

Coliseum. The extra men are standing off to one side, near a chain-link fence. One of them is facing the camera. He's short and over-weight, and when the simulator enhanced the resolution, I discovered that he looks a lot like Lenny Phelps, from the South Carolina Klan. I can't see his companion's face, but he's taller. Thinner, too. It could very easily be Scoggin.

"None of the simulations were able to isolate a change that would have caused all four early deaths," Rich tells Angelo. "We can say with sixty-four percent certainty that it involves a racial hate group called the Ku Klux Klan. The thing that's throwing the calculations off is the attack in March of 1965, since that's *before* Tyson's jump to the graduation speech by Dr. King."

"What about one of the other historians who went out at the same time?" Angelo asks. "Did you factor in their dates and locations?"

Rich nods. "We did—all eleven of them. The closest jumps prior to that were a 1933 jump to Germany by Wallace Moehler to observe the Reichstag fire, and a 1924 jump to Paris by Paddy Dunne, to observe Ireland's first team in the Olympics. Neither of those seemed like logical candidates to us, and the simulator seemed to agree."

"Before that," Katherine says, "we have Saul and Grant's jump to 1911 Atlanta, Georgia. Grant is doing some research that's race related, but Saul is just there for some religious conference looking at evolving views on . . . predestination, I think? It's closer in loca-tion, but further back in time. And the other seven jumps were, like Tyson's, after the events."

"Do you need more time? There's another isolation unit. I can send you back twenty-four additional hours." Angelo looks a little queasy at the prospect. It wouldn't be a big deal for us, as long as we didn't cross our own paths, because we wouldn't be changing anything we did over the past twenty-four hours. Our earlier selves would just be working away in here, oblivious to the fact that there are duplicates working in the unit next door. But that would mean not just double, but triple memories for Angelo, since he's not time traveling, but rather *un*doing things he did before.

"I don't think that will help," Rich says.

Angelo heaves a sigh of relief. "Good. Double memories suck. Triple memories, though? They will flatten you."

"We tried various combinations of changes on those dates and locations," I tell him. "The death of Dr. King alone has a miniscule chance of extending the Vietnam War. It's only when you add in Lennon that it goes up into double digits—a twenty-seven percent chance. We had to drop the deaths at the 1965 rally in Montgomery. Since those were *before* my jump, it caused the simulation to throw an error. The system says the chances of anything I did in Ohio resulting in Lennon's death are . . ." I glance over at the display. "Well, you can see it there. A tiny fraction of one percent."

"And that's only when we factored in this." Rich taps the display to pull up the picture of the seven men, six hooded men and one in a business suit, standing outside Mid-South Coliseum. He points toward the two guys in the periphery of the picture. The shorter and chubbier of the two is in typical Klan garb, but the taller man is dressed in a suit. "Tyson thinks the one facing the camera is a man named Lendell Phelps. He's with the klavern that had the big Beatles bonfire we visited on our first leg of this project."

"I can't tell for certain," I say. "But they weren't in the original photo that was taken, and it looks like him. The guy in the suit standing next to him, the one with his back to the camera, could easily be Scoggin, the South Carolina Klan leader. I don't know why he's not wearing his regalia, but it could be because the green robe would stand out a bit with all of the others in white. And maybe they don't want anyone to know that one of the leaders is participating."

Angelo rubs his eyes. "So do we start with the attack on Lennon?"

"We don't have full consensus on that," Rich says, giving me a slightly annoyed look. "My view is that if we find out who killed

Lennon, and stop it, that *should* prevent the time shift, or at least minimize it. Then we can work our way backward and stop the other deaths. But Tyson thinks we should start with Baldwin and Travers."

I pull up an image of the field where the attack in Montgomery happened. "Part of my reasoning is the crowd size and spacing. Estimates say there were between two thousand and ten thousand people camped out with the Selma march. At the high end, that's not significantly different from the twelve thousand at Mid-South Coliseum to see the Beatles, but they're more spread out. Plus, with Baldwin and Travers, we know with a reasonable degree of certainty where the shots came from, based on witness accounts. There are only about a dozen buildings where the shooter could have been hiding. It will be a lot easier to isolate the location than trying to figure out where a shot is coming from inside a crowded auditorium. But Rich is right that if all of these are connected to the Klan, we might give them advance warning. Working backward means they can't see us coming."

Angelo sighs. "My inclination is to start with the first event. How well coordinated are the actions of the Klan in 1965? I mean, do you think this is something that would have been planned from the top?"

"United Klans of America, the group I was researching, was *not* the only Klan operating in those states at that time. There were a number of offshoot groups, and from what I've heard they're barely organized at all. The United Klans branches were fairly well coordinated in terms of overall strategy. But they usually picked targets of opportunity."

"You have two leaders of the South Carolina Klan at a protest in Tennessee," Angelo says. "Assuming that's them in the photo. That seems pretty coordinated."

"Some things were planned in advance, but most were spur of the moment, like the killing of Viola Liuz—" I stop and go back over to the computer.

"Who?" Katherine asks.

"Viola Liuzzo," I say as I enter the name. "A white woman from up north who volunteered with the Southern Christian Leadership Conference. Killed by the Klan the very next night, after the march was over and they were ferrying people back to Selma. The black kid who was in the car with her played dead. I can't remember his name, but he was only nineteen. He was covered with her blood, so they assumed they'd killed him, too."

Rich looks up at the display. "Not in this timeline. She lived to be ninety-three. But . . . she doesn't show up as a significant alteration."

"Which is weird. They were driving back to Montgomery to pick up another carload of people when some Klansmen chased her off the road and shot her. One of the men in the car was an FBI informant. There was a lot of bad press for the FBI, but the guy's testimony is what resulted in the other three being convicted. That's the case that put the spotlight on the Klan. A key reason Scoggin and several of the others would eventually spend a year in jail for contempt of Congress. This was the first time a white female civil rights activist had been killed. Some of the pictures the newspapers used weren't recent, and Liuzzo actually looked a little like Katherine when she was younger. The photos showed a blond, petite woman, standing next to her young children. And given the prevailing racist views of the time, her image on the news galvanized public opinion in a way that the killing of a black woman probably wouldn't have. It pushed the government to crack down. A lot of people believed her death was the reason the Voting Rights Act passed, so yeah, she was definitely significant."

Rich switches back to the previous display, with the pictures of the five people killed, and points to Mary Travers. Not petite, but very pretty, with long blond hair and bangs. "I'm guessing she became the rallying point, instead."

"And maybe these two, as well." Katherine points to two of the others killed. "Also blond women. Which is odd, given that there were far more African Americans in the crowd than whites."

"So the Liuzzo woman survives because they killed five people the day before," Rich says. "I guess they decided a little caution was in order the next night."

"And if we stop them on the 24th, they'll still be in a killing mood when they see her driving back from Selma." I try to keep the bitterness out of my voice, but it's no use. Liuzzo had five kids, one of them only six years old when her mother was killed.

"Hers is a necessary death, though," Angelo says firmly, and unnecessarily. "You can't stop it."

"I *know* that. Someone apparently has to be the sacrifice that wakes up the middle-class suburbanites. And I'll take one death over five any day of the week. Doesn't mean I have to like the idea of some dumb gox putting a bullet in her head."

Angelo gives me a little nod of admission. "Fair enough. Back to the issue of the itinerary, though. There's only one of these attacks where, at least to my mind, there's much doubt that the Klan was involved, and that's the Beatles concert. I mean, it's *probably* the Klan, but we don't know that for certain. The person who eventually shot this Lennon guy wasn't connected to the organization, so . . . it could just be a random lunatic."

I'm less certain on that point. "The same could be said for the attack on the Selma marchers. Someone who lived in the area might have just decided to engage in some lethal target practice."

"True," Angelo says. "But both are directly connected to the civil rights movement and to Dr. King, so that seems like a stretch. Basically, these first two jumps are intelligence gathering. We need to plan our steps carefully. Set up a base of operations in Memphis 1966 and find out whether that killing is connected to the Klan. Then *one* of you report back and let me know what you've learned. Same thing for Montgomery, although we're going to need to be extra cautious there. Three historians from previous cohorts researched the events surrounding the Selma march. Two of them—William Burke and Mary Margolis—will be with the marchers when they arrive in Montgomery."

Rich gives him a concerned look. "The changes could trigger some major double memories for them."

"It would if they were still alive. They were with the first and second cohorts. But they'll be in the crowd, so you need to avoid interaction. I'll send images of them so you'll know to steer clear. The more pertinent problem is Abel Waters. He did two jumps connected to the Selma march about twelve years back. One jump was actually *in* Selma, investigating the kid who was shot by the police. The other jump was a day trip, to witness the speech when they finally reach the Alabama State Capitol. That's the only reason he's not going with the three of you, or, more likely, instead of you. Having a twelve-year overlap of memories . . ." He shakes his head. "It's going to be bad enough for Tyson when it's a couple of days. That's why I say we save the Antioch jump for last, and you need to keep toward the periphery. I'm *really* hoping when you get back there you don't see those five CHRONOS keys in the crowd waiting for the shooting to start. They complicate the hell out of things. But either way, we do whatever we have to do to stop those four deaths."

"Eight deaths," I say. "There are *eight* total. Two at Antioch, five in Montgomery, and then John Lennon in Memphis."

Angelo nods. "But only four that seem to have had any effect on the timeline. If you stop those four deaths, you'll likely save the others, too, but those four are your priority."

"Exactly *how* are we supposed to stop them?" Katherine asks. "Leaving aside the possibility of other CHRONOS agents in the crowd, the Klan members are using bombs and rifles. I don't think they're going to respond well to us showing up and politely asking them to change their plans."

"We won't be asking politely." Angelo reaches into his bag and pulls out three wristwatches. Katherine's has a thin gold band, and the other two are black leather. Mine says *Timex* across the front, just below the notch for twelve o'clock. "Pull out the button on the side. The one you're supposed to use to wind it. Point at your target, then push the button back in."

"And it does what?" Katherine gives her watch a wary look.

"It sends a short signal that will stun the person you're pointing it at. Should last five minutes at the very most. Enough time for you to disarm and bind someone. Just be aware that it's not precise. There will be some peripheral fallout."

"Define *peripheral*," Rich says.

"Anyone within twenty meters or so. The original purpose was to disorient witnesses during an extraction, so precision wasn't really a priority for the design. The CHRONOS field blocks it, so you'll be fine, but using it in a crowd could be problematic."

"If the field blocks the signal, that means it won't work on those people I saw in Ohio," I say.

"You're probably right. But this will." Angelo pulls something else from the bag. Katherine and Rich both recoil instantly, and even Angelo doesn't look too happy about holding it.

"I'm not using that," Richard says. "I don't have any training."

"You're right." Angelo hands the pistol to me. "The gun is for Tyson, who *has* been trained. And it is a weapon of absolute last resort. Shoot to wound. If *possible*."

I take the pistol, which I've held many times before. It's one of the two weapons I used during my field training with Glen, along with a deer rifle. The system in the klavern wasn't exactly like earning Boy Scout badges, but there were certain things they expected anyone around them to be fairly adept at. In the Pitt County klavern, anyone who showed up who didn't know how to shoot would have been instantly suspect. Most of the members had been hunting and doing target practice since they were little kids. It wasn't at all unusual for a father to start teaching his sons to shoot before they started school. Most of the guys in the Pitt County Klan had been hunting together since they were, in the parlance of the day, knee-high to a grasshopper. We weren't exactly newcomers—or "aliens," in Klanspeak—since Glen transferred in from another branch of United Klans of America, located in Birmingham, Alabama, where he'd been studying the Sixteenth Street Church bombing. He came to Pitt County in 1964 with an actual letter of reference from "Dynamite Bob" Chambliss, and later that year, he vouched for me as his nephew. Bob Chambliss and the others connected to the Birmingham bombing were legendary in Klan circles, so we were accepted pretty quickly. But we still weren't local, so we had to prove ourselves in some ways. We took part in regular training drills, learned how to construct a rudimentary bomb, and even joined them on a few hunting trips. The fact that I was able to bag an eight-point buck on our first outing went a long way toward proving my bona fides.

So, yeah. I know how to use a gun. And thanks to enhanced reflexes and perfect eyesight, I was easily the best shot in our klavern, at least after Glen left. I'd always miss one or two on purpose, though. You don't want to draw too much attention to yourself when you're in the field.

Angelo has read all of my reports. So when he tells me to *shoot to wound*, he knows that my accuracy is such that I can absolutely choose to wound rather than kill. Those last two words—*if possible*—mean something else entirely. He's asking for a judgment call.

Shooting tin cans, paper targets, and even deer isn't the same thing as shooting a person, though. There has never been any reason for me to take a stand on that issue, to draw my own moral line in the sand, because the oversight committee would have a collective aneurysm at the mere thought of a CHRONOS agent using a weapon against a person during a field exercise. Glen and I weren't even allowed to be physically present at any event where the Klan used violence. And moral concerns aside, wounding or killing someone of little historical importance in the mid-1960s probably wouldn't cause the sort of rift that we're seeing right now, but it would definitely cause a few ripples.

Are extraction teams usually armed, though? It's not something I've ever thought about, and Katherine's story about the rumored killings in that French village comes rushing back. I definitely want to know the answer to that question now, given my worry about Toni and her family, but asking seems like a very bad idea. It might lead the conversation down paths I'd rather not travel.

So I nod, and pocket the gun. "I take it I should *dress* accordingly?"

He clearly picks up on the wry note in my question. A white man carrying a gun isn't a problem during most of the twentieth century. For a black man, on the other hand, carrying a gun might not be a wise move. It isn't just a situation where the authorities might shoot first and ask questions later. In 1966 Memphis, there's a damn good chance they might shoot if they so much as suspect you are armed and never bother to ask any questions at all.

"Yeah," Angelo says. "You'll have a security pass for all three events. Rich and Katherine will have press credentials. I'm thinking you go in the day before to get set up and check things out. Get acquainted with the situation. Tyson can touch base with local Klan leaders. Maybe call Glen and see if he has any contacts in the area, since he did a trip to Memphis during this era a while back. But . . . be discreet, okay?"

I nod. Contacting Glen was already on my list of things to do, but I was holding off until just before we left, since it's likely to trigger a double memory for him.

"We need to get this right the first time if at all possible, because . . ." Angelo shrugs. He doesn't really need to finish the sentence. We all know the drill. Going back in at the same location and time period carries the risk of crossing our own paths, and then we'll also be sorting through double memories. "Set a lot of stable points so that if we *do* need to send you back in, you can observe the area and make sure we keep any overlap to a minimum. I will also be instructing Aaron to modify the security settings, in case you can't get back to a stable point. You'll be cleared for jumps back to here from any local point you set, but, again, please try to be discreet about it."

I exchange a look with Rich and Katherine. Judging from their expressions, they didn't know that was possible, either.

"That is *strictly* confidential," Angelo says sternly, looking at each of us in turn, although his eyes linger a bit longer on Katherine. "I didn't clear this with the board, because we're trying to affect as few people as possible, and I'm not even sure they *would* clear it. Treat it as an emergency exit only, because I may have to justify any deviations from standard procedure. And none of this goes beyond the four of us and Aaron. Not even to other historians, or romantic partners. Are we understood?"

We all agree, including Katherine, although she looks a little taken aback by the last stipulation.

"Okay, then," Angelo says. "Any questions?"

Rich says, "I have one. What about the other CHRONOS keys Tyce spotted in 1965? If there were observers around for that event, I'm guessing they'll be at this one, too."

"Avoid them just like the ones from the earlier cohort," Angelo says, but I can tell from his voice that he's winging this. "I'll have costuming give you something to shield the light from your keys, so they shouldn't be able to spot you. And if you can't avoid them . . ."
His eyes shift to me.

"You're kidding?"

"Tyson, it won't matter. I don't know why those people are there, but I can promise you that they aren't CHRONOS agents from our future. If we don't fix this, the government will shut us down and there won't be any CHRONOS agents at all. They may well shut us down anyway. I guess it's *possible* that someone might eventually get hold of the technology for private commercial use. But if so, it's not the CHRONOS we know. We wouldn't allow a kid there. And we wouldn't be simply standing there watching people get murdered."

"Really?" I say. "*Really?* Because at least half the agents I know have done precisely that. How many have made a jump to Ford's Theatre the night Lincoln was killed? Timothy and Evelyn just filed a jump plan for the Kennedy assassination, and they're far from the first. Dealey Plaza probably has a dozen agents in the crowd by now. Moehler went back to view the assassination of Franz Ferdinand, and I doubt he was the first, either. Glen was embedded in the local branch of an organization that killed those four little girls in Birmingham. And none of them ever lifted a finger to stop those murders."

Angelo seems taken aback by my tone. For that matter, so do Rich and Katherine.

"But that's . . . different," Katherine says. "That's *history*. We can't change it without screwing things up, without ending up in exactly the kind of situation we're in right now."

"Yeah, well, maybe this is *their* history. Did you ever think of that? My point is that we've simply observed things that are morally wrong on many occasions. And not just on a small scale. Slavery, war, genocide. And I don't think any of us approved of those things. So we can't discount the possibility that those people are from a future cohort. Maybe they're trying to figure out how we screwed up the situation so badly."

Angelo stares down at his shoes for a moment, and then looks up, meeting my eyes squarely. "Valid point. But if they try to stop what you're doing—if they *interfere* with history—then you'll know, won't you? Rich is officially in charge on this jump, and Katherine is your senior as well, but ultimately, it's your call because you're the one who has to pull the trigger. Use your judgment. And be careful, okay? All of you."

Then he leaves, possibly because he can see that I'm not entirely happy to be the one stuck using my *judgment*, and therefore the one who will potentially have someone's death on my conscience. Katherine also doesn't seem particularly pleased. Her mouth twitched downward when Angelo said Rich would be in charge, and I'm guessing it's because she has exactly the same amount of experience. I jot her reaction down in the column *against* Timothy's theory about her personality traits.

The door has barely closed behind Angelo when three people from costuming show up with appropriate 1960s garb for the three of us. They're also carrying overnight bags, which should have identification, cash, and everything else we'll need for a few days in 1966. The two costume techs I recognize both seem disgruntled, probably because they're used to shoving us into one of the Juvapods to take care of basic chores like hair or makeup, and that's not an available option in the isolation units. The time shift clearly hasn't happened for them yet, and I don't know if they're even in a job category where they'll know about it. CHRONOS bureaucracy can be a bit opaque. Right now, they probably assume we've broken some sort of rule that landed us in the tank.

I'm assigned to the third guy, who is super chatty and introduces himself as Jamal. I don't remember seeing him before, and I soon find out that he's fresh out of training. Jamal is still pretty psyched about the new job and asks if I've ever traveled back to prehistoric times, because there's this neat VR game he's playing where you're one of the dinosaurs. He seems a little disappointed when I tell him that there aren't even stable points going that far back. After a jump of that magnitude, a historian would need to rest up before the return trip. No one is crazy enough to want to spend a day or two in an era where a T. rex might decide you look like a tasty lunch.

Once he has my lenses in and my hair tamed with the gloopy stuff, I go into the back room to change into a rather dull black suit. On the plus side, the jacket has a reinforced pocket to hide the light of my CHRONOS key, and there's a shoulder holster for the pistol.

"There are extra lenses in the overnight bag," Jamal says when I come back into the room. "You might want to carry a pack in your pocket, though. Just in case."

"You look like a cop," Rich says, glancing over at me.

"He's security," Jamal says, a little defensively. "That's what he's supposed to look like. We had a photograph from the event."

"Rich is joking," I say.

Katherine looks at me out of the corner of her eye as her costume tech sprays a toxic-smelling vapor cloud onto her hair. Then the three pack up their gear.

"He's right," Katherine says after they're gone. "You *do* look like a cop. Isn't that going to be a problem if you need to get information from the Klan guys who are protesting out front?"

Richard snorts. "This is Memphis in the mid-1960s. He's got identification as a security officer, and he knows their passwords and hand signs. If anything, being a cop improves his cover."

I nod. "It's true. Scoggin said some of the security at this specific event were Klan or at least sympathetic to the cause when he was talking to his men at the bonfire."

Katherine glances down at the pockets of my suit jacket, and I realize she's looking for the pistol. I pull the coat back to reveal the shoulder holster.

Her brow furrows. "Do you know how to use that thing?"

"Yes."

"And you think you *can* use it?" she asks. "On an actual person? I saw your expression when you were talking to Angelo about it. You looked a little hesitant."

"Of course, I'm hesitant. The truth is, I'm not entirely certain I can shoot those people with CHRONOS keys if they show up. I definitely couldn't shoot the kid, even just to wound. But those two guys in the photograph outside the Coliseum? If that's Phelps and Scoggin, like I think, then yeah. I can absolutely pull the trigger."

FROM THE DIARY OF KATE PIERCE-KELLER

November 19, 2070

Kiernan Dunne died one hundred years ago today, at the age of ninety-two. That information wasn't in the letter that Other-Kate packed away with the photo album she sent when she returned the three medallions. That letter was written when both of them were still alive.

For the longest time, I didn't check online for their obituaries. I wanted to think of them as still alive, somewhere back in time. But eventually curiosity got the better of me.

I think of him often. Not because I wish things were different. Trey has been the best husband, best father, best friend I could ever have wished for. I love him. I would choose him again, even if there had been no alternate version of me, pregnant with Kiernan's daughter who would grow up to be an artist. That talent definitely didn't come from her mother's gene pool. I can barely draw a stick figure, so I'm sure that's true for any alternate versions of me.

My mind naturally strays to Kiernan, and to Other-Kate, anytime I think about alternate paths. Alternate realities. Is there some other timeline where the Harry Keller I met in Delaware was the father of the two little boys running around by the pond—and they will always be little boys in my mind, even though they'd be middle aged by now, with kids of their own, if that reality exists. Is there some splinter universe where Connor was around to see his grandchildren?

I don't know. I suspect that I will never *know*, and it's hard for me to simply accept it on faith. But I desperately *want* to believe. And I keep looking for evidence to give me some grounds upon which to base that belief.

There's a book in the library called *The Physics of Many Paths* by Stanford Fuller. It's not one of the out-of-timeline editions we rescued from oblivion. I picked it up at a bookstore, even though I never paid much attention to Stan Fuller's program when it aired. The book sat in a corner, untouched, like so many of my impetuous bookstore purchases, until last week when I saw something online about the author coming to town as part of a symposium on the Many-Worlds Interpretation.

Stan Fuller claims that he can see the "Many Paths" that gave him the title for his book and his video series. These realities appear as layers, unclear and chaotic until the paths begin to align. Thirty years ago, Stan Fuller made a good deal of money from that purported ability, although I think that was due more to the skill his brother (and cohost) displayed in picking their cases wisely.

I'm having to work my way through the book slowly, but so far, I'm impressed, even though it never sold many copies. Of course, I am probably far more capable of imagining these different paths, these other realities, than most people, because I've seen them, too.

And most importantly, because I want to believe those two little boys still existed, somewhere, even after I fixed the timeline and made them disappear.

∞18∞

"You felt it, too, didn't you?"

Jack and Alex both jump, almost in unison, and turn to face me.

"Damn," Alex says. "Give us a warning next time. First the alarm goes off, and then you scare the hell out of us."

The amber light behind the glass doors of the bookshelves is pulsing as the computer blares out an odd sound. Part of a song, maybe? *Ba dum. Ba dum. Ba dum ba dum ba dum ba dum.*

"How's she supposed to warn us?" Jack asks. "Normally, we'd still be staring at the stable point."

I nod. "Exactly. Why *aren't* you staring at the stable point? It's only been a few seconds since I left. And can you turn that noise off, please?"

"The noise—and the light show—is why we're over here," Jack says, coming toward me. "Are you okay? You don't *look* okay. What happened to your dress?"

I glance down at my torn sleeve. "Oh. I was pushed in front of a parade float. On accident. This kid in a fur hat—the kind with the animal's tail hanging down the back?"

"A coonskin cap?"

"Yeah, I guess? Anyway, he bumped into a fat man, who stumbled into two other people, who then stumbled into me, and I wound up sprawled on the pavement. The truck was able to stop in time. Although I guess that's obvious. Otherwise I'd have far worse than a torn sleeve, wouldn't I?"

I laugh nervously. He reaches out to hug me just as I sink down into one of the desk chairs. The result is an awkward half hug, with my face pressing into his ribs. Crossed signals again.

Alex is staring at the oldest of the computers, an absolute antique, which I'm amazed to discover actually works. I can't see the display, so I wheel my chair a bit closer. "Before you ask," Alex says, "I didn't touch it. We got this weird queasy feeling. Then the lights in the entire room pulsed a few times, and this thing turned on all by itself."

"I felt the same sensation—the queasiness, I mean—as I was about to blink out. Only it started with a feeling almost like a fist punched me in the stomach. A really big one, too. I thought it was a delayed panic attack from nearly being hit by the truck. What does all of that mean?" I point to the display, where lines of data are flying upward.

"We don't know," Jack says. "The program launched automatically when the computer started. That heading at the top, though . . ."

I look closer and see the word *Anomalies*. Below it, new lines of information keep marching steadily toward the top of the screen. Alex taps the display and drags his finger down several dozen times until we see the beginning of the feed. When he lifts his finger, the scroll begins again, so he swipes once more and keeps his finger pressed against the display so that we can read it.

03241965 James Arthur Baldwin 323534539367372976214409017742 ✓

The next line is *03241965 Mary Allin Travers*, with the name again hyperlinked and followed by the same string of digits and a blue check mark. Below that are three more lines with the same date, different names, and the same long number string, but none of these have the little blue check mark.

"I don't know the other names, but Baldwin was a writer. He dealt with race and social justice issues, back in the 1960s," I tell them. "And I'd have to count those to be sure, but those strings look about the same length as the numbers I see in the last part of a stable-point entry. Montgomery was one of the places I popped into that first day with the key. I remember because the stable point was between these two buildings with curved roofs. I didn't go out into the crowd, but a band was playing. They were singing 'This Little Light of Mine.'" I didn't see anyone or say anything. I just stood there for a moment and listened."

"Can you click one of the links?" Jack asks.

Alex clicks the James Baldwin link, and two news articles pop up, side by side. On the left is a biographical piece—born in 1924, died in 1987. The article on the right begs to differ, however, with a headline that proclaims, "Five Killed at Stars for Freedom Rally in Montgomery."

When Alex clicks the link for Mary Travers, we get a similar result. The biography says that she was a member of a folk group called Peter, Paul, and Mary and lived until 2009. Next to it is the same article about the Stars for Freedom concert, which was held where the participants in the Selma march stopped for the night, in the field of a local church in Montgomery. According to the article, Baldwin, Travers, and three others were killed by a sniper. One other person was wounded. All five fatalities died from a bullet wound to the head.

There are no alternate biographies for the others killed, the ones who didn't warrant the blue check mark. Instead, there's the article listing them as casualties of the attack in Montgomery on the right, and very different obituaries, the last one written in 2015, on the left.

The eighth name on the list has a blue check mark, and it's one that we all recognize.

"Is that an anomaly, though?" Jack asks. "Martin Luther King Jr. actually *was* killed in the 1960s. Or maybe in the 1970s, but definitely around that time."

Alex taps the link. Both show that he was assassinated, but the one on the right shows it happening three years earlier, in 1965, and in Ohio, rather than 1968 Memphis.

These events happened in the US, both in 1965. How could they possibly be the result of my jump to Liverpool in 1957? If the time shift had happened during the jump to Montgomery, that might make sense . . . although, even then, I didn't interact with anyone. I was barely there for thirty seconds. And I was never in Ohio at all.

Of course, I'm now remembering Nora's comment about butterfly wings setting off chain reactions, and I'm a little less certain. Maybe the Coonskin Cap Kid grew up, moved to the US, and became a serial killer. Maybe he developed a taste for murder after nearly getting his first victim at age seven. Or maybe someone did see me on that jump to 1965 and was so freaked out that they went on a shooting rampage. And Dr. King was at the rally in Montgomery.

"This can't be anything Madi did, though," Jack says, echoing my thoughts. "She was in the UK. In the present. Right?"

"Umm. Mostly. I talked to my mother, and to Nora, both in the present. But the parade I mentioned was in 1957. I wanted to check out that stable point while I was there, since we were talking about cataloging them. That was in Liverpool, though. All the way across the ocean."

Alex shrugs. "Normally, I'd say it's really unlikely that something a person did in 1957, especially so far away, could have such a major impact eight years later. But you were in the middle of a time jump, and it looks like something is now broken. And you were at one of these locations, even if it was earlier. Seems like a pretty unlikely coincidence, so I'm going to have to assume something you did caused the rift. Probably."

He lifts his finger from the display. As the names begin scrolling again, one of them jumps out at me, probably because he was the next to earn the blue check mark.

"Whoa. Stop." I reach out and tap the name. As with James Baldwin and Mary Travers, two articles pop up. Both newspaper articles say that John Winston Lennon was killed. One is dated 1966, however, and the other, 1980.

A stream of curses that would put Nora to shame flies from my mouth. Jack and Alex both seem a bit surprised. So does Lorena, who is now standing inside the double door that leads to the hallway.

"What happened?" Lorena asks. "I was getting Yun down for her nap when I got that feeling again. Like before, when Madi created the double." She glances around the room, maybe looking for a duplicate me.

"We're not sure yet," Alex says. "But whatever it was seems to have autolaunched a program on this old computer. Want to get RJ in here, too, so we can all discuss this together?"

"He went back over to Joey's house to grab the stroller. We forgot it was in their storage room. He should be back any minute, though." Lorena peers in over my shoulder. "What's this?"

"Anomalies," Alex says. "Which are probably connected to Madi's jump."

"I think you can go ahead and change that *probably* to *definitely*," I tell him. "This guy was at the town festival. In fact, the truck that nearly hit me was the one carrying him and the other members of his band. A group called the Quarry Men, although that's not the name they were using when the group eventually became famous."

"Was this Lennon guy hurt?" Jack asks.

"No. Not at all. He and the rest of the group were out in the churchyard five minutes later, playing for the crowd. I didn't even speak to him. But it must have changed something, somehow, if he died in August 1966, instead of December 1980."

I really wish one of them would argue against my point. Try to convince me that it's not connected to my trip. But, of course, none of them do, because that would be totally irrational. Jack does give me a sympathetic look, though, like he wishes he *could* say it.

The list of anomalies continues to scroll upward, with an occasional blue check mark to break up the black-and-white monotony. We watch for nearly a full minute. I keep thinking it has to stop soon. Finally I can't take any more. I reach out to pause the list again. It's at 796 and the little bar on the side of the window suggests that we've barely scratched the surface.

"Are those all casualties?" Lorena asks.

I can't make myself touch the screen again. Alex is the one who eventually reaches forward and clicks a name.

Willis Martin Parry's two obituaries are side by side. The Willis on the left was an old man when he died in 2025. He was survived by five children, twelve grandchildren, twenty-one great-grandchildren, and one great-great-grandson. The article on the right shows the picture of a young man in uniform. Sgt. Willis M. Parry died in combat in Vietnam in August of 1975, when he was twenty-two years old. He was survived by his parents, a sister, and a fiancée.

"That date," Jack says. "It's wrong. Jarvis, when did the last US soldier die in the Vietnam conflict?"

There's a long pause.

"Oh, sorry," Jack says. "I didn't know it was set for just your voice."

"He's not." I repeat the question anyway, thinking maybe something is wrong with the system.

"Apologies, mistress. I'm attempting to reconcile conflicting data from an external source."

"Explain."

"My local data set indicates that US involvement in the Vietnam War ended with the fall of Saigon to North Vietnamese forces on April 30, 1975. But when I checked for updates from external historical archives, the date given is November 19, 1975."

Alex taps a menu at the top of the display. A summary appears with four categories.

Deaths: 32,714 (Significant: 692)

Erasures: 1,110,563 (Significant: 22,342)

Additions: 1,107,224 (Significant: 21,905)

Alterations to Historical Events: 543 (Significant: 17)

When Alex clicks *Erasures*, we see a list of names with links to birth certificates. In some cases, there's a biographical profile instead. The same is true for the *Additions* category.

"I . . . don't get it," Jack says. "Are these more people who died?"

"Not exactly," Lorena says. "Think back to the two obituaries for Willis Parry. The offspring listed in the first one were never born. They didn't die. They just never *were*. And the fiancée of Sgt. Parry probably married someone else. Any children she had from the new union wouldn't have existed if Parry had lived. Both of those categories are multiplied by several generations."

"And he's not even one who's marked as significant," Alex says. "Wonder what criteria they used to determine whether someone gets one of those little blue check marks? Seems like that would be pretty arbitrary."

"And what constitutes an alteration, let alone a significant one," Lorena says. "You'd think that many changes to the cast of characters would be reflected a bit more in the story line."

Jack shrugs. "Maybe. But very few major events in history can be laid firmly on the shoulders of one individual. A war *might* be averted due to a certain leader in power, but the more likely scenario is that it's just delayed a bit. And you both know from your work that major discoveries are built on the research of many different people. A brilliant scientist might push the work along a bit faster, but someone else would probably make the same breakthrough eventually."

"And yet, somehow, I managed to wreak havoc without even interacting with a musician. Beginner's luck, I guess." I center the CHRONOS key in my palm.

"Wait!" Jack says, grabbing my hand.

"I can fix this, Jack! All I have to do is go back and tell myself not to stop in 1957. To come straight back here. We'll get hit with those weird memories again, but—"

"Yes," he says. "I agree that you have to go back. But let's think this through. Figure out the best time for you to stop yourself. I mean, it's not like there's a huge rush."

"What? Over a million people dead or erased because I decided to check out that stupid stable point. How can you . . . Oh."

He's right. There's no reason to rush in, aside from my eagerness to fix this and get it off my conscience. Those people won't be any more or less dead or erased if I fix this twenty minutes or twenty days from now, although I suspect the list of erasures and additions might grow a bit. Plus, things could get far more complicated if I make some sort of blunder on the first try. I need to get this right.

And then I need to destroy this device. *Both* of the devices.

Lorena reaches forward to tap the link for *Alterations to Historical Events*.

Alex gives her a sideways look. "That seems like a bad idea. Madi's going back to undo anything that was changed, so . . ."

He doesn't stop her, however, and when she opens the section labeled *Scientific Advances*, his eyes are crawling all over the data as greedily as hers.

"No reason we can't at least look," Lorena says. "Maybe get some ideas."

"Except those ideas belong to someone else," I counter. "So it seems a bit unfair."

"Why?" Alex says. "Once you undo the damage, these people will probably never be born."

Jack snorts. "That's technically true, I guess. Hard for anyone to accuse you of stealing from a person who doesn't exist."

It occurs to me then that the same thing could be said for works of art, music, and yes . . . literature.

I laugh and they all turn to look at me. "Oh, it's nothing, really. I'm pretty sure I just solved the mystery of James L. Coleman's exceptional productivity as a writer, as well as the whole plagiarism question. And it's not an answer my thesis committee is going to believe."

Jack seems to be following my line of thought, but Lorena and Alex are giving me blank looks, so I explain further. "My great-grandfather was publishing books from a different timeline. Books written by authors who were never born. Or who took a different path for some reason. He just made a few mistakes, and that cost him the trust of his daughter and very nearly destroyed his career. So you might want to think carefully about possible plagiarism charges before you go rifling through those files."

"I'll take my chances," Lorena says. "There are still variants of cancer that we can't cure. RJ's aunt died from one of . . ." She trails off, her eyes widening. For a moment, she just sits there, her finger poised hesitantly above her comm-band. Then she taps it. "Call RJ."

Nothing happens. She taps again. "Call RJ." There's still no response of any sort, so she takes the band off and shakes it. "It must be dead. Damn it. I've barely had it a year. You call him, Alex."

"Okay." Alex looks a bit nervous, but he makes the call. When RJ's face pops up above Alex's wrist, a collective sigh of relief fills the room.

"Hey, Alex! What's up, man? I haven't heard from you in ages. Don't you ever leave the lab?"

"RJ?" Lorena steps closer to Alex, so that she's within range of his camera. "Are you almost home?"

He frowns. "Umm. Yeah. I'm *at* home, in fact. Have we . . . met?"

The color drains from Lorena's face and she looks faint. I get up and pull her toward a chair while Alex makes a lame excuse, telling his cousin that he'll call him back.

As soon as he cuts the connection, Lorena rushes back to the terminal. "How do you search on this damn thing?"

Alex pokes a few spots on the display experimentally, and finally comes up with a search bar. "I don't think it's finished compiling the list. But I'll try. What do you want me to—"

"Why doesn't he know who I am? Something must have changed for him."

"Okay," Alex says. "But I'm not sure how to search for that."

"Some event must have altered the past three years," she says. "Erased his memory."

I wince when she says *erased* and exchange a look with Jack. He looks as sick as I feel.

"Alex," Jack says, "search the erasures. What is your middle name, Lorena?"

She turns away from the display and stares at him for a moment. Her expression is more resignation than realization, so I think she had already reached the same conclusion but just wasn't quite to the point where she could admit it.

"It's Ann," she says. "Lorena Ann Jeung."

Alex sighs and selects *Erasures* from the menu. Then he types in Lorena's name. It takes a moment, but her information pops up, along with a picture from a few years ago. It's an article from the Georgetown University data bank, profiling several new postdoctoral fellowship recipients.

He quickly types in his own name, but gets no result. No erasure notice for me or for Jack, either.

Lorena sinks back into the chair. "Well, I guess there's no point in searching for Yun Hee," she says in a flat, emotionless voice. "If I'm not in this reality, she certainly couldn't be. And I can't fault RJ. How could he remember a wife and daughter who don't exist?"

"You exist," Alex says. "Just not in this timeline."

"You remember me, though. Don't you? You were at our wedding."

Alex nods. "Yeah. But I'm under the CHRONOS field. I'm in the reality where you exist."

"Does this mean there are other versions of us walking around out there?" Jack asks. "Just as oblivious as RJ?"

"I don't know," Alex admits. "I guess it's possible. Or we might be in the overlap—the envelope, I guess you could say?—where two bubble universes touch. Every time Madi uses that device, it emits chronotron particles. The area around the house emits them, too, but they're more diffuse."

"So what happens if Yun Hee or I step outside this . . . field?" Lorena asks. "If we go outside of this bubble?"

"I don't know," Alex repeats. "But I really don't think that's something we want to put to the test."

Yun Hee chooses that moment to let out a wail from the suite at the end of the hallway, loud enough that we hear her even without Jarvis chiming in to inform us that the baby is awake. I guess she wanted to let us know that she does indeed exist. Or maybe it's her way of letting us know she objects to being indefinitely confined to this house.

"Do you want me to get her?" Alex asks.

Lorena shakes her head as she gets up. "She's tired. I'll try to get her back down." There are tears in her voice, and I reach out to touch her arm as she passes me.

"I'm going to fix this, Lorena."

She jerks away and then turns to face me. "Yes. You *are* going to fix this. And then I am going to personally destroy that abomination, along with any others there may be, and we will *not* be continuing this research. This is . . . playing God."

I nod, even though I can't help but remember that she wasn't nearly as upset about the situation until we found out that she was one of the casualties. Okay, no. That's not fair. She was upset, but not so rattled that she couldn't be pragmatic and look for a silver lining in the massive dark cloud of over a million deaths or erasures.

Jack slips an arm around me and pulls me close once she's gone. "You'll fix this. It's all going to be okay. We just need to figure out the best time for you to make contact. So you can tell yourself not to go."

I think for a moment. "The most straightforward path would be to blink into the stable point in 1957 a few seconds before I arrive. The location is hidden behind a hedge. I can just tell myself to jump straight back to here. That would keep me from interacting with Lennon. We'll have this block of time, from the moment I arrived until I leave again, as overlap. But if experience holds, she—or one of us, at least—will vanish. Alternatively, I could go back further, to before I do any of these jumps, and tell myself to stay here this morning. Take a nap. Go for a swim. But then all of us have overlapping memories. Finally, I could just jump back and intercept myself at Nora's. I set a stable point in her front room. Or at least, I think I did."

My brain feels foggy, and I wonder if this is a side effect of the time travel. I glance back down at the key, and yes, I see a stable point showing the bay window that looks out over Nora's patio. "Yeah. I set it. But I'm a little worried about Nora. If I start acting differently that morning, after my conversation with me, would that give Nora double memories, too?"

Jack and I both look at Alex as I finish the question. He throws up his hands in frustration.

"*I. Don't. Know,*" he yells. "Okay? Yes, I get it. I'm the only temporal physicist in the room, but the research I've done and read about is all theoretical. It's mostly equations, for God's sake! I really don't have much more of an idea than you do about how all of this plays out in practice. Maybe I *would* understand how all of this works twenty years from now, which seems to be around the time that we're supposed to make this discovery. Maybe, by then, I would have a team of researchers. Funding. Safety protocols. Because, as Jack noted, scientific breakthroughs are rarely made by one person. So again, *I don't know.* You're the one with the practical experience, so your guess is as good as mine. Probably better."

It's really not like Alex to totally lose it, and he looks a little contrite by the time he reaches the end of the rant.

"I'm sorry," I tell him. "None of you asked to be in the middle of this mess."

The three of us are silent for a moment, and then Alex speaks again, this time in more measured tones. "Actually, I *did* ask to be in the middle of this. I've spent the last seven years in school working toward the goal of one day creating something like that device. I wanted to be part of the discovery. But if *this* is what we get from time travel . . ." He nods toward the display, which is still scrolling upward. "It's not worth it. So go fix it. Then we'll turn the key and my research over to Lorena and let her blow it to bits."

"Agreed. I'd prefer to avoid confusing Nora, if at all possible, though. She's eighty, and she already jokes about being forgetful. So I'll try the first option. If it doesn't work, if for some reason my simply being in 1957 did this, then I'll intercept myself when I was at Nora's house." I stop, grimacing as a new thought hits me. "Although, I was in Liverpool briefly that first day when I tried out the stable points. Long enough to realize I was really in the past and not exactly dressed for the era. I blinked straight back, but if me simply being in 1957 did this, then I may have to go back to the very beginning. Before I pulled any of you into this."

"How about we cross that bridge when we get there?" Jack says. "If we get there. You'll need to come back to see if things are still . . . broken, right?"

Truthfully, I think there's a very good chance I'll feel another one of those oh-so-fun blasts to my equilibrium if the timeline changes back. But I give him a nod and what I hope is a brave smile as I center the key in my palm.

"Madi?" He tilts my chin up to break my eye contact with the key and then kisses me. Not a quick goodbye peck on the lips, but a full toe-curling kiss that, for one brief second, takes my mind off the apocalypse I've created. When he pulls back, he says, "You'll fix this."

The certainty in his voice brings tears to my eyes. I squeeze them tight and then look back at the interface to pull up the Liverpool stable point—the one for short people who don't want to get poked by pointy leaves—and then set the time for thirty seconds before my previous arrival. As soon as I arrive, I step out of the stable point and crouch down below the line of sight, so that Earlier-Me doesn't see a doppelgänger in the frame and decide not to jump in. The marching band is still playing badly, and I can hear the noise of the crowd gathered near the sidewalk.

Half a minute later, Earlier-Me arrives, again scraping my cheek on the holly leaf. Again cursing under my breath. But this time, I startle because someone—me—reaches out to grab my arm.

"Shh!" I clap one hand over Earlier-Me's mouth, because I can tell that she's a hair's breadth away from screaming. Even with the racket of the marching band, someone would hear a scream, and who knows what kind of impact that might have.

"You need to abort," I tell her. "Jump back home *now*."

To my credit, Earlier-Me doesn't argue or even ask why. She just centers the key in her palm and pulls up the stable point. I don't know if she's getting the same looping sensation that I am. Maybe not, since this is the first time for her. I try to keep my eyes averted, and it helps a tiny bit.

"Wait!" I say, when I realize that this me won't have the same information when she arrives that I had. "Tell them you were nearly hit by a truck. John Lennon was on that truck. He wasn't hurt. Neither was I—or you. We didn't talk to him or interact in any way, but it . . . broke something. Now go."

She nods and pulls up the interface, and then I remember about the second stable point. "Wait, wait, one more thing."

Earlier-Me gives me an exasperated look, and then follows my instructions for setting the location.

"Is that all?" she asks.

I nod mutely, and she blinks out. Once she's gone, I pull up the display. Jack and Alex are at the computer, exactly where they were when I blinked in. This feels like a bad sign, especially coupled with the fact that I haven't felt that gut-punch sensation. Then Earlier-Me joins them.

Too late, I realize that I might have been able to spare them the full impact of the double memory by having her jump in later. But I really don't know how this works, and that seems like more of a risk, so maybe it's just as well.

Since I want to spend as little time as possible in the same room with myself, however, I scan forward to about a minute before I jumped out to intercept her. The look on their faces tells me that nothing has changed, but, like Alex said, none of us really knows exactly how this works. Maybe everything will magically be okay when there's only one of me left in that library.

FROM *THE MANUAL OF THE UNITED KLANS OF AMERICA* (1964)

KLANSMAN'S OATH

Section II. SECRECY.

I most solemnly swear that I will forever keep sacredly secret the signs, words, and grip; and any and all other matters and knowledge of the Knights of the Ku Klux Klan, regarding which a most rigid secrecy must be maintained, which may at any time be communicated to me and will never divulge same nor even cause the same to be divulged to any person in the whole world, unless I know positively that such person is a member of this Order in good and regular standing; and not even then unless it be for the best interest of this Order.

I most sacredly vow and most positively swear that I will not yield to bribe, flattery, threats, passion, punishment, persuasion, nor any enticements whatever coming from or offered by any person or persons, male or female, for the purpose of obtaining from me a secret or secret information of the Knights of the Ku Klux Klan. I will die rather than divulge same. So help me, God. Amen!

OBJECTS AND PURPOSES (Article II, The Constitution)

VI. RACIAL:

"To maintain forever white supremacy." Or as the Declaration proclaims it, "To maintain forever the God-given supremacy of the white race."

∞19∞

Flipping through the *Log of Stable Points*, which looks a lot like a standard-issue diary, is a CHRONOS historian's first step any time we research a new city. And while I've never actually counted, I'd be willing to bet that at least 20 percent of the thousands of locations in the *Log* are inside hotels. It makes sense, if you think about it. There are always a lot of new people coming and going at a hotel, and the buildings are often in the same spot for hundreds of years with minimal renovations to the public areas. You can usually find a helpful concierge to flag you a taxi or give you detailed information about local areas of interest. Plus, if you're coming in for more than just a day trip, you don't have to lug your bags around.

Someone put some major thought and effort into these stable points. The one here at the Peabody, located in downtown Memphis, is a good example. When you jump in, you find yourself in a secluded nook on the mezzanine level where there's less foot traffic, so you're very unlikely to be seen. An early version of the hotel was located a few blocks down the street, with active dates from 1869 to 1924, making it a prime location for historians of the postbellum South. The current location at Union and Second Street opened in 1925, and it's listed as stable until the mid-twenty-first century, with the exception of a brief period in the late 1970s, when the hotel was vacant.

This stable point at the Peabody is one of two active jump locations at Memphis hotels during this time period. The other is just behind the Lorraine Motel, which was a whites-only establishment under a different name from 1925 until 1945, when it was converted into a motel catering to black travelers. Later still, it would become the National Civil Rights Museum, with a wreath marking the approximate spot where Martin Luther King Jr. was shot and killed on April 4, 1968.

Or at least, that was the historical trajectory of that building in the old timeline. I browsed that stable point yesterday, while we were running our simulations, panning around until the word *Lorraine*, in a very midcentury yellow neon oval, came into view. The lights on that sign went out for good in 1976, and the building and sign both came down in 1979. Early the next year, the space was taken over by a Burger King and a gas station.

That has me wondering how many of our stable points are still *stable* for the durations noted in the *Log*. I guess we should have run a simulation for that before we left HQ, although there probably won't be major changes until a few decades from now, once the casualties increase and erasures start to kick in.

Rich and Katherine have already stepped out of the stable point and are at the banister overlooking the lobby. "Come on," Rich says. "We need to hurry or we'll miss it."

"Miss what?" Katherine asks, but he just grabs her elbow and steers her toward the stairs. A crowd is gathering near the large, ornate fountain in the center of the lobby.

A John Philip Sousa march begins playing over the loudspeaker, and a couple of the children start clapping, their eyes fixed on the elevator. The elevator dings, and then the door opens. A man clad in livery steps out and dramatically unfurls a long red carpet. As soon as the path is spread in front of them, five ducks waddle out of the elevator, paying no attention at all to the people gathered on either side of the red carpet. They march down the runway, flapping their wings slightly to steady themselves as they hop up the stairs and dive happily into a fountain lined with small, brightly colored tiles. Marble cherubs support the upper basin, which rains gently down on the green-headed drake and four brown hens.

Katherine grins up at Rich. "What was that all about?"

Rich, who has stayed here twice before, chuckles. "Happens every morning. The ducks own the place. Most of the time, they're in a penthouse suite on the roof, but they take the elevator to the lobby each morning."

She gives him a skeptical look.

"I'm not kidding," he says. "Well, except for them owning the place. The duck march has been a thing since the 1930s. Some say even before that."

Katherine pulls out her key and sets a stable point. "Now I can roll it back and watch it all over again later."

Rich smiles back at her, looking ridiculously pleased at having made her happy.

The hotel has one room with two double beds available. Not ideal, because I have no doubt it means I'll be sharing a bed with Richard, but it will have to do. We take the room, and once we're settled, I scan the yellow pages of the phone book for a rental-car agency nearby.

While Richard calls to reserve a car, I continue thumbing through the phone books, this time searching the white pages. Toni's dad introduced himself as Lowell Robinson when he was thanking me for saving Toni, and, sure enough, there's a Lowell Robinson on Keel Avenue.

"Tyce?" Richard says. "You looking for something?"

"Nope. Just browsing."

"We probably need to get a move on," he says, "if you're still planning to go in search of that contact of Glen's."

Rich knows damn well I'm still going, so the remark is obviously designed to get temptation out of my hands. Which isn't necessary. I wasn't actually planning to call her. I'm just curious. But I slide the phone book back into the nightstand drawer, giving him an annoyed look as I do.

Once we have the car, I drop Rich and Katherine off at a diner a few blocks from the Coliseum. Katherine has pen and paper in hand, and Rich has a massive camera around his neck, which kind of makes me wonder whether there was any room for a change of clothes inside the suitcase he brought along. Their press credentials are with teen magazine *Tiger Beat*, a relatively new publication that probably isn't sending reporters into the field, so there's less chance of them bumping into anyone who can blow their cover. I'm also pretty sure it means no one will take them very seriously, and that's probably a good thing. If they were with the *New York Times*, they would attract a lot more curiosity. The plan is to set a few dozen observation points inside the auditorium—or, as they plan to tell the security guy they'll bribe, get a few photographs of the Coliseum when it's empty to show next to the one when it's teeming with teenyboppers the next day. Since it would no doubt raise some suspicion if they walked around with their CHRONOS keys out, setting observation points with the guard watching, they'll just set a single location. Then, they can go back to the hotel, scan forward to tonight when the place is empty, and set a few dozen more.

Katherine is in a better mood than she's been. I think the idea of sneaking around like a detective amuses her. And Rich is definitely psyched. He gets to spend the day with the girl he loves, while Saul Rand is four hundred miles and more than five decades away. Aside from the fact that we now have a major rift in the timeline to contend with, that's pretty much the scenario he had in mind when he originally set up this research trip.

My task for the afternoon is to drive to Collierville, about forty-five minutes outside the city. The notes I have from field training with Glen included one contact, a guy named Buster Wilson, in the Shelby County Klan.

I called Glen just before we left to double-check the name and see if he had any other information. Glen, who has been in the analysis section since he retired from fieldwork, was a little surprised to hear from me. We were never super close, given the age difference and the fact that Glen was a little disgruntled about being near the end of his time as an active field agent. But normally, I'd have stopped in his office if I had a question, rather than calling. And I'd have chatted with him for a while and filled him in on my latest research. The clock was ticking on our departure, however, so I didn't have the luxury of an extended visit. I'll have to call back and apologize once we fix this, *if* we fix this, although he may have a pretty good idea why I was acting weird by that time.

The trip where he met the contact mentioned in my notes was about ten years ago for Glen, but only a few weeks back in terms of the actual date. Robert Shelton, Imperial Wizard of the United Klans, spoke at a rally in Memphis on July 23. Glen wound up at a bar with several of the men afterward. Buster had a bit too much to drink and missed his connection for a ride home, so Glen offered to drive him—before realizing he'd committed to a two-hour round trip that was much farther away from his stable point than he'd planned to travel. Glen told me the story partly as a cautionary tale, but he also noted that he'd learned a lot about the organization of local klaverns outside of North Carolina during that drive, because Buster was still half-tanked and much chattier than he might have been otherwise. When I spoke with him this morning, Glen said he had no clue whether Buster Wilson has a telephone in 1966, but suggested that my best bet would be to ask around at one of the restaurants on the town square where Buster eats dinner most nights when his shift at the toy factory is over.

Glen sent over his notes from the trip, so I flip my diary to audio mode and listen as I drive. I suspect the section on Buster would be a lot more interesting if Glen had just recorded the man talking, but instead I'm treated to a half-hour discussion on evolving race relations in rural Tennessee, a bit on gender roles, and a side plot on economic development. I wonder if my reports are this boring for those who have to read them. There are only a few things of real use in Glen's narrative. The first is that Buster's wife took up with a sailor from the Mid-South Naval Base a few months back. That's why he's eating out so much these days. Buster apparently spent a good portion of the drive complaining that the Klan needed to focus on all parts of its constitution. That the sections about enforcing morality ought to pertain to whites, too, and maybe then Cindy wouldn't have run off. Because she'd have known there were consequences. She'd have been too afraid to leave. If she'd run off with a black man, the Klan would have helped him, and he's still a little annoyed that they turned him down when he asked for a "corrective action." Even told in Glen's boring academic writing style, it's clear that Buster is one messed-up individual, and I'm glad that this Cindy is free of him.

The second thing I glean from the report is that even though the "more popular than Jesus" quote wouldn't blow up in the US media for another week, several of the men at the bar had been grumbling about flyers they'd seen at the venue for the Klan rally, advertising the Memphis Country Blues Festival being held there the next week. It featured both black and white performers on the roster, and that had gotten one of them who had a teenage daughter talking about how she wouldn't be going to the upcoming Beatles concert for that same reason. There was no talk of sabotage or a protest at that point, however. Or if there was, it's not in Glen's notes.

It's not all that hot for mid-August, certainly nothing like the heat I had to put up with when I worked at Ida's. The air conditioner in the car is feeble, though, so once the audio is over, I strip down to my white T-shirt and crank the windows down instead. When I reach the edge of town, I park near a phone booth, pull my shirt back on, and check the white pages to see if there's a listing for Buster Wilson. There are seven *Wilsons*, none of them Buster. While Buster is probably a nickname, in my experience with southern names, that's not a safe bet.

It's a little before five when I arrive at the town square. There's a small bandstand in the park, so I sit on the edge and smoke one of my bogus cigarettes, mostly because it gives me something to do with my hands while I wait. After about ten minutes, I get bored and start to pace around the perimeter of the park, checking to see how many restaurants I'll need to scope out.

The first one is an ice-cream shop, so it's probably not a candidate. There's also a drugstore, although that seems like more of a lunch thing to me. Dyer's Cafe, which appears to specialize in hamburgers, is almost directly opposite the spot where I parked the rental car, and it seems the most likely candidate until I spot a very familiar sign down the block. A large yellow hen in an apron emblazoned with the Confederate flag is perched atop the words *The Dixie Chicken*.

My first thought is that I didn't realize the place was a chain, but then I remember Phelps's comment about his younger sister living outside of Memphis. It may just be a family business with two far-flung locations. Either way, I know which restaurant I'll be checking first. And even though I hate to give them my money (again), I have to know.

The woman who owns this place apparently isn't as proud as her older sister, or maybe the recipes weren't hers to begin with, so pride wasn't an issue. Chicken, hush puppies, biscuits . . . even the coleslaw is good enough that it could have come straight from Miss Ida's kitchen at the Southside. Or maybe I'm just extra hungry.

No one matching the description Glen gave me enters The Dixie Chicken while I'm eating, so I go back up and ask one of the two people working the counter for a refill on the iced tea. When the guy, who looks like he's still in high school, comes back with the pitcher to top off my cup, I ask him if he knows Buster Wilson.

"A friend of mine met him at an event in Memphis a couple weeks back," I say. "He told me I might want to look him up while I'm in town."

The boy's eyes narrow slightly. "Sure. Buster usually comes in around this time. Although sometimes it's later, depending on when Mr. *Ayak* shuts down the factory line."

He's a good-looking kid, tall and clean-cut, with a friendly grin, and he seems bright enough. But he put such a strong emphasis on the word *Ayak* that anyone listening would have known he was passing some sort of message.

I don't know who came up with the Klan code, but they were pretty awful at it. In this case, the word is an acronym for a question—*Are you a Klansman?*—and I'm expected to respond with some sentence including the acronym AKIA, for *A Klansman I am*. The problem is *AYAK* and *AKIA* aren't easy to work into conversation. You have to treat them as proper nouns, and most towns with an active Klan in 1966 don't have people with last names like Ayak and Akia. Glen searched for options, and said it would have been easier during the resurgence of the Klan in the early twenty-first century, because you could ask if he was "driving a Kia," but by then, they just ask for a token kept on your cell phone rather than these elaborate ruses.

"Isn't Buster working at the Akia factory in Memphis now?" I ask.

The kid smiles when he hears the response and gives me a thumbs-up. I respond in kind, even though that's not the usual hand signal.

"Nah. He's still makin' them bouncy horses here in town. He'll be in later tonight if the weather doesn't turn . . ." His face squinches up, like he's trying to remember something, probably another code; then his voice drops down to where it's almost inaudible. "Six. He'll be here at six with the others." Then he sticks out his hand, and I shake it. "Billy Meeks. My dad's the klaliff."

"Troy Rayburn. Good to meet you."

"You want some banana puddin' while you wait? On the house. Mama made it this mornin', and it's real good."

I say sure, more because I think he'll be offended if I don't than because I'm still hungry. When he comes back with the pudding, he says, "Where you from?"

"Over near Raleigh."

"Dang. Didn't know we had Tar Heels comin' in, too. My Uncle Lenny came in this morning. You may know him . . . He's been in Raleigh a lot lately."

"Lenny Phelps?"

"Yeah."

"Hey, Billy!" a woman calls from the back. "Are you workin' or talkin'? Pam cain't run the counter all by herself."

"Sorry, Mama." He frowns, clearly troubled, then leans forward over the counter and whispers, "This don't mean they're turning tomorrow over to a *wrecking crew*, does it?"

Wrecking crew is code for actions involving death or serious harm. Within United Klans, it's not unusual for a request to come down for a few extra hands to travel for any actions that might get violent. Basically, they pull in outside help for the kinds of things where you don't want to use locals, because they might be recognized by the police or bystanders. The fact that Billy looks worried about the prospect of a wrecking crew, and maybe even a little disappointed, makes me wonder if he has grown up with the Klan but is now questioning it, or at least some of the more extreme actions.

"Not sure," I say. "I'll let you get back to work before your mama gets onto you again."

He hurries back to the cash register, and I return to my table, trying to decide how to play this. On the one hand, the fact that Phelps is here—and presumably Scoggin, too—gives me an excellent opportunity to get inside information. They know me. On the other hand, it could get a little complicated, since Buster hung out with Glen less than a month ago, from his perspective, and the people in the Carolina Klans all think he's been living in Chicago for the past eighteen months. Also, I've got this weird feeling that anything I do could make things worse—what if this attack on Lennon was supposed to be simple harassment and it *becomes* a wrecking crew simply because they now believe they have enough out-of-towners to *make* it one?

But that's stupid. I'm only here because someone *already* decided to shoot Lennon. So there's no way anything I do now causes the rift.

At least, I don't see how it could, but then I'm not the team expert on temporal conundrums. It's still twenty minutes until six, so I head down to the phone booth on the corner and call the hotel room back in Memphis to get Rich's opinion. He and Katherine aren't back yet, which sucks, because a standard phone line is my only way of contacting them in this era, short of sending a message to CHRONOS and having them relay it to Richard via the diaries. Normally, I'd go that route, but given that this isn't a standard mission, I'm not sure how Angelo would feel about me pulling in other support staff. I could also jump back to headquarters and research it myself, I guess, since the usual safety protocol isn't in effect. But I don't know if the override will extend to any local points I set here in Collierville, and I need to get back here, preferably without having to rent another car and drive for an hour. So I just leave a message with the front desk at the Peabody, with the vague statement that I'll be delayed because I have to attend a late meeting, and head back to The Dixie Chicken.

I'm pretty sure Rich and Katherine would both agree that this meeting is my best chance to get information on the plot to kill Lennon, even though I hadn't been expecting to find Phelps and Scoggin here.

Anyway, Angelo said to use my best judgment. It's telling me there's no way anything I do right now, *after* a massive time shift, could have caused the rift. If that's wrong, then our timeline is illogical and should probably end anyway.

Five men, including two who match Glen's description of Buster—fat, tall, and balding—are at the counter placing their orders when I step back inside the restaurant. Billy gives me a little wave and then nods his head toward a door at the back of the room. I'd assumed it led to a storage area, but the door is open now, and I see two long tables inside a dimly lit room. Three men are already seated, digging into their chicken dinners.

I'm a little hesitant about going in, but then my eyes adjust to the lighting, and I realize that one of the three men is Lenny Phelps. He's sitting next to two tall, beefy guys who could be brothers.

"Hey, Troy!" Phelps says. "I'll be damn. What the hell you doin' in Collierville? You planning to sell Roberta some of them Cutco knives?"

The guy on his right snorts. "Roberta don't need no more knives. She's dangerous enough as it is."

That earns a few chuckles from everyone except Phelps, so I'm guessing Roberta is his sister, and the guy on his right is Billy's dad, the klaliff, or vice president, of the group.

"Don't have them with me, but if anyone here's in the market, I'll drive back over with my display case. It's been a slow month. And no, I didn't even know you were here," I say honestly. "I've just gotta kill the weekend in Memphis, due to an appointment Monday morning, and I remembered what Scoggin said about that concert. My uncle told me I might want to look up Buster Wilson while I'm in the area.

Apparently, they had an adventure a few weeks back, and Uncle Glen thought he might be able to help me get in on the action."

"Well, you won't have to look far," Phelps says. "Buster's ordering dinner right now. But I can promise you won't get a decent conversation out of him until he's polished off his fried chicken."

Maybe it's the smell of the fried chicken and hush puppies in the room. Or maybe it's just the way Phelps says the words *fried chicken*. Whatever it is, I get a vivid flashback to standing in front of the courthouse in Spartanburg, holding the bag with the judge's lunch, while Phelps looked at me like I was something nasty on the bottom of his shoe.

Pasting on a big grin, I say, "Can't blame him for giving priority to dinner. Not one bit. Just finished off a three-piece myself." I hold up the paper cup. "Good banana pudding."

We go through a round of introductions, and, as I suspected, the guy on Phelps's right is Bill Meeks, Billy's dad, and the other guy is his brother, Frank. The fact that they don't bother with all of the password-and-handshake hoopla is reassuring. If Phelps had any doubts about me, he'd have at least made a show of it, since he's the one vouching for me.

"Is Scoggin with you?" I ask.

Phelps gives me an odd look. "Why would he come with me to visit my sister?"

"No reason. Just thought after everything he said at the bonfire the other night, he might be interested in helping put a little fear of Jesus into those mopheads."

He laughs. "Nah. That was more to pull out a crowd than anything else. Get a bit more cash into the legal-defense fund. He's happy to leave the piddly crap for you young'uns still tryin' to prove yourselves. And young enough to run so you don't get caught. I'll introduce you to Buster, and you're welcome to join us protestin' out front, but the one you need to talk to if you want in on the real action is out there behind the counter." He nods toward the open door, where I can see Billy Meeks at the soda fountain. "Billy's got the whole thing planned. They picked a box of tomatoes last week and left 'em out in the trunk so they'll be nice and soft. Got some light bulbs to hurl off the balcony. Couple fireworks, too."

"Roberta told Billy he ain't goin'," Bill Meeks says. "She thinks it's too dangerous."

Phelps rolls his eyes. "Let me deal with Roberta. Maybe I need to remind her about some of the shit she got up to when she was his age."

Bill casts an uneasy eye toward his son out in the main dining room. "Well, to be honest, Lenny, I ain't too keen on him gettin' involved, either. He starts classes at UT in a coupla weeks. Some fool stunt like this could keep him out, and then he winds up drafted."

Phelps sniffs dismissively. "Billy's eighteen. I reckon he'll do as he pleases."

Bill seems like he's going to argue the point some more, so I jump in quickly with a question. "So this is just a harassment thing? Rotten tomatoes and the like? You're not here tonight to plan something more . . . substantive?"

"*Substantive*," Phelps says, nudging Bill with his elbow. "I think we got another college boy here. You mean a wreckin' crew?"

"Yeah. After what you said at the bonfire . . ."

Phelps shakes his head. "You think we're going to do something major with the feds watching us this close? You think we'd take that kind of risk over a smart-ass remark by some hippy singer? That's definitely *not* the sort of publicity we need right now. You kids may be all hot-blooded and rarin' to go, but you need to cool your jets. I get it, though. Like I said at the bonfire, I'd just as soon line all four of 'em up and shoot 'em. But this ain't the time."

FROM *THE GENETICS WARS: AN ALTERNATE HISTORY*, BY JAMES L. COLEMAN (2109)

The First Genetics War began in Africa, in 2071, between Akana and the small nation of Tchad, a member of the East African Union (EAU). A series of border skirmishes had been going on for several years, and the Akan government accused Tchadean forces of systematically raping women taken prisoner during their incursions onto Akan territory. The Tchadean government vehemently denied this charge, and the Akan military was reluctant to launch a direct attack, for fear of upsetting their shaky peace with the EAU. An Akan scientist named Elizabeth Forson, whose cousin had reportedly been raped and murdered in one of these attacks, approached her government with an alternative plan for retaliation. She had developed a virus that would genetically target Tchadean males, killing some and rendering many others sterile. According to testimony by her subordinates at the postwar trials, Forson believed the virus to be a very poetic form of justice given the nature of the crime.

Within six months, border incursions ceased almost entirely as the virus swept through the Tchadean ranks. The civilian population, including male children, were also hit hard, and the gender-specific nature of the virus prompted an investigation by EAU intelligence forces. When the plot was revealed in 2073, Tchad declared war on Akana, pulling in the EAU as a result of their collective security agreement. International sanctions were also enacted, because Akana's use of the virus violated a UN biological weapons treaty.

A massive war, using mostly conventional weapons, erupted on the continent. In 2074, the EAU army, bolstered by troops from several UN members, invaded Akana. The government surrendered, but Forson and several other high-ranking officials escaped to the south.

Once the hostilities ended, the UN assumed a peacekeeping role. Angry that Europeans had yet again interfered in African affairs, Forson designed another biological weapon, this one aimed at individuals with specific genetic markers inherited from Neanderthal ancestors. The UN peacekeepers of Asian and European descent contracted the waterborne virus, which mutated within days to airborne transmission. Most of those who contracted the disease died in a matter of days. The vast majority of sub-Saharan people, who lacked the Neanderthal DNA, were untouched. A popular uprising in Akana ejected the remaining EAU and UN forces.

Several infected people traveled back to UN headquarters before the quarantine was put in place, carrying the virus with them. Researchers immediately began work on antiviral countermeasures. By the time they found a cure, the plague had spread to most population centers around the globe. The death toll, which includes casualties from a tactical nuclear attack against Akana in 2079, is estimated at 730,000,000.

∞20∞

The other version of me vanishes a few seconds after I blink into the library. She doesn't look very happy about it, but unlike the first duplicate me, who vanished after my trip to Estero, this one almost certainly understood that she was going to lose this round of quantum Darwinism.

Jack is watching when she disappears. And I'm probably imagining it, but I'd swear he looks a little wistful. Like he'll miss her. And that kind of bugs me, which is truly ridiculous.

One glance at the computer, however, tells me I've got far bigger problems than being unreasonably jealous of my former other self. The *Anomalies* file is still on the ancient display, and the totals don't appear to have budged in the slightest.

"Damn it." I pull up the interface on the key again. "Guess I'm going back to Nora's house."

"You should really take a break first." Jack goes over to the liquor cabinet near Grandpa James's desk. "Maybe a little bourbon. Or brandy?"

"Neither. I need to get this over with." I nod toward the computer. "I'll take a break when that database no longer exists."

He pours the brandy anyway, and I can tell he wants to argue that we need to talk all of this through. Make sure we have the best plan. But he's not the one stuck with making the jump. My hand is already shaking so hard that it's difficult to keep the display stable. And while I know that probably supports his assertion that I should take a break, I need to keep moving. Otherwise, I think there's a very real risk that I'll lose my nerve.

Once my hand is steady, I pull up the location in Nora's front room and begin rolling the time back to last night. The stable point is dark, though, and it shouldn't be, since we were in that room until around midnight. Then I remember that my days and nights are no longer in sequential order. Since I went backward a day when I returned to the present, it's *tonight* that I'll read Kate's diary to Nora. Although the wee hours of tomorrow morning might be the best time to jump in, after Nora is asleep and I'm in bed next to Mercury, watching the video that looks disturbingly like Thea and this Prudence person.

"Is something wrong?" Jack asks.

"Aside from everything?" I shake my head. "It's just that I have a lot to tell you guys once this is fixed. But I can't think about that now."

When I look back down at the stable point, however, I realize that something is wrong. The furniture in Nora's front room is entirely different. In fact, the very shape of the room has changed. Someone has knocked out the wall separating off the dining area, turning it into one large room. And that room is dark. Abandoned, even. I scan forward for days and see no sign of activity, aside from lights coming on at set times, probably due to a security setting.

Nora's not there. This doesn't even look like her house anymore.

And more to the point, *I'm* not there to intercept with the warning.

"Alex, check the database for my grandmother Nora Coleman Grace. Born—"

"Already did that," he says. "She wasn't affected."

"She may not have been erased, but she *was* affected. Her house isn't her house anymore. The stable point I set in the front room looks completely different. And *we're* not there." I stop, thinking back to my weird reactions after the time shift. "But I think I already knew that. Sort of. I kept getting a foggy, disoriented feeling every time I thought about the visit, and I had this really strong sense that I'd never gone at all. That my mother and Nora hadn't been there. That I tried calling, too, but I couldn't find either of them. And now this stable point isn't showing Nora's house."

"That doesn't make sense," Lorena says from the doorway. She has Yun Hee on one hip and a shawl slung over her shoulder. "How can there be a stable point at her house if you were never there?"

"Because there's a CHRONOS field around the key," Alex says. "The stable point is just a geographic location combined with date and time. Even if Madi wasn't there to set the stable point in this timeline, that doesn't change what's on the key."

"But . . . the change is fairly recent. It was still Nora's house two Christmases back. Before I jumped home, I saw myself at her house on Christmas Eve. Nora was there. And my dad. I couldn't hear what we were saying, but everything about that moment was exactly as I remembered it."

I enter in that date—December 24, 2134. Sure enough, the Christmas tree is in front of the bay window. And it's definitely Nora's tree. I recognize the silver garland and the angel on top. I begin scrolling forward to the point where my father and I enter the room, but Yun Hee starts to whimper again, reminding me that my actions *erased* that child. My hand shakes, breaking up the interface.

Lorena sinks down onto the couch and flips the shawl over the baby. After a moment, Yun Hee hushes and begins to nurse. I put the key down on the desk and take deep breaths, searching for some inner calm.

"If you're thinking about going back two years," Alex says, "that's not a good idea. It could make things worse."

I give him an incredulous look. "Worse than this?"

"Alex is right," Jack says. "We need to find a way for you to *undo* what happened. Adding levels of complexity isn't going to help, and it could easily make things worse."

Lorena says, "Go back to this morning. Before any of us woke up. Leave a note on the desk here in the library, telling yourself not to make the jump. We'll all get screwy memories, but I don't see any way to avoid it."

"And then what? Do I just hang around with you guys and the other me?"

"If you want," Alex says. "Personally, though, if I could use that key, I'd spare myself the suspense and agony. Just jump back to now. The other you will vanish."

"You *assume*. The other me could win this toss of the quantum dice."

Alex gives me a little shrug of admission. "Maybe? But that's going to be true no matter what you do."

I sigh. "I'm sorry. I don't mean to be difficult. My brain is all jumbled. And . . . to be honest, being the one who blinks out of existence doesn't sound so bad right now. Seems a bit like poetic justice."

"Stop it," Jack says. "You're acting like you're the only one to blame for this, and you're not."

I'm inclined to argue the point. Yes, the others seemed to be fully on board for the project, but I'm the only one who can actually *use* the key. If I'd been more careful, more cautious, less curious, this wouldn't have happened. I suspect that Lorena might agree with me on that point, since she and Yun Hee will almost certainly cease to exist if they walk outside the front gate.

But laying blame and harping on what I should have done—or should *not* have done—isn't going to solve anything, so I close my eyes and draw a few deep breaths. When I open them, Jack is standing in front of me. He gives me a grim smile and presses the glass of brandy into my hands.

I drink.

My stomach churns, but I manage to keep it down. Then, I cross over to the desk on the other side of the room. There's a notepad on the right-hand side—*From the Desk of James L. Coleman.*

I blink back to the library stable point this morning at five a.m., grab the notepad, and quickly scrawl a message:

> *Don't make the jump to 1957 today. In fact, don't jump at all. Call Nora instead. And Mom—but she isn't going to tell you anything.*
>
> *If I'm the one who disappears, the others will probably remember what happened eventually. But if they don't, just tell them you're not using the key again.*
>
> *And* don't *use it again. Ever.*
> *Destroy them both, along with the diaries.*
> *Madi*

I realize that the signature at the bottom is ridiculous as soon as I put down the pen. I mean, seriously, who else would the note be from? Plus, I'm pretty sure I'd recognize my own handwriting. I'm tempted to tear it up and start over, but I know I'm just stalling. Putting off the moment when I have to go back and see whether this worked.

So I center the key in my hand and scroll forward to my time of departure plus five seconds. Usually, I pan around to check things out, but I don't have the nerve. As soon as I see that there's no physical obstruction at the stable point, I blink in.

When I open my eyes and turn around, the *Anomalies* file is still on the display. The other me must have already checked out. Yun Hee is peacefully sleeping in Lorena's arms on the couch. Everyone else looks slightly ill.

They've had time to get used to the news, however. I barely make it to my bathroom down the hallway before the brandy jumps ship. As I'm splashing water on my face afterward, the tears that have lurked right below the surface since I saw my dad earlier begin to spill over.

I should have gone back to save him. I should go now. What difference would it make, when the timeline is shot to hell anyway?

But Jack and Alex are right. It *could* be worse. The deaths and erasures could be higher. And for all I know, I could be unraveling the timeline more each time I use the key, each time I try to fix what I've already broken.

Jack is leaning against the bedroom wall when I emerge. His face is pale and his eyes are red rimmed, so I don't think I'm the only one who's been crying. When he pulls me into his arms, I break into tears again, pressing my face into his sweater. I'd give anything to just stay here, exactly like this. To never have to go back into that library and see that cursed computer with its millions of wrongs I don't know how to right.

When my tears taper off again, Jack says, "We need to go back to the others. I've . . . I've got something I need to say, and it's going to be hard enough to say it once, let alone twice."

I give him a questioning look and take a step back. Cold fingers of dread grip my stomach. "Okay."

"Wait. There's something I need to tell you first. *Just* you, because it doesn't pertain to the others. This." He points to himself and then to me. "Us. This was real, Madi. *Real.* Whatever else I've done, I never wanted to hurt you. When I agreed to this, I didn't count on falling in love with you, okay?"

I have no clue how to respond to that. After a moment of just staring at him, stunned, I back out of the room and head toward the library.

When he *agreed to this*? What the hell does that even mean?

I hear Jack's footsteps behind me and pick up my pace, because I'm really afraid he'll stop me and say something else that makes my already-jumbled brain even more confused. Lorena is still on the couch, holding the baby as she looks out the window at the bank of trees across the street. Alex is at his computer, not the ancient beast scrolling through the names of the dead and never existed, but the new system he brought in earlier this week. A massive 3-D model of something I don't understand in the slightest surrounds him.

When Jack says his name, Alex holds up a hand. "Give me a minute. I need to wrap this section up."

I sit on the other end of the sofa, avoiding Jack's eyes. I'm certain that I don't want to hear what he's about to say, and equally certain that I have no choice.

Alex moves one of the objects off to the side and enters something into the terminal of the computer with the anomalies database. Then he turns to Jack, who is pouring another brandy. "Okay. What's up?"

"Yeah," Jack says. He takes a chair from one of the other desks and turns it around to face us. "It's just . . . I can't let Madi keep thinking she's to blame for all of this."

Alex says, "You're right. My name is in that book, too, and unless Madi is planning on getting a PhD in temporal physics in the next decade or so, she couldn't have created the device without my help."

"To be fair, RJ's name is in there, too," Lorena says dully. "And we all know it wasn't included just because he handled the business side. If we actually created that thing, it wouldn't have been possible without me working on the genetic side of the equation. The key is useless without someone to use it. So, apparently, Jack and Yun Hee are the only ones in the room who aren't on the hook for this."

Jack laughs. It's a bitter sound. His hand tightens on the glass, and I can tell he'd like nothing more than to hurl it against the wall next to him. But then his eyes fall on Yun Hee, sleeping, and he puts the glass down on the desk.

"You're wrong. I own this every bit as much as the rest of you, if not more so. In fact, if not for me, the three of you wouldn't have met until 2148. You'd have finished work on the time-travel device a little over ten years later. And since there's nothing in *A Brief History of CHRONOS* to suggest otherwise, I'm going to guess there wouldn't have been a time shift. At least, not one like this."

We all stare at him, and then Alex says, "You buried the medallion in the backyard, didn't you? To speed things up. But why?"

"No, actually, I didn't have anything to do with that. The dog threw the team a curveball. They thought there might be a device *somewhere* in the house, but didn't know where. And that setup inside the pool wall disperses the chronotron signal and expands the radius to cover most of the property—which is why Lorena and the baby are still here despite the time shift, but also why most of the team thought the field was being generated by something other than an actual CHRONOS device. No one even knew there was a second key buried out back, because it wasn't activated and therefore didn't send out a signal. My job was simply to get the data from the old project into your hands earlier. To get the three of you talking earlier and see if maybe we could push fast-forward on this research. And if I was successful on that front, they'd pull you in officially and get the device they have in their archives into your hands."

"You keep saying *they*. Who exactly is this *they* that you're part of?"

He's been avoiding my eyes, but he finally looks at me when he answers my question. "I told you I was part of a military family."

"You also told me you weren't *in* the military."

"And that wasn't a lie. I don't even work for the government. I'm a history grad student, just like you. My dad is a civilian now, but he's still a contract worker with the Department of Defense, working on long-range threat assessment. Every indicator they have says the Alliance of the Southern Hemisphere is fracturing, with several of the regional leaders jockeying for power. They can't compete with us in conventional or chemical warfare. Their only edge is biogenetic weapons, and one of the key players in the alliance, Akana, has a history in that regard."

"You're talking about the war with Tchad," Alex says. "In the 2070s."

"Yeah," Jack says. "Although technically it was with the entire East African Union."

This is sounding eerily familiar. I've never tended to remember many details from the war and foreign-policy side of history—it's bloody and it's depressing—so I don't think it's a memory from a world-history class. Also, it feels much more recent. My mind keeps trying to pull up the details as Jack continues.

"Eight months ago, when I was home for a visit," Jack says, "my dad showed me the most recent simulation. That was illegal, to be honest—I don't have any sort of clearance, let alone one that would give me access to that type of information. I thought at first that he just needed someone to talk to about it. To get it off his chest. But..." He shrugs and takes a sip of his drink. "Anyway, when I told you earlier that it *could* be worse, I wasn't kidding. Thirty-two thousand deaths isn't even a drop in the bucket compared to what I saw in that simulation. We're talking hundreds of millions."

"But what does any of this have to do with the CHRONOS device?" Alex asks. "If this hypothetical war hasn't even started yet, why would they need a time traveler to undo it?"

"It's not about undoing anything. The hope is to make sure the balance of power is in our favor from the start. To give us a chance to create antidotes and shore up our defenses *before* the attacks begin."

"I just don't get how your father even knows the keys exist," I say. "You said this group knew there was a CHRONOS key in the house. Has someone been spying on me? I mean, aside from *you.*" He flinches a little at the jab, but I'm actually pretty okay with that.

"They probably detected the chronotron particles," Alex says. "And the US government funded the research back in the 2090s. Like I said before, I think it's possible they had one of these devices."

Jack nods. "They had two of them until the 2092 attacks. The prevailing theory at LORTA—that's what they call the Long-Range Threat Assessment group, which is part of DARPA. That's the—"

"We all know what DARPA is," Alex says, although I'm actually not too clear on that point. I have a vague sense that it's a high-tech research arm of the Department of Defense, but I have no idea what the acronym stands for.

"Okay," Jack says. "Anyway, the analysts at DARPA are pretty much evenly split between thinking the 2092 attacks were by aliens and thinking they were a cover for some group, or possibly a nation, that was trying to destroy the time-travel research."

"Aliens?" I say. "Seriously?"

Jack shrugs, looking a little sheepish. "My dad actually thinks it could be both, as in aliens trying to destroy time-travel research. Or more likely, steal it and cover their tracks. He's never given me a good answer why he believes that, but then he knows a lot more classified stuff than I do, so . . . let's just say I wouldn't discount the possibility. But anyway, the vast majority of people at DARPA would tell you that what happened at the lab was a very *good* thing. I mean, not the attacks themselves. They don't generally applaud things that result in casualties. But they were glad that it put an end to the research. Back in the 2090s, a congressional oversight committee was pushing really hard to terminate the project, arguing that time travel was too risky, that the government wouldn't be able to properly safeguard the technology. They weren't getting a lot of traction, though, because they had classified information they couldn't share for fear that it would leak to the public and cause a mass panic. See, they knew there *had already been changes* to the timeline. Everything was, for the most part, patched up, but it had apparently been a close call. A lot of people could have been killed. And erased."

"How many is a lot?" Alex asks.

"Enough to make this current time shift look like a tiny blip. At least as many casualties as we're likely to see if we end up in a full-scale genetics war. And the simulation my dad showed me . . ." Jack trails off, looking over at me. "You've got to understand that this isn't just idle conjecture. The projections are based on intelligence not just from our own agencies but backed up with data from the entire Northern Alliance."

His eyes stay on me as he speaks, clearly pleading with me to try and understand why he lied to me. To be honest, though, I'm more interested right now in the changes to the timeline that he mentioned than I am in his excuses. So I nudge the conversation back in that direction. "When did this other time shift occur?"

"During the Patterson administration, back in the early 2000s. Only a handful of people in the government knew what really happened. The administration passed it off as a terrorist attack. Which may be why the LORTA crowd is suspicious about the official explanation for 2092—they know it was used as a cover earlier that century. The key they had wasn't found in the rubble. Nor was the body of the guy who'd had some success using it. But the oversight committee had read the classified documents. They knew how close we'd come to a total catastrophe and didn't think it was wise to go down that road again. My dad said he viewed the bombing of the temporal-physics lab as the one silver lining of the 2092 attacks." He glances around the library. "And . . . Kate Pierce-Keller was at the center of the whole thing."

I sit there quietly for a moment and then sigh. "*Of course* she was. I should have known that breaking the timeline would turn out to be a family tradition."

"No," Jack says. "You don't understand. Kate was the one who fixed it."

FROM THE *NEW YORK DAILY INTREPID* (MARCH 27, 1965)

Klan Leader Declares Liuzzo and Reeb Murders a Communist Plot

(Birmingham, Ala.) At a press conference held at the Dinkler-Tutwiler Hotel, Robert M. Shelton, Imperial Wizard of the Ku Klux Klan, claimed that the recent murders of two white civil rights workers were part of a "Communist plot to destroy the right wing in America." Furthermore, Shelton asserted he had specific evidence proving the murders were committed by Communist agents hoping to tarnish the reputation of the Klan.

Rev. James J. Reeb of Boston died on March 11 from injuries sustained when he was clubbed in Selma two days earlier. Mrs. Viola G. Liuzzo, 39, of Detroit, was shot in her car near Lowndesboro, Alabama, on Thursday night. Federal charges were filed yesterday against four Alabama Klansmen in connection with that shooting.

Shelton noted that the $200,000 bail ($50,000 for each of the four defendants) was raised by his organization and "some other of our friends." Collie LeRoy Wilkins Jr., 21, of Fairfield, remained in jail due to violating probation on a previous weapons charge. William Orville Eaton, 41, and Eugene Thomas, 43, both of Bessemer, and Gary Thomas Rowe Jr., 31, of Birmingham were released on bond yesterday.

A preliminary hearing is set for April 15 at 11 a.m.

∞21∞

My shoes squelch in the mud as I round the corner of the building and set another observation point at Campsite 4, located at the Catholic mission in downtown Montgomery otherwise known as the City of St. Jude. The rain has been intermittent since I arrived at the stable point near the state capitol around noon. Just a light drizzle, really, so the weather must have been bad for the past few days, or maybe the field is just perpetually muddy. Tomorrow, when the marchers and the troops protecting them arrive, there will be well over seven thousand people here, by most accounts. These soggy fields will probably look like they were the site of a buffalo stampede by the time the marchers depart Thursday morning.

The City of St. Jude was founded back in the 1930s specifically to minister to African Americans, and the campus is bustling today. School is in session, just as it will be tomorrow when the marchers arrive. It must be recess now, or phys ed class, since a bunch of kids are playing kickball on the muddy field where the marchers will eventually camp, as two nuns watch from a nearby bench. St. Jude's Hospital, the first integrated hospital in the Southeast, has a steady flow of traffic today, as well. It's where Viola Liuzzo will be taken

Thursday night, assuming we manage to set the timeline straight. Otherwise, the medical personnel there will be tending to the sniper's victims after the Stars for Freedom rally.

I suspect that the workers here at St. Jude are on edge today, however. When Dr. King contacted the parish priest to ask if the marchers could camp here on the final night of their five-day journey, there was really never any question that the priest would say yes. There was also never any question that the mission would face a financial backlash for doing so. Many of their regular donors were white middle-class residents of the city who viewed funding a school and a hospital for underprivileged blacks as part of their civic or religious duty. Funding an institution giving open support to black "agitators" working for the right to vote, however, was apparently a bridge too far for many of them. In the previous timeline, the mission nearly closed in the aftermath of the Selma march, until tempers died down and fundraising returned to fairly normal levels.

I'm not sure what happens to the place in this timeline, and that's more than a little disconcerting for me. For the past decade, I've studied race relations in the mid-1960s almost exclusively. I know this period of history inside out . . . or at least I *did*. After tomorrow, I'll be on much shakier ground. I read through a brief revised history of the civil rights movement—one in which Viola Liuzzo lives and King dies three years earlier—while we were getting ready for the trip and added a few other books and articles to my diary so I could consult them while we're here. But it's not the same. I don't understand the connections yet, how one action leads to the next. That's what makes it history. Otherwise, it's just a string of random events.

Before the time shift, thousands of troops, both state and federal, would be guarding the City of St. Jude tomorrow night. In this reality, President Johnson still nationalizes the Alabama National Guard, but a significant number came down with a nasty stomach bug or food poisoning two days ago, just after the march began in Selma.

One newspaper image showed a line of guardsmen standing off to the side, vomiting, while others were carted away in military vehicles. The illness never spread to the federal troops or the marchers, leading historians of this new timeline to suspect that the Alabama National Guard's rations were tainted, possibly on purpose. One of the marchers swore she saw several bottles of ipecac syrup in a ditch before someone came along and scooped them up. It could even have been the members of the guard consuming those rations who did the tainting. Many of them were furious about being called up against the wishes of their governor for a purpose they opposed, and puking your guts out on the side of the road would have been a perfect, if somewhat unpleasant, way to get pulled off the detail without risking a court martial.

Even with the mass defection, this area will be heavily guarded tomorrow night. There will be at least a thousand troops in the area, possibly more. Even so, the sniper was never apprehended. Witnesses believed the shot came from one of the houses across the street from the field, although they couldn't entirely discount the possibility that the shots were fired from a vehicle on one of those streets. If the gunman got away, even when there were hundreds of observers on the lookout for troublemakers, I'm not confident I'll fare any better at finding him.

No one has paid much attention to me wandering around. The cord that holds my CHRONOS key hangs down from my hands, and to a casual observer, I probably look like a guy taking a morning stroll while praying the rosary. The only person who seemed to notice me at all was a girl about my age who was getting out of a cab when I walked by, and that's possibly because I was also looking at her. She was pretty, with blond hair, wearing jeans and a blue flowered shirt. Not a pale blonde, like Katherine. This girl's hair was more of a honey color. But it was still close enough that it got me thinking about the three blond women the sniper will target tomorrow night, which is the reason Angelo changed his mind and let me do this jump solo.

When I returned to the Peabody Hotel after the Klan meeting in Collierville last night, Rich and Katherine both agreed that Lendell Phelps's presence in the area, and his plan to be at the Beatles concert, seems a bit too coincidental not to be connected to the time shift. Something I did or said in my interactions with the South Carolina Klan must have convinced Phelps to change his plans and travel to Memphis. And maybe having Uncle Lenny there to egg him on is the reason that Billy Meeks and the others will decide that they need to do more than simply put a scare into Lennon. Scoggin not being with Phelps in Collierville seems odd, given that they're both in the news photo, but maybe Scoggin comes in the next day, just in time for the concert.

With the Memphis area Klan's involvement in killing Lennon now seeming highly probable, we followed Angelo's direction and one of us—me—reported back to HQ. Katherine and Richard are still at the hotel in Memphis, and Katherine, at least, is going to be pissed at me for talking Angelo into letting me go solo on this jump. I'm to report back once I know the identity of the shooter and the location he's firing from.

I wasn't being sexist, even though I'm sure she will argue the point. It was the combination of listening to Glen's report about Buster Wilson's obsession with getting back at his ex-wife and the pictures of the three women who were targeted by the sniper that worried me. It's entirely possible that the sniper wasn't aiming at a specific target when he hit Mary Travers and James Baldwin. But Travers was a blond woman in the company of a black man. The fact that all three women targeted by the sniper at the concert were blondes just doesn't seem like a coincidence to me, given that whites were a fairly small fraction of the people in attendance. Maybe lighter hair just showed up better under the lights, and the gunman took the easiest targets. Or maybe he's seeking a twisted, indirect sort of revenge against some blond woman in his life. Maybe, like Buster Wilson, he's got a grudge he's looking to settle.

Either way, I don't think it's a safe jump for Katherine. To be honest, though, it's not just her hair. I'm also a little worried about her screwing something up. I fully recognize the irony of that, when we're almost certainly in this mess because of something I did, and I know that Katherine is a damn good historian. I've read reports from her various jumps. She spent several months undercover with abolition and suffrage groups, and also their opposition, during the nineteenth century. And she does learn fast. But she's only made a few jumps to the twentieth century. As quick as she is on her feet, she doesn't know the lingo of this era. This is simply not her time period. That was pretty clear at the Jesus rally in Memphis. Katherine looked the part, and she seemed to fit in at first, but she was out of her element. And in South Carolina, the Klan women weren't even willing to give her a chance until I introduced her—again, not her fault, but simply the reality of being a fish out of water. If we were in 1865 rather than 1965, I'd happily take the bench and follow Katherine's lead. But we're not, and a lot is on the line here.

The same is true, to a lesser extent, of Richard. He's got as much experience in the mid-1960s as I do. Maybe more. But for him, it's all about the music, and he's only dealt with segregation as it pertains to entertainers. The Beatles bonfire was tame. No violence, just a lot of trash talk.

What I said to Katherine the other day at the OC is true—we all have historical tunnel vision. Simply put, our task here is much more within the realm of my training than theirs. I may be the junior partner in this trio, but I'm the only one with relevant experience.

I think Angelo knows that, too, and that's why he was so willing to bench the two of them. All I had to do was mention the unexpectedly high proportion of blond women among the deceased, and

Angelo picked up on my point instantly. He suggested that Richard should stay behind as well, but I suspect it was just as cover to keep Katherine from being too annoyed. And while Rich might be a little pissed off, all I'll have to do is point out that my goal was keeping Katherine safe, and all will be forgiven.

Angelo also didn't get much time to think things through before our first meeting. Maybe he's realized that giving me two partners who are armed only with stun guns disguised as watches could make them as much liabilities as assets. Because even though I hate to admit it, my gut instinct tells me I'm going to come away from this with blood on my hands.

∞

"You happy with the table, hon?" the waitress asks as she lays down a paper coaster and puts my bourbon on top. "'Cause we can move you to another one if you ain't. Place don't usually fill up for another half hour or so."

She's right on that point. The main reason I'm here this early is because the restaurant is more likely to be empty, despite the discounted early bird special. My goal is to set up a few observation points and drop some of the listening devices without being noticed, but I seem to have landed an unusually alert waitress. And I definitely don't want to move. This is the one table in the room that affords me a clear view of the front door, the lobby, and the bar, where I dropped a couple of recorders and set a stable point before I came over to the restaurant.

I give her my best smile and slip into my Troy Rayburn drawl. "The table's perfect, ma'am. I've just been driving all day, and when you spend that much time behind the wheel, it feels mighty good to get up and stretch the legs a bit. Know what I mean?"

She smiles back at me. "I sure do. We drove straight through to Nashville last summer, and it took me a week to get the kinks out of my back. You decided what you want to eat, hon, or you need a minute?"

"Well, I'm starting with the French onion soup, but I need to look at the rest of the menu. Last time I ate was breakfast, and that was before dawn, so I'm gonna be keepin' you busy for the next hour."

"Yessir. You take your time."

I do take my time, working my way slowly through the soup, a lackluster salad, a steak more notable for quantity than quality, and a damn good slice of strawberry shortcake, along with a few more drinks and several cups of coffee. Eating alone always makes me feel conspicuous, so I picked up an Ian Fleming novel at the drugstore on the walk over from the stable point near the state capitol. I keep one eye on the book and one on the door. As the waitress predicted, the restaurant does indeed fill up, but none of the faces are ones I recognize. Families, mostly, along with some singles like me, probably passing through on business.

I'm not sure that any outside Klansmen will be in town tonight, since it's a weekday and a lot of them will have to work. The average member in 1965 doesn't have money to blow on hotels. Leaders do, though, since they tend to consider the Klan treasury their own personal slush fund. Plus, like other organized-crime bosses, they aren't above taking kickbacks from local businesses in exchange for so-called protection.

Rank-and-file members, however, are the ones most likely to be on the other end of a sniper rifle. I doubt they'll stay in town at all after the shooting, if it's the same group that killed Viola Liuzzo in the original timeline. They only live about a hundred miles away, and no matter how inclined the local police might be to turn a blind eye toward a wrecking crew attacking several thousand civil rights activists, you don't tempt fate by staying in the area. The police might feel the need to make an example for once.

And if any Klan members *are* in town, they'll be here at the Exchange. Aside from a bellhop and the young man who bussed my table, I haven't seen a single face that wasn't white. Technically, hotels and restaurants are supposed to be integrated in 1965, but the Civil Rights Act isn't even a year old, and most establishments in the South are dragging their feet when it comes to compliance. If this had been a year ago, I couldn't have ruled out the possibility that any Klan members in town for the march might have stayed at the Jefferson Davis Hotel, which was, after all, named for the Confederate States' president. But the chain that owns that hotel has received a couple of bomb threats over the past year, since they received a personal request to desegregate from Attorney General Robert Kennedy and decided not to fight the new law.

The Exchange has its own Civil War history. Jefferson Davis gave a speech in the old Exchange building, on this same site. And it's widely known that even though official votes are taken at the capitol, the real decision-making happens here, over whiskey and cigars.

A little after seven, when it's clear I can't drag out my stay at the table any longer without incurring the wrath of my waitress, I pay the check and carry my half-finished drink over to the bar on the other side of the lobby. The place reminds me a bit of Campbell's Redwing Room at the OC, all dark wood and burgundy leather. It's a lot smokier than any room at the OC, however, where any toxic fumes are enclosed in ventilation bubbles and whisked up to the ceiling. The smell in this room is a bit like an ashtray filled with whiskey.

As I enter, I realize that I must have gotten a little too involved in *You Only Live Twice*, or else there's a back door I didn't know about. Three men are sitting together at a table at the other end of the bar. I recognize two of them. The first is Robert Chambliss, sometimes called "Dynamite Bob." I suspect he started the nickname. He's as nasty a snake as I've encountered, and not half as smart as he thinks he is. He's one of the guys who bombed the Sixteenth Street Church in Birmingham, killing four girls, in 1963. Chambliss won't be convicted until he's an old man. The testimony at the trial indicated that he'd designed the bomb to go off when the church was empty, not during services, but I'm not sure I believe that.

Officially a member of the Eastview Klavern 13, one of the most vicious in KKK history, Dynamite Bob is also the leader of a rather informal group called the Cahaba Boys. They're sort of a permanent wrecking crew, although I think the more common term around here is "action squad." Most of them are still members of Klavern 13, even though they generally think the KKK has gone soft.

I'm a little surprised to see Chambliss here. He wasn't one of the four men indicted for killing Viola Liuzzo, and nothing I read indicated he was even in Montgomery for the end of the Selma march. I've only met Chambliss once, and we didn't speak directly, so I doubt he'll recognize me. Still, I take a seat at a booth on the other side of the room where the light is dim. Once I'm settled, I tap the disk behind my ear.

When the display pops up, I select the closest of the seven listening devices I've scattered around the building. The only thing I hear is ambient noise and the occasional crunch, because there's a lull in the conversation right now. They're drinking and munching on bar peanuts. Waiting on someone or something, from the looks of it.

Collie Wilkins, one of the men who will be charged with killing Viola Liuzzo, sits on Chambliss's right. Wilkins is a baby-faced guy in his early twenties. His hair is puffed up just a bit in front and slicked down on the sides and back, and a cigarette hangs from his lips. He doesn't really look much like Elvis, but I suspect that's the image he's going for.

The other guy's back is to me, so I can't see his face. When he shifts slightly to the left, however, I see something in the breast pocket of his jacket that nearly causes me to drop the glass I'm holding. Vivid purple light seeps through the holes in the fabric.

I reflexively clutch the CHRONOS key in my own pocket, making sure it's securely inside the pouch the guy from costuming gave me. Then I slide over a bit more into the shadows and set a stable point from this angle. I'm definitely going to want the others to see this when I get back.

The three men are talking about an upcoming boxing match. Wilkins says he's not going to watch it. That Clay, or Muhammad Ali, or whatever you want to call him isn't the heavyweight champion anymore, so it's a pointless fight. Chambliss snorts and says he's damn sure going to watch, assuming they don't cancel, because no matter who wins, he'll get to see an uppity monkey with a big ego hit the ground. He says he hopes it's Ali. Says he's got five bucks on Liston to smack Ali's smart-ass mouth right off his face this time.

The guy with the CHRONOS key asks if they're sure theaters in Birmingham are carrying the fight on closed-circuit. Chambliss says it will probably be downtown at The Alabama, but Wilkins seems convinced it's at a drive-in theater. They're debating whether it's possibly at both when Bob Shelton, Imperial Wizard of United Klans of America, walks past my booth. He claps the mystery guy on the shoulder and motions for him to slide over.

Shelton tells the men he can only stay a few minutes. Then he congratulates the guy next to him for his idea about the Ex-Lax and ipecac combo in the rations. "I think a few of them overindulged," he says, "but it beats the hell out of an Article 15 or worse. Three-quarters of the state guard volunteered for your version of the stomach flu, so we're down to mostly feds. I still think that's too many to plan a major action, unless you guys come up with some ideas tonight. Just let me know through normal channels. But nothin' too blatant, or we'll be callin' *you* Crazy Tommy."

All three of the other men chuckle at that.

There were at least two men called Tommy that some historical accounts connect to Klavern 13 or the Cahaba Boys. But to the best of my knowledge, the only one Shelton ever called Crazy Tommy was Gary Thomas "Tommy" Rowe, who was eventually revealed to be an FBI informant. Glen was with the Birmingham area Klans for several years, and he claims that Rowe never managed to make it into the inner circle. That he found out about a lot of events *after* the fact. Rowe did inform the FBI that some members of Klavern 13 were heading to Montgomery to greet the marchers from Selma, but that was the last they heard from him before he was arrested with the three other men for shooting Liuzzo.

From the way Shelton emphasized the word *you*, however, I don't think this guy is actually Rowe. I shift to try to get a better look, but I can only see his profile. He's about the same build as the images I remember seeing of Rowe, but the face is wrong. I hate using my retinal screen on jumps, because anyone looking at you can see your eyes jerking around, but I risk it this once. And sure enough, the man next to Shelton isn't Tommy Rowe. But then I was sure he was an imposter of some sort as soon as I saw the light from the medallion in his breast pocket.

What's bugging me is that he still looks familiar. I scroll through all of the faces in my files for Klavern 13, and none of them match. I'm almost convinced that he just has one of those generic faces when he picks up the cigar resting on the ashtray and taps it against the edge. It's something about the movement, the way he flicks the tip of the cigar with his thumbnail. And then I see a ruby signet ring on his other hand. I can't get a good look, but I'd be willing to wager that the initials on the side are *OC.*

This man is about seventy pounds thinner and at least twenty-five years younger than the version holding court at the Objectivist Club in 2304. But it's him. I'm certain. The hair is a good bit shorter than the portrait of him hanging in the Redwing Room at the OC, but otherwise it's a perfect likeness.

After all these years of wishing he could time travel, Morgen Campbell has somehow gotten hold of a CHRONOS key. And even more baffling, he's also acquired the genetic enhancement that allows him to use it.

FROM *THE PHYSICS OF MANY PATHS* BY STANFORD FULLER (2032)

I am not a scientist. Anyone who picks up this book probably knows that already. The nature of my gift has, however, made me curious about those fields of science that might explain why I see the things I do. So while my understanding of the theories discussed in this chapter is that of a layperson, not a physicist, it is a subject that I have endeavored to understand as best I can.

I'm not certain if there is a scientific explanation for my seeing The Paths. If so, I fear that it is a very inexact science. The ability has never been something that I can summon at will, and that is why I discourage people who come to me for guidance from raising their hopes too high. The fact that someone is standing before me does not mean that I will see his or her personal crossroads, the alternate paths that might be taken, or the result of those choices. It simply means that there's a chance I'll pick something up. A chance that I might be able to guide that individual toward The Path that will result in their best personal outcome. That's also why I accept no payment, only donations after the fact if someone finds my advice was useful.

The Many-Worlds hypothesis claims that there is an infinite—or at least incredibly large—number of universes branching off from our actions. Every possible option that you could take spins off new possibilities, new realities.

While this concept of multiple universes is a bit overwhelming to imagine, it corresponds very closely with what I have come to call *The Paths*. For some reason, I've been gifted with the ability to catch tiny glimpses of these alternate realities. Some people call these visions, and I suppose they are, in a sense. But I see them as physical paths, much like computer projection models for hurricanes and other unpredictable phenomena. The most likely outcomes cluster into a few thicker branches, but there are also offshoots that fan out in every direction.

When the paths first appear, they are blurry, almost too blurry for me to make out details. Each possible outcome is a separate layer, and with so many layers it's hard to see anything clearly. Sometimes the paths seem to be on the same plane. Other times they intersect at odd angles. Occasionally paths will loop, intersecting at an earlier juncture in time. Those paths are very unstable, and I'm always glad when they finally resolve and I stop seeing them.

∞22∞

I tiptoe down the stairs and into the kitchen, not bothering with the light, and key in the code for pasta Alfredo with broccoli. It usually comes out half-decent and only takes a few minutes. I'm pouring myself a glass of wine, with just three minutes left on the timer, when a shadow falls over the kitchen counter. I know without even turning around that it's Jack.

"Can we talk?" he asks.

"I just came down to get dinner."

"Yes," he says. "I know. It's the *only* time you come down. This is *your* house, Madi. You don't have to hide in your room to avoid me. I'll stay out of your way."

"I'm not hiding."

We both know it's a lie. I'm not sure why I bother denying it. Pride, I guess. If there was a food-processing unit in my bedroom, I wouldn't be here right now.

"I've just been busy," I say. "And I *have* been outside my room. I went for a swim. I even watched Yun Hee for Lorena so she could shower in peace."

Both of those things are true, but they don't disprove Jack's claim about me hiding. The swim was when I knew he was asleep. And Lorena actually brought Yun Hee to my room. The baby was in a much better mood—apparently her tooth finally pushed through—and we watched some animated videos on the wall screen and played peekaboo games until Lorena came back to get her.

Although I don't mention it to Jack, I think Lorena had a secondary motive for leaving the baby with me. Yes, she probably did want a few moments alone, but what she really wanted was for me to bond with Yun Hee. To feel personally connected, so that I'd be willing to go the extra mile to fix this catastrophe. I'm a little insulted that she would think she needed to do that. Every time I look at either one of them, my stomach clenches and my resolve to undo this time shift kicks into turbo. But hey, if Yun Hee were my kid, if my existence and hers hinged on the goodwill of some person I barely knew, I'd probably do the same thing.

To Jack's credit, he doesn't press me. He stands in the doorway, watching silently as I place a stopper in the wine bottle and turn toward the food unit. There's a book in his hands. It's one he was looking at earlier in the library, which I know because there's a stable point in the library that I've been able to view from my room. That's how I know that everything seems fairly normal between Jack and Alex. This fact kind of has me wanting to smack Alex, since his willingness to forgive and forget makes it look like I'm being unreasonable. I don't see how he can be so blasé about the whole thing. True, he wasn't one step away from tumbling into bed with Jack, but the man was his roommate. Jack faked a friendship with him, at least at the beginning. He used all of us to get information, and no matter how sound his reasons may have been, it makes it hard to trust him.

"Did you ever manage to get up with your mom?" Jack asks.

Yesterday, when we spoke briefly in the hallway, I told him I'd managed to locate Nora, but not my mom. Finding Nora was actually easy. Her comm-band account is still the same, which is probably a good thing, since I am on her account and would be screwed otherwise. It was an odd conversation, with me saying only vague things, waiting for Nora to fill in the blanks and confirm what I already strongly suspected. Our conversation at the cottage never happened in this reality, even though I have a blood sample from her downstairs that begs to differ. The cottage was sold last spring, and Nora is living in a rented flat in Bray with a woman who is—or perhaps I should say was—a friend of hers. The arrangement isn't working out at all.

Finding Mom wasn't all that difficult, either, once I thought things through. If Nora's finances are worse, maybe Mom's are a bit better.

In this reality, she got the slightly better end of the financial negotiations after we lost almost everything, because she's in our old house and Nora is in a shared flat. I didn't find out exactly how or why that happened. I think maybe Thea is involved, because when I asked if Mom had heard from her, she said Thea was expected back in a week or two.

"She's still at the address we lived at in London before my father died," I tell Jack. I don't add that the first few minutes of my conversation with her were among the hardest of my life, partly because she was sitting in Dad's old study. But more to the point, I realized that Nora hadn't mentioned Dad when we spoke. Neither of us had. For a full five minutes, as Mom chattered on, I held my breath, wondering if it was possible that he was still alive. But then she said something about the memorial service, and I knew.

"Did you ask her about the genetic enhancement?"

"No," I say. "I didn't see the point, since we intend for this timeline to be temporary."

A long silence follows, in which he just looks miserable. I can tell he's trying to think of something else to ask, so I decide to save him the trouble.

"I'm just not ready to talk yet, okay, Jack? And I'm definitely not ready to talk about anything that doesn't pertain directly to the problems at hand. I mean, it's not like I don't have plenty to keep me occupied right now."

That came out a little more accusatory than intended, but it's true. I'm the only one who can use the stable points, so I had to scan through to find a good time to go back and discuss this current situation with Kate. Alex says it needs to be very close to the time she dies. I've been hunting for a good opportunity in her last few weeks of life, even though that isn't the Kate I want to visit. I'm sure she's a perfectly nice old lady, and she'll probably have some sage advice to offer. But what I want is to go back to when she was younger, when she could actually *use* the key. If she fixed the time shift last time, maybe she could help me now. But Alex says that's too risky, and I suspect he's right. I can't afford to do anything that makes things worse, or that causes my name to appear along with Lorena's on the *Erasures* list.

I've also been going through Kate's and Katherine's diary entries. The goal is to understand as much as I can about what happened in her time before I jump back to talk to her. We won't have much time, so I need a way to quickly let Kate know that I've read—and hopefully, understood—the information she left behind for me. Unfortunately, two days in, I feel more confused than when I started.

"I *know* you're busy," Jack says. "That's what I want to talk about. You can give one of the diaries to me."

I'm about to protest that it would be pointless, but something about his expression stops me. He looks like he's bracing for a blow, and I get the sense he's just confessed to another lie. But if he can't use the key, how can . . .

That's when I remember that first night when we found the diaries. The interface didn't seem to respond nearly as well for Jack, but it *did* respond. And when he realized that it was something that worked better for me—when he realized that it was reacting to the

CHRONOS enhancements—he couldn't get it out of his hands fast enough.

"Yes," he says, before I can get the question out. "I can't jump, but I can see the interface."

"How do you know you can't jump?"

"Because I spent several weeks trying. Not with *your* key. With one that's been in a LORTA vault for the past four decades. I should have told you everything at once, but . . . my father and the colleague who helped him could easily end up in prison if anyone finds out they let me handle it. My sister could be at risk, too, if they find out about me, since she's also enhanced, although I don't have the slightest idea whether the gene is expressed in her case."

This isn't making any sense to me. "So your parents had both of you enhanced?"

"No. Like I told you, I'm from a military family, going back generations."

"Yeah. I remember that part. You're the black sheep because you decided to study history. But what does that have to do with being enhanced?"

"My granddad was one of several dozen military test subjects back in the 2070s. He was in the first round of time-travel guinea pigs, before they figured out that the genetic tweaking had to be in vitro."

"How did they even know what to tweak?"

"They had blood samples from some guy who was imprisoned after the first time shifts happened. I think there was some blood at a crime scene at the Cyrist Temple, too. They developed a serum from those samples. All my grandfather or any of that first group could do was see the light from the key, and he told my dad that he thinks some of the participants may have been lying about that, because having any sort of ability kept them off active duty while the researchers continued trying different formulas. After that, they shifted over to in vitro test subjects. Most of the volunteers were low-income pregnant women whose babies had some sort of problem. Something that could be fixed if they had the money for prenatal gene therapy. The government coerced them into signing their kids up to be test subjects, although they had no clue for what, in order to make sure their babies were born healthy."

"That's . . . awful," I say. "Not the parents. I mean, you'd probably do whatever you had to do in that situation. But it's pretty damn reprehensible on the part of the government to put that kind of condition on the deal."

"Exactly. Anyway, they had to wait for these kids to reach an age where they were responsible enough that they felt comfortable testing them. Or, more to the point, old enough that they understood that there could be repercussions for their families if they misused the device. Only one of the first group seemed to have any real ability, and then 2092 comes along, and he's wiped out, along with the lead researcher."

"That's the researcher Alex mentioned. So, were you part of a second batch of subjects, or . . . ?"

"No. I got the genetic boost the same way you did—inheritance. Only it's coming from just the one side for me, and two generations back. My parents have known that I inherited some enhancements since my birth, but one perk of being a military test subject is that the government doesn't tend to hold things you volunteered for against your offspring, and the program was discontinued long ago. I didn't find out until eight months ago, when my father dropped all of this on me . . . and dropped that damn CHRONOS key into my hand. The hope was that I'd be able to use it. When that failed, he convinced me to pursue Plan B. A few years ago, one of their researchers started picking up the signals that Alex mentioned from the chronotron particles. They were probably here all along, but the research wasn't far along enough to detect it."

"So why didn't they just come get the damn thing?"

"They . . . uh . . . tried," he says, hesitantly. "About six months before you moved in. But they couldn't find it. The signal was dispersed through the house. They thought it might be in the basement, because it seemed a bit stronger down there. But the scientists finally decided that there wasn't actually a key here. That someone had just figured out a way to put the house under a chronotron field without one."

"Is that possible?"

Jack shrugs. "Alex thinks so. He says that these diaries emit the chronotron particles, too, so he's examining one to see how that works. He can't risk opening up one of the medallions to examine it. I mean, you obviously need yours in order to travel back to fix this, and we can't leave the place unprotected now, because of Lorena and the baby. That's what he's been working on the past few days—trying to extend the field from one of the diaries without diluting it too much. Well, that's one of the things he's working on. He's also discovered what he says are weird surges in the field at the times when you jumped to Liverpool and to Montgomery."

I start to ask for more information, but he cuts me off. "That's the only thing I understood from what Alex told me, and he talked for a good five minutes. He didn't seem to think the field around the house was in any danger of collapsing, though. He was pretty excited about the possibility of stabilizing that surge."

"If the diaries have a CHRONOS field, maybe we should have Lorena carry one. And Yun Hee, too."

We had talked about pulling the key out of the device in the basement and having Lorena wear it, but that's risky, since the house would no longer be shielded. If there's another shift, Alex or Jack might be affected, and we kind of need everyone to keep their memories intact.

Plus, after this latest time shift, some of the books in the library would also pop out of existence if they're not under the CHRONOS field. That's a minor consideration compared to protecting Lorena and the baby, but I suspect James Coleman would have an entirely new crop of orphaned works to adopt as his own if he were still alive. I'll admit that I feel a slight twinge thinking about this. What if it is *Flowers for Algernon* that is unwritten? Or the Harry Potter books I loved as a child? Suddenly I'm a lot more sympathetic to Kate and James's plan to ensure that certain works weren't erased along with their authors. If what I assume is correct, *Flowers for Algernon* and the other books James published *were* erased in an earlier time shift. Faced with the choice of those books never being written, never being read, I'd probably have done the exact same thing my great-grandfather did. And it wasn't just the fiction. Those odd alternative histories are probably from other timelines. They are dry, almost unreadable— but the same can be said of most actual history textbooks.

"I still don't think we could chance them going outside of the house," he says. "Even if that field around the diaries is stable, it would be too big of a risk."

"True. Since Alex needs an extra key to experiment on, maybe you could go grab the one from your dad?"

Jack rolls his eyes at the hint of sarcasm in my voice. "It's back in the vault at DARPA. His successor risked a lot letting him borrow it the first time around. And anyway . . . I haven't actually told my dad that you can use it."

The food unit finally beeps, and I'm glad to have something else to focus on while I think that last comment through. Jack's purpose was to get this research fast-tracked. Why wouldn't he tell his father that I can use the key?

My plan had been to take the pasta and my glass of wine back up to my room, but I carry them over to the octagonal table that is recessed into the kitchen wall. The table and benches are made of dark, heavy wood. I've sat here often while eating breakfast, but now, for the first time, I wonder if the table was here when Kate or

Katherine owned this house. Did they sit here around this table, trying to sort out how to undo the last temporal catastrophe? Did Kate and her husband take their meals here with their children and grandchildren?

Jack is still standing in the doorway. "Grab a glass and the rest of the bottle," I say, nodding toward the bench across from me.

I'm still angry with him. In fact, there's a part of me that's even more angry now, because when he was supposedly coming clean with me, he was still holding this back. On the other hand, I'm apparently not the only one who has recently discovered they're genetically altered. That was a tough pill for me to swallow. I'm sure it was the same for Jack.

He pours himself some wine and then hovers the bottle over my glass. When I nod, he tops it off.

Once he's seated, I pull the CHRONOS key out and hand it to him. "What *really* happens when you hold it?"

He colors slightly. "I'm sorry I lied to you—"

"Not now. Just tell me what you can see."

He centers the key in his palm. "I see the light, but not like you do. It's sort of a turquoise color. And I can keep the interface steady, even scroll through the stable points and set the time. If I watch the stable points long enough, things change—people walking past, and so forth. But I can't blink into the location. Not even really short jumps—in terms of time or distance. Absolutely no luck."

"Can you set a new stable point?"

"I haven't tried. Didn't even know you could do that until you mentioned it."

My stomach responds with a very audible growl.

"You should eat," he says. "It's going to get cold."

"What have you found out from the diary you're holding?" I dig into the pasta as he talks.

"Actually, I don't think it's a diary. I've spent the past two days going through the stacks in the library. There were two more of these books tucked away inside the shelves, but they don't appear to have belonged to anyone in particular, since there's no name written inside the cover. One says *Book of Prophecy* on the front. That's one of the Cyrist religious texts. Not the *Book of Cyrus*—they distributed that one far and wide—but the other one that the clerics kept mostly secret."

"Yeah. I spotted that one on the shelves the other day. I think it's a joke of some sort, though. It's blank."

He nods, placing the diary he's holding on the table. "This one is blank, too, but you may find the title interesting."

He slides it over to me. There's barely enough light in here to read, but I make out the words *Log of Stable Points*.

"I think we owe RJ credit for that title," he says.

It takes a moment, but I remember. "That's right. That first day that I demonstrated the key to him and Lorena, he said we'd need to put together a log of stable points, to present to buyers along with the device."

"Do you think maybe the book is blank because RJ is no longer part of the team?" Jack asks.

I consider it, and then shake my head. "Doesn't make sense. The book has been under the CHRONOS field the entire time. His name is still in that *Brief History of CHRONOS* book, isn't it? Also, Kate mentioned this in her . . ." I stop, remembering that I couldn't view the videos or other linked files in the diary until I started using the eardisk. "Hold on. Maybe it's not blank."

Pushing my half-eaten pasta aside, I hurry upstairs to grab the disk and diaries from my nightstand. Then I dig through my bag and find the vial with the rest of the disks. If Jack can use the equipment even a little bit, maybe it will be enough for him to see the videos and scan through events occurring at stable points.

When I get back downstairs, I toss Jack the vial. He gives me a questioning look.

"I figured out what these were for while I was gone, but with everything else going on, I forgot to mention it. Also, I didn't have any idea you could use it. Just peel one off and press it into the little hollow behind your ear. It's . . . kind of a speaker, but it must be sending a signal to the optic nerves, too, because that's how I can see the videos."

While he's figuring out how to adhere the disk behind his ear, I open the *Log of Stable Points* and discover that it's exactly what the title claims. Flipping through, I see that there are hundreds—no, it's easily thousands—of locations. As with the key, they all have date ranges during which the spots are viable. A lot of them are dark, but I'm guessing that's because they're tucked away in an alley or a closet or whatever. None of them go past 2160, which seems to be a strict cutoff date for time travel.

"Okay, here's what I don't get," I say to Jack. "If the title is based on what RJ said that day in the living room, who created all of these stable points? Who tested them to make sure the dates were accurate? That's what I was supposed to do, right? I was supposed to come up with a menu of jump locations as part of this package we'd deliver along with the key."

Jack gives me a weak smile. "Looks like you already did it. So I guess you can skip that step."

"But the work has to be done at some point, or the book will cease to exist. Right?"

"Not if some other version of you in another timeline already did it. Like I said, the diaries have a CHRONOS field, so they're protected even in this timeline. Or at least, that's my best guess."

I start to say, yet again, that it doesn't make sense. Because it truly doesn't. But I'm starting to feel like that song is stuck on repeat, so I just ask the question that's still circling in the periphery of my mind.

"Why didn't you tell your father that I can use the key?"

Jack is quiet for a moment, staring down into his wineglass. "Remember the day when we were sitting in the quad eating lunch, about a month after we met? A squirrel came over and swiped a piece of your bread. You told me how different the squirrels here look from the red squirrels in the nature preserve where you used to hike with your dad. At Glen . . . something."

"Glendalough."

"Yeah. And we started talking about coping with losing someone you loved. About the way it carves out a hole inside of you."

I nod, because I do remember the conversation, vividly. I'd spoken with people who had experienced grief, but our conversations had been fairly superficial. They'd all said it gets better with time. Which I had found to be true, for the most part, but also *not* true. Jack was the first person who understood that. *The hole gets smaller every day,* he'd said when he told me about his mother dying. *But it never fully heals. And maybe you don't want it to heal completely. At least, I don't. I want that space inside of me to be the one place where she still lives.*

In that moment, I'd felt like we really connected. But then Jack looked away and shifted the topic abruptly. A few minutes later he'd shoved his things back into his pack, saying he needed to stop at the library before class. I'd tossed the last of my pita to the squirrel as I watched him walk away, mystified by his sudden change of mood.

"I was already attracted to you," he says, with his eyes still locked on his glass. "That was true from the beginning, even though I knew it wasn't smart, given the reasons I was seeking you out in the first place. But I can pinpoint that afternoon in the quad as the moment I fell in love with you."

Jack's hand moves almost imperceptibly toward mine, and then he moves it back to his wineglass in silent acknowledgment that he knows things have changed. That I will have to be the one to make that first move, to give him the green light.

"But the other reason is because what you said in the basement is dead on," he adds, looking down at the table. "My father is a good man, but he's got a very *utilitarian* point of view, like pretty much everyone else in the military. They'll give lip service to the whole thing about no soldier left behind, but it doesn't disguise the underlying core belief that the good of the many outweighs the good of the one. If I let them know you can use that key, you will more or less be drafted into whatever they think we need to do to prevent our enemies from launching a global pandemic. Most likely, that will include you being sent back to kill Elizabeth Forson or erase—" Jack stops suddenly. He stares at me for a second and pushes up from the table.

I follow Jack as he runs toward the staircase that leads to the library. "Elizabeth Forson?" I ask. "I've heard the name. Who is she?"

"It's *they*, actually. Elizabeth Forson developed an ethnic bioweapon in the early 2070s. She's dead, but one of her two cloned daughters, Liza Forson, is carrying on her work. And based on the intelligence my dad has seen, she's ratcheting things up a notch."

Alex is at one of the tables, running a tiny scalpel along the edge of the binding of a CHRONOS diary, as we enter the library. The computer I've come to think of as the *Anomalies Machine* is dark. Jack pokes at the display, and when it comes up, he opens the database.

He types in the name *Forson* and selects search all.

Two entries pop up:

Elizabeth Anne Forson II

Elizabeth Anne Forson III √

Both erased. One significant.

"What are you guys looking at?" Alex asks, glancing up from his book surgery.

Jack slides down into the closest chair and gives me a look of abject misery. I hold his gaze for several seconds and discover several very important things in that silent moment.

First, everything Jack has been telling me is true.

Second, despite the fact that this time shift conveniently wiped away a genocidal maniac, he agrees with me that we can't let it stand. That we will have to find another way.

Third, I'm in love with him. That's probably been true for quite some time, but it's a crystal-clear fact at the very front of my mind now. Undeniable. Big, bold, flashing letters. I'm not sure if I've entirely forgiven him for not telling me the truth from the beginning, but I *will* forgive him. Because I'm in love with him.

And finally, I realize Jack and I are doing that same couples-telepathy thing that Lorena and RJ are always doing. That last flash of insight comes, in part, from Alex's expression, which I catch out of the corner of my eye as he goes over to inspect the Anomalies Machine. He looks annoyed and more than a little baffled.

"Could one of you please explain who Elizabeth Forson is?" Alex asks. "And maybe what she did to earn that blue check mark?"

"She killed nearly a billion people," Jack tells him. "The time shift erased her. And unfortunately, we're going to have to risk *un*erasing her."

FROM THE *NEW YORK DAILY INTREPID* (AUGUST 20, 1966)

(Memphis, Tenn.) The second of two performances by British singing sensations the Beatles was disrupted on Friday when a man tossed a cherry bomb onto the stage. A crowd of 12,500 fans, many of them teenagers, attended the show at Mid-South Coliseum last evening.

An individual in the regalia of the Ku Klux Klan told a television reporter earlier this week that his organization took issue with Lennon's statement and were planning a few "surprises." Tomatoes and light bulbs were tossed at the stage prior to detonating the cherry bomb.

Members of the audience near the front stated that they were initially concerned that the explosion was a gunshot. Security personnel apprehended the culprit, and the concert continued without further incident.

∞23∞

The four Klan members drop their voices almost to a whisper, forcing me to crank the volume up all the way on my earpiece in order to hear them. It's hard to filter out the background noise at this setting. Each time they put a glass down, it sounds like someone dropped an anvil onto the table.

"I got two devices in a suitcase in my trunk," Chambliss says. "All I gotta do is connect some wires and we're set."

Collie Wilkins's eyes grow wide. I'm guessing he rode down from Birmingham in that car without any clue what Dynamite Bob had packed for the trip.

"And where are you thinking of placing them?" Shelton asks. "The march is supposed to end on the steps of the state capitol. The governor has been pretty good about giving us cover, but that won't extend to blowin' shit up on his front steps."

"Then we hit 'em before they get to the capitol."

"During the march?" Wilkins asks. "Wouldn't that be a little hard to set up?"

"Well, no," Chambliss admits. "*During* the march ain't a good idea, since we don't know exactly what route they'll take. But we do know where they're stayin' tomorrow night."

Shelton snorts. "Yeah. On church property. Because blowin' up a church went really well for us last time. And now you want both dead kids *and* dead nuns? The press will crucify us, even if they can't prove anything. The feds, too, for that matter."

Chambliss is silent for a moment. "So you're sayin' we should just pack it up, then?" he asks sullenly. "Let the feds, the NAACP, the *Reverend Doctor*, and the rest of those commie bastards just take over the goddamn state? Hell, they even got celebrities comin' in. I thought you said—"

Shelton leans across the table. "Lower your damn voice, Bobby. You know full well I ain't sayin' that."

Campbell has been quiet up to this point. "I think what he's saying is that we need to do *something*, but it needs to be a little more strategic."

The look Chambliss gives Campbell is downright poisonous. And while I can barely see Shelton's face from this angle, his spine definitely stiffens as he glances over at Campbell. Despite the ludicrous titles, the United Klans of America claims to operate within a military structure. As Imperial Wizard, Robert Shelton considers himself the commander in chief. I doubt he's a big fan of one of the troops cutting in to interpret his words for him.

Campbell doesn't seem to pick up on that, though. "The FBI's got experts who look for bomb signatures," he continues. "They'll recognize yours and tie it back to Birmingham. I'm thinking it needs to be more of a surgical strike. Something that makes a strong statement about all the sympathizers flocking into the South instead of minding their own damn business. We got pissed off men all over the state who agree with us, but they're too chickenshit to take a stand. That includes all of the little splinter Klans. Wouldn't mind seein' one of the other groups catch some flak for a change. What we don't need is something that can be tied back to us."

Am I the only one noticing the way Campbell's accent comes and goes? And is his comment about the FBI analyzing bomb signatures even accurate in 1965? They may have been looking for commonalities in the design of explosives, but I doubt they called them *bomb signatures* back then.

I've been trying to push my questions about what he's doing here aside for the time being, partly because I need to focus on what they're saying, but also because I still can't entirely wrap my head around the fact that Morgen Campbell is using a CHRONOS key. Or rather, he *was* using a key a few decades back, since the Morgen across the bar looks like he's thirty, max. Although, the guy could be a clone, I guess.

I don't have any questions at all about how he got a key. You can buy almost anything on the black market when you're as wealthy as Campbell. But you have to acquire the CHRONOS gene before you're even born. Plus, the key doesn't function on its own. He'd have to have bribed one of the techs—or, more likely, a bunch of them—along with security personnel, and who knows how many others in order to pull this off.

"Sounds like you got somethin' in mind, *Wayne*," Shelton says softly. "Why don't you enlighten us about your plan?"

Campbell must notice the undertone of venom in Shelton's voice. "Well, it ain't really a plan," he says, his accent miraculously in place again. "More of an idea I just had. Maybe a sniper would be better this time. They expect us to use a bomb, so instead we take up position in one of the houses across the street and just pick off a few people. Maybe one of their celebrities, even. I got an old army buddy I served with in Korea. He's over in Prattville now. He'd take care of it for fifty bucks, no questions asked."

"R-i-i-ght," Chambliss says. "He gets caught and suddenly he's singin' like the goddamn Beatles."

Shelton shrugs. "No more of a risk than one of you doing it. Why does this guy work so cheap?"

I get a good look at Campbell's face this time, because he turns to give Shelton a grin that sets my teeth on edge. "Let's just say my friend loves his work. He'd do the killing for free. The fifty bucks is for the no-questions-asked part."

"And he's available?" Shelton asks.

It's Campbell's turn to shrug. "Won't know 'til I ask. He'll want payment up front, though."

Shelton stands, pulls out his wallet, and tosses some bills onto the table. "That should cover the tab, too. And, Wayne?" He waits until Campbell looks up at him. "You'll be payin' the treasury back that fifty bucks if I ain't happy. And don't use the damn phone. Drive over and ask him."

After Shelton leaves, the other three order another round. I debate going back to HQ to tell them about Campbell. But I still don't know for certain who the shooter is, or where he's firing from, and Angelo said we need to minimize the back-and-forth jumps as much as possible. So, I head up to my room to scan the stable points and see what information I can find on this Wayne guy that Campbell is impersonating and why he's here with Collie Wilkins tonight, instead of Tommy Rowe. It's not like I can follow him to his war buddy's house. I don't have a rental car, and I'd look kind of conspicuous tailing him in a taxi. Plus, I've got a sneaky feeling this whole thing with his homicidal friend was already arranged.

Once I'm in the room, I scan through my files for Klavern 13, to see if there's a Wayne mentioned. The only one I notice is about sixty years old, so I don't think it's him. What jumps out at me, though, is the information about Gary Thomas Rowe. He's mentioned only in passing as a suspected informant for the FBI who the United Klans ran out of the state, along with his wife and kids, in November of 1964. I'd bet a significant amount of money that he was ratted out by Campbell. That would have allowed him to gain credibility with the group in pretty short order.

No one with either the first or the last name Wayne is mentioned in the newspaper accounts of the shooting at City of St. Jude. No one with that name is in the transcripts of the House Un-American Activities Committee hearings, either. There is one significant thing in that account, however, that has changed—only Robert Shelton winds up with a prison sentence. Both Scoggin and the North Carolina Grand Dragon Bob Jones pay a fine, but escape jail time.

That makes me want to put my fist through the hotel wall. And while that might be a decent stress reliever, it doesn't seem likely to change anything, so I take out my CHRONOS key and get to work. My best bet is to figure out which house they're planning to use, jump in early, and set up a stable point. Then I'll come back to the hotel and watch the events unfold, just to be certain, before going back to clear things with Angelo and the others. Because I want their official buy-in if it actually comes down to killing someone.

I open one of the stable points on the athletic field at City of St. Jude and scan forward to tomorrow night at 9:20 p.m., which is when the shooting begins, according to the newspapers. The place looks very different. For one thing, the lights surrounding the field are on now, casting an odd, yellowish glow over everything. There's also a decent-sized temporary stage on the field. I know from my research that it was built from the boxes that coffins arrive in, with sheets of plywood nailed to the top. In the previous timeline, that was just a quirky factoid. In this one, it's downright macabre.

I pan around, looking at the crowd, until the first shots ring out at exactly 9:22:38. While I can't hear them, of course, I can tell from the reaction of the crowd. Since I really don't want to watch the bodies fall and people screaming, I pan over to where the military vehicles are parked to see the reaction from the security forces. Something else catches my eye, and I pan back a bit. It's the blond girl I saw getting out of the cab yesterday. I think she's even wearing the same clothes. She's not with the rest of the crowd. Her back is pressed against one of the buildings, and she's looking toward the houses across the street, probably trying to figure out where the hell the shots are coming from. I hope she stays put. She doesn't really look like the pictures of either of the two women who were killed along with Mary Travers, but those both looked like yearbook photos, so they might have been a few years out of date. I scan forward a couple of minutes, relieved when I see the girl retreat into the shadows between the two buildings.

I switch over to the stable points I set along Oak and Stephens Streets. All of the houses on these streets are small, neat single-story buildings. The newspaper accounts of the attack noted that the sniper was probably on a rooftop or possibly in an attic, based on the angle of the shots.

The house that seems most likely to me is the one with the *FOR SALE* sign jammed into the front lawn, so I jump to 9:22 p.m. and wait. Lights are on in one of the back rooms of the house, and two people are sitting on the unlit front porch. I can't really tell anything about them, except that they're in rocking chairs and must be listening to the concert across the street, because one of them is tapping out a rhythm against the arm of the rocker. Both of the people on the porch spring to their feet at 9:22:39. The woman scoops up something next to the rocker closest to the door. Neon-green eyes reflect back from her arms—is it a dog or a cat?—as the couple takes cover inside the house.

There's no movement on the roof. So apparently the shots didn't come from there. I move on to the next house, the next observation point, rolling the time back to 9:22, and again see no sign of the shooter.

On the fifth house, however, I notice something I hadn't seen when I was there in person. When I zoom in, a handwritten sign is propped up inside the screened porch. *For Rent—Inquire Two Doors Down.* Below the words, an arrow points to the right.

I don't see anyone on the roof, but at 9:22:10 one of the slats from the ventilation window in the attic pops out and pings off the sloped roof to land in the bushes below. Twenty-eight seconds later, I see the first muzzle flash.

Eight more flashes and then it ends. I continue watching, looking for a shadow inside the house or someone running off through the neighborhood. But I don't see anything. The street looks eerily quiet until I pan back around to the City of St. Jude. Several men with guns are running toward the gate of the chain-link fence surrounding the field, which seems to be locked. Two of the armed men decide not to wait. They scale the fence and come storming across Stephens Street, so clearly I'm not the only one who saw where the muzzle flashes came from.

I really want to jump forward to tomorrow and go set up the stable point. But I remember what Angelo said about having to explain every one of the extra jumps when this is over. I don't want to make it harder for him than it has to be. And I've been awake for at least twenty hours, maybe longer. I put the key aside and settle in to get some sleep.

∞

I sleep restlessly. Around three o'clock in the morning, I wake and realize I've dozed off with the stupid blue lenses still in my eyes. After I remove them, it's hard to fall back asleep. I keep seeing Campbell's expression when he told Shelton that his sniper friend enjoyed his work. Something about that smile makes me wonder if Campbell's friend is imaginary. Maybe Campbell himself is the one up in that attic with the rifle?

I toss around for a bit more, but eventually get tired of fighting it, so I grab the key and scan the stable points in the lobby. Campbell left the building around eleven. Chambliss and Wilkins stayed in the bar a bit longer, staggering off to the elevators around a little after one.

Campbell won't come back until a little after nine, when he'll join the other two men in the restaurant for breakfast. They have the same waitress I did last night, which makes me wonder how many hours a day that poor woman works. Although I guess she could have split shifts like I did at the diner.

My mind keeps wandering away to totally pointless thoughts like that one, but I still can't sleep. I finally pop one of the sleep aids in my briefcase, and after a few minutes, I doze back off.

Setting an alarm would have been a good idea, in retrospect. I wake around noon, with barely enough time to get a shower before housekeeping taps on the door to say it's time to check out. I dress quickly, pop the lenses back in, and make it out the door in five minutes.

When I arrive at the City of St. Jude, I find that it's a bit more active today than it was yesterday. There are kids out on the play-ground, but they're having a hard time focusing on their kickball game, because they keep craning their necks to stare at the police and military vehicles parked on the far side of the chapel. Just two of each for now, although I know from my surveillance earlier that they'll be joined by many more once the marchers arrive. A few dozen men in military uniform are hanging around the vehicles now. Not patrol-ling. Just waiting.

And that same blond girl is here. At the bus stop today, rather than getting out of a cab. It's around the same time as yesterday, so I guess it's not that odd. She's reading a newspaper, and she must not like what she's reading, because she looks upset. I fight the temptation to stop and tell her to steer clear of this area tonight. Yes, I know she doesn't get shot, but being there, hearing the gunfire, knowing that people are being murdered not fifty feet from where you are standing is pretty traumatic in and of itself. But I can't imagine how I'd explain that, so I just keep walking.

I'm definitely not criminal by nature, and I wasn't looking forward to doing it, but my original intention had been to go around to the back of the house, check for open windows or doors, and barring that, do a little discreet breaking and entering. But as soon as I turn onto Stephens Street, I can see that's going to be a problem. For one thing, there's a woman next door hanging out her laundry. I might be able to wait that one out, but the contingent of federal troops and police officers across the street is only going to get larger. Instead, I follow the instructions of the sign and go to the second house to the right to ask about renting the place.

A middle-aged black woman opens the door almost immediately. She's wearing a dress and holding a purse, so she must be heading out. When I ask her about the house, she cocks her head to the side and peers closely at me.

"Yes. It's available. The rent is seventy-five a month, unfurnished. You sure you don't want to look over on the other side of Cleveland, though? I saw a place over on Douglas Street that probably wouldn't be much more expensive than this."

It takes me a moment to realize that she means Cleveland *Avenue*, which will be renamed Rosa Parks Avenue later this year, rather than the city of Cleveland. I'm still not quite sure why she's pointing me to a different house, though.

Something about my expression must change her mind, because she laughs and gives me a more genuine smile. "Guess maybe you do belong over on this side. Those baby blues threw me off."

Damn. I hadn't even thought about the contacts. The school over at St. Jude is predominantly black, but as a private religious institution serving the poor, they have a few white students, too. The nuns I saw yesterday were white, too. But the rest of this neighborhood is black. The color line cuts both ways, and there are fairly distinct racial boundaries for housing in this city long after 1965.

"I don't suppose you could come back around five thirty?" she asks. "I'm due back from lunch in twenty minutes, and it's almost that long a walk."

"No, ma'am. I work evenings."

"Okay." She sighs and begins rummaging around in her purse as we walk toward the other house. "The key has to be in here somewhere. I'm guessing you're married?"

"Yes, ma'am. Two years ago next week. We're expecting in July, so I'm looking for somethin' a little bigger."

"Well, it's a good little house, and you'd have good neighbors. St. Jude's across the street don't mind in the least if kids around here use the playground, although I guess it will be a few years before you need to think about that." She opens the door to the tiny porch and then steps inside and slides the key into the lock on the front door. "Tell you what, I really don't want to be late, so I'll just let you in. You can take your time that way. Not like there's anything in there you could run off with, aside from a can of paint. Just be sure to pull the door all the way closed when you leave, to make sure it locks. If you decide the house suits you, pop into the library, and we can talk about the deposit and other details. If I'm not at the desk, tell them you need to speak to Bertha Williams."

"Yes, ma'am. Thank you, Mrs. Williams. I sure do appreciate it."

She smiles again. "Tell your wife I said congratulations on that baby."

I thank her again and step into the tiny living room, which smells of fresh paint and Pine-Sol. Despite the shaky start with Mrs. Williams, having her leave me here alone is an excellent bit of luck. I was thinking I would have a prospective landlord staring over my shoulder the entire time and would have a tough time managing to even set a stable point so that I could return later. Getting up into an almost-certainly-unfinished attic to set the observation point I'll need to see who is doing the shooting would have been out of the question, so I'd resigned myself to racking up one more jump that Angelo would need to eventually explain or cover up.

It takes a few minutes, but I finally locate the entrance to the attic on the ceiling inside a bedroom closet. There's a small stepladder folded against the wall. The door has one of those cord pulls, and I yank to tug it down. It's stuck, apparently painted shut. I yank again, harder. This time, it cracks open slightly. Finally, I shove the door upward, and it opens far enough to reveal a bunch of boxes near the edge. Apparently, no one wanted to actually climb up inside, so they just stood at the top of the ladder and jammed the boxes into the attic when they needed to store something. As my eyes adjust to the dim light, I make out a disassembled crib propped up against the exposed beams of the sloped wall, and a large, dust-covered metal footlocker a few yards into the attic. It looks like it's military issue.

I move one of the boxes away from the opening, stirring up a cloud of dust as I pull myself up. Even at the highest point, the room is only about five feet tall. As much as I'd just like to set the stable point here and be done with it, the window that the sniper uses is at the far end and there's no guarantee I'll be able to see his face. That wouldn't be a big deal, really—it might actually be better not to see the face of the guy I'm almost certainly going to have to shoot. But I still think there's a decent chance it's Campbell, and if so, that's something I'm going to need to see up close.

So, I set the first stable point and push the attic door back into place. Then I begin crouch-walking toward the vent window at the front of the narrow attic. The plywood doesn't seem to be nailed down, because it keeps shifting as I move forward. When I reach the window, I set the observation point and then start making my way back to the door.

I'm about six feet from the doorway when the plywood cracks and my heel slips down into the crevice. Already slightly off-balance from being crouched over, I pinwheel my arms, trying to stay upright. But it's a lost cause. I pitch backward, smacking my head hard against the metal trunk.

I have just enough time for the fleeting thought that this is not a good thing, and then everything goes dark.

FROM THE DIARY OF KATE PIERCE-KELLER

January 19, 2089

To the person who now holds my key:

I've had the strangest sense these past few days that I'm being watched. Not in a sinister or intrusive way. Just curious eyes, and I have no doubt that they are yours, staring into the stable point. Maybe even here in this house, if it's still standing.

At first, I kind of hoped you'd visit. Are you the one who caused the shift? Are you the one stuck fixing it? The two aren't mutually exclusive, I know, and the fact that you are almost certainly someone with my DNA, one-quarter of which I inherited from Saul Rand, is a little troubling. I suspect that there is a genetic component to his insanity, a component he passed along to Prudence and to Simon, although they were both shaped by their environment, as well.

And still, even when they were manipulated by Saul in so many ways, they both retained the capacity to love, something that I'm quite certain Saul lacked.

I hope you were raised with love. I also hope that the awful traits Saul Rand possessed have withered away on our family tree. To be honest, I'm gambling quite a lot on those two hopes. I had three other grandparents, all of whom were good people. Good historians, too. None of them were into mass murder, nor would they have considered playing games with the timeline to further their own interests. My children had a good man for their father, and they were good men, too, so barring some bizarre throwback to the genocidal maniac we share as an ancestor, I believe the odds are in my favor.

If you haven't read my earlier entries, you should do that now. Otherwise, most of what follows will make little sense. You *do* have time to read the entire thing. Yes, the circumstances are dire. I knew that when I entered the library several weeks ago and heard the theme from *Jaws* playing as that damned list of anomalies scrolled across Katherine's ancient computer. But you have a tool in your hands that can pack a whole lot of time into any given day. It's not unlimited time, obviously. You'll still grow old just as I have. But that key can help you shove extra hours into the days that need them, and that can tilt the playing field in your direction when everything seems to be stacked against you.

If you've already read my story, you have a better understanding of why I would leave behind that key for you to find. Why I didn't destroy every last one of the damned things. We tried, but I knew we didn't have *all* of them. The Cyrists were still in control of the government . . ."reformed" Cyrists, but still, I didn't trust them. I *don't* trust them. They also had two, maybe three CHRONOS keys that I had no way of getting.

Simply put, I wanted to know if they changed something. If they reneged on their promises, if one of them started screwing around with the timeline again, God help me, I wanted to *know*. Even after I could have used the key to stop them, I wanted to know. Even when the Cyrists had devolved into little more than an isolated cult of greed, I *still* wanted to know.

And that made everyone around me less happy. Myself included.

Before you write me off as a crotchety old bigot, I *do* know that all greedy bastards aren't Cyrists. And I know that there are good people who get pulled into their cult. Some very good people are born into it, as well, including one of my oldest and dearest friends. The members with good hearts pick and choose from the teachings in the *Book of Cyrus*, ignore or reinterpret the horrible parts, and manage to live good, productive, even helpful lives. But I'd maintain that they do this *despite* their affiliation with Cyrist International, not because of it.

It took a long time, but I finally reconciled with the fact that there will *always* be Cyrists. Even if I'd found a way to completely erase that foul excuse for a religion from this timeline, there would still be Cyrists, because there will always be people who put their own wealth over everyone else's well-being, even the well-being of the planet, shouting all the while that their big, fat bank accounts prove that they are the Blessed. That they know The Way. That their own personal god has shown them favor. There will *always* be Cyrists.

Whether this time shift was caused by something you did after finding the key or something they've done, you'll obviously have to fix it. Or undo it. You have my sympathy for the double memories that are going to hit you if it comes to that.

And you have my sympathy for the dreams that may follow. Strangely enough, the dreams of the bodies that I saw at Six Bridges and elsewhere faded more quickly than the dreams about the people who vanished. Maybe it's because we are conditioned for death, but nothing in my experience had prepared me to see someone simply blink out of existence when they were no longer under a CHRONOS field. Mostly I dreamed about Connor, reaching for the key a second too late. Eve, too. And yes, even Saul. It was poetic justice, but it haunted me. Hopefully the key will be kinder to you in that regard.

But here's my advice: Change the things you can, but once you've done your best, even if there are pieces that don't fit, you can't spend your entire life blaming yourself. Get on with the business of living. Blame me if you need to. I'm the one whose final wish put the key into your hands. One of my sons, possibly both if they actually managed to work together on something, agreed to grant that wish. We took a risk, and it may have been an unwise one.

But either way, I believe the lion's share of blame rests on the people who use the key for personal gain. And unless we can find a way to stuff the genie back into the bottle, someone must keep them in check.

I've scanned the list of anomalies, and I can't figure out how the Cyrists are involved. But you need to assume that they are. I suspect they have a few people who can jump, and I'm fairly certain they have at least one key. But they've been reluctant to use it, because there was a CHRONOS in the previous timeline. There's a CHRONOS in this one, too. Otherwise, I'd have blinked out of existence when I left the house to visit the doctor earlier this week. But there's no guarantee that will be true with every time shift. If CHRONOS never exists, Saul Rand can't go back in time to start their religion, and most of them will never be born. So the practical Cyrists have no desire to change the timeline. The true believers, however? The ones who thought Saul's idea for the Culling was the best hope for humanity? They're the ones you have to watch out for.

The fact that you *are* watching me, that you didn't simply jump in without considering the consequences, gives me hope that you will be wiser than I was. I don't mean in terms of how you fix the immediate crisis. All these years later, I'm still not sure what else I could have done. The real test is how you face what comes after.

Because there will be no perfect answer. Whatever you choose, you *will* be playing God. Some people in this reality will never breathe life if you restore the previous timeline. And some who are alive in the other timeline will be ghosts who exist only in records protected by a CHRONOS field if you choose to do nothing.

You'll have to make that decision based on your conscience. The greatest good for the greatest number is a good rule of thumb, but I can't decide for you. The power is now in your hands, and for the role I played in putting it there, I am truly sorry.

∞24∞

I place the CHRONOS key on the nightstand, remove the little disk from behind my ear, and rub my eyes. The sun has gone down since I came in here a few hours ago, and the light from the holographic display against the dark room leaves an afterimage on the back of my eyelids. I've spent almost an hour staring at the stable point where a ninety-year-old Kate Pierce-Keller is napping on a sofa in this very room, her head tilted onto her shoulder. Whatever she was watching continued to play long after she nodded off. I could see the reflection of her wall screen in the glass table in front of the sofa, distorted into a hypnotic dance of shapes and colors as the sun outside the window slowly dropped behind the trees across the street. She looked old and frail, but she also looked at peace. And I can't bring myself to change that. It feels selfish. And I'm no longer certain that it's needed.

"So . . . are you going?" Jack gives me a sympathetic smile and puts Katherine Shaw's diary aside. He's currently on a couch in almost the same spot where Kate was sitting, in front of the very same window. It's night outside, however, and the room is lit for reading.

"No. There's nothing I can think of that she could tell me that's worth stressing out a ninety-year-old woman in her final days of life.

That's why she left the diaries in the first place. So that I'd know everything. So that I wouldn't have to risk jumping back and screwing something else up."

So she could die in peace, I think.

Or at least, that's what I assume. Alex said earlier that even if she wasn't wearing a key, the house must have been under a CHRONOS field when the time shift happened for Kate. Otherwise, he claims, the Anomalies Machine wouldn't exist and some of the books in the library would be different. That hurts my brain a little, but I *guess* it makes sense. If Jack and the others felt something when the timeline changed in 2136, it was probably even stronger in 2089. And it was far from the first time shift she'd experienced, so Kate would have certainly known what was happening. From what I've read in her diary, she felt the time shifts even before she was under a key. She just didn't know what they were.

All of that had me leaning away from making the trip anyway, but the thing that clinched it was Kate's final diary entry. Her *final* final entry, written several years after the one I read last week, where Kate said she was going to London to visit Nora and leaving the key behind. That she was done obsessing over things she couldn't change. I'm certain that one really *had* been the final entry in the diary before the time shift, because I flipped to the back. No, I'm not one of *those* readers, at least not with fiction. It simply stood to reason that she might have left a message at the back, some sort of specific guidance for the unlucky fool who inherited the key.

And then today, this new entry was there. Targeted at me, although not by name. Confirming Alex's belief that Kate had felt the time shift.

"If I can't figure out what happened on my own," I tell Jack, "then I may have to reassess. Or maybe I'll go in search of this Other-Kate person and ask for her help."

Jack starts to get up and join me on the bed, but then thinks better of it and slides over, patting the spot next to him on the couch. He's right. We've moved past most of the tension of the past few days, but him sitting next to me on the bed would still be a bit awkward, more because I don't trust myself than because I don't trust him. I'm feeling miserable. So is he. It would be all too easy to rush in, to seek comfort where we can find it.

But it *is* nice to feel his arm slip around my shoulders when I sit down. Nice to lean my head against his chest and feel his heartbeat against my cheek.

"You don't have to convince me, you know. Alex and I have been the ones trying to talk you *out* of visiting her. Interacting with family just seems . . . risky."

What he's saying is true, although it's been mostly Jack trying to talk me out of going. Maybe it's the curse of knowing more than any of us do about the mechanics of time travel, but Alex spends a lot of time second-guessing himself. One minute, he's stressing out about the many conundrums and quandaries that might be unleashed if I interact with Kate Pierce-Keller, and the next he's handing me a list of important questions that I should ask her when I go.

"You mentioned seeing your dad through the stable point you set at Nora's." Jack hesitates, probably trying to think of a tactful way to ask the obvious question.

"Yes. I was tempted. Very tempted. To be honest, the one thing that pulled me back from the brink was knowing that you were here. And then . . ."

"And then you discovered I'm a duplicitous asshole who has been deceiving you," he says.

"Something like that."

"I wish I could use that key so that you didn't have to," Jack says. "But if I could, I know I'd still be tempted to go back. To see if there was any way to save my mom. Or even just to see her again. Even though it was fifteen years ago. Even though that hole is no longer gaping. So I know it must be agonizing for you."

"It's a little less tempting now," I admit. "Given that I know it's possible to thoroughly fuck up the timeline. But there's still a part of me that holds that back in reserve. If I can't fix things, then why not go back, get him to a cardiologist? Roll the dice again. Because this timeline kind of sucks."

A faint ding sounds, and Jarvis says, "A delivery has arrived for Master Jack."

Jack laughs and turns to me. "Seriously?"

I give him a wicked grin. "Hey, I'm not going to change his programming, but I don't want the rest of you to feel left out."

"Well, in this case, I get the last laugh," Jack says. "The package is actually for *you*. And I'm pretty sure you're going to hate it."

Lorena and Yun Hee are in the living room when we go downstairs. I'm glad to see them outside of the suite where they're sleeping. It isn't tiny by any means, especially now that it's just the two of them. But it's not like Lorena can take the baby outside for a walk around the neighborhood. At least they can take advantage of the common space in the house. Yun Hee gives us a mostly toothless grin when she looks our way. She's standing up, holding on to the edge of the coffee table as she watches a dancing rabbit on the wall screen.

The box Jarvis mentioned is on the delivery pad outside. When I bring it in, Lorena says, "Jack picked what he thought you'd hate the least out of the options, and I guessed at your size. Jarvis said it should fit based on your previous purchases."

I hadn't even thought about what I would wear when I finally make these jumps to the 1960s. Inside the box is a navy skirt and a blouse, with tiny flowers in varying shades of blue, along with matching shoes, tights, a purse, and accessories. I've seen enough photographs in the past few days to know it's the height of fashion in the mid-1960s, but it's truly not me.

Jack grins when he sees my expression. "See. I told you you'd hate it. You should have seen the other options. Seriously, this was the least offensive of the bunch."

"The blouse is fine," I say. "But I'm wearing pants and shoes I can run in. Not the trainers I wore to Estero, but definitely not these fake leather things. A pair of jeans and basic flats won't get me burned at the stake in 1965. And I don't need a purse. The CHRONOS key will be around my neck, and anything else I need for the hour or so I'm there to observe each event, I can stash in my pockets."

"Maybe," Jack says. He goes over to the hall closet and pulls something from his coat as I stash the skirt and tights back into the box. "You're right about wearing something you can run in. We don't know what you'll be up against. But even though this is pretty small, I'm not sure how well it will fit in a pocket."

"What exactly is it?"

The gray object takes up most of his palm and looks more like one of those old-fashioned remote-control devices than what I suspect it is—a weapon. It's not like anything I've seen for personal defense. I'm not even sure it's legal. It looks more like something you see in VR games that have military or police elements.

"I went to pick this up from a friend of my dad's the day you were helping RJ and Lorena move," Jack says. "The night before, I called my father and said there were some people tailing you. That I suspected they were planning to kill one or more of you to stop the research. His head nearly exploded, because even though he's convinced now that speeding the research up may be our best hope, there's a part of him that I'm pretty sure still thinks *preventing* the research is a good thing—"

"By killing us?"

Jack makes a slightly sick face. "I told you he was utilitarian. Lethal force would never be the *first* recourse for General John Merrick, and he'd make every effort to resolve the issue short of that point, but yeah. It would be on his list of possible options, if all else failed. Anyway, I asked him to get me a weapon."

"And he just agreed?"

"Of course. The man has been trying to put a gun of some sort into my hands since I was eight years old. He probably danced a fucking jig after we ended the call, happy that the wayward son had returned to the fold."

I take the gun—if you can call it that—from him, examining it cautiously.

"It's not on right now. See the tiny red *X*? But I can show you how to use it. I have a couple of targets we can set up in the basement. The thing makes a popping noise, and there's a bright light when you fire it, so we probably don't want to do it up here where there are windows."

"But this isn't historically accurate. They had actual guns, with bullets, back then. What if I'm caught with this thing in 1966? If me simply being in the same place as John Lennon back in 1957 somehow broke the timeline, I can't even begin to imagine what sort of impact me being caught with an electrolaser weapon in the mid-1960s might have. It was a good idea, though—as much as I hate it, I'm probably going to need something. Maybe the gun in Grandpa James's desk still works."

"There's a *gun* in his desk?" Jack says.

Lorena chuckles softly. It's the first time I've heard anything close to a laugh from her since the time shift. "Why are you surprised? Alex found a decades-old banana peel in one of those desk drawers."

"Good point," he says. "You should have seen it, Mads. It looked like some sort of alien spawn. The only reason we know for certain it was a banana peel is because Lorena snipped off a bit and ran a chemical analysis."

We leave Lorena and Yun Hee to the antics of the dancing rabbit and head to the library. Alex is in his usual spot, encircled in his own personal data cave.

"When did you last eat?" Jack asks him as I rummage through the desk in search of the pistol.

Alex doesn't look away. "Um. Earlier today. I think. When I made coffee."

"So, a granola bar. Nearly fifteen hours ago."

"I'm busy," Alex says. "I'll eat later."

I find the gun and a box of cartridges under a stack of papers and place the gun on the desk. It's a squared-off black pistol with pearl grips.

"This was mentioned in one of the diaries," I say. "I think it was Kate's."

"That thing is ancient." Jack picks it up and inspects it, looking at an inscription along the side. *Automatic Colt Calibre 32 Rimless Smokeless.* On the reverse, it reads, *Browning's Patent. Apr.20.1897, Dec.22.1903.*

The ammo box is stuck to the bottom of the desk drawer. When Jack tries to pull it out, the box crumbles and shells come tumbling out. I ask Jarvis for info on the model, and we find out that it was manufactured into the mid-twentieth century.

"Yeah," Jack says, looking at the thing dubiously. "So it *might* be only two hundred years old, rather than two hundred and thirty. I don't know enough about this thing to be sure it's safe. We'd need to find an antique-firearms dealer and . . ." He shrugs and hands the gun back to me. "You'd be as likely to end up killing yourself."

"Got it." I place the gun back inside the desk. "Looks like I'll be carrying your mini laser gun or whatever it is. You said you have targets?"

Jack nods and we're about to leave, but Alex waves us over. "Come look at this. Both of you. You won't have any idea what you're seeing, but I need to show someone."

Coming from anyone else, that last sentence would be insufferably rude, but Alex is simply stating a fact. I have no clue what we're looking at as we approach his computer station, and I can tell from Jack's expression that he doesn't, either.

"It looks like . . . bubbles?" I say. "When I was a kid, I had this wand thing that Nora bought me. It was sort of a mesh pattern, and when you dipped it in the soap solution, it would make dozens and dozens of bubbles. They weren't exactly different colors, like the ones here, but some of them overlapped a bit, like these two." I point to two bubbles that share a side, creating something that looks a bit like a three-dimensional Venn diagram, although the clear bubble is slightly larger and slightly more oblong in shape. "And those over here," I add, pointing to a second pair.

Alex nods. "Good. You've homed in on the important part. This is a close-up of my representation of the chronotron pulses emanating from a twenty-kilometer radius around DC." He scrolls out briefly, revealing that the portion we were seeing was just a small section of a much larger grid of bubbles. They look more like grains of sand when he zooms out.

"That's thousands," Jack says.

"Hundreds of thousands, technically. Just over two hundred thousand."

"When did these pulses occur?" I ask.

"In *every* time. Well, okay. Not technically. The first one is in 1608." He zooms in to the extreme upper-left sector, and we see four bubbles. "This cell is 1600 through 1610, but all four occurred in 1608. The key thing of historical note in this area in 1608 was a visit by some European explorer, John Smith. Then, if we go all the way over to here . . ." Alex zeroes in on a square near the extreme bottom right. "This is April 27, 2305. There are twenty-three pulses that day. Prior to that, there had been twelve to twenty-four pulses twice, or occasionally three times, a week. Almost always twelve at a time, and always precisely on the hour. They were—or, I guess, *will be*—morning people. Out at ten a.m., back at eleven. If there was a second group, they usually went out earlier. After that we have a tiny flurry of pulses here and there"—he clicks a few squares and I see blue bubbles, some lime green, and a few deep green—"and then nothing at all between 2307 and 2385. I still haven't checked the years after that."

"What do the colors mean?" Jack asks. "Did you assign them? They seem kind of random on some dates, but those last few—"

"It's part of the information that I pick up in the pulse," Alex says. "Both the color and the size, although I did choose to graphically represent them as bubbles. I'm a visual thinker. And spatial. Seeing things in three dimensions always helps me."

"Really," Jack says, glancing around at the multiple screens. "I would never have guessed."

Alex gives him a slightly confused look, the sarcasm lost on him. "I'm pretty sure I've mentioned that before. Anyway, no. I don't think the color is assigned randomly, because . . ." He types in the year 2136. There are maybe twenty-five large orange bubbles, along with a few tiny aqua dots so small that he has to zoom in again for me to be sure they're even bubbles.

Jack laughs. "Yep. That's the color I see the light. So I'm guessing this is a graphic representation of my ability with the key versus Madi's?"

"That's my guess, too," Alex says. "Good thing you're going into this with a strong self-image, Jack. Although to be fair, I think the size is more a reflection of the pulse surge than of ability, and these dots are just from you activating the diary's CHRONOS field. Each of the larger bubbles represents a time jump. And some of those squares had hundreds of bubbles. From about 2250 to the point where things begin tapering off, there were sometimes three thousand in a single year. But no overlapping bubbles. The only overlaps I saw that occurred in the DC area were the two Madi noted—"

"Which were both orange, the same shade as I see the key. Well, one side was orange. The other was clear. So what are the clear bubbles?"

"Hold on," Alex says. "Let me finish. There are the two that you noted. Both of them originated on November 4, 2136."

"That first day I was experimenting with the key."

"Yes," he says. "And there are two others, both in 2304. The first is June 19, 1965."

When he drills down to that year, and then that month, and then that day, there are twelve bubbles. Only one, which is sort of a violet shade, has a twin. He opens another date. This one has twenty-three bubbles. The lone double bubble is violet on one side, and the other is clear. Again, both of the clear bubbles seem slightly misshapen, instead of the perfectly round globes scattered elsewhere on the screen.

"Can you tell where the purple jumper was going?" Jack asks him.

Alex shakes his head. "No. Or at least if you can, I haven't figured it out yet. There could be something else encoded and I'm just not picking up on it. What I can do, however, is isolate the locations of all the jumps that individual took. It's only a few hundred."

"*Only?*" I say.

"Yes, I know that's a lot. But I picked a few dates out that may interest you. March 24, 1965. June 19, 1965. And several jumps to August 19—"

"1966," the three of us say in unison.

"Can you tell the end point of the jump?" I ask.

"Not directly," Alex says. "It's just a surge in the location from which the jump originates. But we're assuming round trips, and we know the location of the anomalies. So I ran the same sort of scan for the three cities and . . ." He spins his chair to grab one of the holoscreens and flips it toward us. "We have a pulse leaving each of those cities on the same day the anomaly occurs there. Occasionally, it's more than one pulse, but one of them is always that purple shade."

A surge of relief flows through me. Apparently, Jack feels it, as well, because he says, "So none of this is Madi's fault. Well, aside from whatever role she plays in creating this technology. But it's not something she did on those jumps."

"Probably not. Although, I can't entirely rule it out, since her jump was chronologically the first, in terms of both origin and destination, to attract this tagalong pulse."

"Okay, you lost me," Jack says.

"Her year of origin was 2136, and theirs was 2304. Her first destination was 1957, and their earliest destination with a hitchhiker was 1965."

I look back at the display, at the bubble overlapping with the violet one. "But what *are* they? The clear bubbles?"

"I'm not sure," Alex says. "It's like something latched on to you. Not on to your body," he amends, probably picking up on my shudder. "It latched on to the signal from your key."

That's not really much better. "Did it make the return trip, too?" I ask, glancing around the library. I know he said it was just a pulse, but still . . .

Alex shakes his head. "One-way trip."

"Can you track where or when this hitchhiker originates," Jack says, "like you did with the purple jumper?"

"No," Alex says. "I tried. Not only is there no color embedded in the signal, there's nothing else embedded, either. It's almost like the shell of a parasite that attached itself to a host. They've either got some method of cloaking their signal that I can't detect, or else . . ." He shakes his head.

"Or else what?" I ask, not really liking his expression right this moment.

"Nothing. It has to be that they're cloaking and somehow distorting the signal. Because the other option is that the hitchhikers aren't simply not from this *time*, but from this entire *timeline*. This reality. I don't even want to think about what that might mean. The simplest answer is usually the right one."

Jack and I exchange a look. None of this sounds at all simple to me, and I'm guessing he's feeling the same. And even though Alex is using a voice clearly designed to reassure us, and probably himself, he can't really hide the undercurrent of panic.

Alex clears his throat and continues. "I would have just chalked all of this up to some sort of quantum-level—I don't know, static, I guess?—if we didn't have historical aberrations in three of the four locations. I don't see how that could be a coincidence."

I'm tempted to note that he said basically the same thing about my jump to Liverpool and triggering the time shift not being coincidence, but this seems far more clear-cut. It's not just a minor interaction with John Lennon, years before any of the anomalies began. These are jumps to the actual events.

"So there's nothing Madi can do then, right?" Jack says. "We just have to wait for them to fix it."

"You're assuming they find it," Alex says.

Jack raises an eyebrow and looks around at the motley assortment of equipment in the library, some "borrowed" from Alex's employer and the rest ancient. "No offense, but if you found it, why wouldn't they? I know you're the brains behind this, but if this CHRONOS place is sending a dozen or so professional time travelers out multiple times a week, I'm guessing they have better equipment. And that's leaving aside the fact that they're over a hundred years into our future."

"True," Alex says. "But watch this."

He switches to 2-D. Flat color dots replace the bubbles. The clear bubbles vanish.

"Now you see them. Now you don't," Jack says.

"I'm sure their system is still picking up *something*," Alex says, "because . . ." He zooms in on one of the orange dots, and you can tell that the color is ever-so-slightly faded compared to the one next to it. He shrugs. "As you can see, though, it's just a blip when you display it any other way. So unless there's someone there who uses my specific visualization technique, it might just seem like random fluctuations. I mean, they'll know there was a time shift, but they may not know why. Although I guess we really don't know why, either, but I do think we need to get what information we have to them, just in case."

"None of the stable points go beyond 2160," I tell them. "I've checked on both the *Log* and with the key itself. It's true for the ones that I set locally, as well."

"Then I guess it's a good thing that we know where and when the other traveler will be," Alex says. "And it's somewhere you're already going."

I groan. "Which means I need to get into my new traveling clothes."

"Maybe a little target practice, first?" Jack suggests.

"I guess. Although I'd really rather do a recon trip first. See what we're up against. I don't need a weapon for that, do I? Maybe I can just drop in, let the professional time travelers know what we've found out. And maybe let them take care of it?"

Jack shakes his head. "What if this is intentional? This purple person may *know* they're carrying baggage when they travel. What if it's some sort of sabotage, purposefully changing the timeline like that Saul guy did?"

He's right, of course. I know he's right. I'm just putting off dealing with the lethal aspects of this trip.

"You should have plenty of time to practice," Alex says. "I've got to figure out a way to get RJ back into the house before you make the jump. Just in case. It's possible that the first event is what triggers the other two and stopping the shootings in Montgomery will reset the timeline. I doubt it, partly because those phantom pulses are at all three locations. To be on the safe side, though, RJ needs to be inside a CHRONOS field when the shift happens."

"Is that the only way he gets his memory back?" I ask.

"Hell if I know." Alex throws out his hands. His eyes have a slightly manic look that suggests to me that the man needs food and at least twelve hours of sleep. "We already know that the timeline isn't altered every time you do something different. Otherwise, we'd have had shifts each time you went back and changed something—telling yourself not to do the jumps, for example, or going back to get your shoes. What we got instead was a temporary clone of you that vanished. That tells me the timeline resists change. It will resist changing back, too. So, like I said, I think it's unlikely that just stopping one of these events will fix things. And there's always the chance that he'll be the RJ we know even if he's outside of a field when you do fix it. But since I don't know that for certain, I think we'd be stupid not to have him here, just in case."

"You're right," I tell him. "But you might want to give Lorena a heads-up on that? She may need a little time to adjust to the idea before the husband who doesn't know her drops by."

$$\infty$$

MADI
MONTGOMERY, ALABAMA
MARCH 23, 1965

The sneeze hits almost as soon as I land, wiping out all hope of a quiet entrance. I shouldn't really be surprised, since the stable point sits in the middle of a bank of flowering bushes. Azaleas, I think. I also think I'm allergic to azaleas. Who knew?

I should have just blinked in directly to the City of St. Jude. Last night, I scanned through a seventy-two-hour period at the stable point where I jumped in while testing out the key. The maintenance sheds looked quite different in the old satellite photographs that Jarvis pulled up during our research. They were called Quonset huts, and with their rounded roofs and walls, Jack said they looked a bit like a sausage split lengthwise, the halves side by side on a grill. I'm guessing they're used mostly for storage, because there are no windows. The space between the two halves forms an oddly shaped tunnel so narrow that I could almost touch the two sides if I spread my arms out.

But no one used the location—or rather no one else. I saw myself jump in briefly and then jump out. Nor did anyone use the next closest stable point, which is nearly three miles away, near the state capitol.

At first, I was perplexed. If Alex's information is correct, the jumper represented by the purple bubbles should have arrived. But then I realized that the local points I've set with this key aren't in the *Log*, either. Kate's diary said something about sharing stable points with other keys, too, so the book is most likely just a bare-bones collection for first-time travelers to an area. The purple jumper must have come in via a local point not listed in the *Log*.

All of this made me nervous, although I suspect that's at least partly because I've never jumped into a location where I was worried about encountering another time traveler. Before now, I'd had the luxury of thinking I was a rare beast. Simply put, I'd have felt a lot better if I'd been able to see this other person jump in. To know that I was the one tracking them, and not vice versa.

Jack and I debated the pros and cons of both stable points and finally decided that it's less likely someone will be watching the location near the capitol grounds than that they'll be watching the stable point at St. Jude, given what we know is about to transpire there. The downside is that I'm not comfortable enough with this era to walk the roughly three miles between here and there, risking interactions with God knows how many people. So I hail a cab and tell the driver, a middle-aged man puffing on a cigarette like it's his life support, to take me to the City of St. Jude, please.

He turns back to look at me, snorting a cloud of smoke through his nostrils. "You sure about that? Not the best place for a girl your age, especially on your own. I got nothing against Cath'lics, but that place is on the wrong side of town, if you know what I mean."

From what I can see of the man's expression in the rearview mirror, I should probably be glad that he's sticking to vague euphemisms like *wrong side of town*. Having read the background of the mission, I know exactly what he means. In 1965, Montgomery is divided into eight different wards. The vast majority of black citizens live in two of those wards, and the City of St. Jude sits near the middle of the largest.

"City of St. Jude," I repeat, this time without the *please*, as I crank down the window. In retrospect, I should have walked. Even with all the auto exhaust from passing cars, the air is less toxic outside.

Thankfully, the driver decides he doesn't want to talk to me. He turns up the radio, where some guy is wailing for the bartender to pour him sorrow on the rocks. That segues into another drinking song about grape wine and moonshine and chug-a-lug, and another about wine (type unspecified), women, and song. I'm sensing a theme here.

The musical theme actually ties in quite nicely with the cover story that we came up with to lure RJ inside the CHRONOS field. Alex claimed that he had this friend who was looking for volunteers to test a new alcohol-blocking pill. It paid $750, definitely on the low end for any research study I've ever seen, but Alex told RJ that he'd signed up for it and they needed one more person because somebody dropped out. Food and alcohol were being provided, so it was just a matter of hanging out, drinking, and watching vids for the weekend.

Why any sort of experiment like that would be done at a private home, rather than in a lab, I have no idea, but RJ was happy to take him up on it. I feel sorry for Lorena, since she'll probably need to interact with him. But at least it won't be for long. No matter how long these jumps take *me*, I can wrap things up in a matter of minutes from the point of view of anyone back—or I guess, forward?—in 2136.

I pay the cabdriver, magnanimously telling him to keep the change, since it will be precisely two pennies. Even in 1965, that has to be an insult. But while the driver's comments annoyed me, I'm a little worried that he's right. My blond self is probably going to be conspicuous in a segregated neighborhood.

As soon as I turn back to the sidewalk, however, I see that the driver was wrong. It's not exactly a diverse area, but of the seven people in sight, two are white, including a guy around my age with a friendly smile and vivid blue eyes. I return the smile and he heads off toward the chapel. Maybe times are changing faster than the driver wanted to admit. Come to think of it, that's probably why he was so surly.

But it's still true that the longer I spend hanging around here, the more likely it is that I'll have to explain my presence to someone. My first order of business is to find a safe spot, in a location that won't be in the line of fire tomorrow night. My second task is to jump forward and pinpoint the house across the street from which the shots are coming. Once I'm certain, I'll go back fifteen minutes, find a police or military officer who looks competent and reasonably kindhearted, and tell him I saw someone in the yard of that house when I walked past, aiming a rifle at this field. That it looked like the guy was drinking, too. That he seemed really angry.

There are several holes in this plan. Based on everything I've read, there will be a lot of guards patrolling the fence area once the marchers arrive tomorrow. Convincing those guards that I saw something they didn't probably won't be easy. Also, the occupants of the houses across the street are, almost certainly, not white. Odds are pretty good that they're in favor of this march and Dr. King's agenda of racial justice, so barring mental illness or other issues, they wouldn't be inclined to open fire on the people attending this concert.

I'm really hoping they won't dissect my story too carefully, however. I need Plan A to work. Because if it doesn't, I'll have to move on to Plan B, which requires me to jump back again, break into the house where the sniper is hiding, and shoot him with what I'm sure everyone in 1965 would call my ray gun.

The ray gun isn't so bad, actually. It took a few tries to get the aim right, but once I did, I discovered that I could hit the target with an uncanny accuracy. I've always been good at VR games that require hand-eye coordination. While I never really took pride in that the way I did in my swimming prowess, I'm again wondering whether I truly have any *native* talents. Is this an ability that some genetic designer cooked up? How many of the things that make me *me* were created in a lab a century and a half from now?

The other issue, of course, is that we were shooting at *targets*. Can I actually kill another human being? I'm not entirely sure on that point. Maybe, if I'm certain that I'm saving the lives of the people on that field and, hopefully, setting the timeline straight. But I'd really rather not put it to the test.

As soon as the cab pulls away from the curb, I walk quickly to the rear of the campus, toward the stable point. The athletic field is empty. If anyone is watching, they're doing a good job of staying undercover.

I slip into the shadows between the two sheds and roll the time forward to 9:18 p.m. on March 24th, just in case the papers were wrong and the gunfire starts earlier than reported. Then I take a deep breath and jump in.

The music, loud and a little tinny, is the first thing that my senses pick up when I arrive, followed by the scent of mud and a faint feeling of dampness against my skin. It's not exactly raining, but a fine mist hangs in the air, permeating each breath I take. The song that's playing is vaguely familiar. I think I may have heard it in school as a kid. After a few more bars, I place it. "If I Had a Hammer." It's one of the songs that the group Mary Travers was with sang at the concert.

At the end of the tunnel between the two sheds, I now see at least a dozen vehicles—jeeps, cars, and a few trucks. Most have military markings, but some appear to be police cars. Uniformed men are gathered around, some talking, some listening to the music.

I press my back against the side of one of the huts and set the key for a return trip thirty seconds after I left, just in case I need to return home quickly. Then, I begin inching toward the edge of the tunnel, hoping to avoid catching the attention of any guards. One of the musicians tells the audience to sing along, and a huge swell of voices joins in for the chorus.

Once I'm a few yards from the edge of the building, I stop and wait, glancing down at the CHRONOS key. It's 9:20 now, and I wish I hadn't given myself so much time. My heart is pounding in my ears so loudly that it almost drowns out the music. I close my eyes and focus on breathing slowly as I wait.

The song wraps up and there's applause, followed by a man's voice. He's introducing the next act, James Baldwin, who will read selections from his latest book, *The Fire Next Time*. The crowd applauds again, and then there's a loud crack. Another one follows, and the crowd is no longer applauding. Someone screams, and other voices join in that chorus, too.

The attention of the guards is now on the crowd, so I step toward the edge of the hut-tunnel and scan the houses across the street. Eyewitness reports said there were at least ten shots—some said as many as fifteen—so I have several chances to isolate the location of the sniper.

Another crack of gunfire. I don't see the flash of light Jack told me to look for, so I move a few steps closer. One of the guards yells at me as he runs past, telling me to find cover. He's also scanning the tree-lined street.

Shouts of *run* compete with the advice to *get down*. Another shot rings out, and I see a man fall to the ground. I don't know if he was wounded or if he just decided that hitting the ground was safer than running.

And then I see the flash, almost hidden behind the leaves. A second flash. I'll need to be certain, and check from another angle, but the house should be easy to spot, because it has an odd roof. There are two peaks in front, like a letter *M*, with a slightly higher peak, like an upturned letter *V*, behind them.

So I slip back into the tunnel, pull up the preset stable point, and blink out. The quiet is sudden, like the screams from the crowd were pouring from a faucet and some cosmic hand reached out and cut them off with the twist of a knob. I stand there for a moment, waiting for my pulse to return to normal so that I don't go bolting across the field like a startled rabbit.

When I finally step out into the sunlight, I find I'm no longer alone. Off in the distance, the guy I saw when I got out of the cab is pacing around in the field. For a moment, I think he's just getting a bit of exercise. But then he turns toward me, and as I duck back into the tunnel, I catch a flash of orange light rising up from his hand.

He's setting stable points. *Multiple* stable points, every few yards along the side of the field where the shooting will occur. The locations are out in the open. I can't imagine anyone would use them to jump in, so they must be observation points, like the ones I set in my room to watch Kate.

The bigger question is *why*. I can think of two very different possibilities. One is that he's here for the same reason I am—to look for the killer who screwed up the timeline. The other is that he *is* the killer who screwed up the timeline, and he wants an up-close and personal view of the killing field, so that he can view the scene later, at his leisure, over and over again.

Which, to use Nora's phrase, would make him one sick fuck.

He doesn't *look* like a homicidal maniac. In fact, he seemed nice. But many of the sickest ones do.

What truly annoys me is that after all of those hours of sitting on my bed watching Kate, watching Jack and Alex in the library, and even watching my dad at Nora's house, I didn't think about using the stable point for surveillance the way he is. There was no need for me to be in the middle of the chaos. I didn't have to hear their screams.

The fact that I screwed that up, that I put myself at even a slight risk of getting shot when there was a much safer alternative, reminds me that I really don't know what the hell I'm doing. Katherine Shaw had years of training with CHRONOS. Kate had the advantage of that training secondhand, with Katherine as a teacher. All I have are their diaries. I am in so far over my head that I might as well be back off the coast of Estero Island, staring at that underwater crypt.

I push the controls forward to noon on the 24th, about seven hours before the concert begins. The marchers won't arrive for a few more hours. As soon as I see that no one is watching, I step out of the tunnel and walk quickly toward Stephens Street. I set three locations in front of the house, which I can now see has a *For Rent* sign in front. When I'm done, I walk around the block and set three more so that I'll be able to see if anyone goes through the backyard. Then I walk back down to the hospital on Fairview Avenue. There's a bus stop, and someone left a newspaper behind. I can sit here and pretend to read while I'm watching through the key to see who goes in and out.

The first thing I do is scan forward to 9:22 p.m. That's definitely the house where the sniper was hiding. It looks like the shots are coming from the attic. Then I start scrolling through backward, to see when the sniper enters.

An elderly couple joins me on the bench for a bit. They chat about doctors and the woman's next appointment, then catch the bus when it arrives. A few minutes later, a man approaches from the same direction. I can see from the corner of my eye that it's the guy I saw yesterday with the CHRONOS key.

Folding the newspaper tightly around my own key, I pretend to be engrossed in reading something called Hints from Heloise on the best way to poach an egg. I feel his eyes on me, but he doesn't stop. When he reaches the end of the block, he turns right, onto Stephens Street.

I quickly scan forward on the key, and, sure enough, five minutes later, he's standing outside the door of the house with the triple-peaked roof. A neatly dressed middle-aged woman is with him. She opens the door and lets him in, then begins walking at a rapid pace toward Oak Street, like she's running late.

He definitely wasn't carrying the weapon that the newspapers said was used in the shooting. Jarvis pulled up photos of that rifle. It was more than a meter long, and there's no way it would have fit inside his coat. I suppose the gun could already be in the house. But that doesn't really fit with the woman unlocking the door for him.

At this point, I can't rule out the possibility that we're on the same side. I also can't rule out the possibility that he's planning to kill five people tonight. But either way, Mr. CHRONOS Key and I need to have a little chat.

∞25∞

TYSON
MONTGOMERY, ALABAMA
MARCH 24, 1965

I come to slowly, drifting in and out. It doesn't take long for me to remember what happened—the blood on the floor and my aching head bring the answer crashing back pretty quickly.

I'm relieved to see that it's still daylight, although that doesn't really narrow it down that much. My best guess is that it was around one fifteen when I climbed up here. It's not quite one thirty now, according to the Timex on my right wrist. I vaguely remember yanking that arm up in an attempt to shield my head, and apparently it did absorb some of the hit. A thin crack runs across the glass face, but the hands are still moving merrily along. I'll just have to hope that means the other equipment inside the watch is still working, since there really isn't a way for me to check it out.

I push myself up to sitting and lean back against the damned trunk that cracked my head. A tentative exploration reveals a cut running along the back of my head, near the base of my skull. It's bleeding, but not badly. Should be something that the CHRONOS med can patch up in a couple of minutes. And maybe they can give me something for the headache and dizziness.

As I'm reaching for my key, someone sneezes loudly.

I startle, and even that small movement sends a bolt of pain through my skull. "What the fuck?"

A woman's voice says, "Don't move."

When I turn toward the attic door, the girl from the bus stop is sitting next to one of the boxes, pointing a device at me. It looks more like there are two of her sitting there, however, overlapped. Two devices pointed at me. Two of everything in the attic.

And two overlapping versions of my pistol in her lap.

I squeeze my eyes shut, hoping that it will clear my vision. But everything is still blurred, almost doubled. The one thing I can see, however, is a faint purple glow coming from beneath her shirt. She has the key in some sort of case, but it doesn't fully shield the light.

"Why are you here?" she asks.

"I'm here on official CHRONOS business. What year are you from?"

Her back stiffens slightly, and she glances down at the weapon in her hand. "I'm asking the questions. You're answering. What year are *you* from? And . . . what color is the light for you?"

I don't respond for a moment, trying to figure out how to handle the situation. It's possible that she's one of the two historians that Angelo warned me about, who were with the last stage of the march. But she doesn't match the picture at all, and the marchers aren't due to arrive for another couple of hours, so I don't think so. She's definitely not one of the five people with CHRONOS keys that I saw the day King was killed, but then neither was Campbell and he's here. I'm not sure why she's asking the second question, though. I mean, sure, that's the CHRONOS equivalent of the 1970s *What's your sign?* But I can't imagine how the information could be important enough to her that she'd ask while she has a weapon pointed at me and there's blood running down my neck.

But maybe it was a smart move, because it's the oddity of the question that makes me decide to just tell her the truth. Well, that and the fact that my head is throbbing too badly to come up with a decent lie. "I'm from 2304. We have a . . . situation that I'm trying to resolve. And the light is purple for me. What color is it for you?"

Her shoulders seem to relax when I say it's purple, although she seems a little confused by my slightly snarky tone on the last question.

"It's orange. An amber color like a caution light. And I'm coming from 2136."

I snort. "That's not even a good . . . lie," I begin, and then realize that I don't know for certain that the date she gave is impossible. Rich, Katherine, and I spent the short amount of time we had checking out the changes that were most relevant for these jumps. I didn't check on CHRONOS history, and I don't know if the others did, either. So I don't really *know* when the program started in this timeline. "Would you mind telling me *why* you're here?"

"Because someone is going to jam a rifle through that metal grate over there," she replies, jerking her head toward the ventilation window, "and kill five people over at St. Jude tonight. And I still think there's at least a slight possibility that you're the someone who will do that."

I glance down at the gun in her lap. "They weren't killed with a pistol, though, were they? It was a Remington pump-action. Thirty-aught-six. The shots will start at 9:22:38. And you'll be standing between those two Quonset huts near the field when they do."

Even with double vision I can tell she's surprised I know that.

"If you're not the sniper, why are you up here?" she asks.

I shrug. "Could ask the same of you. Listen, you don't happen to have a handkerchief or anything inside that purse, do you? I don't know if you noticed, but I'm bleeding."

She shakes her head. "Sorry. And yes, I actually thought you were dead. How long were you out?"

"Ten, maybe fifteen minutes. I'm Tyson Reyes, by the way."

"Madison Grace."

"Oh. So, we're going with bullshit names. Fine. I'm Abraham Lincoln."

There's a long, silent standoff, and then I say, "Listen, whoever the hell you are, I'm up here trying to find out for certain who *does* kill those five people, so I can prevent it. I think I know who it is, but the guy has a lot of political pull in my time and . . . I need solid proof. I set a stable point over there by the window. If you'll let me check my key . . ."

"If I let you check your key, you'll jump back to CHRONOS or wherever. And then I'll have to track you down all over again, so . . . no."

"Why didn't you just take the key when you swiped my gun?" I ask.

"Because you might *not* be the sniper. You *might* be an ally. And I've just seen someone get his memory wiped in a time shift." She's quiet for a moment, then tugs on the cord around her neck and pulls her key from a small pouch. "But I suppose we could risk it for a moment. Toss me your key, and I'll transfer the stable point."

"First, how do I know you'll give it back? And second, it doesn't work that way. It's *my* key. I have to transfer the point."

That's something anyone would know before beginning field training. Which now has me worried that Angelo is right about the technology being used for time tourism in the future.

Or she could be telling the truth. I stare at her face for a moment, trying to get the images to resolve so that I can see her more clearly. Madison Grace was the most reclusive of the three inventors, but there are a few photographs. She was a lot older in those pictures, though. Plus the attic is dimly lit and my vision is shot to hell right now.

She sneezes again and wipes her eyes with her sleeve. "You out-weigh me by at least fifty pounds. Even bleeding from that cut on your head, I'm pretty sure you could overpower me, so I'm not coming close enough for you to take my weapon."

It's probably more like sixty pounds, and rationally, I know she has a point. But my head hurts and I don't have the patience for her annoying rationality. "Then we're at an impasse, aren't we? Guess we'll just wait here and see if Morgen Fucking Campbell walks through the goddamn door."

Her eyes widen when I say Campbell's name. "He doesn't have the CHRONOS gene."

"If you're Madison Grace from 2136, how do you know Morgen Campbell? There are no stable points after the mid-2100s."

"I don't know him *personally*." She's quiet for a long while, and her expression shifts several times, like she's trying to think through every angle. Finally, she says, "You say you're with CHRONOS, and if I tell you too much, it could screw up the timeline even worse than it already is. I mean, probably not in 2136. But things could be really different in your time. So, let's just say I found a couple of diaries and Campbell's name was mentioned. He seemed like a pompous, egotistical ass, but I can't say I imagined him to be the type to get his hands dirty with actual murder. And both of the diaries made it very clear that he does *not* have the CHRONOS gene. I suppose that could have changed in this new timeline, but that explanation doesn't work if he's the one who *changed* it. He would have already had to be able to time travel in order to do that, right?"

"Right," I say, trying to sound more confident than I actually am on that point.

"Why do you think the sniper is Campbell?"

"Because I've been following a group of Klansmen who seem to be connected to the time shift."

"Klansmen? Like . . . the actual KKK?"

"Yeah. And Campbell—a younger version of Campbell, at any rate—was with them last night. Said he had a buddy he could hire to pick off a few of the marchers. And maybe he does have a buddy, or maybe Campbell has just decided to travel back a few hundred years and hunt people, instead of terrorizing animals on a game reserve like he usually does. Why did you ask what color the key is for me? I didn't get the sense that was idle chitchat."

"It wasn't. We have a theory about how the timeline was broken. Not who broke it, but how." She sneezes again, twice. "Oh hell, just check the damn key and find out if Campbell's the sniper. I can tell you about our theory once we're out of here. You're bleeding and I'm tired of breathing in all this dust."

I center the key in my hand, thinking that she's played this well, although I'm not sure it was intentional. Even if I were tempted to blink back to CHRONOS now, I'm not likely to do it until I find out what she knows. I glance down at the key and the display pops up. But it's blurred like everything else. I squeeze my eyes tight, rub them, and then try again.

"What's wrong?"

"If I had to guess, I'd say I have a mild concussion. Everything is blurry. Doubled, almost. You can either throw me your key and I'll transfer the stable point, or come close enough for me to tap the key to mine."

"Yeah. Like I'd give you my bloody key and strand myself in 1965." She stares at me for a long time, clearly trying to gauge whether I'm lying. Then she taps the device she's holding. "Fine. I had this set to stun. Now it's at max and my thumb will be on the button."

She begins sliding across the floor toward me, stirring up dust as she goes. When she's close enough, she stretches her key out toward mine, keeping her tiny little gun pointed at me. There's a dark red smear on her sleeve. Blood. *My* blood.

I really hope she doesn't sneeze while her thumb is on that thing.

Fortunately, there's not much to navigate in transferring a stable point, although I still manage to transfer the wrong one the first time.

Once I'm done, she slides to her original spot on the floor. I lean back against the footlocker and close my eyes, dizzy and a bit queasy from even that mild exertion.

"What does he look like?" she says as she pulls up the display. "All I remember is a vague description of him as a *fat gox*, and I really don't know what that means."

"Like I said, he's younger. Thinner, but still pretty beefy. Dark hair, cut short. He's probably wearing a red signet ring. And he'll be carrying a CHRONOS key."

After a moment, she says, "It's two people. They *both* have CHRONOS keys. Both have those rings you mentioned, too. The other one is a short, thin guy. He has the rifle."

"What time do they come in?"

"Three nineteen. Which makes sense. St. Jude is crawling with security forces once the marchers arrive around four. I think they'd notice someone carrying a gun that large." There's a pause as she scans forward. "They both jump out at three twenty-five. The short guy sets a stable point and . . ." Another, much longer pause. "He's back at nine twenty. Alone. And yeah, he's definitely the shooter."

Her eyes move slowly to the right, not the quick jerk you use when swiping, but the slow and steady motion of panning the stable point. "Most of the boxes have been moved to the other side of the attic door, except for a few that are where you are right now. The other boxes are stacked on top of each other, not scattered around."

"Why did they take the time to do that?" I ask.

"I don't think *they* did. You can't use the key. You said you're seeing double, and you're covered in blood. Getting you out of here is going to be a little problematic."

She has a very good point. One that I'd like to imagine I'd have thought of myself if I weren't dizzy and bleeding.

"Well, if you're not the sniper, I guess you're an ally," she says. "And you're the only ally I have who can actually time travel, so I'd better start moving boxes. Otherwise, you're going to be victim number one."

Five minutes and several sneezes later, she's relocated most of the boxes to the side of the attic opposite from the vent the sniper will use. She saves one extralong box and pulls it toward me.

"What's that one for?" I ask.

"To cover up the blood. Hopefully. I'll get something to wipe it up, but there will likely be a wet spot on the wood. Are you still bleeding?"

"A bit." I press my hand to the back of my head. "It seems to have slowed."

"Good. Otherwise, you're going to leave a trail. Come on. Your palace awaits."

She ends up having to help me walk. I'm so off-balance that we nearly fall twice.

I sink into the corner and take deep breaths, fighting back nausea. "Thank you," I say once I'm steady enough to speak. "You're right. I wouldn't have made it out of here. How long do we have before they arrive?"

She checks the key and then sets a stable point. "About an hour. Be right back. I'm going down to move the ladder back against the closet wall. And do what I can to hide the blood . . ."

I close my eyes and rest my head against one of the wooden beams. There are some scuffling noises and some cursing as she fights with getting the sticky attic door to open, several loud sneezes, and then she's gone. When she pops back in, her shirt is clean and there's a cloth bag over her shoulder. She puts it down next to me and pulls out a first aid kit, a jug of water, a small pill container, and a few other items.

"My virtual assistant says that your symptoms do indeed sound like a concussion. This is pretty pathetic, as painkillers go." She hands me the pills. "But my friend Lorena said anything stronger might interfere with your ability to use the key. She said the same about the antihistamine I wanted to take, so you'll have to put up with me sniffling. But these pills should help with the swelling, too."

"Is this Lorena a doctor?" I ask as I pop three of the pills and wash them down with some water from the jug.

The girl laughs. "*Technically*, I guess, since she has a PhD. She's a geneticist. But her . . . husband got a mild concussion last year when he tripped on the soccer field."

Her face falls slightly when she mentions the geneticist's husband. I suspect there's a story there.

"This may sound like a stupid question," she says, "but I could have sworn both of your eyes were blue when I saw you yesterday. Were you wearing lenses?"

"Yes. Are they out?"

"Just one," she says, tapping below her left eye. "Should I go look for the other one?"

"No." I take the right lens out and toss it into the bag. "I have another pair in my pocket. So what's this theory you mentioned?"

"Let's get you patched up first, and then I'll let Alex explain it."

Once the cut is clean and bandaged, she pulls back her sleeve and taps something on her wrist. A small holoscreen recording pops up, showing her next to an ancient computer. I've never seen one that old, even inside a museum, just pictures in books. The label at the top of the screen is very familiar, however—*Anomalies*.

"This kicked on right after the time shift," the girl on the holoscreen says. "I'm guessing you've seen something similar, since you knew to go to Montgomery 1965, so I won't belabor the point. I'll just turn things over to Alex." She nods toward one of the two guys, who is sitting in front of a more modern system. It's still far behind anything at CHRONOS, but at least it's recognizable.

The guy gives me a perfunctory nod and then begins demonstrating a bunch of tiny globes on the display, which he says are graphic representations depicting chronotron pulses coming from the Metro-Washington area. "These orange bubbles are Madi. Note the clear bubbles. We don't know what the hell those are, but . . ." He zooms out on the screen and selects a quadrant labeled *2300*. The section he pulls up includes several globes that are exactly the same color I see with the CHRONOS key. "You'll notice we have another cluster here. And here. Those both seem to correspond to the jumps you took on the days that Martin Luther King and John Lennon were killed in this timeline. Note that this is just a graphic representation, something that I put together so I could visualize it. When you look at this in two dimensions—or as a wave—it's barely perceptible."

He's right. I can't see anything different when he flattens the display.

"Again, I don't know what these things are or where they're coming from. I'm certain that I'm working with really primitive equipment compared to what you have in 2304, however, so maybe you could get your people to look into this. My best guess is that something or someone was . . . well, piggybacking on your signal." He puts the display back to 3-D. "Or maybe a better analogy would be that they're caught in your wake. Because if you turn the globes this way, you can see the clear side is stretched out a bit. I don't know what that means, but again . . . something you should probably mention to your technical crew. It's possible that it represents a slight distortion in the field to keep them from jumping in while you're still at the stable point, but that's just a guess. And what kind of worries me is that even if you reverse these changes, we don't know where or when these people are coming from or how they managed to get in. Which means there's a hole that somebody really needs to get to work on patching."

Madi cuts the video. "Did that make sense to you?"

"Kind of?" I say. "You're really Madison Grace? I pictured you as older."

She sniffs, and seems to be holding back another sneeze. "I'll be older at some point. At least, I hope so. Listen, there's a lot of stuff that I'm not going to go into. Like I said before, it could cause problems."

"I'm the one from *your* future. I should be giving the spoilers speech."

"Maybe. But here's the thing. You're from 2304. How many historians are at CHRONOS then? Thirty-six, right?"

I nod. "Yeah. Thirty-six active agents. There are others working in research and archives, but they've retired from the field."

"So it's a small enough group that you know them all, then, right?"

I nod again.

"Let's just say I have some ancestors in that group. *Several* ancestors. If the course of their lives changes, I won't exist. And since I seem to be the one who creates this damn key, that could mean CHRONOS doesn't exist, and therefore—"

"None of the historians exist," I say. "No CHRONOS, so no CHRONOS gene. Got it. But there's a huge conundrum right smack in the center of that claim, Madison. Several of them, in fact."

She gives me a grim smile. "It's Madi. And what would time travel be without conundrums? If you think you're confused, imagine stumbling across this thing, having it dump you into the freaking ocean in 1906, and then discovering you—or at least some version of you, in some timeline—created the damn thing a few decades from now." She waves a hand. "Or rather, a few decades from *my* now. That's all been in the past two weeks for me."

I'm quiet for a moment, because she's gone above and beyond by getting me patched up and hidden, and I really don't want to offend her. But the question has to be asked.

"You've just started using the key, and suddenly we have a time shift. Has it occurred to you that—"

"That I'm the cause? Of course. In fact, I was convinced it was *entirely* my fault until we noticed those odd deviations in the chronotron pulses, which seem to be people hitchhiking on our signals. Not just mine, but yours, too. And now you have someone who we know doesn't have the CHRONOS gene in the other timeline popping in to murder people. I'm not sure how my jumps could have affected either of those things. That's based on less than two weeks of practical experience, however, combined with Alex's theoretical background."

"So the two guys in the video are your partners?"

"One of them. The other is a friend. My second official partner had his memory wiped in the time shift. He's Alex's cousin, but the main reason he was pulled in was because he was married to Lorena, the geneticist I mentioned. She and their daughter don't exist in this timeline. Lorena and the baby were under a CHRONOS field when it happened. He wasn't, so he's off somewhere, totally oblivious to the fact that he has a wife and child."

I have a ton of questions, but when I open my mouth to ask them, she cuts me off.

"Let's focus on fixing the timeline. We can figure out the rest of it later."

She nods toward the bag. "There's an apple in there. Some crackers, too, if the nausea comes back. I have to go. The last thing we need is for me to sneeze and give your position away. Your gun is in the bag, but . . . you're not going to be able to see well enough to use it."

"You skipped ahead and checked?"

"Yes. I'll be back at 9:22." She looks slightly ill at the thought.

"Do you think you can do it?" I ask.

"Do I have a choice?"

∞

Even though the weather isn't especially warm, the attic is stifling. My head throbs miserably, and I'd like nothing more than to curl up on the floor and sleep. All it would take is one loud snore to give me away, but if that were going to happen, Madi would have seen it, right?

All thoughts of a nap vanish, however, as soon as I hear Campbell's voice floating up from below.

". . . other three. More than that is overkill. Pun definitely intended."

Someone laughs, although it sounds a bit forced to me. I've heard this kind of laugh before from the lackeys who hang around Morgen at the OC hoping he drops a few crumbs their way. Maybe if they laugh at his stupid jokes, he'll grant them access to the members-only rooms. More gaming credits. A high-status job once they're no longer in the field. It's the laugh you put on for the boss, so I have no doubt who's in charge here.

The attic-door hinge creaks loudly, and then I hear the sound of the ladder scraping across the closet floor. I tap my eardisk. It doesn't respond at first, and it's still hard to navigate any sort of visual interface, but I finally get the thing set to record, and then shift slightly so that I can peek through a gap between the boxes. My line of sight is poor, but at least I'll have the audio. If nothing else, Angelo should be able to run a voice analysis to show that it's Campbell.

The first thing I see is the faint purple glow from their CHRONOS keys, followed by the barrel of the rifle, and then a man's head and shoulders. He pulls himself up and moves aside for Campbell to follow. It takes a bit more effort for Campbell. Once he's in the attic, they both crouch down and head toward the window.

"You really think this location will work?" Campbell says, peering through the slats. "There's a lot of tree cover. I still think the other place—"

"Maybe," the other guy says reluctantly. "I just worry about being out in the open like that. If it was only a shot or two, a rooftop might be okay, but it's kind of risky when I'm taking out this many.

Especially when you're being picky about my targets. If it was King and some *random* people . . ."

"Just a matter of precision. Do you want to get docked for unintended consequences again?"

"No," the guy says. "That's why I think this location is better, though. And see, it's a pretty straight line to where they'll place that stage they're building."

"Fine," Campbell says. "You're the marksman. It's your call."

The second guy pulls out his key and sets a stable point. "Are you going to be up here?"

"We'll meet back at the hotel after," Campbell says. "I want to be down where the action is. And if you shoot me, I will absolutely haunt your ass."

The other guy snorts. "No worries. You're the one with the strategy skills. I can't win this on my own."

Campbell gives him a little nod of admission. "We make a good team, Bailey. Leave the gun and let's go get a beer."

"Do you think this will flip it?" Bailey asks as he props the gun against the wall.

"Unlikely. I'm fairly certain it will take both events. But the other one should be easy. And even if it doesn't flip, I think we'll win this round on points alone. If we take Lennon out in '57, there's no way Rand's team can do it in '66."

I center the key in my hand and try to pull up the jump room again. It's an improvement over an hour ago. I can see the platform, can even make out Angelo standing on the other side. But I still can't lock it in.

Should I get the gun? It's tempting, but in the end, it seems like a bad idea. It will tip this Bailey guy off that someone has been here. Given that he has a CHRONOS key, he can blink out and get another gun. If he pans around the stable point carefully, he might even realize it's gone before he jumps in. So, the gun stays against the wall, taunting me.

I stash the key back in its case and manage to doze intermittently. But that last bit that Campbell said keeps circling in my mind.

Teams. Rounds. Points.

He's treating this like a game of time chess. Just without the damn simulator this time.

And apparently Saul Rand is playing, too.

FROM *TEMPORAL DILEMMA USER'S GUIDE*, 2ND ED. (2293)

While there are many variations, a standard *TD* game consists of two rounds of play for each team or individual player. In each round, you are allowed five moves in one or more of the categories. Game play is sequential, with opening play determined by virtual coin toss. The first team or player to flip the timeline wins. Their opponent may, however, use any remaining move(s) to undo that change to the timeline.

Most games do *not* end with a temporal change. This is true in individual play, but even more frequently when competing as a team. In such cases, victory is determined by the player or team amassing the most points. For a full listing of points, please see Appendix A (Game Points) and Appendix B (Style Points).

∞26∞

To his credit, Tyson Reyes does try to take the shot. He points his gun at the sniper at 9:21. He takes aim and very nearly pulls the trigger. I'm thankful for the gesture, for his attempt to keep me from having to do it, although I can tell that his aim is off, just by watching through the key. In the end, he realizes it's too big a risk and pulls the gun back down at almost the same instant I blink in.

Would he have tried the shot if I hadn't told him he failed? Alex says no, and he's probably right, since I watched the events play out both before and after telling him, and the outcome was the same.

I've watched the rest of the scene through a stable point half a dozen times now. Jack watched it, as well. I can't help feeling that the only reason I'm able to even contemplate doing this, to contemplate blinking in and ending someone's life with the press of a button, is because I've *seen* myself do it over and over again. Alex says that's nonsense, too. He claims my decision to act is what sets the event in motion, and I must have already decided to do it, already been determined to press that button, or I couldn't see myself doing it through the key.

He's probably right. I just know that's how it feels.

I will have less than a second before the man notices the glow of my key. I don't know if the light is reflected somehow, if he catches it in his peripheral vision, or if it's just that vague sense that someone is behind you. Watching. Whatever the reason, he turns, and that's when I press the button that kills him.

Yes, I'm doing this to save the lives of the people on that field. To save the lives of those who die in the extension of a war that was already senseless, and to save those who are erased, even though I know I'm erasing all of those people who are listed in the files under *Additions*.

I, Madison E. Grace, being of sound mind and body, do hereby declare myself God almighty. Judge, jury, and executioner.

An overstatement, perhaps, but it feels like I'm veering way out of my lane on this one. But as I said to Tyson earlier, Do I have a choice? That final diary entry of Kate's springs to mind again, with her caution to change what I can and not spend the rest of my life questioning my actions. I hope I'm able to follow that advice.

Jack has been watching me stand here, staring at the key, trying to work up my nerve, for the past few minutes. I lean over and give him a quick kiss.

And then I lock the stable point.

Blink in.

Aim.

Fire.

There's a popping noise, and the beam hits the man exactly where I've seen it hit every time—just above his left ear. He crumples and falls.

That much is a direct replay of what Jack and I watched through the key.

What we didn't see, due to the position of his body, was his finger squeezing the trigger as he fell. I didn't hear it, either, because some damn fool—possibly me or Alex—decided in the original variation of this timeline that we didn't *need* an audio track.

It's just one shot, and the barrel of the gun was shifting upward as he fell, so I can't see how he could have hit anyone.

But the guards across the street will have heard that shot. Someone may even have seen the muzzle flash, given how many people are there. Either way, they're going to come investigate.

I can blink out, but Tyson can't. And that means he's stuck up here with a dead body.

Tyson is clearly thinking the same thing. "Just go. If they take me in, I'll manage to blink out later. Or CHRONOS will send an extraction team." He doesn't sound very confident on that last point. "There's no reason for both of us to get caught up in this. Go."

"The police aren't our only concern, though, and you know it. Campbell could beat them here. He didn't set a stable point, but the other guy could have given it to him. And he'd probably just kill you."

I stare at the body lying at the other end of the attic for a moment. I've gotten this far without knowing his name or getting a clear look at his face. My hope was that keeping it vague would make it easier. Make it less likely that I would have the haunted dreams that Kate talked about.

There's really only one option, now, and if Kate is right, this isn't likely to improve my chances for restful sleep. I'm not even sure it will work.

I make my way toward the body, trying not to see the mangled flesh at the back of his head. Clenching my teeth, I reach inside his shirt and find the CHRONOS key. I yank, but it's on a chain, so I have to pull it over his head.

Once I have it in my hand, I take a step back and the body vanishes. The gun is still on the floor, so they must have picked it up locally.

"Where the hell did he go?" Tyson says. "And how did you know that would happen?"

"I *didn't* know. It was a hunch, from something I read in one of the diaries I mentioned." I shove the guy's key into my pocket and grab the rifle. "And I don't really know where his body went, but the only logical conclusion is that he didn't exist in this timeline."

"Then how was he here?"

"Maybe he was a splinter. Or he wasn't under a CHRONOS field when the time shift happened."

"No. I don't think so. Not if they *caused* the time shift by killing King, Lennon, and the others. And they were talking about all of this like it's a time-chess game."

I'm scanning backward on my key as he talks, looking at the field at 9:23. Everyone is standing still, looking around. Probably trying to figure out if that was a gunshot or a car backfiring. James Baldwin is on the stage, looking nervous. He must make a joke, because the audience laughs, and then everything seems to go back to normal.

The military crowd doesn't seem nearly as relaxed, though. Several of them are gathered at the gate. I scroll forward quickly and see that they'll get the gate open in about two minutes, and then several dozen armed men will start combing the neighborhood. Knocking on doors. And I think someone must have seen the muzzle flash or else has a good ability to pinpoint where the sound came from, because this is one of the first houses they'll hit.

"I need to get downstairs. They're coming. I'll tell them I saw someone hop off the roof."

Tyson nods, wincing slightly at the movement. "Say he ran through the backyard toward . . . Council Street. That's the one behind Stephens. Do you have time to scan this room first, though? We need to see if Campbell comes back. Because you're right. He's a bigger threat than the cops."

Scanning quickly through the next fifteen minutes, the only persons in the attic are me and Tyson. "It's clear. I'll be back in a second."

I take the normal exit, through the attic door, since I don't have a stable point downstairs. None of the lights are on, and I toy with the idea of just staying quiet. But if they saw the shot being fired, that won't work. So, I open the front door and wait on the porch. Across the street, the concert continues. I don't know the singer or the song, but it's something about freedom.

When the armed man comes up the sidewalk, I speak first. "Did you see him, too?"

"See who, ma'am?" His voice is a slow drawl, and as I answer I'm painfully aware of my own accent. It has only a tinge of Brit, but it's completely out of place here. No point in faking it, though, since I already started speaking and I'm crap with accents.

"I thought it was fireworks or something, but then this guy jumped down from the roof and took off through the backyard. He had a gun. Hopped the neighbor's fence, too. I was going to call the police, but our phone's not hooked up yet. Was anyone hurt?"

"No, ma'am." He shifts the rifle to his other shoulder. Its appearance is just as menacing as the gun in the attic, far more menacing than the tiny and at least equally lethal device I have in my hand. "Did you get a good look at him?"

"Short guy. White. Kind of thin. Might even have been a teenager. Had on a . . . flannel shirt, I think. Jeans."

He nods, then sticks two fingers into his mouth and whistles. "Do you mind if a few of us cut through your yard?"

I tell him I don't mind at all. Six or seven guys respond to his whistle and begin tramping through the yard. When I try to go back inside, I realize the door has locked behind me, so I reach inside my shirt for the CHRONOS key.

As I'm locking in the attic stable point for thirty seconds after I left, I see a flash of orange light across the street. It's Campbell.

"That key in your pocket belongs to me," he says. "Give it to me, and then you can go back and tell Saul we're even now. Although, like I told him before, the player he lost was an accident. If you don't hand over the key, they'll dock points. The rules are clear. Don't you blink out on—"

I *do* blink out on him, which is nothing short of a miracle, given how badly my hand is shaking.

Tyson opens his now-brown eyes, which I like better than the blue. "What happened?"

"Maybe you should finish what you were saying about time chess. Because I've never heard of it. Campbell seems pissed—okay, *mildly* pissed—that we killed his player. And he seems to think I'm playing for Saul Rand's team."

"You know Rand, too?"

"He was in the diaries. And . . . is this time chess the same thing as The Game?"

"Yeah," he says. "That's what we tend to call it at CHRONOS. A lot of the historians play. But . . . it's done with a simulator."

"What's the objective?"

He makes a sick face. "Changing history. Causing a time shift. You get a set number of moves in each round. Concrete actions you can take. You alternate moves with your opponent, trying to be the first to flip the timeline to achieve a concrete goal. But getting back to Rand, he's an asshole. There's no doubt about that. But I don't think he'd be part of anything like *this*. CHRONOS runs us through a whole battery of psychological tests. They don't send murderers back in time."

I make an extra effort to keep my expression neutral, but it's probably a good thing that Tyson's vision is blurred. Whatever psychological safeguards CHRONOS may have, Saul Rand evaded them. He would *definitely* be part of something like this.

"Anyway, he's in Atlanta right now. In 1911, I think."

"But this is a *younger* Campbell," I say. "Maybe it's a younger Saul, too. Maybe this is something they did years ago—"

"First, there's like a thirty-year age gap between the two of them. Maybe more. If Campbell is in his twenties, Saul hasn't even been born. And second, like I said before, the time shift means that can't be the case. The shift just happened. Everyone under a CHRONOS key felt it at the same instant, no matter what time they were in."

"That makes absolutely no fucking sense," I tell him, as I fight an ultimately losing battle with another sneeze.

"Gesundheit," he says. "The way it was explained to me is that each key has a chronometer showing how long it has been in operation. They were turned on at the same time."

"But if the people who caused the shift were wearing a key, they'd have felt the shift when all of us did. Wouldn't the game be over, and they'd go home?"

"Yeah," he says. "You'd think so."

I shake my head to clear it. "Let's untangle this later. I need to take this key back to Alex. Campbell was pretty insistent that I give it back to him, so maybe it will tell us something. I can check the stable points, too."

"How are you going to unlock it?" he asks.

"Um . . . the same way I unlocked the one I've been using? By placing it in my palm."

"Valid point. Guess that's a security feature that doesn't apply to you."

I hadn't really thought much about the various security protocols that were mentioned in the diaries and how they might affect Tyson. It's stupid, but I keep thinking of both diaries as things that happened strictly in the past, probably because the women who wrote them are both long dead in my time.

"Can you even jump out from here?" I ask. "Or do you have to get back to a stable point?"

"Normally, no," he says. "That's the one security protocol that Angelo waived for this trip. We've generally been trying to use the stable points because that will be less he has to explain to the board eventually. He said to consider it an emergency exit. And ironically, it's done me absolutely no good in that respect. The one emergency I land in and I can barely see the thing. Although it seems to be clearing up a bit."

"You're going to get it checked out before you make the next jump?"

"I won't have any choice. Angelo will make certain it's healed before he lets me join Rich and Katherine." He stops and looks at me, head slightly tilted. "And like I said, my vision is clearing up. Is it Katherine or Rich?"

"What?"

"You flinched when I said their names."

"I'm not answering any questions about that. Maybe when this is all over, but—"

"I think it's Katherine. I mean . . . logistically, if you're in the past and you have an ancestor at CHRONOS, it would have to be a guy. We don't stay in the field nine months. But Rich isn't really the type. It's not Rich, is it?"

"God, you're really not going to give this up, are you? No. Okay? It's not Rich. But he's in love with Katherine, even if it's not requited. I don't think it's a good idea for me to interact with him, either."

"Poor Rich," he says. "Is there anyone across space and time who doesn't know he's in love with Katherine? And I see your point. But she'll be in Memphis. She'll be in Ohio. They both will. The only reason she and Rich aren't here with me now is I realized the sniper was targeting blondes. And she and Rich are only on this assignment because they were part of the original Memphis jump, and because they were two of the twelve agents who weren't in the field when the shift occurred. Neither of them is going to be much help, since they're only armed with these." He taps the watch on his wrist and then adds, when he sees my expression, "There's some sort of neural disruptor inside. But the CHRONOS field blocks it. Generally, that would be a good thing, but it's kind of a mixed blessing in this case. My point is, they'd be okay as backup if we were facing the Klan, which is what we thought to begin with. This is a whole new wrinkle, though. Neither of them has weapons training, and we're kind of trying to solve this quietly. There's already some political pressure to shut down CHRONOS, and—"

"And you want backup that can actually back you up. Understood. Which trip are you tackling next?" I change the subject in part because I want to know, but also because I really don't want to talk to him about shutting down CHRONOS. Undoing CHRONOS, never creating these keys in the first place, is still my primary objective when this is all over. Of course, I have no idea how I'll accomplish that, if the technology was created by some future version of AJG Research in the timeline next door.

"I'm not sure yet," Tyson says. "The original plan was to hold off on Ohio until the end. We need to tread lightly, because I was there when the shift happens—and oh, wow. I forgot to tell you there were five people with keys there, although I don't see how they were with CHRONOS. They had a kid with them. It's like they were *observing* Dr. King get shot."

"Damn. How many people could coast in on a single one of those bubbles that Alex spotted? Now I'm feeling like I carried in an entire caravan on my back."

"Yeah. I don't know. I'm not even sure how to factor them or the whole Campbell situation into the simulations we were running. Anyway, the plan was to do Memphis first, but these events may change that."

"That's the Beatles concert, right?"

"Yeah. But when Campbell and Bailey were talking, he said something about killing Lennon in 1957 instead. He said that Saul wouldn't be able to kill him in 1966 if they did it in 1957."

"That was my other jump! The one with the clear bubble. Liverpool, 1957. And . . . you mentioned a kid. What did he look like?"

"Preteen. Kind of pale. Dark brown hair. Dark eyes."

"I *may* have seen him, too. But Lennon wasn't killed in 1957. We know that. Otherwise he wouldn't have been around in 1966. Maybe Campbell is planning on doubling back and trying again?"

"Maybe. But I'm still not seeing how Saul could be part of this. I suppose it could be his father, or . . ."

"Is his father named Saul?"

He shakes his head. "I don't think so, but Campbell just said Rand."

"And outside in about . . ." I glance at the time on my key. "In about two minutes, he's going to say *Saul.*"

"Okay, then. I still don't see *how* it's Saul, given the restrictions on us when we jump, but okay. Anyway, to get back to your question, in The Game they don't have to tackle the challenges in chronological order, but they can't double back. You're not allowed to make the same move twice. In some scenarios, you can go back to get your wounded, but if you screw it up during your turn, there are no do-overs. That basic rule applies even in some of the more flexible expansion modules, so if these players are following—"

"I think we can safely say they're *not* following the rules if they're sacrificing . . ." I stop. "Wait, if it's time *chess*, are you suggesting that they have pawns? You guys play a game that has actual human pawns?"

He sighs. "It's normally a *simulation.* But yes. I've played. I guess I've even been used as a pawn the few times I've played with a team, although they don't use that term. It's an extremely complicated simulation, and I haven't played much. Katherine could probably explain it better than I can."

I ignore that comment, because I think he's trying to get more information out of me. "Why wouldn't Campbell's team have done the earlier jump first?"

He shrugs. "Maybe for the style points?"

"*Style* points?"

"Yeah. If you don't actually succeed in making the historical change you wanted—stopping the Civil War or whatever—in a given round, then the winner of that round is determined by points. Same for the game as a whole. Going backward chronologically, playing with a smaller support team—of virtual players, I mean—really, there are dozens of ways to get style points. I saw someone win one time because she managed to have a dog play a pivotal role in delaying the Industrial Revolution. That was Campbell's daughter, actually. Aside from Saul, I think that's the only time anyone has beaten Campbell—in public, at any rate."

We spend the next hour swapping information—with him telling me what he knows about this time-chess game and me answering a few of his questions about information in the diaries. I try to keep it vague, but probably end up spilling more than I should. Every few minutes, I scan forward to make sure that nothing has changed, that Campbell or the police aren't lurking outside. Tyson tells me about the original project they were on, about his undercover work with the Klan, and about the jump to Ohio where he saw Dr. King get killed. I get the sense he's holding something back about that jump, but I don't press. There are plenty of holes in what I told him, too.

While I'm hesitant to bring up Katherine at all, I need to know how big of a sea of conundrums I'm sailing into. Based on both of the diaries, anything that drives a wedge between Katherine and Saul before New Year's Eve is likely to result in my erasure. So I grit my teeth and ask, "Are you going to tell Katherine that Saul is involved in this?"

"Well, if it's him, if he's somehow managed to break the rules this badly, she'll have to know eventually. She's his partner. They *live* together. And if it *is* Saul, he'll be in Memphis, based on what Campbell said. So will Katherine. It's going to be a bit hard to hide. But I think we should hold off on telling her what we suspect until we have some proof, partly because I don't even know what I suspect at this point. It's just Campbell's word, and that's not worth much."

"Okay." I pile the first aid kit and other items back into the bag. "You should try the key again. When I scanned forward earlier, you were gone about ten minutes from now. But first, we need to establish a place and time to meet in Memphis. Privately."

He transfers a batch of stable points to my key, most of them at the Coliseum, but also one for the Peabody Hotel. "Let's make it eleven," he says, "just to be safe. Katherine and Rich will have to head to the airport shortly after ten, in order to be there when the band's plane touches down. And I have to meet up with the Klan at two."

"Are you still meeting them? I think we can assume the Klan didn't kill Lennon, based on what we've seen here. Right?"

"Maybe. Again, though, if whatever game these people are playing follows roughly the same rules as time chess, there's a huge points difference between taking an action directly with one of your team members and convincing an actual historical character to take that same action. That's almost as important as how many moves it takes you to accomplish a change. So I'm almost certain that goading members of the KKK into killing Lennon would be Saul's first choice. And sadly, they're pretty damn easy to goad."

∞

Yun Hee is snoozing on the couch next to Jack, who has been tasked with babysitting while Lorena is with RJ and Alex. Lorena debated taking her downstairs. Alex pointed out that RJ loves kids, and he'd probably enjoy having her around. And Yun Hee clearly misses her daddy.

But the man downstairs isn't really her daddy. He won't scoop her up in his arms and tickle her feet. He won't know to call her June bug. And even at ten months old, she'd probably sense the difference.

"Are you okay?" Jack says.

I half nod, half shrug, and he motions for me to come around to the other side of the couch so he doesn't risk waking the baby. Before I sit down, I pull the extra key out of my pocket.

"I brought back a present."

He takes the key and examines it. "This belonged to the sniper?"

"Yeah. And . . . he vanished when I yanked it. At least now you'll have one if you need it when I'm away."

"You're only away for a few minutes at a time."

"You want me to stay gone longer?"

He presses a kiss against my temple. "Nope."

I give him an overview of what happened, including Tyson's description of the game.

"How long were you in 1965?" Jack asks.

"Between the two jumps? About nine hours total."

I center the new CHRONOS key in my palm. There's a slight tingle, but nothing happens. I pick it up, wipe the back off against my sleeve, and then try again, thinking maybe it's still damp . . . although I've definitely used the other key when it was wet or I'd never have gotten back from Estero.

Still nothing.

"Can you try this?" I hand the key over to Jack. It doesn't work for him, either. We can both see the light, as we do with any other key. But the interface won't open.

"I'm going to carry Yun Hee to her crib," he says. "Then I'll see if I can get Alex to take a short break, so I can catch him up and maybe get him to take a look at this key."

"Is Lorena doing okay?"

"Yeah. I was down there for a few minutes earlier, and she was in the living room. Talking to RJ about old movies. They seem to have hit it off rather well."

"Which probably shouldn't be a surprise. And it's not making Lorena crazy?"

"She said she was going to basically treat this like a first date. Do you want me to bring you up anything?"

"Some herbal tea, maybe? I know it's not that late here, but I'm kind of wiped out. I need to get a shower. And at least try to get some sleep."

I crank the water up a few degrees higher than normal, scrub my skin until it's nearly raw, then slip into my favorite nightshirt, the one I've had since my teens, now so old that it feels like a second skin. I'm exhausted, but my brain is still buzzing. Part of me wants to jump straight to Memphis, and then to Ohio. To get this over with, one way or another. But I need to recharge. I need to untangle my brain. I need to forget the sight of that man as I pulled the key over his head. The sight of him dead. The sight of him erased.

When I step out of the bathroom, Jack is waiting with a tray. There's the herbal tea I suggested, as well as a bottle of Shiraz, a wedge of cheese, grapes, and a bar of dark chocolate.

"I was going to add ice cream," he said. "The ultimate comfort food. But the food unit spat out something that looked a bit like frozen calf slobber."

Tears are very close to the surface, and I do *not* want to go down that path. So I opt for levity, instead. "Are you going to spoil me like this every time I have to shoot someone?"

"Sure. As long as you keep it to single digits."

I take a long sip from the glass of wine he hands me. Then I place it on the dresser and glance down at my nightshirt, which is purple with tiny orange witches on brooms. "I should have worn something nicer."

"I don't know. It looks pretty comfortable."

"It is," I agree. "But it's not really the visual I want either of us to have from the first time we make love."

He smiles softly. "I can think of an easy fix for that. If you're absolutely sure it's what you want."

"I'm absolutely sure." I whisper the words against his neck.

Jack's arms tighten around me, and then he takes the hem of the nightshirt and lifts it over my head. As I begin unbuttoning his shirt, he slides his hands along the sides of my body, his thumbs grazing the edges of my breasts. I arch into him and everything dissolves into a delicious, mindless blur. There's little of the awkward fumbling that so often happens the first time, or maybe it just doesn't *feel* awkward. It feels like an exploration. I want to know what he likes. What makes him happy. We strike an easy balance of give-and-take. The tense threads in my body and mind slowly untangle, and thoughts of the past few weeks fade until there is nothing but me and him, and much later, a dreamless sleep.

∞

Jarvis awakens us with a notice that Alex needs us in the lab.

"It's six in the morning," I mumble into Jack's shoulder. "Doesn't he sleep? And it's a frickin' library, not a lab. There are books *everywhere*."

"I think it's kind of both at this point," Jack says.

"True. And I guess I need to get moving anyway."

Jack pulls me back down. "Jarvis, tell Alex we'll be there in twenty minutes."

"Yes, Master Jack."

Jack groans and whacks me with one of the pillows. "You programmed him to do that, didn't you? He never calls you Mistress Madi."

"He calls me mistress."

"That's not the same thing. Master Jack makes me sound like a street urchin in a Dickens novel."

I fight to keep my face straight. "You don't know what Jarvis calls me in private. And we have twenty minutes. Do you really want to spend them discussing my virtual assistant?"

He does not, as it turns out. And it's more like forty minutes before we finally make it to the library.

When we join Alex in the library or lab or whatever, he is in his swimsuit, with his hair sticking up wildly. "Finally," he says. "Everyone in this house needs to get their libidos under control."

"You're kidding?" Jack says. "Lorena and RJ? From his perspective, they just met."

"So? The exact same thing happened when they *just met* at a party five years ago. They're very decisive. When they see something they want . . ." Alex shrugs. "Anyway, I was going to get Madi to do this, since she can hold her breath for longer, but I got tired of waiting. Here." He hands Jack a CHRONOS key. "This is the one from the pool. I swapped them out. The other one works perfectly well for maintaining a protective field around the house, but there are some weird differences. Look at this."

"Hold on a second." I tap my comm-band to start recording. "Otherwise you're going to have to repeat it all so that I can share it with Tyson."

Alex waits until I'm ready and then flips one of his holoscreens toward us. "These are the two keys, front and back. The first is the key that was in the shielding device in the pool. The other is the one you brought back from Montgomery."

There are two sets of side-by-side images of CHRONOS keys on the screen. One is a front view, and the other is the back. Almost every detail is the same on the pictures of the front of the key, but the hourglass in the middle is more curved in the image on the left. There's also a tiny ridge that runs through the spokes that come out from the middle of the medallion. The back of the key is blank on the left-hand image, just as it is on the key I've been using. In the second image, however, there's a single word engraved on the back. *CHRO-NOS*.

"They could have been made at different times, I guess?" Jack says. "Or customized? The hyphen seems odd, though. Haven't seen that in any of the diaries or in *A Brief History of CHRONOS*. It's always one word."

I shake my head. "Tyson says the keys were all created at the same time. Or at least all activated at the same time, and they have a chronometer of some sort on the inside. That's apparently so that every key gets a notice about a time shift at the same instant."

"Normally, I wouldn't put much stock in stylistic differences," Alex says. "But the CHRONOS field on the other key is slightly different, too. I had to make some minor adjustments in order to get it to work with our shielding setup."

"So, do you think this is from some later version of CHRONOS, where they use slightly different equipment?" Jack asks. "And where they like hyphens in their acronyms? Or maybe an earlier iteration, since Madi says this Morgen Campbell guy is younger."

"That's a reasonable explanation. But I don't think it's the right one. Look at this." He spins another one of his data-cave screens and expands a chart at the bottom. "The thin red lines there show the interference I picked up in the chronotron field the times that Madi spun off a clone. Or a splinter, as I guess they call them. The blue line is what I'm picking up from the new key now that it's activated by the device inside the pool wall. The lines are different in terms of their strength and consistency. You can see how the red ones grow thinner, and then vanish. But . . ."

"The pattern is the same," I say. "So, what does that mean?"

Alex points toward the red lines. "Each of these were an attempt at spinning off a different reality, right? An attempt that eventually failed, but still an attempt. I could be totally off base here, but my best guess is that this key comes from a *stable* alternate reality. That's kind of freaking me out, because it shouldn't be possible. And also because, if it happened once, what's to stop it from happening again?"

∞

Jack and I spend the next few hours combing through the stable points that Tyson transferred to my key last night, and that I transferred to the spare key, looking for any odd flashes of light. We sync up the time and go through together, so that we can double-check. If Jack sees something as aqua and I see it as orange, we add it to the list.

Tyson said the observers were wearing their keys out in the open at the event where Dr. King was killed, but maybe they realized the medallions are a bit odd looking for mid-1960s jewelry, because the only two keys we're certain we spot are a bit muted. We do locate seven other blips of light that we're fairly sure are from keys. All of them occur during the time that the Beatles are onstage for the evening performance, so we could have skipped scanning through the matinee and the roughly two hours in each show where the four opening acts perform. The lights we've found are never visible for more than a few seconds, though, because the place is packed with kids waving posters and albums in the air. This is one time I'm quite glad there's no audio on the key. Not because of the music. I've had Jarvis play some of their songs. They're actually quite good. But I'm pretty sure you'd never be able to hear the music over the screams. Every girl—and a few of the guys—that I've seen has either been screaming, laughing, or in tears since the Fab Four came onstage in their snazzy dark-green suits. I'm getting a much better sense of why the press at the time called it Beatlemania.

The task feels a little futile, to be honest, like we're searching for a needle in a frantic, wildly gyrating haystack. Even going through at double speed, there are dozens of these locations, and we have to take the time to pan around almost 360. Some stable points we've been able to eliminate entirely—many of the ones Rich and Katherine set near the center of the auditorium only work sporadically in terms of viewing and aren't available at all for jumping in, which makes me wonder if they're smack in the middle of some teenage Beatles fan. As a result, we've stuck mostly to the locations on the perimeter of the audience, but it's still a lot to scan.

And there are *so many* other flashes of light in the auditorium that it's hard to pinpoint anything, even with the color difference to guide us. I wasn't sure what the other flashes were until I had Jarvis look up portable cameras from the era, and I saw the little flash cube on top. Between those and the professional photographers, the lights are making my head pound.

Jack rubs my shoulder. "We could take another break," he says, grinning.

"A break, hmm? Is that what the groovy kids are calling it these days?"

When break time is over, he says, "We'd best get back to it." I groan and he adds, "Hey, I'm just glad for something I can *do*. You have no idea how helpless I feel each time you jump out. I don't know what sort of danger you might be jumping into, and there's not a damn thing I can do to help you."

I want to tell him that it helps just to know he's here waiting for me. But that sounds a little like I'm casting him in the role of the faithful Penelope, waiting for Odysseus to return from his journeys. So I just snuggle closer, and we start on the next stable point. About ten minutes in, Jack says, "Did you see that? Two flashes."

My key must be a smidgen behind his, because it's still a second before I see what he's talking about. It's the clearest flash of orange I've noticed. And he's right, it's actually two flashes, one slightly higher than the other, in the last row of the balcony section just to the left of the stage, which is only about half-full, due to the fact that the view of the stage is partially obstructed. The two amber lights are fully visible for a few seconds. Then it looks like they drop their keys inside their shirts. They stand there for about a minute, before they begin moving closer to the edge of the balcony.

I zoom in as much as possible, but between the kids jumping around and the fact that the couple is moving, I can't tell much aside from the fact that it appears to be a man and a woman. They push through the sea of screaming girls, thoroughly pissing off one tween who whacks at the man with a magazine she's holding. He ignores her and moves on, but the woman—tall and very pretty, with vivid auburn hair—turns around and lunges at the girl, teeth bared. The girl, who looks stunned, cowers back toward the group she's with. For a second, the woman holds the snarl, then she laughs and joins the man. The couple moves out of my sight for a moment, and then the man turns back and I get a clear look at his face.

The first thing that strikes me is that this very easily could be Saul Rand, based on Kate's description in the diary, on the stylized paintings of his Brother Cyrus alter ego that I found online, and on the one brief glimpse I got of him in Katherine's video diaries. He's tall and thin, with dark hair, light eyes, and pale skin. The second thing that strikes me is the scar running down his right cheek. None of my sources mentioned that. Nor did they mention his right eye, which doesn't look entirely natural. The pupil widens all the way, completely covering his iris and part of the white as well, as he scans the auditorium.

He turns to the woman and whispers something to her. She laughs. Then he reaches into his jacket and whips out a pistol that looks quite a bit like the one in the desk downstairs.

∞27∞

I curl up on my side, wishing the headache would go away. The concussion was bad enough. CHRONOS med patched that up in fairly quick order, but this? They don't have a cure for this. The only thing is to get through it. Angelo said it would take a day or two, but that was probably only a guess on his part. Double memories are bad enough. But, like Angelo said before, a triple memory will lay you out flat.

He wasn't wrong.

The only good thing about the entire situation is that I was here at HQ when the triple memory hit. I'm not sure I could have jumped back otherwise. It's still hard to sit up without feeling like I'm going to hurl.

A voice on the other side of the room says, "You alive?"

"Yeah. Not particularly happy about it, though. What about you?"

Timothy Winslow chuckles softly. "I'm doing okay, actually. It's just one little bit of overlap for me. It kind of tickles the front of my brain if I think about it too long, and not in a good way, but I've had worse. Never had a triple memory, though. That takes some doing."

I'm tempted to tell him that it really didn't take much doing on my part. Just him going back to 1965 to deliver an anonymous tip. But I'm not sure how much Angelo has told him about the time shift or even how much the rest of CHRONOS will know when all of this is over, so I just say, "You got that right."

When I showed up in the jump room last night—or technically, *tomorrow* night—covered in blood, Angelo checked the anomalies list and discovered that most of the events surrounding the Selma march were back on track. There were some disturbing ripple effects, however. Viola Liuzzo was killed the next night, exactly the way it happened before, except some other member of Klavern 13 was in the car, instead of FBI informant Tommy Rowe. The young man who was in the car with Liuzzo described their attackers to the police, but it was the word of a nineteen-year-old black man who had been in the company of a white woman who was now dead, so the cops weren't inclined to take his word. They even tried to pin it on him, but the charges didn't stick. Without the testimony of a white witness to back him up, the case was pushed under the rug. The Voting Rights Act was eventually passed, but it took longer. And the HUAC hearings never really got off the ground.

I told Angelo that I'd go back and take care of the problem, but the med tech said I'd need at least twenty-four hours before she'd clear me to jump. So Angelo reluctantly called Timothy in. He was sent back to Montgomery with an anonymous tip about some Klansmen he'd overheard talking in a bar, who planned to kill Mrs. Liuzzo. To back up his claim, he mailed the FBI and the *New York Times* a cassette tape, fairly new technology at the time, containing a heavily edited audio version of the recording I made in the bar when Shelton and the other Klansmen were talking about stirring up some trouble. While I really *don't* think the Liuzzo killing was premeditated, there are plenty of other things those men have done without any repercussions, so I don't feel too bad about them facing a false charge.

The timeline didn't shift back entirely, but then we never really expected it would. It took a lot to shove the timeline off its track. It will likely take just as much to shove it back into place. As best we can tell, there's only one change to the *original* timeline . . . Dynamite Bob Chambliss spends eleven years longer in prison than he did before. No clue why, but having him behind bars could only be an improvement. And we're now back to Scoggin and Jones spending a year in jail along with Robert Shelton.

The unexpected, but definitely not unwelcome wrinkle was that it also halted the murder of Dr. King at the event at Antioch. That's why I'm in the isolation tank recovering from the triple memory that hit me like a truck just as Timothy returned. Because Dr. King wasn't killed, there were no observers wearing CHRONOS keys. No one tumbled from the roof screaming. I never tackled Antoinette Robinson to the ground, so she was never in contact with my key. In the new version of events, when I spoke to her outside the drugstore, she looked healthy and happy. Her smile lit up her entire face, just like the first time.

In some sense, the new memory is very similar to the story she told me about graduation day, and it does solve the mystery of how I helped the Robinson family with their car. I wasn't the only one helping, and it didn't require any knowledge at all about automobiles, just strong legs. Six of us pushed the car so that her father could pop the clutch and start it. I was, however, the only one unlucky enough to slip as the car cranked, landing square on my ass in a patch of mud. So I'd been standing there, mud splattered, when her dad pulled back around to thank us. Her little sister had laughed, and Toni had elbowed her, then flashed me a sympathetic smile as they drove away.

These memories joust in my head, each trying to knock out the other two. But as uncomfortable as that may be, I'm glad I'm battling them and not Toni. Everyone around her must have thought she was crazy. At least I know what's happening.

"Is that all of the story I'm going to get?" Timothy asks. "No humorous tales of how you screwed up so bad that you're juggling three memories?"

"There's nothing at all humorous about any of this. Just take my word that Angelo has the situation marked need to know for a reason."

He's quiet for a moment, which is a bit unusual for Timothy. "I'm getting the sense that this wasn't entirely a screwup on your part. Angelo was off in the corner talking to Aaron when I got back, and both of them looked like—"

I roll over so that I can look at him. "Tim. I'm sorry. I *can't* tell you."

He smiles and waves me off. "Nah, that's okay. You know me. Evelyn says I'm too damn curious for my own good."

I think Evelyn is right, but it's impossible to be annoyed at him for long. Katherine's comment about Saul being like an overgrown pup is actually a much better description of Timothy Winslow.

"Hey, curiosity isn't always a bad thing," I say. "If you want to know more, though, you'll have to take it up with Angelo. He knows everything I do."

That's *mostly* true. I told Angelo the full story about Madi after the med tech finished patching up my head. While I may end up regretting that, I didn't see any other option. There was no way he'd have believed I just came up with the information about something hitching a ride on our chronotron pulse. I don't think there's a single historian at CHRONOS who has more than a rudimentary under-standing of how the technology works. That's partly because we're customized for our work in the field, but I suspect it's also to avoid anyone becoming too curious about the safety protocols, whether they might be tweakable, and so forth.

I didn't tell him about Toni, though. In retrospect, that's a good thing, since it resolved on its own, although I know it's a bit hypocritical to trust Angelo on the other issues and not trust him about her double memories. The difference is that he has a vested interest in protecting CHRONOS. I also suspected that he could do some checking to find out whether Madi was telling the truth. Turns out he didn't even have to check. He already knew that the history of CHRONOS had changed slightly prior to the time shift. It was nothing that caused a major rift in the timeline, however. They sold the technology a few decades earlier, but the government decided it was too risky to use, and they shelved the project. There's a picture of the three founders of AJG Research, and even though Madi and the temporal physicist both look a little older than they did in the vid, it's definitely them.

Angelo agreed about keeping Madi's role in this to a strictly need-to-know basis. The only thing he was perturbed about was me letting her take the key back with her. To be honest, it wasn't even something I'd given much thought to, possibly because my head was killing me. He said they might have a better idea what's going on if some of the tech people could examine the key, so when I see her this afternoon, I'm going to ask if she'd be willing to let us have it.

The other thing we agreed on was that I would not mention Saul to Katherine. Truthfully, I think the fact that Saul might be part of this is the only reason that Angelo didn't decide to call Rich and Katherine back from Memphis and let me and Madi deal with the Lennon assassination. There's not a whole lot they can do to help in Memphis. But if Saul is there and he's part of this, Katherine would be a powerful witness against him with the board. And she's unlikely to believe any evidence against him unless she sees it with her own eyes.

∞

Tyson
Memphis, Tennessee
August 19, 1966

"I just don't understand why you would take that kind of risk," Katherine says as she pushes aside her mostly uneaten breakfast. "For that matter, why would Angelo let you?"

"Because it was the most sensible thing to do. If you couldn't be with the marchers, there really wasn't much either of you could have done in Montgomery."

Rich rolls his eyes. "You mean aside from realizing you hadn't reported back to the hotel? That you might be bleeding out somewhere?"

"I managed, okay? The sniper is dead, and no one at the rally was killed. Everything seems to be back on track in 1965. And it's done. We need to focus on 1966. And we have to figure out what all of this stuff with Campbell means. Angelo is going to get some people working on that."

"You *certain* it was Campbell?" Katherine asks, even though they've viewed the stable point twice. "The lighting was horrible in that bar. And those candles on the table tinted everything, so I honestly couldn't tell whether he was carrying a key."

"He's definitely carrying a key," Rich says. "Inside his jacket. But I'm still not one hundred percent convinced that it's Morgen."

"You've both been in the Redwing Room more times than I have," I say. "Are you telling me you never noticed the portrait over the fireplace?"

"Which one?" Richard asks. "There's like . . . a dozen portraits over the fireplace. All the glorious leaders of the glorious Objectivist Club."

I rub my temples. Even though the med tech cleared me for duty, my head is still tense, and arguing—even over minor stuff like this—isn't helping. "It's Campbell, okay? Angelo agrees with me. He managed to view the stable point for a few seconds. It kept breaking up, but he got enough of a look to compare it to the portrait, which was done when Campbell took over from his grandfather, at around age forty. The guy in the bar was a lot younger than that—maybe twenty-five—but it's Morgen Campbell. Did you see the way he flicked the cigar? And his ring. Plus, it sounded like Campbell."

I'm wishing now that I'd had Madi slip that ring off the Bailey guy's finger, although she looked ill enough at having to lift the chain over his head. And the ring would probably have vanished, anyway, just like the guy's body did, if it was ever outside of a CHRONOS field.

"The ring does look like his," Katherine admits. "And I do remember the portrait you're talking about now that you mention it. I guess I just can't stand the idea of there being two of the pompous fool running around. But I don't understand how he could use the key without the equipment in the jump room."

"The safeguards to the system apparently aren't as ironclad as we thought," I tell her. "Otherwise, Angelo couldn't have given us this emergency-exit option. And Campbell's family is disgustingly rich. Maybe they purchased some deluxe package not available to the rest of us."

"So all this time Campbell has been yakking about how lucky we are that we can actually travel, how he wishes he wasn't stuck in one time, and he was actually using the damn thing when he was younger," Rich says, with a disgusted shake of the head. "It figures."

"Are you going to shoot him?" Katherine asks. She doesn't sound nearly as horrified at the idea as I would expect from someone who blanched when Angelo handed me the gun.

"Wouldn't it be nice if it were that easy?" Rich says. "Just go shoot the stupid gox and be done with it. I doubt anyone would miss him."

"Saul would," Katherine says under her breath.

I don't argue either point, but the truth is, Campbell's not stupid. He's got an ego the size of a mountain and social views I find personally abhorrent. But he's actually well above average intelligence. On the few occasions I have actually watched him play time chess, he's usually two or three moves ahead of his opponent. Unless he's playing Saul. They're pretty evenly matched. One of their games went on for thirty-seven hours.

"I'm not supposed to shoot him unless it's completely unavoidable. For one thing, can you imagine the double memories anyone under a CHRONOS field would be stuck with? Every one of us has interacted with him. But we do need to figure out what's going on, how they managed to use the equipment, and so forth. Angelo even debated asking Sutter to go question Campbell—by which I mean the older version of Campbell holding court over at the OC—but there's no way he'd keep this under wraps."

"Oh, Sutter would keep it secret," Rich says, smirking. "For a while. Until it was in his best interest to blackmail you with it."

Katherine and I both nod, although I'm going on the basis of legend, not actual interaction with him, and I'm pretty sure both of them are, too. Sutter is head of CHRONOS security and, rumor has it, an excruciatingly by-the-book sort of guy who gets his jollies from interrogation. I don't know what his genetic tweak is, but he has ocular implants that can spot a lie at fifty paces. He was the boogeyman that teachers threatened us with as kids. *Do you want me to call Sutter?* The answer was always *no*, followed by a noticeable change in attitude. I don't think Sutter could actually inflict physical punishment—in fact, I never heard of anyone getting any sort of behavior modification beyond that vague Sutter threat. Which is weird, come to think of it. Rebelliousness must have been one more thing they tweaked while they were playing around with our genomes. Saul has definitely been called in a few times, but even he tries to avoid being too flagrant about flouting regulations.

"I'm not sure Campbell would keep quiet about being questioned, though," Rich says. "The thing that bugs me about all this is Campbell being younger. The guy in the video is at least thirty, maybe even thirty-five, years younger than Campbell is now. If his actions caused the time shift, it should have been detected at CHRONOS *when* he did it, before the three of us were even born. It's got to be a clone."

"You're overcomplicating things," I say. "There's no reason it has to be a clone. If he managed to get a key to a younger version of himself, and also arranged for the CHRONOS gene as his chosen gift, then it could just be a younger Campbell."

"I still think it's a clone," Katherine says. "He couldn't use the key, so he cloned a version of himself that could. And now that version is involved in some sort of sick game that's screwed up the timeline. I just hope both of them pay for this, not just the clone. I mean, there should be some sort of penalty for black-market enhancement and, for that matter, having the damn clone in the first place."

"There *should*, but I think all three of us know that's very unlikely to happen," Rich says. "If we manage to fix this, Campbell will probably deny all involvement and maybe spread a little cash around to make the problem go away."

I shake my head. "Sorry, but I still don't think it's a clone. Morgen Campbell could have bought the CHRONOS gene for his daughter. He didn't. I'm not sure why he'd see a clone any differently. The man is inherently selfish. He wants the experience for *himself*. He'd be jealous of the clone getting to experience everything that he didn't."

"Okay," Katherine admits grudgingly. "That's a valid point. So . . . maybe we just table the whole clone-or-not question. Either way, we're dealing with a younger version of Morgen. What worries me are the *others* we saw wandering around."

I've already viewed the eight stable points, out of at least a hundred that they set in the Coliseum last night, where Rich and Katherine found evidence of someone with a CHRONOS key. They admitted that there could easily be more, and looking at the lights in the auditorium, it's easy to see why they can't be entirely sure. Once the Beatles take the stage, there's so much movement that it's a bit nausea inducing.

We do know the time of the shooting, though. The last of the opening acts leaves the stage at 10:17 p.m., and the emcee goes on to announce the Beatles two minutes later. Flashbulbs begin popping so fast at that point that the stage takes on a weird strobe-light effect. Unless we manage to stop it, at 10:38 tonight, about a minute into the third song, "If I Needed Someone," John Lennon will stumble forward, drop his guitar to the stage, and pitch forward into the pit, inches away from a line of uniformed cops standing at the fence surrounding the stage.

I glance at my watch. It's nearly time for me to meet Madi. "Listen, I'm going to head back to the room and look over a few things before I meet up with Meeks and his buddies. I'll just catch a cab."

Katherine excuses herself for a trip to the ladies' room while we wave down the waiter for our check. As soon as she's out of sight, Rich leans forward. "I didn't want to say this in front of Katherine, but I think Saul's in this, too." He holds out his key to transfer a stable point.

The man I see when I pull up the stable point definitely *could* be Saul. He's around the same height. There appears to be a woman with him. Both are in the section directly behind the stage. The angle is bad, and if I didn't already suspect Saul was involved, I'd probably hold off, but . . .

"It's Saul." Then I tell him what I heard Campbell say when I was stuck in the attic.

"If Campbell is younger here," Richard says. "Saul would be a toddler. No, I don't think he'd even be born yet. And he's fully grown. So that's more evidence for the clone theory."

"Not really. Maybe it's a greatest-of-all-time championship of some sort? I keep getting stuck on the age thing, too, but they're time traveling as part of The Game. Saul could just as easily have jumped back to compete with Campbell when he was in his prime. Do you have any other stable points in that section?"

"I checked the locations I set. Katherine created some, as well. I have those on my key, but since they were transferred, they're not in the same order. I haven't found anything that gives a clearer view. Katherine shouldn't be here, though. Angelo should have pulled her out as soon as he suspected Saul was involved in this. And you should have told me."

"When? This is the first chance I've had. And you suck at keeping secrets from Katherine."

"The hell I do. She doesn't know I'm in love with her."

I sigh, because I really don't want to do this. He's going to totally blame the messenger. "Rich . . . she *knows*. She doesn't want to admit it to herself, but she knows."

As expected, he looks pissed and miserable and sad. But not surprised. Deep down, he *knew* that she at least suspected. "Why didn't Angelo call her back to HQ, then? If you told him Saul was there, why—"

"She needs to see for herself, Rich. And she'll be the best witness against him if it comes down to that."

Katherine is on her way back. Rich takes one look at her, and then pushes away from the table, mumbling something about getting the valet to pull the car around.

"What was that about?" Katherine asks. "He looks angry."

"Don't know. We were talking about Campbell, and I think he's still a little pissed about being benched on the Montgomery trip."

She nods. "He has a valid point. If he's pissed at you, though, it's mostly because he's worried. You need to check in with us a bit more often. And yes, Tyson, we're both well aware that we kind of suck as backup. But Rich is your best friend. It bothers him not to be of more use."

"You guys are doing all of the grunt work, though. Setting all those stable points. And then going through them. That has to have taken most of the night."

She rolls her eyes. "While you're bashing your head open in strange attics, shooting people, disposing of the evidence, and so on. My point is we may suck as backup, but we're what you have, and we may surprise you. Don't get yourself killed by trying to do it all on your own. Because if this really is Campbell and he's playing The Game, he's going to take it seriously. And judging from those other blips of light we spotted, he's not the only one you need to be watching out for."

When she's gone, I pay the check, then head up to the stable point on the mezzanine to intercept Madi. She arrives promptly at eleven. That's not exactly a surprise. When you have a key that will let you arrive on time no matter when you leave, it takes a conscious effort to keep someone waiting.

"The elevator is around the corner," I say. "If you don't mind talking up in our room, that is."

"I think I can trust you." She gives me a wry grin and pats her pocket. "And if it turns out I can't, you already know I'm armed."

"That's an excellent point."

Madi tucks her key inside the leather pouch as we turn toward the bank of elevators about halfway down the curved hallway. As we're about to step inside, I spot Rich downstairs near the concierge station, looking up at me. He's wearing a curious expression, so I wonder how long he's been watching us. There's no law against talking to a stranger while you wait for the elevator, but if he's been standing there for more than about ten seconds, he could very well have seen Madi tucking her key back into the pouch.

I give him a wave as the doors close.

"Who was that?" she asks.

"Richard."

"I thought you said they'd be gone by now."

"Yeah. They should have been. He and Katherine were waiting outside for the valet to bring the car around. Must have been a delay of some sort."

"Did you tell him about me?"

"No. I had to tell Angelo, though." Her shoulders sink, and I continue quickly. "I didn't have any choice, Madi. There's no way he'd have believed I had this random thought that they might want to check our chronotron pulses for stowaways. It's not something I'd ever have come up with. He's known me since I was ten, so there's no way I could sell that story. He has a vested interest in making sure that nothing changes your development of time travel, so he's not going to be a problem. His only concern was that you don't need to take any risks. If something happens to you, I think there's a decent chance we might have another timeline shift. And he agreed that Katherine and Rich need to be kept in the dark about your role in all of this, at least for now."

"Okay," she says, as we exit the elevator and head down the hallway toward the room. "I guess that will have to do. Do you think Rich saw my key?"

"Probably. He's pretty observant."

"Great. I'm not used to this whole undercover thing," Madi says. "You guys train most of your lives for this sort of stuff."

"True. But you've handled yourself pretty well so far. That's the only reason I didn't wind up as a mystery corpse in that attic."

I unlock the door. Once we're inside, Madi pulls her communications band out of her purse and snaps it to her wrist. "I remembered to take this thing off for once, but then I go waving the damn key around," she mumbles as she taps the wristband. "Anyway, Alex has been busy."

"Wait," I say. "Do you mind if I record this for Angelo?"

She looks hesitant, and then says, "Sure. Go ahead. If he knows anyway, I guess there's no harm in making sure he gets accurate information."

I touch the eardisk.

"You can record video with that?" she asks.

"Not without the lens implants."

"Your blue lenses?"

"No, those are just cosmetic. The communications implants are beneath. Everyone has those, from the time you're around eight or nine. They have to be changed out every year or so, but they work in conjunction with the eardisk. Okay, you can start."

She begins the recording, and I watch as her partner demonstrates some minor physical differences between the two keys, which he argues could easily be explained away as them being from different time periods. The next part, however, is far more interesting.

"That's bizarre," I tell her. "And your partner there—"

"Alex."

"Yeah. He's right that the interference pattern looks similar, but . . . there could be other explanations for that. It's been accepted science since—well, since before your time—that there are indeed parallel universes. But they spin off from actions taken in this universe. You can't travel between them."

"Except," she says, "I kind of know of someone who *did* that. Not purposefully. It happened because there was a time shift. She was under a key, and so was her grandmother . . . who was pregnant at the time with her mom and her aunt. So there were eventually two of her in the same timeline."

That doesn't make sense to me. "Then why don't splinters continue to exist?" I ask. "They're under a CHRONOS field."

"Because . . . they don't actually come from a *stable* reality, maybe? And quantum Darwinism . . . I think. I'm not claiming to understand it. Even Alex doesn't fully understand it, but that's what I've been able to piece together from what he told me. It wasn't just that one example, either. There were a few other cases, too—they're why I decided to try pulling that guy's key, to see if his body would vanish."

"Speaking of, do you have the other key with you?"

"No. Like Alex said, it's powering the shield around my house."

"Um . . . Angelo's going to want it when I go back, in order to test out your theory. That's the one thing that he was kind of pissed about. Me not bringing it back, I mean."

Madi looks a little perturbed at that. "We might be able to *loan* you the key, briefly, but we need it. We've got two erased people to protect. One is a baby, and I'm pretty sure that CHRONOS will never exist without the other one. And since Angelo isn't the one who had to kill a guy to get it . . ."

I nod. "Understood. I'm just telling you what he said."

"We'll see. So, now that science class is out of the way, I need to see if you can identify someone. The easiest way would be for me to transfer the stable point back to you, rather than you wading through to find the right one."

Once we make the transfer, she waits for me to pull it up and then says, "Is that him?"

I see the person—or rather, persons—in question a moment later. A man and a woman. The guy is definitely Saul.

Although, as he comes closer, I amend that. He's a version of Saul.

"Yes," I say. "But unless he's had some major plastic surgery, that's not the Saul I know. That scar, for one thing. And he's got one of those eyes like Sutter, the head of security at CHRONOS."

"Maybe it's a future version of Saul?"

"I don't think so. If anything, he looks younger here. So, I'm kind of coming around to this whole visitors-from-another-dimension theory."

"The gun looks a lot like one in my great-grandfather's desk. His had pearl grips, though."

I shake my head. "Do you have any idea how many of these were made? A huge proportion of police officers carried that model during the first half of the twentieth century. It's really, really common."

"Okay. What about the woman? Is she a historian?"

"I know her, too." What I don't add is that I know her in the biblical sense. Even once when she had her hair this exact shade of red. "She's not a historian, though. That's Alisa Campbell, Morgen's daughter."

"But if Morgen and Saul are opponents, why would she be on Saul's team?"

I laugh. "If you knew them, you really wouldn't have to ask that question. What's the time when they arrive?" Glancing down at the display, I see 10:33:21. "A little less than five minutes before the shooting. This is a good find, Madi. At least we have a backup option."

"*Backup* option? Why? Not only do we know where he's going to be, we know he has a gun out a few minutes before Lennon is killed."

I raise my eyebrows and wait.

She sighs. "And . . . it's in the middle of over twelve thousand people. Plus a massive security battalion. But . . . there will be security around all day, right? From the moment the Beatles arrive."

"Yes, but not as many as there will be for the evening show. If we can catch them before the Coliseum fills up, that's the goal. If not . . . well, hopefully my Timex can buy us a few minutes to get the two of them out of there. Also, I'm not convinced yet that it's Saul pulling the trigger. I definitely think he will do it if no one else does, but . . ."

"Style points," Madi says.

We're both silent for a moment, and then she says, "So . . . what's the plan?"

"Rich and Katherine are out at the airport where the Beatles' plane should be landing soon. We're supposed to meet up at five thirty, just before the Beatles finish their set for the afternoon show, over at the press entrance on the north side, to discuss anything we've seen or heard. The two of them will then head to the press conference between the matinee and evening concerts, keeping an eye out for people with keys. This"—I reach into my pocket and pull out another press pass—"is for you."

"So I'll be in the same area as Katherine? Bad idea."

"It's just to cover you if anyone asks why you're backstage. But there's a separate event for school journalists and fan-club leaders that starts at six. Maybe check that one out? Those rooms were locked when Katherine and Richard came in to set stable points, so we didn't have any way to scan them. Other than that, circulate and look for Saul, Alisa, or anyone else who might be wearing a key."

"How am I supposed to let you know if I spot one of them?"

She has a point. Rich, Katherine, and I have a short-range communicator inside our eardisks. About a square mile range. Standard protocol is that it's for emergencies only, up until 2010. By that point, no one thinks twice if someone starts walking around talking out loud. Everyone else just assumes they're talking on a device.

"Hold on," I tell her. "Let me check something." I pull up my display and search for available communicators. There's one listed for Katherine. While it's possible she has an extra disk in her luggage, it shouldn't show up unless it's currently activated. Which I'm pretty sure means that Madi's disk once belonged to Katherine. I send her a little ping.

She jumps and then laughs. "Oh. Okay. So it's kind of like my comm-band."

"Yes. Tap behind your ear to talk. Tap again to cut the transmission. Try it."

We test it out, and then I tell her, "I'll let you sit in on my conversation with Rich and Katherine through the disk. Likewise, you can use it either before or after to let me know if you have anything to add. One other thing. I doubt Campbell will show, since this is Saul's round of play. But it's not explicitly forbidden, as long as he doesn't interfere. So he might be in the audience. You said that gun of yours has a stun setting?"

She nods. "I don't know how effective it is. And for all I know, the CHRONOS field might block it, too, just like your watch gadget."

"Hopefully not. If you get a chance to disable either of them, especially before the concert, do it. Just be discreet. Then tap the eardisk and let me know what section of the building you're in."

"Should I pull their keys?" she asks with a slightly sick look.

"Not unless you have to. We need to get answers, and that's not going to happen if they literally vanish into thin air. Plus it could be hard to explain, if someone happens to be watching."

"What will you be doing? Just pretending to be security?"

"Not exactly. I'll be spending the afternoon with Billy Meeks and his racist friends who are plotting, at a minimum, to terrorize not just the band, but an entire auditorium full of fans. I have a security pass, so I told them my uncle has a friend who got me a temp job. I'll probably let them think I'm keeping the actual security at bay by being on lookout, but it's them I'll be watching. As long as they stick to the cherry bomb and other low-level harassment, I won't do anything. But if they're doing anything beyond that, the plan is to use the disruptor"—I tap my Timex—"to knock them out and disarm them. Then I'll get actual security people in there to deal with them. And hopefully blink out before they decide to start checking *my* credentials too closely."

"What a fun way to spend an afternoon," she says dryly. "But they should be fairly easy to outwit, right?"

"Maybe. Ignorance isn't stupidity, though. Yes, there are some Klan members who are dumb as the proverbial stump, but many of the ones I've met are far from stupid. That's especially true of the leaders of the movement—men like Robert Shelton, Bob Scoggin, Bob Jones—"

"That's a lot of Bobs," she says.

"No kidding. Every parent with Klan sympathies must have named a son after Robert E. Lee. Anyway, all three of them have been savvy enough to make a comfortable living from dues paid by local members, along with the occasional bit of extortion. It's not so much that they're stupid as it is that they're hampered by the ideological blinders they've been wearing their entire lives and a pervasive fear that their position at the top of the food chain might be slipping away. Billy Meeks didn't strike me as stupid, either. I didn't even get the sense that he was all that angry. But he's barely eighteen, and I haven't met his buddies yet. Peer pressure can be a powerful drug at that age."

∞

My cab arrives outside a dive called the Hubcap, about a half mile from the Coliseum, around two fifteen. Traffic has already begun to pick up around the Coliseum. A small cluster of fans was waiting outside for the afternoon show, which begins at four, when we drove past. The cabdriver said his wife and daughter are going. His daughter had asked for tickets for her birthday last month, although God help him if he could understand what she liked about that racket. But he guessed most parents felt that way.

Billy Meeks had referred to this place as a diner when his dad was within earshot, but it's clearly a bar. He waves me back to a booth in the rear, where he's seated with three other guys working on their second pitcher. Luckily for my still-lurking headache, it's early afternoon and no one seems interested in feeding coins into the jukebox.

Two of Billy's companions seem to be about his age, maybe even a little younger, which leads me to think this place doesn't bother with piddling things like ID, although the drinking age is eighteen in many states. The third guy seated with him is in his twenties, tall and beefy, with red hair and skin that would burn to a crisp after five minutes in the August sun. He looks vaguely familiar. I don't think he was at the meeting in Collierville, though.

It's clear that some sort of argument is going on. Billy doesn't pause for introductions, so I pull a chair over from a nearby table.

"I don't see what the issue is," the redheaded guy says. "You said last week the only thing stopping you was getting a weapon past security. I solved that problem. Now you're backing out. I took you at your word, on your oath."

"I never took no oath," Billy says.

The redheaded guy stares down into his beer for a moment and then says softly, "A Klansman's *word* is his oath. Our nighthawk went to a lot of trouble to get that weapon in place. He coulda been caught." When he finishes, he glances over at me for the first time, and his face finally clicks. His name is Corker, or something like that. He's a CHRONOS tech. *Not* a historian. I can't see his key, though, so he must have it inside a pouch or something.

If he recognizes my face, he doesn't let on. He just asks Billy if he's vouching for me.

"Yeah. He's from North Carolina. Uncle Lenny knows him."

"Your uncle's word any better than yours, or is your whole family a bunch of chickenshit liars? Maybe your whole damn klabern."

Billy clenches his fist. The kid next to him, who looks a bit like a French bulldog took human form, says, "Damn, Billy. You gonna let him talk about you like that?"

"Troy is cool," Billy says through gritted teeth. "He's the one I told you about who's working security today. Uncle Lenny says he worked with Dynamite Bob on that church thing a few years back."

That's such a massive overstatement of my fake credentials that I very nearly laugh. Even Glen didn't claim to have been in on the Sixteenth Street bombing. I think there's a good chance Billy is inflating my reputation on purpose, hoping the other guy will back down if he believes Billy has connections to the inner sanctum of United Klans. But it wouldn't be the first time that something has been blown way out of proportion by the time it made the rounds of the Klan grapevine, especially when you've always got people bragging about who they know and what they did.

So I don't correct the record. I just nod and extend a hand. "Troy Rayburn."

"Nelson Crocker," he says, pumping my hand once. "What you think about your little buddy here . . . goin' back on his word to take out that . . . Jesus hatin' faggot?"

"I wasn't here to witness what you said or what Billy said, so I don't actually have an opinion on the matter."

Bulldog chugs the last of his beer. "He said it."

The other kid says, "Shut up, Turley. Billy was drunk! You know it. So does Crocker. You want somebody holdin' you to account for every single stupid thing you say when you're drunk?"

"No exceptions in the Koran . . . about mouthin' off when you're drunk," Crocker says.

I'm beginning to think Crocker is drunk, himself. That's two words he's mispronounced—*klavern* and *Kloran*. And he keeps pausing in the middle of his sentences. They're not long pauses, but they give his speech a sort of singsong effect.

"Billy told me that if he had a way to get a rifle . . . into the Coliseum . . . he'd gladly shoot John Lennon. Said he'd never see the inside of a jail . . . because his daddy and his uncle have both got friends . . . in Memphis. When I told him I thought I could . . . manage the rifle, he said fine . . . 'You set it up, and I'll do it.' I think that is what they call a *verbatim* quote." Crocker ends with a slow, mean smile, tipping his mug toward Billy.

Billy's face turns so red that I have no doubt Crocker's telling the truth.

I shrug. "Even if he said it, he'd have to clear it with his klavern. And I can promise they're not gonna authorize anything like this right now. There's too much focus on Shelton and the others with this whole HUAC thing. It's fine to give the bastards a little scare, but there's no way they'd approve an assassination right now. No way."

There's an extralong pause, then Crocker says, "I don't give two shits about . . . HUAC or the UKA leadership . . . You think those old men are the future of this country?" His eyes narrow slightly each time he pauses, like he's listening for something. "They're makin' compromises while the government gives rights away . . . rights that white men like me have fought hard to protect . . . If Billy wants to back out, fine . . . but at least he can admit he's a fuckin' coward."

Someone is feeding this guy his lines. I have a strong urge to reach behind his ear and yank that disk. Or just yank his key. But maybe tipping my hand isn't the best idea. He doesn't seem to recognize me, so playing along to find the ventriloquist behind this dummy is probably a better idea.

"No need to be so hard on Billy," I tell Crocker. "He'd have been stupid to take on something like this on his own, but now he has backup. His buddy here"—I nod toward Bulldog—"seems eager, and I haven't had a bit of excitement in a while. You're right. The guy—hell, the whole band—needs to be taught a lesson. So if you've got a weapon stashed away *and* we can actually get to it *and* I think we stand a reasonable chance of getting out alive, we'll do it."

The look Billy gives me lands solidly between fear and gratitude. Bulldog, on the other hand, looks like he's about to crap his pants.

"That's a lot of conditions, but it's better than I was gettin' from Billy." Crocker smiles broadly and reaches into his jeans pocket. "Here's the map. It'll take you right to the gun. It's . . . near an exit with a clear shot at the stage."

He drops the folded paper and a five-dollar bill onto the table. "You boys have another round on me. Not too much, though. One of you needs to be able to shoot straight."

FROM *TEMPORAL DILEMMA USER'S GUIDE*, 2ND ED. (2293)

Team Play: Temporal Dilemma teams may be composed of up to eight players. The strongest and most successful teams are those that include players with a wide array of skills.

There are many strategies and techniques involved in creating a winning team, but the most important thing to remember is that the team cannot win without the leader. This is similar to the game of chess, where the king must be protected. It does not matter how many players remain in the game or how many points have been accrued. A team loses by default if the leader is no longer in the game at the final tally.

∞28∞

John Lennon has changed quite a bit in the last nine years. He's still rather gangly, but his hair is longer, and he's wearing tinted glasses. In Liverpool, he didn't wear glasses at all when he performed. Glasses weren't cool back then, I guess, but today, he's setting the fashion.

I'm having less luck in that regard. Women do wear jeans in the 1960s, although they were often called dungarees, for some reason. Jarvis pulled up dozens of pictures when I was researching. But I've yet to see a single jean-clad female. Only one of the girls seated in the rows of folding chairs is in pants. Most are wearing skirts or dresses, in brightly colored plaids or florals. I'm half wishing I'd done the same, because it is wicked hot, despite the air-conditioning.

The first press conference is strictly for teen journalists and fan-club presidents. Apparently, I look young enough to pass, or their security just doesn't give a damn, because I pushed through the door with the rest of the teens, a little over half of whom are female. There are a lot of photographers, including one wielding a contraption that must be a reel-to-reel movie camera. Even more of them have audio recording equipment, although I suspect they're going to have a hard time hearing the proceedings. The door is closed, but the music of the opening acts currently performing in the auditorium still makes it a little hard to follow some of what's being said.

The band sits at a long table covered with a white cloth. John Lennon is at one end, Paul McCartney at the other, with George Harrison and Ringo Starr in the middle. All four are dressed neatly in sports jackets. Paul and Ringo are both smoking, which I find a little amusing, since they're seated right in front of a massive wall-mounted fire extinguisher. Paul keeps idly running his thumb across the edge of a paperback in front of him. I don't know what the title is, but I get the sense he'd rather be reading.

All of the chairs are taken, so I join a small group pressed back against the beige tile walls. Most of the questions asked so far have been about their music or their upcoming album. The questioners have all been proper young professionals, for the most part, although you could tell that quite a few of them were nervous, and one poor girl froze for several seconds when the emcee pointed to her. One of the budding journalists has now ventured into dangerous territory, however, by asking about John's recent remarks on Christianity.

A chorus of boos fills the room.

"I don't *agree* with them!" the girl says, clearly hurt by their reaction. "I only want to know how it's affecting the tour."

Lennon waves for the others to settle down. "Cut the girl a bit of slack, okay? It's all been blown out of proportion, really. I didn't mean it as disrespectful, or anythin'. Jesus had some really good ideas. My point was that most people aren't listenin'. Otherwise we wouldn't have wars and those KKK people chanting out front. We've got our rights, you know."

I came in through a stable point, so I didn't actually see the cluster of protesters outside the building. Unless something has changed dramatically since Jarvis and I researched the event, there are a few people carrying signs—*Beatles Go Home, Memphis Does Not Welcome Communists,* and *God Forever, Beatles Never*. There's also a small cluster of robed KKK members, just as one of their leaders had sworn there would be in an interview with a TV reporter a few days before. It seems like a pretty pitiful showing for the *Ban the Beatles* movement.

Paul McCartney jumps in. "When you're a celebrity, they come at you with all these questions, and they want to know your opinion—on war, and religion, and things like segregation. Then they get angry when you tell them what you think. We're entitled to have views on these things. It's not really fair to expect us to lie."

Just beyond McCartney, I catch a brief flash of orange light. A boy of maybe twelve, with dark hair and eyes, is standing off to the singer's left, just behind a uniformed police officer. His key is tucked inside his shirt, but otherwise, no attempt is made to shield the light. He's focusing mostly on Lennon and the other members of the band, but he occasionally turns to glance at the others inside the room.

The boy is the first traveler that I've spotted so far, but I know from listening in on Tyson's meeting with Katherine and Rich that they've seen three others. One of them is the woman who's with Saul, because Katherine said the girl she saw "looked a bit like a younger, red-haired Alisa." The faint sniff she added after the woman's name makes me think Saul and Alisa have been companions in this time-line, too. Tyson tells them about someone he saw at the bar, someone they know who shouldn't be able to use the key.

"Okay, we've got time for just one more question," the emcee says. This is met by a disappointed sigh, and then he points to a girl near the back who begins to ask the group about plans for their next album.

The dark-haired boy, who has moved back a few steps, taps his ear and then turns his head to look directly at me. I hear a ping and then his voice in my ear.

"You interfered in Montgomery," he says. "That's against the rules."

"Our timeline is not your playground," I reply, keeping my voice as low as possible. "We play by our own rules."

The boy's mouth tightens in a disappointed frown, and he taps his earpiece again. Guess our conversation is over.

I'm tempted to contact Tyson to ask what he wants me to do about the kid. But I can't think of any other option aside from following him. The room is too crowded to confront him here, and, truthfully, I feel a bit odd even following a child, so I hope he leads me to his parents. But when the press conference ends, the kid simply takes out his key and vanishes.

And I'm not the only one who sees it happen. One girl in the front row near McCartney rubs her eyes and blinks a couple of times, looking baffled. The police officer, who would have had the boy in his peripheral vision, seems a little confused as well, but he shakes it off.

We're asked to clear the room so the next group can enter. As soon as the door opens, the sound blast gets louder, including what sounds like thunder. Then the girl group on the ticket, the Ronettes, begin singing "Walking in the Rain." Katherine and Rich are in the line waiting to get in. He has a large camera around his neck, and she's wearing a spiffy little suit, complete with a hat. Katherine's back is to me, but Richard is looking right at me, and I'm now certain that he saw my CHRONOS key in the hotel this morning. For a moment, I think he's going to come after me, but when I glance back, he and Katherine are heading inside.

I try paging Tyson, not really caring if anyone thinks I'm crazy for talking to myself. He doesn't respond immediately, which isn't surprising, given that he's undercover.

What I really want is to find a secluded spot so that I can scan that location in the balcony and see if anything has changed with Saul and his companion. If Nora's point about butterfly wings has even the slightest bit of truth to it, there are several people in this building, including myself, who really aren't supposed to be here. We're a lot bigger than butterflies, so I'm expecting at least a few changes.

I *could* blink home to do this. That's really, really tempting on several levels. But the place is beginning to fill up, and I'm worried about finding a good time to jump back in. The ladies' room is up ahead, and—potential privacy issues aside—a bathroom stall would be a perfect location for a stable point. Close the door, blink out. You'd have at least a few minutes before anyone would think to peek under the door to see if it's occupied. But the line stretches halfway back to the press-conference room.

Anyway, Jack is already on edge. He doesn't need me bouncing to and fro. Assuming we can wrap this up fairly quickly, I'd love to be able to just go home and stay home.

It occurs to me that another option would be to stay *here* but leave *now*. Finally, I spot a block of vending booths hawking shirts, posters, and albums. I step behind one of them, glance around to be sure that no one is watching me, set a return point, and then roll the time back to early this morning. A cluster of girls hurries past, probably on their way to the bathroom, and then I jump into the empty balcony where Saul, Alisa, and about fifty Beatles fans will be later tonight.

The silence is heavenly. Even the darkness is nice, after the intense glow of the fluorescent lights and the incessant pop of flashbulbs. I sink down into one of the seats and begin scanning the stable point. For the most part, everything is the same. The only difference is that the girl that Other-Saul bumped into is standing slightly to the right this time. She still looks annoyed that the two of them are blocking her view, but she doesn't get a chance to smack him, and Alisa doesn't snarl at her. I have no clue what caused that to change, but here in the dead silence of the Mid-South Coliseum at a little before seven in the morning, I can almost hear the sound of butterfly wings.

I'm about to blink back to this evening, thoroughly dreading the noise and lights, when a movement across the auditorium catches my attention. It's a door opening in the blue section of the balcony almost directly below the press box, three columns over. I tuck my key into its pouch, slide down behind the row of seats in front of me, and peer through the gap between the chairs. Two people, one CHRONOS key. Both are men, and neither of them looks like Saul. The one without a key is too short, and the other is way too beefy. Could be Campbell, but Tyson said he's not supposed to interact with anyone. The man without the key—or at least, without a key out in the open—is holding a large flashlight, and his face is the only one that I can see right now. He looks bored and sleepy. I can't see much of what he's wearing, but it looks like a uniform.

The one with the CHRONOS key bends down to stash something under the seat. Then he follows the guy with the flashlight back through the entranceway. I wait until their footsteps disappear and then begin creeping slowly, crouched down, toward the first row of blue chairs.

When I finally reach the end of that section, I reach down and find a rifle wedged beneath the seats. No need to think twice on this one. The man was clearly leaving this here for someone, and even if he hadn't been wearing a key and I didn't know what's going down tonight, there's no scenario I can imagine where there's a noble purpose for hiding a gun here.

Since I really don't want to stress Jack or myself out with another goodbye, I jump to the attic stable point in Montgomery, where the rifle Campbell's team intended to use is still on the plywood floor, now covered with a thin coat of dust. I put this one down next to it. At some point, when the owner of this place decides to clean out her attic, she's going to have a rather interesting mystery to solve.

I really didn't think through the creepiness of being in the dark attic where I recently killed a man and disposed of his body, however.

My feet are almost exactly in the spot where he fell when I shot him, and I take a reflexive step backward. But if there are any ghosts here, they don't seem to be restless. The only things stirring are the dust motes dancing in the amber light of the medallion. And since I have no clue whether the house is currently occupied, I need to get out of here before I sneeze.

When I arrive back at the vendors' booths in the Coliseum, I hear Tyson's ping over the noise of the music. The bathroom line is still massive, but there's a bank of phone booths up ahead. I step into one and lift the receiver, then tap the eardisk. When Tyson answers, I report on the past half hour.

"The thing with the kid is weird," he says. "But yeah, sounds like the same boy I saw at Antioch. As for the gun, that explains a lot. Crocker gave me a map. I've been looking all over for the damn thing, trying to figure out what purpose Crocker could have had for lying about it."

"Should I go back and stun him? It's just one guy with a key and a guard. I think he was building security."

"It's probably the same guard Katherine and Rich bribed to get into the building last night. He's making a bloody killing off this. But no. If we intercept them, I'll have double memories from when I met Crocker at the bar. Plus, it might alert Saul to the fact that we've removed the gun."

"Here's what I don't get. Why convince the guard to let you stash a *gun*? Why not do what Katherine and Rich did, since they have CHRONOS keys, and just get him to let them set a stable point so they could return later? Seems like they were opening themselves up to a lot more potential trouble."

"Yeah . . . but also, more potential points. The guard would count as a historical accomplice, just like Billy Meeks or anyone else would if they agreed to shoot Lennon. Not as big as swaying a *major* historical figure, but the points add up. That's why Campbell pulled in

Shelton and the other Klan members in Montgomery, although he left a lot of points on the table when he decided to have one of his own team do the actual shooting. Guess he decided having control was better, so that he wouldn't be docked for unintentional consequences. Those can wreck you."

"I need a rule book for this goddamn game."

He snorts. "You'll need several to fully understand it. Anyway, you removing the gun is good. This way, we know Saul will have to take the shot on his own, even if it costs him the style points. And we know where he's going to be. Now all we have to do is stop him."

∞

Neither the matinee nor the evening performance was sold out, thanks in part to the negative publicity from the Klan and other activists. The evening show did still manage to set an attendance record for the Coliseum, though. Most sections of the auditorium are full, with the exception of the tier behind the stage, which is fairly empty, and four sections—two on the left, two on the right—where you only have a side view of the performance. After I ended my call with Tyson, I jumped forward to just before they let the audience in for the second show and claimed a seat close to where Saul and Alisa will enter. I scanned through a couple of times, and at least for now, nothing has changed aside from the mini confrontation with the girl in the third row. And I have a lot less sympathy for her now than I did watching through the key. She's bumped into the people seated in front of her on several occasions, and while she's jumping around like water on a hot skillet, she gets mad anytime someone blocks her view in the slightest. Maybe she deserves a little scare.

Thanks to a tip from Tyson on reducing background noise, sitting through the opening bands has been much easier. The music comes through clearly, and the roar of the audience is reduced to a mellow buzz. If I could close my eyes and block the flashing lights from the cameras, it would be almost pleasant.

But that's not an option. I'm scanning for amber light. More specifically, I'm scanning for five amber lights together. I want to know what those people are doing here. As it stands, this will be two on two, with Rich nearby for backup. I have no clue where Katherine will be, although I got the sense they're tasking her with some distraction until we have Saul subdued, at which point they'll page her to join us. And at which point I'll be making myself scarce.

The plan is fairly simple. Tyson will join me here around 10:20. Rich will be one aisle over. When Saul and Alisa arrive, I'll wait until they pass my seat, follow them to the end of the aisle, and stun them. Rich and Tyson will drag them into the entranceway. It *may* not attract much attention. True, I haven't seen a man faint yet, but several young women have been carried off to first aid stations. If there's too much focus on the incident, however, Richard will use the neural-disruptor thing to knock out witnesses. I don't really like that part. There are a bunch of kids here, and it would be all too easy for one of them to get hurt. But we may not have an alternative.

A little after 10:15, the Cyrkle finishes the last chords of "Red Rubber Ball." The band is apparently a pretty big deal right now, because they get more screams and squeals than the other opening acts from the girls in this section. When the applause ends, the lights go down and the audience goes wild with anticipation as the crew begins moving things about. One of the crew bumps the cymbal as they're setting up Ringo's drums, sparking another frenzy. The Beatles finally take the stage for the opening song, "Rock and Roll Music," at 10:24. By that time, the roar is so loud that it's almost impossible to make out the song.

The second song, "She's a Woman," is a little more low key, but I'm beginning to get worried about Tyson. At 10:27, I check the key one more time, shielding it below one of the programs scattered about on the floor. I skip forward in ten-second increments, just like I did before, but now when I get to the part where Tyson and Richard are supposed to grab the bodies, they're nowhere to be seen.

Tyson should be here by now. He's supposed to take up position on the other side of the aisle across from me. I wait another minute and tap the eardisk.

It pings, but all I can hear is a roar. I sit up in my seat to see if maybe he's just in the wrong spot, but I don't see him. I don't see Rich, either.

But I *do* see Katherine. She's alone, standing at the entrance tunnel two sections over, watching the back wall where Saul and Alisa will soon appear. Someone spilled the beans, or she's been watching this stable point, too.

Katherine tucks her key inside her blouse and begins making her way over, looking carefully up each row as she walks. I slump down in my seat. This is bad. If she's been watching the stable point, and I have to assume she has, she's seen me approach Saul. She's seen him go down. Hell, she may even have seen the device in my hand.

She'd also have seen the gun he pulls, and it wouldn't take a rocket scientist to figure out that he's part of this. But I have no idea how she'll react. Is she going to help me stop *him* or try to stop *me*?

A flash of orange light reflects in the cement floor. I force myself not to turn around, not to look back at them, and keep my eyes pinned on Katherine. She's not trying to get out of sight, but rather just standing against the railing in front of the balcony. Several people shout for her to get out of the way.

Alisa and Saul pass me. Both of them can see Katherine, but neither of them pays her the slightest heed. They simply look straight past her. And now they're almost to the end of the balcony, so I have to make my move. I push my way through, bumping into the girl in the third row. Her rolled-up magazine whacks *my* shoulder this time, and I really want to turn and snarl at her exactly as Alisa did.

On the other side of the auditorium, in the section directly across from this one, five orange lights blink into view.

Saul turns toward Alisa and whispers something, and she laughs.

But he doesn't reach into his coat. He doesn't pull out the pistol. Instead, he snakes an arm around her waist, and they move toward the tunnel.

I glance over my shoulder at Katherine, and she looks as baffled as I am. So yeah. She's definitely here because she watched the stable point and saw him pull the gun.

Is it still inside his jacket? I don't know. Truthfully, I don't care at this point. He's part of this and we have to stop him.

I aim the device at Saul's back and press the button. The popping noise isn't even audible over the cacophony in the auditorium, and the bright light is simply another flashbulb. He jerks once, grabs at the railing, then begins to sink to the concrete floor. Alisa's mouth flies open, but before she can scream, I aim at her and fire again.

When I turn toward Katherine, she's yelling something at me. Pointing.

And then there's a noise that *does* cut through the music, but only just barely.

A single gunshot. And now I'm the one falling to the floor.

FROM THE *NEW YORK DAILY INTREPID* (JUNE 26, 1995)

An Explanation for Mass Fainting?

When Frank Sinatra performed at the Paramount Theater in the 1940s, dozens of girls swooned. A generation later, it was Elvis. Then came the Beatles, where first aid workers were bombarded with fainting fans at nearly every performance.

The latest issue of the *New England Journal of Medicine* may provide some answers as to why. The researchers examined forty girls, between the ages of eleven and seventeen, who attended a New Kids on the Block show. While many have chalked this up to mass hysteria, the researchers noted a variety of physiological symptoms, including low blood sugar, exhaustion, and hyperventilation, which is often brought on by screaming. The brain doesn't receive enough oxygen, which can reduce carbon-dioxide levels and induce fainting.

Researchers acknowledge that more study is needed, since this does not explain all cases of mass fainting. The most notable instance was a Beatles concert in 1966, where approximately 10 percent of those in attendance briefly lost consciousness in the middle of the show. Most were young women, but numerous adults, including some security personnel, were also affected.

∞29∞

I stand at the edge of the balcony behind the stage, scanning the masses pouring in through the doors at the front of the auditorium. Looking for a girl in a bright-orange dress, with an even brighter smile, coming in with her sister and her friends. I need that one last bit of confirmation to put a stake through the heart of the other memory, where it seemed like she was dead inside and only going through the motions.

What I see instead is Billy Meeks and his two friends at one of the front entrances. Bulldog—I know he has a name, but I can't remember it—has a bag flung over one shoulder. Even from this distance, it looks suspicious. But the security guards at the door either aren't expected to scan the bags as people come in or else aren't taking their jobs very seriously. Billy shows one of them his ticket, and the guard motions toward the section of balcony one over from where I'm standing. Then he points them back into the corridor, where there's a flight of stairs leading to the upper concourse.

I take one last look at the entrance. I already know Toni is okay. One of my dueling memories says I saw her barely an hour ago—at least from her perspective—standing outside the drugstore. There's really nothing I need to confirm. Might as well quit lying to myself and just admit that I want to see her again, and this may well be my last chance.

But I need to *focus*.

Meeks and his buddies come up through the entrance tunnel a couple of minutes later. He spots me and I head over to break the news. I'm not entirely sure whether they'll view it as good news or bad. Probably a mixed bag.

"Nice hat," Billy says, nodding toward the policeman's cap that all of the temporary security guards were given at our briefing earlier to make sure we could be spotted easily in the crowd.

"Thanks. Crocker's a liar. I followed his map, and when that turned out to be useless, I searched the whole damn balcony. There's nothing here."

"You're sure?" Billy asks.

"Yep. Feel free to poke around yourself if you want, but you might want to do it quickly. Seats are going to start filling up soon. There will even be people sitting in this section."

As I'm saying it, I remember that this is something I know only due to viewing the area through the stable points. But they don't have a clue. They probably think all eighty-plus people working security tonight were given detailed seating charts of every section of the Coliseum.

Billy sinks down into one of the chairs. "That settles it, then. If he didn't keep up his end of the bargain, then I can't be expected to keep up mine, now can I?"

I'm pretty sure his remarks are aimed more at his friends than at me, but I say, "I think he was pulling your leg. Just trying to see if he could get a rise out of you."

The thin kid says, "Something about him felt off to me anyway. I told Billy maybe he was a cop. One of those undercover guys with the FBI, trying to get more information for those HUAC hearings."

Bulldog snorts. "Crocker's not a cop. I've seen him at three rallies. Gimme the map. I'm gonna check it out myself. Come on, Jesse."

I hand him the map. Bulldog stares at the spot on the map oh-so-cleverly marked with an X, looks around to get his bearings, and then takes off. The thin kid looks like he'd really rather stay in his seat, but he follows. I get the sense he's been following orders for many years.

"I'd have done it," Billy says once they're gone. "I'd have kept my word."

"Not a big deal. Like I said before, United Klans isn't too crazy about people makin' a big stink right now, anyway. There are gonna be over twelve thousand people in here tonight. And I've had a chance to look the place over more carefully now. There are no exits from this level that don't go past at least a few guards."

"Why'd you tell Crocker we'd do it, then?"

"I didn't," I tell him, smiling grimly. "I said *if* he left the weapon, which I didn't really think he'd do. *If* we could find it, which I didn't, and your buddies won't, either. And finally, *if* I thought we'd have a decent chance of getting out alive, which I don't, now that I'm inside the place. The only thing I agreed to do was consider it. Anyway, you're heading off to college soon, right? You really want something like this on your record?"

He rolls his eyes. "Me going off to college is part of the reason I said I'd do it. I'm tired of catchin' shit from Turley and the others."

"You mean Bulldog over there?"

Billy smiles. "Yeah. You're not the first to call him that. Anyway, he's enlisting next month. Says he'd rather get it over with. Have some say in his assignment, you know? But he's sure he'll end up in 'Nam, and he never misses the chance to tell me it must be nice to have a coward deferment—his term. Uncle Lenny doesn't call it that, but he thinks the same thing. He fought in Korea and always says it teaches you more than college. Anyway, Turley said if he was goin' over there to defend the country, least I could do was defend it back home. And he's right. We got a war right here that's every bit as important."

I start to say something in character, but at this point, I'm ready to be done with all of them. The gun isn't here for them to use, and I'm better off combing the auditorium, looking for Saul and whoever else might be here, than babysitting a trio of delinquents. If it weren't for the fact that somebody needs to launch that cherry bomb at Lennon in order to keep the timeline on track, I'd be tempted to turn the whole lot of them in.

"Yeah, well, that's bullshit, Billy. Maybe the best way for you to defend the country is to become a doctor. A scientist who cures cancer. The guy who *teaches* the kid who cures cancer. No matter how much you disagree with the man, killing John Lennon isn't going to make you a hero or save the country from anything. Enlist if you want, but don't let some numb-nuts bully shame you into doing stupid things that could land your ass in jail."

Billy looks a little surprised, but his two friends are back, so he doesn't respond.

"It's not there," Bulldog says.

I raise my eyebrows sarcastically. "No shit. I've got places to be to keep my cover."

I tell them I'll check back later. But, to be honest, I don't think I will.

I spend the next two hours doing pretty much the same thing as the other guards. Walk around the auditorium. Hang out by the fence a bit. Go outside for a smoke break. Visually inspect rows of mostly kids who are more or less enthusiastically listening to the opening acts while they wait for the Beatles to play. The key difference is that the others are looking for pot or alcohol. I'm looking for purple rays of light.

The plan is for me to meet Madi at 10:20 in section N-North, which is where Saul and Alisa will blink in shortly thereafter. Richard will be joining me. We tried to think of some distraction for Katherine, but it turned out not to be necessary. She told Richard she was going over to sit with some of the other women journalists near the press box and scan from that direction for a bit.

What's bugging me, though, is the direction of the shot. It hasn't changed. Someone will shoot Lennon from this side—the south side—of the auditorium at 10:38. It's entirely possible that it's Crocker, or that Saul simply comes over to this section.

At 10:18, as I'm making my way over, I see Saul leaving the men's room in the lower concourse, heading toward the north side of the building. Rich is supposed to meet me at the midpoint in two minutes. I tap my earpiece and tell him I'm following Saul, but as I pass the men's room door, someone yanks me backward and inside. His elbow wraps around my neck, pinning my arm against his chest.

"What'd you do with my gun, asshole? That thing cost me nearly fifty bucks."

"Don't have it," I manage to squeak out. "It wasn't there."

I try to reach for my own gun, but Crocker squeezes tighter. He's got a good four inches on me, and maybe seventy pounds. Unfortunately, more of those pounds seem to be muscle than I would have expected from looking at him, and with him pulling up on my neck, the best I can do at this point is flail and hope I land a solid kick. I tuck my chin into his arm, trying to keep a little space open for air, and manage to do little more than knock the cap off my head. The noise from the auditorium increases by an order of magnitude as I struggle with him, and then I hear the opening bars of "Rock and Roll Music."

Is this really about the stupid gun, or has Crocker clued in to the fact that I'm CHRONOS?

The instant that thought enters my mind, I feel something sliding upward between Crocker's chest and my back. Crocker must feel it, too, because he freezes and then his head jerks backward. He loosens his grip on my neck, and I pull the gun as I slip to the floor.

Richard yanks again on the leather cord that holds his CHRONOS key, and Crocker drops to his knees. "Might want to get a chain for this thing," Rich says.

"Yeah." I swallow hard, rubbing my throat. "If someone yanked it really hard, you might pop out of sight, just like Bailey did."

There's a flash of recognition in the man's eyes. Surprise, too, so I guess his attack really *was* about a stupid gun that wouldn't even cost a dollar in our time if you adjusted for inflation.

I grab the police hat off the floor. "Yeah. You *know* who Bailey is, don't you?"

Rich twists the cord again, and the metal case surrounding his medallion presses into Crocker's neck.

Three boys come running into the restroom, laughing. The oldest is maybe sixteen. All three of them come to a skidding stop when they see the gun and my hat.

"He tried to sell me pot," Rich says, "so I called security. Go find another place to pee."

The kids back out of the doorway, eyes wide. I grin at Rich. "I think you're kind of getting into this."

"Maybe," Rich says. "What are we going to do with him?"

"Can't shoot him in cold blood. Anyway, I want him to take a message back. I know you're not worried about the stupid gun," I tell Crocker. "You're worried about losing the damn style points for your team. We're onto your asses. Tell Saul he's going to lose The Game this time. He's not quite the chess master he thinks he is. In fact, he and Campbell are *both* going to lose. This isn't your chessboard."

In the auditorium, the band moves on to the next song, "She's a Woman." I keep the gun pointed at Crocker as Rich loosens his hold on the cord and the key drops back down to Crocker's chest. As Rich backs toward the door, Crocker looks up and gives a mirthless laugh.

"If you think Saul is going to back off after he and Campbell have invested this much time, this much money, to breach that barrier—well, you don't know them, do you? Guns are *cheap*. Real easy to get inside, too, once you have a stable point set. And that kid is itching to prove himself."

I back out of the restroom, and Rich and I take off running to the south side, where Billy and his friends were sitting. As we head upstairs, I glance down at my watch. 10:26.

Tapping my eardisk, I call Madi. It makes a connection, but I can't hear her. So I leave a message. "Problem on this end. Be there as soon as I can." I have no clue whether she can hear me over the crowd noise.

This section isn't nearly as packed as the ground floor, but teenyboppers still clog the arteries at the front of the balcony, trying to get a closer look at their idols, even if it's only at their backs. The security briefing I attended today told the guards not to allow dancing, crowding into the aisles, or pressing up against the gates, and that they should arrest anyone breaking the rules, but I've only seen a couple of people dragged out. The main strategy I'm seeing with security personnel is sticking their fingers in their ears, because even though some have earplugs, the noise level is torture.

I shift course and begin running through one of the upper rows, trying to see over the heads of the crowd. Rich follows behind me. He says something that I can't make out and then points across the auditorium. I can't see Madi, but she's probably behind the kids who are standing up. I see Katherine, though, right near the entrance tunnel. I'm not sure whether this is good or bad, but I have to focus on the main objective. I just wish I knew whether that means finding Saul or finding Billy.

The song ends, and the band barely pauses for applause. There's little point, since it's nonstop screaming. George just steps to the microphone, and they begin "If I Needed Someone." That's the song that was playing when the cherry bomb was tossed onto the stage back in the other timeline. I want to check the key to see if it still shows Lennon being shot at 10:38, but I can't risk stopping.

When I turn back to see where Rich is, I spot them. Not Billy and his friends, but five purple lights, seated in the very back row.

Watching.

One of them seems to be watching *me*, but they don't move to intercept us. They just sit there.

Rich sees them, too. "Go!" he screams into my ear. "You're in uniform. Get Lennon offstage. I'll keep looking for the shooter. I can stun him, at least."

He doesn't have a clue what the Klan guys look like, aside from my mention of the one favoring a bulldog. But most of the audience is female, and they're hopefully the only ones he'll see carrying a gun. I mouth the words *good luck*, and he gives me a thumbs-up.

I glance at the two closest entrance tunnels. Getting to either of them will take too long. I go to the edge of the balcony and drop about two meters down to the mezzanine level, then work my way down to the main floor and begin pushing through the crowd, watching the balcony above me as I go. The purple lights remain exactly where they were. Rich continues squeezing through the rows of stadium chairs, moving toward the entrance tunnel that juts up into the balcony sections. One section over, the three young Klan members are now on the mezzanine level. Billy and Bulldog look like they're arguing.

A popping noise, audible over the roar, causes me to look over to the north side. I don't see Saul and Alisa, but Madi is standing on the aisle stairway. Crocker, who is directly behind her, dives forward, and they fall. And then, at almost the same instant, everyone in that section of the auditorium and half of the one next to it crumples to the ground.

I keep pushing forward, elbowing my way through a sea of screaming girls. The band starts the next song, "Day Tripper," which is also the standard CHRONOS nickname for people doing a one-day jump.

Glancing up, I see Bulldog snatch the gun from Billy and head to the railing, just as I reach the fence around the stage. I tell the guard at the end that I heard a gun go off, and that I think it was in N-North. And then I hop the fence and run to the stage.

I tackle Lennon, taking the mic down with us, just as two shots ring out in rapid succession. Turning my head, I see a body tumble from the mezzanine. Billy stands at the railing. The thin kid, whose name I never did catch, is next to him, so the body that fell must be Bulldog.

The next minute or so is a blur. I help Lennon up and he thanks me. I'm not sure how the band continues after that, but after saying a few words to the audience, they do. They launch into "I Feel Fine," and you can actually hear the music now. The gunfire seems to have doused the frantic shrieking like a spray of cold water. There are still a few screams, and quite a few of the attendees are in tears, but the noise level is down by almost half.

First aid workers rush down the aisle toward the kid sprawled on the floor, who is, unbelievably, trying to sit up. His shoulder is bleeding, so I think he took at least one bullet. A gun that looks exactly like the one we saw Saul with is in his hand.

I'm on the steps when the time shift hits, and I barely make it to the bottom before collapsing. Several of the other guards look around nervously, probably thinking I've been shot, too, and wondering why they didn't hear it. I tell one of them it's just a panic attack, before realizing that's not really a thing people say in 1966.

And despite the nausea that grips me, it's not panic I'm feeling. It's relief.

The five purple lights in the balcony are now gone.

Two guards, one about my age and the other one in his forties, help me up. I'm pretty sure they're taking me to the first aid station, and I'm completely sure that I'm going to have a hard time answering any questions they have. Girls reach out toward me, and there's a chorus of thank-yous as we pass by. Just as we reach the exit into the lower concourse, though, I hear a familiar voice call my name.

I turn to see Antoinette Robinson behind me, looking perfectly lovely in her bright-orange dress. Her smile is a bit perplexed, though. "I thought you were going to the thing at Ellis Auditorium."

"No. I got called into work." Which is a truly stupid answer in an era without mobile phones. Or for someone supposedly passing through on his way back to college.

One of the two guards tugs at my arm, but I shake him off. "I'll meet you at first aid." They both back off, but the older one's lip curls into a sneer as he stares at Toni.

She isn't paying him any attention. Her smile widens. "Good thing they called you, I guess! That was . . . incredibly brave."

Then she stares at my eyes, and her jaw drops. She looks over at the two guards who are standing in the concourse. And then back at my eyes, as realization dawns.

"Oh God, I'm sorry. I didn't mean to get you in trouble."

"No, no. Don't be sorry. It's just . . . they're not hiring black cops for this, and I needed the cash for school."

Toni nods. "I understand. That's why I can't start at Antioch until next year. Listen, I've got to get back to Jo, but . . . look me up next fall. Or next time you're in town. We're in the book under Lowell Robinson."

I nod. "Sure thing."

She leans in and tiptoes up so that her breath tickles my ear. "But lose the contacts. I like your eyes just the way they are."

∞30∞

I hit the concrete steps hard, with most of my weight landing on my left hip and shoulder. For a brief second, I lie there, stunned. There was a noise. A gunshot, I think, although I suppose it could have been the cherry bomb that was reported in the newspaper. But I can't move. It's like a massive weight is holding me down, pressing me into the sharp edges of the steps.

Was I shot?

I open my eyes and see that I'm not the only one on the floor. The girl in the third row is draped over the chair in front of her, with her head in the lap of the occupant, also unconscious, whose arm hangs out into the aisle. Her hand, which hovers just inches from my face, has a heart drawn on the back, with the name *Paul* in the center.

But it's George singing lead right now, on "If I Needed Someone." That's the last song of the set in this timeline. The last song the band will ever play together. The last song Lennon will ever sing.

Shiny white shoes click up the steps, pausing near me for a second, and then continuing upward. I try to turn my head to see where the shoes are going—Katherine's shoes, I think—but my view is blocked by a large arm, covered with reddish-gold hair and tiny crimson specks. It takes a major effort, but I manage to shake the arm loose enough that I can wriggle the top half of my body free.

My jeans are drenched in blood. I'm fairly certain it's not mine. The man lying facedown on the bottom half of me has a small hole in the back of his head. Judging from the sheer quantity of blood I'm wearing, I'd guess that the exit wound is much larger.

All around me, people are slumped onto the floor or in their seats, with their heads lolling in all directions. The music plays on, as if nothing has happened. In fact, the security forces seem to be running to the *other* side of the auditorium.

I pull my legs out from under the man, and nearly tumble down the last two steps when I break free. When I look up, I'm face-to-face with Katherine.

"Which cohort are you?" she yells into my ear.

I search my brain, trying to remember what Tyson said about cohorts. Every two years, I think. It takes a moment, but I stammer out an even number, hoping I've guessed right. "2318. Where's Tyson?"

She frowns, although I'm not sure whether it's because she doubts I'm from a future cohort or because I know his name. "He and Richard must still be trying to save Lennon. I don't know how long we have. I can handle Alisa, but I'm going to need help with that . . . *man*." She glares down at Other-Saul.

"What are you going to do with them?"

"Drag them into the tunnel for now. But go check on your guardian angel up there first. I think he's in shock. And hurry!"

I have no idea what she means, but I scramble up the stairs to the back row. When I look to the left, I find Jack on the floor, wedged between the seats, staring down at the CHRONOS key in his hand. A white leather purse, which I'm pretty sure is Katherine's, is next to him.

"Jack? How—"

There's a sharp intake of breath when he hears my voice, and then he reaches out with both hands and pulls me toward him. "You didn't come back. I waited and then I started checking the key, because you were late. He killed you, Madi, he fucking *killed* you. I got the gun out of the desk, and then I watched again, and . . . you were just lying there, and I don't know how I did it, but—"

"Where's the gun?"

He points to the purse. "The other woman . . . Katherine?"

I nod. "Listen to me, you need to go back, okay? Take the gun and go. I'm not sure how long we can hold off security."

"That's what she said, too, but, Madi, I can't even pull up the interface now. I can still see the light, but I'm getting *nothing*."

I glance over to see Katherine dragging Alisa down the short flight of stairs to the tunnel. She's not being very gentle, although that could be due in part to the fact that Alisa is a good deal bigger than Katherine. Beyond that, on the main floor of the auditorium, I see an armed guard near the stage, pointing up at this section of seats, which is totally still. The same is true for most of the section to the right, and the others seated there are noticeably subdued, with several of them now ignoring the concert and trying to wake up the people around them. A couple of them appear to be screaming, but then a good third of the audience is screaming.

The band plays on. "Day Tripper." Which means something has changed. Something, but apparently not enough to budge the timeline.

I turn to Jack. "Give me the gun. I'll jump back and dispose of it. If they find you here with it and the body . . ." I stop, very tempted to smack my head. "Never mind. Stay here."

"No," he says. "I'm fine. Go help Katherine. I'll get rid of it."

Hurrying down the steps, I dodge two girls who are lying halfway in the aisle. One of them stirs slightly as I pass. The guard who was pointing at this section a moment ago is no longer in sight. It looks like he may have convinced a few others to peel off from protecting the stage, as well, because this side is looking a little bare.

As I run past the dead man, I remember that I'm covered in his blood. I start to tell Jack we need to change assignments. He's wearing fabrics that won't be invented for another century, but that will raise fewer eyebrows than my blood-drenched jeans. But when I look back, I see Jack just behind me. His hand is wrapped around the thick black cord holding the man's key. He yanks once and blood sprays onto the row of seats behind him. A second yank and the body is gone. The blood is gone. Even the blood on my jeans is simply *gone*, as though it never existed.

He shoves the key into his pocket, hurries down to the bottom of the stairs, and hooks his hands under Saul's armpits. As we round the corner, three security guards are heading toward us from the other end of the short tunnel.

"I think there's a . . . some sort of chemical . . . gas leak?" I say. "Dozens of people are passed out. We're trying to get them clear."

Katherine gives me an incredulous look and then does something with her watch. All three security guards stop and then fall to the tunnel floor.

"Why did you do that?" I scream.

"Because there's a body in the aisle, in case you didn't notice!"

Jack holds up the man's CHRONOS key. Or, I guess in this case, CHRO-NOS key. "We need to get out of here. I doubt those are the only security guards who—"

Two shots ring out, one after the other, and the music tapers off to a discordant squeal. I push past Jack, rushing to the balcony wall. John Lennon is flat on his back. A security guard is on top of him, with the neck of Lennon's guitar sticking out between them. Maybe ten meters away, a third man is sprawled on the ground, faceup. Ringo is crouched behind his drums, while Paul and George stare, openmouthed.

For a moment, there's an odd hush, and then someone screams. Others join in, and a wailing chorus rises up from the auditorium. Some of the audience members look like they're trying to get to the exits, but others are pressing toward the stage.

The guard on top of Lennon moves aside. It's Tyson. He glances back at the body on the floor, then gets to his feet and offers Lennon a hand up.

McCartney walks across the stage and says something to Lennon, who nods. Ringo gets back onto the drum stool, and then McCartney yells into the mic. "Just a scare, people. Give us a sec and we'll finish the show."

The pronouncement is met with applause and cheers.

John Lennon steps up to the microphone and says, "The next song is 'I Feel Fine,' which I'm dedicating to this man and the other security officers who took action just now. Because I don't think I'd be feelin' fine at all if they hadn't acted so quickly." There's more applause, and Tyson nods to the audience. Lennon says something else to him off-mike, and then Tyson moves off the stage.

He takes the last step at a stumble, the time shift hitting him at the same instant the three of us at the edge of the tunnel feel it. I sink down against the rounded wall, holding my stomach. Head between knees. Deep breaths.

I've never been happier to feel so absolutely miserable.

"What's going on?" a voice yells from the end of the tunnel.

Jack is the only one able to muster a response. "Gas leak, maybe?" He nods to the two guards. "Almost everyone in our section fainted. We were trying to evacuate them."

The police officer unclips a massive communicator from the side of his belt and starts yelling into it. "Get these people out of here," he says to two men who join him a moment later. "Take the unconscious ones first."

My reaction to the time shift is starting to fade. Jack is already standing. He helps me up and then Katherine, as the two guards begin dragging Saul and Alisa up the tunnel and into the corridor.

"What are we going to do with them?" Katherine asks. "I don't know if that's Alisa Campbell or not, but I can promise you whoever that is, it's *not* Saul."

The two guards come running back toward us. "Ladies, I need you to clear out if you can. You, too," he says to Jack, "although, if you're feeling okay, we could use some help."

"Grab the purse," I tell him.

He nods, and heads back into the auditorium.

As we head toward the concourse, Katherine gives me a tiny smile. "I'm Katherine Shaw, by the way. 2300."

Telling her my real name would raise all sorts of questions, so I opt for a pseudonym. "Max Coleman. 2318."

When we reach the concourse, a boy and girl of maybe fourteen are staring at an empty spot on the floor. The girl clutches his arm as he points a shaky finger. "There were two people, lying right there. They just vanished."

Katherine sighs and reaches toward her watch. I slap her hand away.

"*Stop that!*" I hiss, then step toward the couple. "First aid has received reports of people hallucinating. They think there may be a chemical in the water supply . . ."

"Oh, wow!" the girl says, as a grin spreads across her face. "Like LSD? That's *so* cool."

The boy gives his companion an odd look, and then they head off in the other direction.

"Do you really think that story was an improvement?" Katherine asks. "This is how urban legends get started."

"We can't zap everyone in the building. That's just kicking the can down the road."

She huffs, then glances at the blank spot where Saul and Alisa were. "That *wasn't* Saul. He doesn't even like Alisa."

The first guard who went in comes back, talking into his radio. "No, sir. Not at all. I don't smell a thing. Most of 'em are back on their feet shrieking again. Maybe it's just that Beatlemania crap, bunch of them copycattin' each other. If the girl next to you faints and you don't, guess she must love them Beatles even more than you do, know what I mean? Although we got three guards apparently hit with the same thing, so I don't know. Your call."

Jack emerges, carrying a little girl, whose mother follows behind, still looking a bit dazed. Katherine's white purse hangs from Jack's arm. One of the security guards sits a girl down against the wall. She's conscious, but her nose is bleeding, so she has her head tipped back, trying to stanch the flow with a handkerchief.

"Where'd the other two go?" the guard asks, staring at the spot where he and his buddy just deposited Saul and Alisa.

I shrug. "They left."

And I'm not the least bit unhappy about that, to be honest.

I hope they *stay* gone.

But I really don't think they will.

∞

MADI
MEMPHIS, TENNESSEE
AUGUST 20, 1966

I drop the suitcase onto the bed. Like Jack's clothes, it's probably made of materials that won't be invented for another century, but with any luck, he won't be staying in 1966 for very long.

"You're going to need to keep this thing locked if you step outside the room for food," I tell him. "Your toothbrush and reader would definitely raise some eyebrows with the cleaning staff. There's a portable charging unit in there, too."

"What about *your* toothbrush?" he asks. "Are we going to share?"

I give him a pained look. "Lorena says I can't stay. She says if you're too comfortable, too happy here, you'll never manage to jump back."

"Oh, really?" Jack frowns, sinking down onto the bed. "And she knows this how?"

"It's more of a . . . theory, I think, but it's really all we have to go on. She believes your system was flooded with a cocktail of fear chemicals—cortisol, adrenaline, glucose. Neurotransmitters. Maybe some anger chemicals, too. Testosterone, catechol-something. I need to record what she says next time."

"Well, she's right on the fear part. I freaked the hell out. I'm holding the key, watching the stable point, and he just kills you. He bashes your head on the steps while I'm watching. I rolled it back and was almost to the point of shooting the interface when I blinked, and there I was, in the auditorium. I just pulled the trigger."

There are tears in Jack's eyes. If he thought I was dead, it occurs to me that Lorena might need to test whatever chemicals are released by grief, as well.

We rode back to the Peabody Hotel in the rental car with Katherine and Rich last night. Tyson was waiting when we arrived at the hotel. He'd been forced to take an emergency exit back to CHRONOS in order to avoid a confrontation and, most likely, some pesky questions about why the head of security had no record of him ever being hired.

There were no other rooms available, probably due to a certain concert at Mid-South Coliseum. It didn't matter, though. Richard had this room rented for the night, and they weren't staying. Katherine still thinks I'm from a future cohort, but Tyson seems to have told Rich some version of the truth. He extended the room rental for a week, saying he could expense it and it was the least CHRONOS could do under the circumstances.

I'm really hoping we won't need the room for that long, but it's not looking good.

Jack spent a few hours trying the key last night, but we were both exhausted and he gave up around two in the morning. When we woke up, we ordered room service, praying that the fact that Jack hadn't eaten for the better part of the day was the problem. Then he tried again.

And again.

After dinner, I went back home to pack him a bag. When I first pulled up the stable point, I saw Jack in the chair behind Grandpa James's desk, holding the gun. He looked so anguished that I wanted to jump back to that second and tell him I was fine. But I knew I couldn't.

Jack had told me that Lorena, Alex, and RJ were in the library, watching as he tried to use the key. But when I pulled up the stable point and jumped back in, they were all across the room, staring at the computer. The Anomalies Machine, now anomaly-free. And Yun Hee was in the side carrier, sleeping with her head against her daddy's sweater. Those two sights told me almost everything I needed to know.

Even though I was fairly certain of the answer, I asked Jarvis for information on Liza Forson. She's alive and well again, probably cooking up bioweapons to start a world war. Which means we have some big decisions to make about how we handle this technology.

Before I came back here, to Jack in 1966, I called Nora. She's at the cottage in Bray, and after a few questions that she may have found a bit odd, I was able to deduce that she has no memory of my visit last week. My mother didn't answer, but her virtual assistant took the call at her London flat. If Nora doesn't remember, I'm sure Mom won't, either. I'll need to get up with her soon, though. I've got a lot of questions about her mother and the Cyrists.

I snuggle up next to Jack on the hotel bed, and he says, "So Lorena thinks I'm stuck here until I get angry or scared enough to blink back? Like that Hulk guy in the old comics?"

"Something like that. She's going to try to make something to help you. I need to take back a blood sample so that she has a base to start from. But she says we need to be careful. Too big of a dose of adrenaline can kill you. Some of the others are dangerous, too."

"Great," he says. "I'm going to be Lorena's lab rat."

I shrug and give him a smile. "We could try her other suggestion."

"Why do I get the feeling I'm not going to like this?"

"Oh, I think you'd like it if it worked. She said I just need to get you really worked up here, and then jump back to my room at home. And . . . um . . . wait for you to join me."

"I like the first part," he said. "But I don't think it will work. I remember how I felt just before I managed to make the trip. It had nothing to do with sex."

"Still," I say, "it might be fun to try."

"And what happens if I can't join you?"

"Then I guess I'll be spending a lot of time in 1966."

∞Epilogue∞

TYSON
CHRONOS HQ
WASHINGTON, EC
NOVEMBER 9, 2304

At eleven a.m., twelve CHRONOS agents return from the field.

If the others notice that I seem a bit worse for wear, they don't mention it. Most are too busy bombarding Angelo with questions. They tell him they felt something odd, which hit them in two waves. Delia Morrell says it was like when you cross your own path, only more intense. Angelo apologizes, blaming the issue on a minor equipment malfunction. He's a pretty smooth liar, as it turns out, which makes me wonder how often he's practiced that particular talent.

Everything is fixed now, he tells them. Which is true, up to a point.

The only two who aren't asking questions are Saul and Grant. They look at least as ragged as I feel, especially Grant, who is led off to the med unit ahead of us. Saul says Grant got a case of food poisoning in Atlanta. Messed up both of their research agendas. And after making that pronouncement, Saul storms out, not even waiting for the Temporal Monitoring Unit check, which is mandatory. I fall into line with the others, going through the med pod and then waiting for clearance from Timeline Consistency.

There's a slight difference today, but I don't think anyone else notices. Usually when Marcy calls our names and says, "You're free to go," she takes us in alphabetical order. With the name Reyes, I'm always near the end. But today, she clears me first.

When I step outside the TMU, Angelo is waiting. The side door opens and one of the techs steps aside to let Rich and Katherine, who weren't on the jump schedule and therefore had to return to the isolation tank stable point, into the room.

Before I lose my nerve, I hold out the contacts that I stashed in my pocket. "I just wanted to let you know that I'm not using these anymore."

"Why? Are they bothering your eyes? I can get—"

"No." I glance over at Rich for moral support. "I mean that I'm not going to be part of this social experiment anymore. I've spent the better part of the past two years embedded with groups who think I'm a lesser human being. Any interest I had in learning more about what makes those people tick is long gone. I *know* what makes them tick. It's not a complex mix—mostly intolerance, anger, and a hefty dose of ignorance. So, I'm not doing it anymore. If that means the board decides to sit me out, stick me in some place like the archives, then . . . so be it."

Angelo sighs. "I don't think it's going to be a problem, Tyson. At least not in the short run." He ushers us into a side room with two desks. The SimMaster 8560 is in the middle of one of them, and the display is active. A globe circles in the background, with the Temporal Dilemma logo at the top.

Superimposed over the globe is a message in big block letters:

SINCE YOU SEEM TO WANT TO PLAY . . .

**OUR OBJECTIVE: PREVENT THE US FROM
ENTERING WWII**

LENGTH: THREE ROUNDS

RESTRICTIONS: FOUR-PLAYER TEAMS, CONTINENTAL US, NO PLAYER SUBSTITUTIONS, NO WEAPONS OF MASS DESTRUCTION, FIVE OBSERVERS PER TEAM

TEAM ONE: MORGEN CAMPBELL, SAUL RAND, ALISA CAMPBELL, ESTHER SOWAH
TEAM TWO: TYSON REYES, MAX COLEMAN, KATHERINE SHAW, RICHARD VIER

STAY TUNED FOR OUR OPENING GAMBIT!

∞Acknowledgments∞

When I wrapped up the CHRONOS Files in 2015, I joked that I needed a time-travel break to unravel my brain. I also had another series that I'd begun writing in 2013 (the Delphi Trilogy), whose characters had been waiting somewhat impatiently for their chance to get out of the confines of my imagination. But I always knew I'd be coming back to CHRONOS. There were other stories I wanted to tell, other historical events that I wanted to explore through the lens of time travel. And so, here we are.

In keeping with tradition from the CHRONOS Files, I want to start out by sorting fact from fiction. The lines can be a bit blurry, and, as with any historical fiction, I've taken some liberties with the real-life historical figures who are in this book. That said, I've done my best to stay true to the character suggested in interviews, both print and video.

- There are numerous articles by fictional newspapers tucked between the chapters. Any articles with dates prior to 2000 are based on actual newspaper accounts of the events described.

- The selection from the Records of the House Un-American Activities Committee and the excerpt from *The Manual of the United Klans of America* are both verbatim transcripts.
- Madi's trip to the church festival in 1957 Liverpool was the first time that Paul McCartney played with John Lennon's skiffle group, The Quarry Men. The two would later go on to form another, somewhat better-known, band. The description of the parade that day is based on photographs of the event and flyers posted online at various Beatles fan sites.
- The actual concert playlist for the Beatles performance in Memphis (prior to the cherry-bomb incident) provides the musical backdrop for Madi and Tyson's final push to restore the timeline.
- Information about the Beatles' 1966 American tour and the public reaction is very close to the historical record. John Lennon's comments about the relative popularity of his band and Jesus Christ were taken somewhat out of context by some politicians and media outlets, especially in the South. On their previous tour in 1964, the Beatles had not endeared themselves to segregationists when they refused to play at the Gator Bowl in Jacksonville, Florida, unless the venue allowed people of all races to attend, and band members, especially Lennon and Paul McCartney, had made statements highly critical of Jim Crow laws still prevalent in the 1960s South.
- I made extensive use of online videos of the Memphis press conference with the Beatles and also a television interview with a KKK leader who claimed that they were planning a surprise for the band. The incident with the cherry bomb, which many believed to be a gunshot, was reportedly instrumental in the band's decision to make the 1966 tour their last.

- Record burnings and KKK rallies were staged throughout the South and elsewhere to protest the tour. One of these was led by South Carolina United Klans of America leader Robert Scoggin. Three other Klan leaders have brief dialogue in the book: Robert Shelton (Imperial Wizard of United Klans), Robert "Dynamite Bob" Chambliss (responsible for the Birmingham Church bombing), and Collie Wilkins (charged with the killing of Viola Liuzzo).
- Reverend Jimmy Stroud organized the Memphis Christian Youth Rally to coincide with the Beatles concert on August 19, 1966. The original plan was to hold it at the Memphis Memorial Stadium, which stood only a few hundred yards from Mid-South Coliseum, where the Beatles would play. As the projected size of the counterrally dwindled, however, it was moved to Ellis Auditorium.
- The Antioch College speech by Dr. Martin Luther King Jr. took place on June 19, 1965. An Ohio branch of the KKK planned an assassination attempt for that day, but it was canceled.
- Individuals who marched from Selma to Montgomery in March 1965 camped on the final night at the City of St. Jude. A Stars for Freedom concert was organized for the marchers that evening. In our timeline, no one was killed, and thousands of troops were on hand to provide protection. They were not, however, able to save the life of Viola Liuzzo, who was murdered while transporting marchers back to Selma.
- The ducks still do their daily march from the elevator to the fountain, if you'd like to visit them at the Peabody Hotel in Memphis.

I think that pretty much covers the historical backdrop, but I'd also like to take a brief moment to talk about the other setting for this book and the two that will follow—the future. Much of the story revolves around CHRONOS, an organization that engages in extensive genetic alteration. While manipulating someone's genetic makeup to allow him or her to time travel is still firmly in the realm of science fiction, most of the other genetic tweaks will be in the far less distant future. The desire to correct for abnormalities that cause suffering or early death would be hard to deny, but parents who currently buy their children's way into elite universities would surely be willing to invest a bit before birth to ensure an intelligence boost. And since it's unlikely that any of this would be free, the gap between the rich and the poor would become a widening chasm.

Why pay for plastic surgery later, when you could ensure that your child doesn't inherit Grandpa's nose, or any other physical trait deemed undesirable? All of the biases in our society—sexism, racism, homophobia, and so on—could potentially be reflected in the types of things that parents might choose to tweak.

All this is to say that I hope readers will view my description of the genetic "enhancement" at CHRONOS as a cautionary tale. I believe we will face some very difficult choices in the coming decades, as we examine what sorts of genetic changes will be permitted. As our understanding of the human genome and how it can be altered grows, we need clear ethical guidelines, both at the national and international level.

And on that cheery note, I'd like to turn to the long list of people to whom I owe a debt of gratitude. First, a big thank you to my team at 47North. Adrienne Procaccini has shepherded this book from start to finish with exceptional care and patience. Mike Corley has produced another gorgeous cover. Tegan Tigani and I shared multiple time travel headaches during the developmental edit. Special thanks as well to the dedicated group of copyeditors and proofreaders who patched up my assorted gaffes.

If you're among my friends on Facebook or Twitter, or in one of my online author groups, thanks for keeping me informed and entertained, and reminding me to get back into the Writing Cave. My trusty CHRONOS Repo Agents and beta readers deserve a special mention for their detailed feedback and support. While not all of them contributed to this particular book, their feedback and friendship helped me grow as a writer, so I won't be "culling" any names, just adding a few who have joined the chaos more recently: Cale Madewell, Chris Fried, Karen Stansbury, Karen Benson, Ian Walniuk, Mary Freeman, Meg A. Watt, Hailey Mulconrey Theile, Billy Thomas, Erin Flynn, Margarida Azevedo Veloz, Summer Nettleman, Heather Jones, Meg Griffin, Kristin Ashenfelter, Lacey Waits, Shell Bryce, Fred Douglis, Jen Gonzales, Donna Harrison Green, Dori Gray, Susan Helliesen, Chelsea Hawk, Mikka McClain, Alexa Huggins, Stephanie Johns-Bragg, Cody Jones, Christina Kmetz, Jenny MacRunnel, Trisha Davis Perry, John Scafidi, Antigone Trowbridge, Jen Wesner, Dan Wilson, Jessica Wolfsohn, Tracy Denison Johnson, Mark Chappell, Becca Porter, and Sarah Kate Fisher. And, as always, apologies in advance to the person—or more likely, persons—I've forgotten!

Thanks to my family—immediate, extended, and chosen. Extra special thanks to Pete for being my sounding board and to the three lovely people to whom this book is dedicated. You guys keep me (relatively) sane, even when I'm in the middle of book frenzy—which is pretty much all the time lately—and you have my unending gratitude.

And finally, thanks to the readers of the original CHRONOS series around the world. Writing the book is only the first part of the creative process. It takes a reader to fill in the blanks and make the story their own. Thanks for lending me your imaginations . . . and I hope you'll join me for the rest of journey.

∞About the Author∞

RYSA WALKER is the bestselling author of The Delphi Trilogy (*The Delphi Effect*, *The Delphi Resistance*, and *The Delphi Revolution*) and the CHRONOS Files series, which includes *Timebound*, winner of the Grand Prize in the 2013 Amazon Breakthrough Novel Awards, *Time's Echo*, *Time's Edge*, *Time's Mirror*, *Time's Divide*, and *Simon Says: Tips for the Intrepid Time Traveler*. Her career had its beginnings in a childhood on a cattle ranch, where she read every book she could find, watched *Star Trek* and *The Twilight Zone*, and let her imagination soar into the future and to distant worlds. Her diverse path has spanned roles such as lifeguard, waitress, actress, digital developer, and professor—and through it all, she has pursued her passion for writing the sorts of stories she imagined in her youth. She lives in North Carolina with her husband, two youngest sons, and a hyperactive golden retriever. Discover more about Rysa and her work at www.rysa.com.